CONFESSIONS OF A SCIENCE FICTION WRITER:

"I have never read one H.G. Wells 'romance of the future' from cover to cover. When I was thirteen somebody gave me Verne's **Twenty Thousand Leagues Under the Sea** and at page two hundred I balked. I never **have** finished it!"

"I write books I have an overwhelming desire to read but cannot find."

"Unlike many writers I can re-read **all** my published work with delight."

"Several times I tried to tell stories. People fidgeted. I kept forgetting the plot. I suppose that's why I became a writer."

THE JEWEL-HINGED JAW

Samuel R. Delany

Notes of the Language of Science Fiction

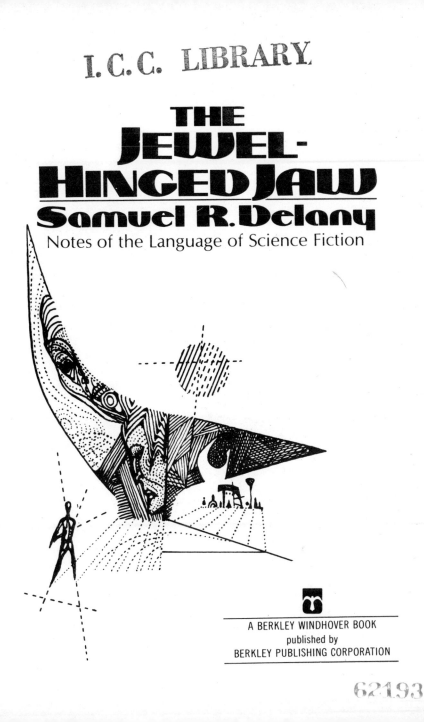

A BERKLEY WINDHOVER BOOK
published by
BERKLEY PUBLISHING CORPORATION

Berkley Publishing Corporation
200 Madison Avenue
New York, N. Y. 10016

SBN 425-03852-1

BERKLEY WINDHOVER BOOKS are published by
Berkley Publishing Corporation
200 Madison Avenue
New York, N. Y. 10016

BERKLEY WINDHOVER BOOK ® TM 1062206

Printed in the United States of America

Berkley Windhover Edition, June, 1978

Interior art © by Richard M. Powers

Letter to a Critic first appeared in *The Little Magazine,* David Hartwell, ed., Vol 6, No 4, New York, 1973.

About Five Thousand Seven Hundred and Fifty Words grew out of a talk presented at the Modern Language Association Meeting in New York, December 27, 1968, and was published in *S-F: The Other Side of Realism,* Thomas D. Clareson, ed., Bowling Green University Popular Press, Bowling Green, Ohio, 1971.

Shadows first appeared in two parts, Part I in *Foundation 6* (May, 1974) and Part II in *Foundation 7/8* (November, 1975), Peter Nichols, ed., North East London Polytechnic. Parts of it also appeared as "Appendix A" in *Triton,* by Samuel R. Delany, Bantam Books, New York, 1976.

Critical Methods/Speculative Fiction and **Quarks** appeared respectively in *Quark/1* and as editorial notes in *Quark/1, Quark/4,* and *Quark/3,* Samuel R. Delany and Marilyn Hacker, eds., Paperback Library, New York, 1970, 1971.

Teaching S-f Writing first appeared under the title *Reading Between the Words* in *Clarion,* Robin Scott Wilson, ed., Signet Books, New American Library, New York, 1971.

Thickening the Plot first appeared in *Those Who Can: An S-F Reader,* Robin Scott Wilson, ed., Mentor Books, New American Library, New York, 1973

Faust and Archimedes, Characters (under the title **Two Points on Characterization**), and **On Pure Story-Telling** appeared in *The Science Fiction Writers of America Forum,* Terry Carr seq. George Zebrowski, ed., New York between 1966 and 1970. The last of these was first presented as a talk at the Nebula Awards Banquet in Berkeley, California, 1970.

Alyx first appeared as an introductory essay by Samuel S. Delany in *Alyx,* by Joanna Russ, Gregg Press, Boston, 1976.

Prisoners' Sleep was first delivered as a lecture at the State University of New York at Buffalo, April, 1975, and is printed here for the first time.

To Read *The Dispossessed* appears here for the first time.

A Fictional Architecture that Manages only with Great Difficulty Not Once to Mention Harlan Ellison first appeared in *Lighthouse,* Terry Carr, ed., Vol. 3, No. 1, New York, 1967.

All pieces that have previously appeared have been somewhat revised for this edition.

Of course for
those without
whom:
        Damon Knight,
        Judith Merril,
        Algis Budrys,
          et in memoriam
        P. Schuyler Miller
        and James Blish.

Contents

Preface

The following essays circle about, hover over, and occasionally home in on science fiction. Four—and only four—examine individual science-fiction writers' works; the last three of these presuppose recent if not repeated intimacy with the texts. This book is not an introduction to its subject.

The fourteen pieces here were written from 1966 to 1976. They are not a unified project, and there is terminological inconsistency from one to the other—the more confusing, I'm afraid, because I have not presented them in that strictly chronological order which would allow a reader to follow the terminological development. But I have chosen to group them (somewhat) according to subject because that arrangement seems to afford them and the reader the greatest service in other ways. Some minor inconsistencies I have been able to bring into line—along with the excision of some minor infelicities of style and analysis. The major inconstant terms, however, "science fiction," "speculative fiction," and "s-f," I could not integrate without major surgery—plastic rather than radical, I suspect, but still beyond my current energies if not skills. I must therefore assume those interested enough to read these pages most probably bring their own ideas on how the terms' thrusts differ, as well as where their loci overlap.

For science fiction, here we must make do with Damon Knight's ostensive definition: "Science fiction is what I point at when I say 'science fiction'"—with the rider that after we have said a great deal more and, besides pointing, have handled and examined and taken some apart, even if no strict definitions are forthcoming, we shall still know a great deal more *about* what we are pointing at than we did before.

Speculative fiction, roughly between 1964 and 1972, was an active term among a number of science fiction writers (borrowed, in some cases unknowingly, from Heinlein a decade and a half earlier) in their talk with one another about what they and a number of other writers were doing. Since then, it has by and large passed out of the talk of these same writers, except as a historical reference.

S-f, happily or unhappily, is the initials of both.

For our purposes, this explanation for when each term appears and when it does not, however inadequate, must suffice.

The recent passage from "mainstream" to "mundane" as a term to designate that fiction which is neither science nor speculative strikes me as a happy gathering of generic self-confidence. (I first came across "mundane fiction" in a 1975 *Galaxy* essay by Roger Zelazny.) Yet the insecurity it remedies is part of our genre's history. Though a comparison with the original of some of these pieces might suggest that I have shamelessly rewritten it other places, here at least I have avoided the temptation to revise that insecurity out and let "mainstream" stand in the older essays—only noting that we have all been unhappy with the term as far back as I can remember.

Rereading the pieces for this edition, I am pleased with a consistency in their movement toward a language model that all of them, for all their different levels, their different methods of approach—intuitive, thematic, textural, or structural—ascribe to. And that model is, after all, their object.

Intensive criticism of science fiction is a comparatively new phenomenon. Its most effective organizing principles have not been established. Also, I emerge into such criticism from a most subjective position: a practicing science fiction writer. The center provides a fine view of certain aspects of our object of consideration and a very poor one of others. Among the poorest it provides is a view of that object's edges. In the s-f world of readers and writers, we are all used to the phrase, "Fandom is a way of life." Being an s-f writer is a way of life too: it is a way of life which courts all the traditional problems of the artist as well as those problems unique to an artist socially devalued in a particularly systematic way—a way that has nothing to do with the family's disapproval of John for enrolling at the Art Students'

League, or with the neighbors' suspicions that the Colton girl has not only been writing poems again but sending them to magazines that actually publish them. The Rimbaldian intensity with which our writers are forever abandoning the s-f field is, I suspect, emblematic of the process by which s-f writers, along with losing sight of the edges of their object, tend to loose, by the same process, their own edges as well. And if money is a reason frequently cited for these defections, well, money is our society's most powerful symbol: it exists at points of social and material vacuum; its trajectory has seemingly infinite potential; its strength is measured by all that moves in to displace it: food, sex, more money, shelter, art, or anxiety.

There are places in these pages where I have exceeded my object's edges (for my own are no more intact than any of my colleagues'), notably in *Shadows* and the closing *Autobiographical Postscript*. "What," my reader may ask, "does Quine's hesitation to quantify across predicates *or* the play of light on Mykonos in winter have to do with science fiction?" My answer is simply: I don't know. Yet the ontology suggested by much in the Quinian position as I understand (or possibly misunderstand) it seems an ontology that much of what I value in science fiction strives to reinforce; and the particular analytic flight the light on that most lovely of Greek islands called from me in the winter of '65/'66 seems a fine topos for a kind of thinking that goes into the richest science fiction. Thus the inclusion of these and similarly "unrelated" bits of speculation and/or autobiography.

In a sense, then, this is the most subjective of books on science fiction—by someone who spends much of his subjective energies analysing the s-f phenomenon. But the discourse of analysis must not be confused with some discourse of privileged objectivity. Such privileges in our epoch have less and less place.

Here I must thank the people who first requested that some of these essays be written, oversaw their publication as editors, or to whom they were written in response: Terry Carr, Thomas Clareson, Leslie Fiedler, David Hartwell, Peter Nichols, and Robin Scott Wilson.

Finally I must thank the students of my two extremely astute classes at SUNY Buffalo during the winter '75 term (particularly Jane Nutter, Mayda Alsace, and Charles Thomas, III); and also Randson Boykin, Eugenio Donato, Marc Gawron, Carol Jacobs, Judith

Kerman, Maureen O'Merra, Paul David Novitsky, Judy Ratner, Robert Scholes, Janet Small, Eric Steis, and Henry Sussman for everything from stimulating converse over these and related subjects to detailed response (in person, letter, or fanzine) to various of the pages here, the results of which are evident in minor revisions of the older works and hopefully inform the newer. Needless to say, errors and eccentricities are all my own.

MARCH 1977

For this Berkley Windhover edition I must also thank—for myriad microimprovements—Camilla Decarnin of San Francisco, Florine Dorfmann of New York City, and Professor Teresa de Lauretis, Assistant Director of the University of Wisconsin—Milwaukee's Center for Twentieth Century Studies, where I was so happily a Fellow in 1977.

MARCH 1978

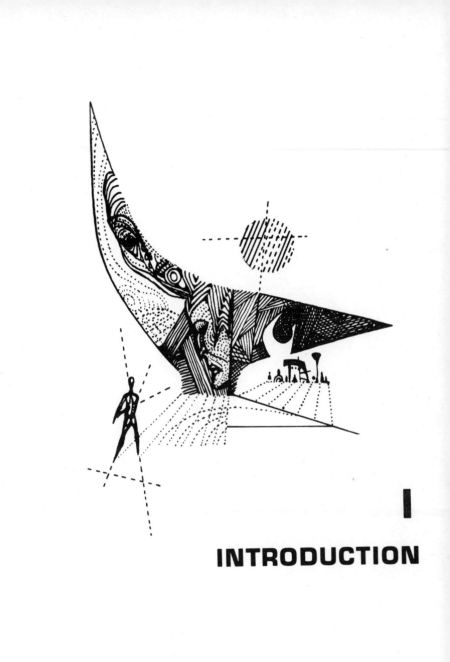

INTRODUCTION

Letter to a Critic: Popular Culture, High Art, and the S-F Landscape

Dear Sir:

How happy I was to have someone of your academic background and accomplishments turn his attention—as more and more of your co-freres seem to have been doing of late—to my sequestered precinct of genre writing, science fiction. And how exciting it was to hear you begin your evening talk: "Pornography, comics, science fiction, poetry, westerns, mysteries, and the serious novel *all* can and must be examined seriously by the serious critic." And as a comic book artist worthy of such examination you cited, with a great grin, S. Clay Wilson! My reaction was, blatantly, "Right on!"—right up till your summation: "I hope science fiction does not lose its slapdash quality, its sloppiness, or its vulgarity."

There, I grew angry.

Articulating it may sound self-righteous, but it comes down to this: Slapdash writing, sloppiness, and vulgarity (unless one means [and you didn't] the sophisticated vulgarity implicit in Durrell's "Good taste is the enemy of great art.") are, no matter how you catch them, fat, diseased lice.

Some art survives in spite of them (Dreiser, Dickens, Dostoyevsky...); in some, the good is so infested with them you cannot separate it out (Edgar R., and William S., Burroughs, gnawing at the idea of civilization from their respectively fascist and radical positions); but slapdashery, sloppiness, and vulgarity only have camp value—where we giggle at what we or our parents were

3

taken in by. That giggle is embarrassed nostalgia for lost ignorance.

Sometimes writing is good in spite of sloppiness.

It is never good because of it.

Some time before this passion for popular culture seized you, you yourself wrote an incisive description and appraisal of the psycho/social mechanics of its purveyors (you talked of Hollywood film producers and studio executives of the fifties), explaining how they were intimidated by, hated, and tried to subvert (all with the best intentions) anything they suspected to be art.

The identical mechanic operates in the publishing/editorial complex that handles "popular genres" like science fiction. And *every* science-fiction writer at one time or another has conflicted with it.

You would be appalled how closely your summary remarks (even to the tone of voice—a little too friendly, a little too cheerful, as if nothing really serious were being said) echo what comes from these well-intentioned people whose motivating processes you once so succinctly described.

Well—there is my anger: spent.

In the hope that some larger cultural points will fall out, I'd like to talk specifically about science fiction—not about what motivates a given writer to create a given story, or even how a particular story may be constructed, but rather about the attitudes and values of the people who contract and pay for it, and publish it once it is written, as well as those who read it and make it profitable to publish—the landscape in which I work. For an understanding of science fiction that will keep usefully fixed to its object the more "rarefied" criticism that, yes, must be done, that landscape has to be explored, if only to define the pressures it puts on production within it. It's a landscape I feel ambiguous before. Much in it, even as I dislike it, stimulates me. Much in it that is comfortable is also destructive. And it is a landscape in change.

Forty-nine out of fifty s-f novels are bought before they are written.

The good and bad points of this situation clear quickly: an editor, having paid money for a book, is more likely to put up with a certain amount of texture or substance experiment not specifically spelled out in the outline. On the other hand, the quality of the final product is never a factor in setting the price. That is left up to the individual writer's integrity (or ability); so that "fine execution," without which, Emily Dickinson claimed, "nothing survives," is not economically encouraged.

A friend of mine—a Yale Younger Poet five or six years ago—published a delightful book of experimental fictions with Atheneum a few years back (sales to date are near three hundred copies). She is at work on a novel (about a werewolf). Her husband is a corporation lawyer; they live back and forth between Europe and the United States. She is an avid science-fiction reader.

I read two or three books of current poetry each week. I have for the last four or more years. I was in a remedial reading class in elementary school; reading for me has always been hard work. I want a lot out of it because I don't do it easily. I don't get a lot from most fiction: I do from poetry.

My friend and I were familiar with each other's work when we met. *She* was surprised to find someone who knew hers... At any rate, we delight in talking about writing till all hours over the bathtub Calvados she and her husband smuggled in from Norway. We agree about most things. And she worries over the reaction of her readers, using the same vocabulary and syntax I use worrying over mine... an odd matrix of care-passionately/don't-care-at-all.

But for all our temperamental congruence, matched tastes, and shared aesthetic concerns, she and I are in *very* different professions.

Despite her awards and publications, she feels chances for the publication of her new novel or a new book of poems are more against than for her. But when, and if, she publishes again, she has no worry that an editor will force upon her *his* concept of what *her* audience wants.

I have made my living as a science-fiction writer for nearly fifteen years. I can say nothing about the golden-age editorships of Campbell, Gold, or Boucher. They were over when I entered the field. *Most* science-fiction writers today have not known them either. I can only talk about the editorial realities I have known.

Science fiction *is* a wanted commodity: publication *per se*, as long as my work stays within the loose bounds of s-f, is not something I have had to worry about for five or six years. But all editors have their idea of what "the audience" (never themselves) wants. With a few glorious exceptions, most s-f editors' sensibilities are the result of having had to read incredible amounts of bad work in a genre that they never particularly enjoyed in the first place. So each book is a battle with an atrophied editorial image of what the editors think someone who is not them is going to like and buy.

If it stopped there, winning that battle in the court of sales would be very rewarding.

But science fiction is commercial writing in a way that Literature with a capital L has never been, even in the days of the blue-paper-covered editions of Dickens or George Eliot. Science fiction, with its set, small sales, is considered the lowest rung on the commercial publishing ladder. (To argue whether s-f is the lowest or the next to lowest rung within that is a masochism we can avoid here.) The point is that in overall form, editorial policy must reflect this, even if the personal preferences of a given editor do not.

A Doubleday editor told me recently that a large publisher with good distribution can expect to sell between two and five hundred copies of a first novel in a hardcover trade edition, even one by a writer with a good reputation in the little magazines and quarterlies—five hundred if they can pass the book off as a romance that might appeal to some distorted image the sales department has of "the average housewife."

A trade edition hardcover, first s-f novel by an unknown writer with no previous magaine publication will sell between twelve and eighteen hundred copies.

The break-even point on a six or seven dollar book is around nine hundred.

Science-fiction novels make money on the average. Ordinary novels, on the average, do not.

And the s-f money made is small.

Nevertheless, since 1965, the s-f audience has created a sellers' market. Publishers have taken on some fairly far-out books to fill up their lists; and the experimental work usually seems to sell well above the break-even point, both hardcover and paperback.

"We've been instructed to suggest to some of our young, literary novelists," another editor told me more recently, "that they let us bring their work out as Science Fiction—especially those whose work has a more imaginative, surreal, or experimental bent." Then he frowned: "I feel pretty bad about having to do that."

I know very well why he feels bad about it.

The best-selling hardcover science-fiction novel for 1968, John Brunner's *Quicksand*, sold seven thousand copies. No trade edition, hardcover science-fiction novel has ever sold more than twelve thousand—except *Stranger in a Strange Land*, to which I'll return.

Only one of New York's six Doubleday Bookstores stocks any hardcover s-f regularly. Scribner's Bookstore may have as many as five titles at any one time—two of the titles on their s-f shelf are always *Stranger* and *2001*. Brentano's stocks none—though recently it has been taking one or two s-f titles with a clearly ecological slant. The Eighth Street Bookshop carries none. Marboro carries none.*

And *2001* and *The Andromeda Strain* aren't s-f anyway: Neither the words *science fiction* nor the initials *s-f* appear anywhere on the hardcover or paperback editions—not even in the blurb recounting author Clarke's past achievements. Booksellers don't stock books labeled s-f. Book distributors don't distribute them.

They'll tell you as much if you ask.

A crate of books reaches a distributor. The first stock boy who rips off the crate cover also removes any and all "science-fiction" books and puts them in a separate pile for special, limited distribution: this is before anyone looks at author, title, or cover. Only after that pile has been made (a similar one is made for "mysteries" and "westerns") are the books looked at and further specialization decided on. A brochure accompanying the s-f books, from publisher to distributor, telling how wide an appeal this or that particular title should have, may mean the distributor will put a little more pressure on the highschool libraries or specialist bookstores which normally take these books.

If *science fiction* should appear only on an inside blurb and not on the outside jacket (e.g., "J.G. Ballard has been the author of some of the most acclaimed science fiction of the past years..."), the distributor's incensed reaction is: "What are you trying to do? Sneak this by? Will you please label the books clearly so we can get them where they ought to go. We know how to sell books, it's our business!"—I quote, from memory, a memo to the Doubleday art department.

People have criticized Vonnegut for not calling his books science fiction. But frankly, his publisher wouldn't let him even if he wanted to. One editor has estimated that if Vonnegut's next novel were to bear the words "science fiction" or the initials "s-f," simply because of

*I am happy to report that the situation is somewhat changed for the better since this letter was written in 1972.

the distribution machinery, his sales would be cut—even today—
perhaps seventy-five percent. The distributor's reaction would be:
"For some reason, Vonnegut has decided to write a science-fiction
novel. Well, when he comes out with another, real one, we'll put it in
the stores." A children's book or a cookbook by Vonnegut would get
wider distribution: Doubleday, Eighth Street, Brentano's, Marboro,
and Scribners all have wide selections of both.

Back as promised, to *Stranger in a Strange Land.*
It sold some ten thousand copies in its initial trade edition in
nineteen sixty. It was kept alive in hardcover through a nontrade,
book-club edition for ten years, where its sales approached three
hundred thousand despite a simultaneous paperback sale in the
millions. After ten years the publishers finally decided, since the
book-club edition was selling as well as ever, to release a new trade
edition—with only the smallest "s-f" in the corner of the jacket.
It sold another ten thousand copies, was unavailable in
Brentano's, Doubleday, etc. So *Stranger*, one of the most popular
books of the last decade, has still only sold twenty thousand in a trade
edition. And the trade edition of *Dune*, by the way, has still sold
under twelve thousand.
An editor (or writer) who suspects (or even hopes) he has a book
that might approach twenty-five thousand sales—and that's not
tickling the bottom rung on the ladder to best-sellerdom—would be
an idiot to label a book "science fiction," even if the hero graduated
from the Space Academy in the first chapter and squelched the Bug
Men of Uranus in the last.
Here is a synopsis of a talk I recently heard Isaac Asimov give:
James Blish, some years ago, in response to Vonnegut's "disavowal"
of science fiction (and as a slap at some writers somebody or other,
around nineteen sixty-six, called "the New Wave") suggested that all
true and loyal ("loyal" to what, I remember wondering) science-
fiction writers insist that their s-f books be clearly marked as such—
for the prestige of the field. Ike had just published his first novel in
sixteen years, *The Gods Themselves*, a story set in the future about
the transfer of elements from universe to universe via black and white
holes, and the multisexed aliens from the other universe who are
involved. He was astonished, then, when Doubleday suggested the

book "not be published as science fiction."—i.e., not have the tell-tale words or initials anywhere on the book.

Ike, recalling Blish's campaign, protested: "But it *is* science fiction! I'm a science-fiction author! Put *science fiction* on it!"

Doubleday refused.

Over the last decade, with talk shows, popular science books, the reissue of his forties and early fifties science-fiction novels, Asimov has become a familiar enough name so that a new novel by him might break that twelve thousand sales barrier the distribution machinery of s-f imposes. Therefore, s-f it cannot be.

Ike finally went along.

I saw the book in Brentano's this afternoon. But, as the clerk told me when I went up to him five minutes later to ask, as I do periodically, "No, Brentano's stocks no hardcover science fiction. The paperbacks are downstairs..."

You can understand my ambiguous feelings: I am delighted that the s-f audience will absorb new works similar to Barthelme's or Coover's without any of the critical ballyhoo that the non s-f audience demands before it will pay attention to anything "experimental." But I am also painfully aware of the inequity of the labeling and distributing process that keeps the s-f writer/reader concert so limited.

Practically speaking, however, this is the position I must finally take: Words mean what people use them to mean. When editors, distributors, and, when all is said and done, science-fiction writers say "science fiction" or "s-f," they mean a distributor's category synonymous with "not of interest to the general public."

Although this does not define the field aesthetically, it certainly defines it economically.

Easily three hundred s-f books are published each year. But because s-f is "not of interest to the general public," the price of an s-f novel to all but about ten authors is $1,250.00 to $3,000.00 for a book, paperback or hardcover.

Therefore, you can make a decent living writing s-f—if you write a lot of it: four to six novels a year. (The magazines pay so little you couldn't possibly live on story sales, even if you were Robert Silverberg or Randall Garrett who, in the fifties and early sixties, were responsible for whole issues of s-f magazines each, the stories appearing under various pseudonyms.) Many s-f writers work at this rate—for years. Four such I know well are among the most intelligent men I've ever met. One began writing at age forty in 1962: He produced between four and ten books a year until he had a stroke in 1971. Two others, in their middle or late thirties today, having kept this pace up for six and ten years respectively, are now in the middle of year-plus writing blocks.

But virtually every great name in s-f—Sturgeon, Bester, Bradbury, Knight, Merril, Leiber, Pohl, Van Vogt, Asimov, Tenn, del Rey, Clarke—any writer, indeed, who began publishing in the thirties or forties when these high-production demands became tradition—has had at least one eight-to-sixteen-year period when he could write no science fiction at all. (Heinlein seems to be the one exception: A few writers who first began writing in the fifties—Anderson, Dick, and Farmer—seem to have gotten by so far with only one or two two/three-year blocked periods to date.) A handful of writers, during these decade-plus dry spells, turned to other kinds of writing, or editing. The lives of most, however, during these years are an incredible catalog of multiple and exploded marriages, alcoholism, drugs, nervous collapses, and stays in mental hospitals. A third of the writers I've named are still "blocked." Perhaps the same could be said of any group of creative temperaments. Still, the number of writers, age fifty, appearing at all the conventions, busily autographing reprints of their books, who consider themselves, in the blurred and boozey conversations of the "pro" parties at the worldcon, "primarily science-fiction writers," but who have written no s-f since they were thirty-five (one runs out of fingers and toes) is a frightening prospect for a writer between twenty and thirty beginning in the field.

Well, H.G. Wells himself wrote no "romances of the future" after age thirty-six.

Still, it makes you wonder.

But while we are wondering, editors want/demand/connive for, and generally presuppose that your work will be turned out at, this rate. And there is a crop of young writers already—Dean R. Koontz (age twenty-four with fourteen s-f books), Mark Geston (twenty-two with six books), Brian Stableford (twenty-four with six books)—who produce. Indeed, my own first five s-f novels were finished while I was still twenty-two.

Then I spent a summer in Mt. Sinai mental hospital: Hallucinations, voices, general nervous exhaustion...even at that pace, I did three complete rewrites on each book.

Here is what editors and older writers who should know better have told me till I am ill with it:

1. You are not an artist, you are a craftsman.
2. You should be able to take any idea ("...like that nutty one I just suggested to you...") and make a "competent" story from it.
3. Science fiction is ideas, not style. What do you care about a few words here and there; whether I cut or rewrite a paragraph just to make things fit?
5. You're a great writer: you get your work in on time.
6. You can be as sloppy and as slapdash as you want: just tell a good story.

The whole vocabulary of "competent/craftsman/salable" and the matrix of half-truths, self-deceptions and exploitation that it fosters are rabid making.

There are very few "ideas" in science fiction.

The resonance between an idea and a landscape is what it's all about.

S-f writers survive entirely as verbally discrete personalities— what are 'Bradbury,' 'Sturgeon,' 'Cordwainer Smith,' 'R.A. Lafferty,' 'Roger Zelazny,' 'Heinlein,' and 'Jack Vance' if not, essentially, the individual narrative tones with which their ideas are put? You'd have to be style deaf to mistake a paragraph of Asimov for a paragraph of Clarke, Phil Dick, Phil Farmer, or Bob Silverberg. You'd have an easier time mistaking a sentence by Christina Stead for one by Malcolm Lowry.

Once a writer has written one good book or, often, one good story, there is an active demand for the s-f audience that will absorb years of mediocre production waiting from the next high point. "Look," I heard an agent tell his s-f writer client, "if you write six books a year, I can sell them—considering you've just won the Hugo for best novel of the year—for two thousand dollars apiece. If you write two books a year—like you've always said you wanted to—I can sell each for fifteen thousand!"

I mentioned that there were approximately ten authors who can command (though they don't always) a price of more than twelve hundred to three thousand per book. I'm one.

My last published s-f novel, *Nova*, probably made more money than any of Asimov's (discounting *The Gods Themselves*, which, as we noted, is not "s-f"), including their numerous reprints. That would be an outright crime if the criminal act had not been committed by the publishers who bought Asimov's books in the fifties.

Nova's paperback sale in 1968 marked a record paid by any publisher, hardcover or paperback, for an s-f novel. Since then, that record has, happily, been broken several times. Admittedly, I have a sharp agent. But, essentially, what brought about that record price was very simple, though it goes back several books.

When I got out of the mental hospital, I decided that to write the next science-fiction novel *I* wanted to write, I would have to take in the neighborhood of a year to do it. I never announced this to anyone. Besides my editor, I knew no one to announce it to.

The book won a Nebula for best s-f novel of the year.

The book I worked on for the next year, while I was living in Europe, won a second Nebula.

Publishers, with standard two- and three-book contracts, began to bob up here and there, wondering why I didn't sign them all.

"I'm sorry," I said. "I'm not going to *have* a half dozen new novels finished any time soon. When I have one, I'll show it to you and you can tell me how much you want to pay for it."

And the offered price began to rise.

My not having a bale of manuscripts lying around to be sold off like yard goods, I'm sure, pushed it higher.

No author can make a sane comment on the quality of his own book, whether he has worked on it three weeks, three years, or three decades. But if a book is sold *after* it is written, whatever quality it does have is there to be judged, however accurately or inaccurately, by the editor buying. My book was bid for, bargained over, and eventually sold—and sold well. The only thing I did personally, however, was to stay out of the way of as many people in the field as possible while bargaining was going on. I've developed a reputation for being hard to find. I don't like the editing/publishing attitudes the people who edit/publish s-f have to hold, personally or practically: I stay hard to find. What they want, essentially, is reassurance they're doing nothing wrong. And that I can't give.

*   *   *

I'd like to move on to a couple of points about the general rise in intelligent interest in "popular culture"—of which the rise in interest in s-f is just a part.

The first of these points must be made often:

The only reason to be interested in popular culture today is because—today—so much is being done here with vitality, skill, intelligence, and relevance.

In underground comics, there is the work of S. Clay Wilson, Richard Corben, De Spain, Bodé, Crumb...

In overground comics, there is the work of Neil Adams, Denny O'Neil, Jim Aparo, Barry Smith, Mike Kaluta...

More important, as the underground artist will be the first to tell you, you can't really appreciate one without the other. The dialog between them is constant.

In pornography, there's Michael Perkins, Marco Vassi, Dirk Vandon (as well as the reprints of Alexander Trocchi)...

About s-f itself, Clifford Simak, who began writing science fiction in the thirties, said recently:

> I would hazard a guess that if a panel of competent critics were to make a survey of science fiction through the years, they would find far more praiseworthy pieces of writing in the last few years than in any previous period. And that does not exclude the so-called golden age of science fiction.*

But the current excellence, which has produced the current interest, in comics and pornography (to cite two fields with which I am somewhat familiar) must be emphasized again and again; if it is not, the historically minded critic, busily "reevaluating the traditions," even if he is aware of the present vitality, usually ends up talking only about *Fanny Hill* and *Little Nemo in Slumberland*.

My next point is also one I deeply feel the critics coming from "High Art" to "Popular Culture" must keep before them if their statements are to have any proportion. To make it, however, I must go somewhat afield.

Let's take a quick (and admittedly biased) look at British poetry in, say, 1818—the year Keats finished *Endymion*, Byron *The*

*From a speech given in Boston, 5 September 71, reprinted in *Extrapolation*, Vol. 13, No. 2.

Prisoner of Chillon, and Shelley the first act of *Prometheus Unbound*—and American poetry now.

In 1818 the population of England was near twenty million, eighty percent of whom were functionally illiterate. The literate field, then, was approximately four hundred thousand. This was not only the maximum poetry audience; more germane, it was the field from which the country's poets could come.

How many poets were there?

Coleridge-Wordsworth-Blake-Byron-Shelley-Keats...? Certainly. But we can pull out over another dozen without even opening our *Palgrave:* Crabbe, Hunt, Reynolds, Campbell, Scott, Moore, Southey, E.H. Coleridge, Landor, Darley, Hood, Praed, Clare, and Beddoes were all writing that same year. And at this point we've pretty much scraped the bottom of the barrel for acceptable thesis topics in British poetry for that decade.

Twenty all together!

And if you can think of five more British poets of any merit what-so-ever who were writing in the year of Emily Bronte's birth, good for you! Out of a field of four hundred thousand, that's six poets of major interest and fourteen of varying minor interest.

In the United States today we have nearly two hundred and twenty-five million people. Perhaps eighty percent are literate, which gives us a literate field of one hundred eighty million from which we can cull both our audience and our poets—a field fifty times as large as the field of Great Britain in 1818.

Forgive the litotes, but it is not unreasonable to suppose that where there were six major and fourteen minor poets in England in 1818, today there are fifty times six major poets (about three hundred) and fifty times fourteen (about seven hundred) of merit and interest in America today.

The blunt truth?

These statistics are about accurate.

Three or four months ago, Dick Allen in the sacrosanct pages of *Poetry (Chicago)*, without recourse to any statistics at all, said: "Let's face it. There are well over a thousand fine poets working in America today." I am, as I said, an avid poetry reader, and my own reading for pleasure certainly bears those figures out, even though I doubt I read ten percent of what is published. Certainly, somewhat more than half of what I read is bad. This still leaves a staggering amount of incredibly fine work—most by people whom I have never heard of before and, after I've read another fifty books of poetry, whose names I will not be able to recall without a trip to the bookshelves or the cartons in the closet. Browsing through a bookstore, I am far more likely to find good poetry from a small, or even vanity (!) press than I am from Doubleday, Scribner's, Harper & Row... I am as likely to find it in a mimeographed or offset pamphlet as I am from Black Sparrow, Oyez, or Wesleyan. I don't write poetry—I doubt I ever will. But, short of modern science fiction, current poetry is the most exciting reading adventure I've ever had.

Now the academic establishment, for years, has invested amazing energy, time, money, and (above all) mystification in perpetuating the view that, somehow, Eliot, Auden, and Pound form some mysterious qualitative analog with Byron, Keats, Shelley, while (and I quote the list from the opening pages of Howard's *Alone with America:*) "Berryman, Bishop, Jarrell, Lowell, Roethke, and Wilber" start to fill, along with Frost, Stevens, and Hart Crane, the places left vacant by the minor romantics of 1818. Waiting below, the hordes...

This, to anyone who *reads* poetry, is ridiculous. Even among the recently dead (O'Hara, Olsen, Plath, Spicer...) there are who-knows-how-many who were doing as (or more, or simply different) fine poetical work as any of the living or dead already mentioned. In general, the standards of poetry are far higher than in Shelley's time. Few little magazines today will accept verse with as much padding as the lines that filled *The Edinburgh Review.* Many people will admit, in an anti intellectual moment, that they can't tell why the latest bit of Lowell in the New York Review of Books is any better than the latest poem by their twenty-four-year-old graduate student or poet-in-residence. Like as not, though, the reason is that both poems really are just as good. Still, most people would rather not respond to a poem at all without the reassurance of critical approbation/mystification... that element so necessary if a writer is to be, to whatever degree, "famous." Fame has been used, by the academic, as a sort of mineral oil to make works of culture slip down the throats of students a bit more easily. But fame is a matter of individual attention/fascination. And, at present, there just isn't enough of it to go around—not if you want to dole it out to poets according to merit. I think people have known this in a vaguely inarticulate way for years: it has resulted in an immense effort to propagate the lie that while the population rises geometrically, the amount of poetic excellence remains an arithmetic constant.

But, at the risk of impugning the Emperor's tailor, barring a fantastic decrease in population and/or literacy, no one person will ever be familiar with the scope of American Poetry again. Nor can anybody be familiar with more than a fraction of the best of it—unless he or she makes that an eight hour a day job, and even then it is doubtful. Consider becoming thoroughly familiar with the work of—and the influences on—300 writers:

So: One classic job of the (poetry) critic—the establishment of *the* canon of excellent work—is undoable . . . and uncheckable should someone claim to have done it.

Some nineteenth-century-oriented academics still uphold the sacred tenet of the arithmetic stasis of excellence. But to anyone who can multiply, much less read, they begin to look like fools. Yes, ninety-nine percent of what is written is awful. And perhaps seventy-five percent of what is published—a microscopically small fraction of what is written—is trivial. But what *is* good *and* published would fill barns.

There are hundreds on hundreds on hundreds of American poets.

Hundreds among them are good.

One critic cannot even be *acquainted* with their complete work, much less have studied it thoroughly.

And I suspect one can find analogs of this situation with the novel, the theater, the dance . . .

Which brings us back to Popular Culture.

The Cartoonist Workers of America (the underground comic-artist guild) has some fifty members. A completist collector of underground comics tells me that well under a hundred artists' work has appeared in anything that could be called a professionally printed, underground comic.

ACBA, The Academy of Comic Book Artists (the overground comic artists' guild), has approximately one hundred fifty members, about a third of which are writers and editors, and about two thirds of which are artists, colorists, letterers. A former member of the ACBA board tells me *well* under two hundred artists' work appears in professional, overground comics today.

I have no figures for pornographers.

The SFWA, however (the Science Fiction Writers of America), lists some four hundred fifty active and associate members. Associate members are editors, publishers, teachers of science-fiction courses, libraries interested in more extensive science-fiction collections. Active members are currently working writers of which there are approximately two hundred fifty. Slightly under one hundred are full-time, working writers. Of these, there are perhaps fifty who make the bulk of their living writing only science fiction.

And there are more comic-book artists, pornographers, and s-f writers today than ever before. Still, despite venerable histories, the current production in the areas of popular culture, compared to current production in the areas of high art—poetry, for instance—is rather small.

The various areas of Popular Culture are knowable.

The various areas of contemporary High Art are not.

And this is one attraction Popular Culture has for the modern critical mind.

Artists, already working in the popular fields, have perhaps been attracted for similar reasons. As fame is a goad to art, there is, obviously, less competition. I can more or less keep up with the work of the fifty who, full time, write science fiction—and read poetry too. Indeed, the real competition, I feel, is with no more than ten of these. Also, I suspect, the personalized response from a specialized and enthusiastic audience is more important than the necessarily limited fame available to an artist in such a field. The artists here feel more comfortable in areas with more defined yet ultimately more flexible traditions than seem to be available in High Art.

But, abandoning the abstract for the personal: I began writing science fiction because a handful of writers I read in my adolescence (Sturgeon, Bester, Heinlein, and McLean) wrote a few books and stories that I found more moving and stimulating than anything I'd ever read. (Other things I was reading and liking? Genet's plays, Beckett's novels, "San Francisco renaissance" poetry, Camus, Baldwin's essays.) A few other science-fiction writers (Asimov, Clarke, Bradbury, and Leiber) were managing to hew clumsily—and I was aware of the clumsiness even then—great, mysterious shapes of mind, lit here and there with the coalescing energies of our new technology, but, for the most, black and unholy with mythic resonances. Their scientific, or pseudoscientific, explanations seemed to have made them brave enough to venture a step or two closer to the dark, lithic mysteries—while they shouted back descriptions of what they saw.

That was the potential and the accomplishment of science

fiction. Without either, I doubt I would have wanted to write it.

I write books I have an overwhelming desire to read but cannot find on library shelf or bookstore rack. (Unlike many writers, I can reread *all* my published work with delight.) And I am sentimentalist enough so that when yet another bright-eyed sixteen-year-old runs up to me at some convention and blurts, in confession, that he has read my last book over five times (this is the way I read "More Than Human" and "The Stars my Destination") I feel quite warm. And, though such an occurrence makes no comment at all on one's aesthetic success, at least one can feel, for a moment, one has done something humane.

Last summer, in the mail, I received a copy of a master's thesis concerned with "mythical" imagery in two of my books. Flattered as I was by the attention, I still cannot remember the author's name or college. Most of his sixty-odd-page paper was, at worst, irrelevant, at best, amusing. He did point out two typographical errors in one of the books—he, however, did not recognize them as errors and made much of them. I have a note to myself giving the page on which they occur and will correct them next edition.

From here I turn to the buzz behind me: critics, scholars, and even some writers, asking among themselves in concerned voices whether the advent of serious criticism will "corrupt" science fiction. To me this sounds like critical megalomania. The tidal wave of well-being that sweeps from the avid fourteen-year-old who has read and reread one lovingly and hopelessly—I recall one girl who had memorized (!) a short story of mine and quoted half of it back to me till I made her stop—is more corrupting than any possible scholarly examination. (I assume "corrupting" for the writer is synonymous with "distracting.")

I suspect the critics are in far greater danger of corruption than we are: I have run across a fair number of "corrupt" critics—that is, critics who praise worthless writers for nonexistent reasons. The amount of wordage writers of science fiction (or poetry) spend praising *any* kind of critic is negligible.

BEST WISHES—

SAMUEL R. DELANY
NEW YORK 1972

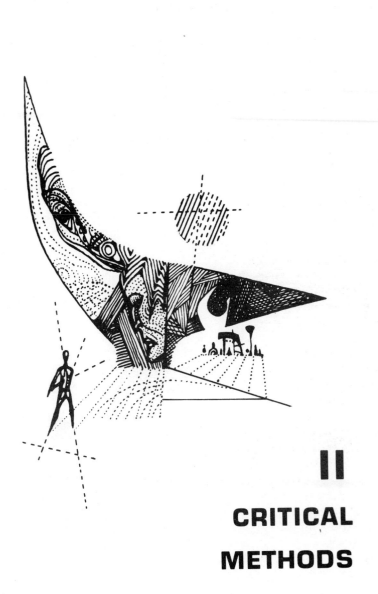

II

CRITICAL

METHODS

About Five Thousand Seven Hundred And Fifty Words

Every generation some critic states the frighteningly obvious in the *style/content* conflict. Most readers are bewildered by it. Most commercial writers (not to say, editors) first become uncomfortable, then blustery; finally, they put the whole business out of their heads and go back to what they were doing all along. And it remains for someone in another generation to repeat:

Put in opposition to "style," there is no such thing as "content."

Now, speculative fiction is still basically a field of commercial writing. Isn't it obvious that what makes a given story s-f *is* its speculative content? As well, in the middle and late Sixties there was much argument about Old Wave and New Wave s-f. The argument was occasionally fruitful, at times vicious, more often just silly. But the critical vocabulary at both ends of the beach included "...old style...new style...old content...new content..." The questions raised were always: "Is the content meaningful?" and "Is the style compatible with it?" Again, I have to say, "content" does not exist. The two new questions that arise then are: (1), How is this possible, and (2), What is gained by atomizing content into its stylistic elements?

The words *content*, *meaning*, and *information* are all metaphors for an abstract quality of a word or group of words. The one I would like to concentrate on is: *information*.

Is content real?

Another way to ask this question is: Is there such a thing as verbal information apart from the words used to inform?

Most of the vocabulary of criticism is set up to imply there is. Information is carried by/with/in words. People are carried by/with/in cars. It should be as easy to separate the information from the word as it is to open the door of a Ford Mustang: *Content* means something that *is contained*.

But let us go back to *information*, and by a rather devious route. Follow me:

red

As the above letters sit alone on the paper, the reader has no way to know what they mean. Do they indicate political tendencies or the sound made once you pass the *b* in *bread*? The word generates no significant information until it is put in *formal relation* with something else. This formal relation can be with a real object ("Red" written on the label of a sealed tin of paint) or with other words ("The breeze through the car window was refreshing. Whoops—red! He hit the brake").[1]

The idea of *meaning, information,* or *content* as something contained by words is a misleading visualization. Here is a more apt one:

Consider meaning to be a thread (or better yet, the path) that connects a sound or configuration of letters called a "word" with a given object or group of objects (or better, memories of those objects). To know the meaning of a word is to be able to follow this thread from the sound to the proper recollections of objects, emotions, or situations—more accurately, to various image-modes of these objects/emotions/situations in your mind. Put more pompously, meanings (*content* or *information*) are the *formal relations* between sounds and images of the objective world.[2]

Any clever geometry student, from this point, can construct a proof for the etymological tautology, "All information is formal," as well as its corollary, "It is impossible to vary the form without varying the information." I will not try and reproduce it in detail. I would like to say in place of it, however, that "content" can be a useful word; but, again, it becomes invalid when it is held up to oppose style. Content is the illusion myriad stylistic factors create when viewed at a certain distance.

When I say it is impossible to vary the form without varying the information, I do not mean any *formal change* (e.g. the shuffling of a few words in a novel) must completely obviate the entire information-al experience of a given work. Some formal changes are minimal; their effect on a particular collection of words may be unimportant simply because it is undetectable. But I am trying to leave open the possibility that the change of a single word in a novel may be all important.

"Tell me, Martha, *did* you really kill him?"
"Yes."

But in the paperback edition, the second line of type was accidentally dropped. Why should this deletion of a single word hurt the reader's enjoyment of the remaining 59,999 words of the novel...

In my second published novel I recall the key sentence in the opening exposition described the lines of communication between two cities as "...now lost for good." A printer's error rendered the line "not lost for good," and practically destroyed the rest of the story.

But the simplicity of my examples sabotages my point more than it supports it. Here is another, more relevant:

I put some things on the desk.
I put some books on the desk.
I put three books on the desk.
I put Hacker's *Presentation Piece*, Ebbe Borregaard's *Sketches for Thirteen Sonnets*, and Wakoski's *Inside the Blood Factory* on the desk.

The variations here are closer to the type people arguing for the chimera of content call meaningless. The information generated by each sentence is clearly different. But what we know about what was put on the desk is only the most obvious difference. Let's assume these are the opening sentences of four different stories. Four tones of voice are generated by the varying specificity. The tone will be heard—if not consciously noted—by whoever reads. And the different tones give different information about the personality of the speaker as well as the speaker's state of mind. That is to say, the *I* generated by each sentence is different.

As a writer utilizes this information about the individual speaker, his story seems more dense, more real. And he is a better artist than the writer who dismisses the variations in these sentences as minimal. This is what makes Heinlein a better writer than Van Vogt.

But we have not exhausted the differences in the information in these sentences when we have explored the differences in the "I . . ." As we know something about the personality of the various speakers, and something about what the speaker is placing down, ranges of possibility are opened up about the desk (and the room around it) itself—four different ranges. This information is much harder to specify, because many other factors will influence it: does the desk belong to the speaker or someone about whom the speaker feels strongly; or has she only seen the desk for the first time moments before laying the books on it? Indeed, there is no way to say that any subsequent description of the desk is wrong because it contradicts specific information generated by those opening sentences. But once those other factors have been cleared up, one description may certainly seem "righter" than another, because it is reinforced by that admittedly vague information, different for each of the examples, that has been generated. And the ability to utilize effectively this refinement in generated information is what makes Sturgeon a better writer than Heinlein.

In each of those sentences the only apparent *formal* variation is the specificity of what *I* put on *the desk*. But by this change, the *I* and *the desk* change as well. The illusion of reality, the sense of veracity in all fiction, is controlled by the author's sensitivity to these distinctions. A story is not a replacement of one set of words by another—plot-synopsis, detailed recounting, or analysis. The story is what happens in the reader's mind as his eyes move from the first word to the second, the second to the third, and so on to the end of the tale.

Let's look more closely at what happens in this visual journey. How, for example, does the work of reading a narrative differ from watching a film? In a film the illusion of reality comes from a series of pictures each slightly different. The difference represents a fixed chronological relation which the eye and the mind together render as motion.

Words in a narrative generate tones of voice, syntactic expectations, memories of other words, and pictures. But rather than a fixed chronological relation, they sit in numerous inter- and overweaving relations. The process as we move our eyes from word to word is corrective and revisionary rather than progressive. Each new word revises the complex picture we had a moment before.

Around the meaning of any word is a certain margin in which to correct the image of the object we arrive at (in the old grammatical terms, to modify).

I say:

dog

and an image jumps in your mind (as it did with "red"), but because I have not put it in a formal relation with anything else, you have no way to know whether the specific image in your mind has anything to do with what I want to communicate. Hence that leeway. I can correct it:

Collie dog, and you will agree. I can correct it into a *big dog* or a *shaggy dog*, and you will still concur. But a *Chevrolet dog*? An *oxymoronic dog*? A *turgidly cardiac dog*? For the purposes of ordinary speech, and naturalistic fiction, these corrections are outside acceptable boundaries: they distort some essential quality in all the various objects that we have attached to the sound "dog." On the other hand, there is something to be enjoyed in the distortions, a freshness that may be quite entertaining, even though they lack the inevitablity of our big, shaggy collie.

A sixty thousand word novel is one picture corrected fifty-nine thousand, nine hundred and ninety-nine times. The total experience must have the same feeling of freshness as this turgidly cardiac creature as well as the inevitability of Big and Shaggy here.

Now let's atomize the correction process itself. A story begins:

The

What is the image thrown on your mind? Whatever it is, it is going to be changed many, many times before the tale is over. My own, unmodified, rather whimsical *The* is a grayish ellipsoid about four feet high that balances on the floor perhaps a yard away. Yours is no doubt different. But it is there, has a specific size, shape, color, and bears a particular relation to you. My *a*, for example, differs from my *the* in that it is about the same shape and color—a bit paler, perhaps—but is either much farther away, or much smaller and nearer. In either case, I am going to be either much less, or much more, interested in it than I am in *The*. Now we come to the second word in the story and the first correction:

The red

My four-foot ellipsoid just changed color. It is still about the same distance away. It has become more interesting. In fact, even at this point I feel vaguely that the increased interest may be outside the leeway I allow for a *The*. I feel a strain here that would be absent if the first two words had been *A red*... My eye goes on to the third word while my mind prepares for the second correction:

The red sun

The original *The* has now been replaced by a luminous disc. The color has lightened considerably. The disk is above me. An indistinct landscape has formed about me. And I am even more aware, now that the object has been placed at such a distance, of the tension between my own interest level in *red sun* and the ordinary attention I accord a *The*: for the intensity of interest is all that is left with me of the original image.

Less clearly, in terms of future corrections, is a feeling that in this landscape it is either dawn, sunset, or, if it is another time, smog of some sort must be hazing the air (...*red* sun...); but I hold all for the next correction:

The red sun is

A sudden sense of intimacy. I am being asked to pay even greater attention, in a way that *was* would not demand, as *was* in the form of the traditional historical narrative. But *is?*... There is a speaker here!

That focus in attention I felt between the first two words is not my attention, but the attention of the speaker. It resolves into a tone of voice: "The *red* sun is . . ." And I listen to this voice, in the midst of this still vague landscape, registering its concern for the red sun. Between *the* and *red* information was generated that between *sun* and *is* resolved into a meaningful correction in my vision. This is my first aesthetic pleasure from the tale—a small one, as we have only progressed four words into the story. Nevertheless, it becomes one drop in the total enjoyment to come from the telling. Watching and listening to my speaker, I proceed to the next corrections:

The red sun is high,

Noon and slightly overcast; this is merely a confirmation of something previously suspected, nowhere near as major a correction as the one before. It allows a slight sense of warmth into the landscape, and the light has been fixed at a specific point. I attempt to visualize that landscape more clearly, but no object, including the speaker, has been cleared enough to resolve. The comma tells me that a thought group is complete. In the pause it occurs to me that the redness of the sun may not be a clue to smog at all, but merely the speaker falling into literary-ism; or at best, the redness is a projection of his consciousness, which as yet I don't understand. And for a moment I notice that from where I'm standing the sun indeed appears its customary, blinding-white gold. Next correction:

The red sun is high, the

In this strange landscape (lit by its somewhat untrustworthily described sun) the speaker has turned his attention to another gray, four-foot ellipsoid, equidistant from himself and me. Again, it is too indistinct to take highlighting. But there have been two corrections with not much tension, and the reality of the speaker himself is beginning to slip. What will this become?

The red sun is high, the blue

The ellipsoid has changed hue. But the repetition in the syntactic arrangement of the description momentarily threatens to dissolve all reality, landscape, speaker, and sun, into a mannered listing of bucolica. The whole scene dims. And the final correction?

The red sun is high, the blue low.

Look! We are worlds and worlds away. The first sun is huge; and how accurate the description of its color turns out to have been. The repetition that predicted mannerism now fixes both big and little sun to the sky. The landscape crawls with long red shadows and stubby blue ones, joined by purple triangles. Look at the speaker himself. Can you see him? You have seen his doubled shadow . . .

Though it ordinarily takes only a quarter of a second and is largely unconscious, this is the process.

When the corrections as we move from word to word produce a muddy picture, when unclear bits of information do not resolve to even greater clarity as we progress, we call the writer a poor stylist. As the story goes on, and the pictures become more complicated as they develop through time, if even greater anomalies appear as we continue correcting, we say he can't plot. But it is the same quality error committed on a grosser level, even though a reader must be a third or three-quarters of the way through the book to spot one, while the first may glare out from the opening sentence.

In any commercial field of writing, like s-f, the argument of writers and editors who feel *content* can be opposed to *style* runs, at its most articulate:

"Basically we are writing adventure fiction. We are writing it very fast. We do not have time to be concerned about any but the grosser errors. More important, you are talking about subtleties too refined for the vast majority of our readers who are basically neither literary nor sophisticated."

The internal contradictions here could make a book. Let me outline two.

The basis of any adventure novel, s-f or otherwise, what gives it its entertainment value—escape value if you will—what sets it apart from the psychological novel, what names it an adventure, is the intensity with which the real actions of the story impinge on the protagonist's consciousness. The simplest way to generate that sense of adventure is to increase the intensity with which the real actions impinge on the reader's. And fictional intensity is almost entirely the province of those refinements of which I have been speaking.

The story of an infant's first toddle across the kitchen floor will be an adventure if the writer can generate the infantile wonder at new muscles, new efforts, obstacles, and detours. I would like to read such a story.

We have all read, many too many times, the heroic attempts of John Smith to save the lives of seven orphans in the face of fire, flood, and avalanche.

I am sure it was an adventure for Smith.

For the reader it was dull as dull could be.

The Doors of His Face, the Lamps of His Mouth by Roger Zelazny has been described as "...all speed and adventure..." by Theodore Sturgeon, and indeed it is one of the most exciting adventure tales s-f has produced. Let me change one word in every grammatical unit of every sentence, replacing it with a word that "...means more or less the same thing..." and I can diminish the excitement by half and expunge every trace of wit. Let me change one word and *add* one word, and I can make it so dull as to be practically unreadable. Yet a paragraph by paragraph synopsis of the "content" will be the same.

An experience I find painful (though it happens with increasing frequency) occurs when I must listen to a literate person who has just become enchanted by some hacked-out space-boiler begin to rhapsodize about the way the blunt, imprecise, leaden language reflects the hairy-chested hero's alienation from reality. He usually goes on to explain how the "...s-f content..." itself reflects our whole society's divorce from the real. The experience is painful because he is right as far as he goes. Badly-written adventure fiction is our true antiliterature. Its protagonists are our real antiheroes. They move through unreal worlds amid all sorts of noise and manage to perceive nothing meaningful or meaningfully.

Author's intention or no, that is what badly written s-f *is* about. But anyone who reads or writes s-f seriously knows that its particular excellence is in another area altogether: in all the brouhaha clanging about these unreal worlds, chords are sounded in total sympathy with the real.

"...you are talking about subtleties too refined for the vast majority of our readers who are basically neither literary nor sophisticated."

This part of the argument always throws me back to an incident from the summer I taught a remedial English class at my Neighborhood Community Center. The voluntary nature of the class automatically restricted enrollment to people who wanted to learn; still, I had sixteen- and seventeen-year-olds who had never had any formal education in either Spanish or English continually joining my lessons. Regardless, after a student had been in the class six months, I would throw at him a full five hundred and fifty page novel to read: Dmitri Merezhkovsky's *The Romance of Leonardo da Vinci*. The book is full of Renaissance history, as well as sword play, magic, and dissertations on art and science. It is an extremely literary novel with several levels of interpretation. It was a favorite of Sigmund Freud (Rilke, in a letter, found it loathsome) and inspired him to write his own *Leonardo da Vinci: A Study in Psychosexuality*. My students loved it, and with it, lost a good deal of their fear of Literature and Long Books.

Shortly before I had to leave the class, *Leonardo* appeared in paperback, translated by Hubert Trench. Till then it had only been available in a Modern Library edition translated by Bernard Gilbet Gurney. To save my latest two students a trip to the Barnes and Noble basement, as well as a dollar fifty, I suggested they buy the paperback. Two days later one had struggled through forty pages and the other had given up after ten. Both thought the book dull, had no idea what it was about, and begged me for something shorter and more exciting.

Bewildered, I bought a copy of the Trench translation myself that afternoon. I do not have either book at hand as I write, so I'm sure a comparison with the actual texts will prove me an exaggerator. But I recall one description of a little house in Florence:

Gurney: "Gray smoke rose and curled from the slate chimney."
Trench: "Billows of smoke, gray and gloomy, elevated and contorted up from the slates of the chimney."

By the same process that differentiated the four examples of putting books on a desk, these two sentences do not refer to the same smoke, chimney, house, time of day; nor do any of the other houses within sight remain the same; nor do any possible inhabitants. One sentence has nine words, the other fifteen. But atomize both as a series of corrected images and you will find the mental energy expended on the latter is greater by a factor of six or seven! And over seven eighths of it leaves that uncomfortable feeling of loose-endedness, unutilized and unresolved. Sadly, it is the less skilled, less sophisticated reader who is most injured by bad writing. Bad prose requires more mental energy to correct your image from word to word, and the corrections themselves are less rewarding. That is what makes it bad. The sophisticated, literary reader may give the words the benefit of the doubt and question whether a seeming clumsiness is more fruitfully interpreted as an intentional ambiguity.

For what it is worth, when I write I often try to say several things at the same time—from a regard for economy that sits contiguous with any concern for skillful expression. I have certainly failed to say many of the things I intended. But ambiguity marks the failure, not the intent.

But how does all this relate to those particular series of corrected images we label *s-f*? To answer that, we must first look at what distinguishes these particular word series from other word series that get labeled *naturalistic fiction, reportage, fantasy.*

A distinct level of subjunctivity informs all the words in an s-f story at a level that is different from that which informs naturalistic fiction, fantasy, or reportage.

Subjunctivity is the tension on the thread of meaning that runs between (to borrow Saussure's term for 'word':) sound-image and sound-image. Suppose a series of words is presented to us as a piece of reportage. A blanket indicative tension informs the whole series: *this happened.* That is the particular level of subjunctivity at which journalism takes place. Any word, even the metaphorical ones, must go straight back to a real object, or a real thought on the part of the reporter.

The subjunctivity level for a series of words labeled naturalistic fiction is defined by: *could have happened.* Note that the level of subjunctivity makes certain dictates and allows certain freedoms as to what word can follow another. Consider this word series: "For one second, as she stood alone on the desert, her world shattered and she watched the fragments bury themselves in the dunes." This is practically meaningless at the subjunctive level of reportage. But it might be a perfectly adequate, if not brilliant , word series for a piece of naturalistic fiction.

Fantasy takes the subjunctivity of naturalistic fiction and throws it into reverse. At the appearance of elves, witches, or magic in a nonmetaphorical position, or at some correction of image too bizarre to be explained by other than the supernatural, the level of subjunctivity becomes: *could not have happened.* And immediately it informs *all* the words in the series. No matter how naturalistic the setting, once the witch has taken off on her broomstick the most realistic of trees, cats, night clouds, or the moon behind them become infected with this reverse subjunctivity.

But when spaceships, ray guns, or more accurately any correction of images that indicates the future appear in a series of words and mark it as s-f, the subjunctivity level is changed once more: These objects, these convocations of objects into situations and events, are blanketly defined by: *have not happened.*

Events that have not happened are very different from the fictional events that *could have happened,* or the fantastic events that *could not have happened.*

Events that have not happened include several subcategories. These subcategories describe the subcategories of s-f. *Events that have not happened* include those events that *might happen:* these are your technological and sociological predictive tales. Another category includes *events that will not happen:* these are your science-fantasy stories. They include *events that have not happened yet* (Can you hear the implied tone of warning?): there are your cautionary dystopias, *Brave New World* and *1984.* Were English a language with a more detailed tense system, it would be easier to see that *events that have not happened* include past events as well as future ones. *Events that have not happened in the past* compose that s-f specialty, the parallel-world story, whose outstanding example is Philip K. Dick's *The Man in the High Castle.*

The particular subjunctive level of s-f expands the freedom of the choice of words that can follow another group of words meaningfully; but it limits the way we employ the corrective process as we move between them.

At the subjunctive level of naturalistic fiction, "The red sun is high, the blue low," is meaningless. In naturalistic fiction our corrections in our images must be made in accordance with what we know of the personally observable—this includes our own observations of others that have been reported to us at the subjunctive level of journalism.

Considered at the subjunctive level of fantasy, "The red sun is high, the blue low," fares a little better. But the corrective process in fantasy is limited too: when we are given a correction that is not meaningful in terms of the personally observable world, we *must* accept any pseudoexplanation we are given. If there is no pseudoexplanation, it must remain mysterious. As fantasy, one suspects that the red sun is the "realer" one, but what sorcerer, to what purpose, shunted up that second, azure, orb, we cannot know and must wait for the rest of the tale.

As we have seen, that sentence makes very good s-f. The subjunctive level of s-f says that we must make our correction process in accord with what we know of the physically explainable universe. And the physically explainable has a much wider range than the personally observable.[3] The particular verbal freedom of s-f, coupled with the corrective process that allows the whole range of the physically explainable universe, can produce the most violent leaps of imagery. For not only does it throw us worlds away, it specifies how we got there.

Let us examine what happens between the following two words:

winged dog

As naturalistic fiction it is meaningless. As fantasy it is merely a visual correction. At the subjunctive level of s-f, however, one must momentarily consider, as one makes that visual correction, an entire track of evolution: whether the dog has forelegs or not. The visual correction must include modification of breastbone and musculature if the wings are to be functional, as well as a whole slew of other factors from hollow bones to heart rate; or if we subsequently learn as the series of words goes on that grafting was the cause, there are all the implications (to consider) of a technology capable of such an operation. All of this information hovers tacitly about and between those two words in the same manner that the information about *I* and *the desk* hovered around the statements about placing down the books. The best s-f writer will utilize this information just as she utilizes the information generated by any verbal juxtapositioning.

I quote Harlan Ellison describing his own reaction to this verbal process:

> ... Heinlein has always managed to indicate the greater strangeness of a culture with the most casually dropped-in reference: the first time in a novel, I believe it was in *Beyond This Horizon*, that a character came through a door that ... dilated. And no discussion. Just: "The door dilated." I read across it, and was two lines down before I realized what the image had been, what the words had called forth. A *dilating* door. It didn't open, it *irised*! Dear God, now I knew I was in a future world ...

"The door dilated," is meaningless as naturalistic fiction, and practically meaningless as fantasy. As s-f—as an event that hasn't happened, yet still must be interpreted in terms of the physically explainable—it is quite as wondrous as Ellison feels it.

As well, the luminosity of Heinlein's particular vision was supported by all sorts of other information, stated and unstated, generated by the novel's other words.

Through this discussion, I have tried to keep away from what motivates the construction of these violent nets of wonder called speculative fiction. The more basic the discussion, the greater is our obligation to stay with the reader in *front* of the page. But at the mention of the author's "vision" the subject is already broached. The vision (sense of wonder, if you will) that s-f tries for seems to me very close to the vision of poetry, particularly poetry as it concerned the nineteenth century Symbolists. No matter how disciplined its creation, to move into the "unreal" world demands a brush with mysticism.

Virtually all the classics of speculative fiction are mystical.

In Isaac Asimov's *Foundation* trilogy, one man, dead on page thirty-seven, achieves nothing less than the redemption of mankind from twenty-nine thousand years of suffering simply by his heightened consciousness of the human condition. (Read "consciousness of the human condition" for "science of psychohistory.")

In Robert Heinlein's *Stranger in a Strange Land* the appearance of God Incarnate creates a world of love and cannibalism.

Clarke's *Childhood's End* and Sturgeon's *More Than Human* detail vastly differing processes by which man becomes more than man.

Alfred Bester's *The Stars My Destination* (or *Tiger, Tiger,* its original title) is considered by many readers and writers, both in and outside the field, to be the greatest single s-f novel. In this book, man, intensely human yet more than human, becomes, through greater acceptance of his humanity, something even more. It chronicles a social education, but within a society which, from our point of view, has gone mad. In the climactic scene, the protagonist, burning in the ruins of a collapsing cathedral, has his senses confused by synesthesia. Terrified, he begins to oscillate insanely in time and space. Through this experience, with the help of his worst enemy transformed by time into his savior, he saves himself and attains a state of innocence and rebirth.

This is the stuff of mysticism.

It is also a very powerful dramatization of Rimbaud's theory of the systematic derangement of the senses to achieve the unknown. And the Rimbaud reference is as conscious as the book's earlier references to Joyce, Blake, and Swift. (I would like to see the relation between the Symbolists and modern American speculative fiction examined more thoroughly. The French Symbolists' particular problems of vision have been explored repeatedly not only by writers like Bester and Sturgeon, but also newer writers like Roger Zelazny, who bring both erudition and word magic to strange creations generated from the tension between suicide and immortality. And the answers they discover are all unique.) To recapitulate: whatever the inspiration or vision, whether it arrives in a flash or has been meticulously worked out over years, the only way a writer can present it is by what he can make happen in the reader's mind between one word and another, by the way he can maneuver the existing tensions between words and associated images.

I have read many descriptions of "mystical experiences"—many in s-f stories and novels. Very, very few have generated any *feel* of the mystical—which is to say that as the writers went about setting correction after correction, the images were too untrustworthy to call up any personal feelings about such experiences. The Symbolists have a lesson here: the only thing that we will trust enough to let it generate in us any real sense of the mystical is a resonant aesthetic form.

The sense of mystical horror, for example, in Thomas M. Disch's extraordinary novella, *The Asian Shore,* does not come from its study of a particularly insidious type of racism, incisive though the study is; nor does it come from the final incidents set frustratingly between the supernatural and the insane. It generates rather in the formal parallels between the protagonist's concepts of Byzantine architecture and the obvious architecture of his own personality.

Aesthetic form...I am going to leave this discussion at this undefined term. For many people it borders on the meaningless. I hope there is enough tension between the words to proliferate with what has gone before. To summarize, however: any serious discussion of speculative fiction must first get away from the distracting concept of s-f content and examine precisely what sort of word-beast sits before us. We must explore both the level of subjunctivity at which speculative fiction takes place and the particular intensity and range of images this level affords. Readers must do this if they want to fully understand what has already been written. Writers must do this if the field is to mature to the potential so frequently cited for it.

NEW YORK
DECEMBER 1968

Notes

¹ I am purposely not using the word "symbol" in this discussion. The vocabulary that must accompany it generates too much confusion.

² Words also have "phonic presence" as well as meaning. And certainly all writers must work with sound to vary the rhythm of a phrase or sentence, as well as to control the meaning. But this discussion is going to veer close enough to poetry. To consider the musical, as well as the ritual, value of language in s-f would make poetry and prose indistinguishable. That is absolutely not my intention.

³ I throw out this notion for its worth as intellectual play. It is not too difficult to see that as *events that have not happened* include the subgroup of *events that have not happened in the past*, they include the subsubgroup of *events that could have happened* with an implied *but didn't.* That is to say, the level of subjunctivity of s-f includes the level of subjunctivity of naturalistic fiction.

As well, the personally observable world is a subcategory of the physically explainable universe. That is, the laws of the first can all be explained in terms of the laws of the second, while the situation is not necessarily reversible. So much for the two levels of subjunctivity and the limitations on the corrective processes that go with them.

What of the respective freedoms in the choice of word to follow word?

I can think of no series of words that could appear in a piece of naturalistic fiction that could not also appear in the same order in a piece of speculative fiction. I can, however, think of many series of words that, while fine for speculative fiction, would be meaningless as naturalism. Which then is the major and which the subcategory?

Consider: naturalistic fictions are parallel-world stories in which the divergence from the real is too slight for historical verification.

Shadows

Criticism of science fiction cannot possibly look like the criticism we are used to. It will—perforce—employ an aesthetic in which the elegance, rigorousness, and systematic coherence of explicit ideas is of great importance. It will therefore appear to stray into all sorts of extraliterary fields, metaphysics, politics, philosophy, physics, biology, psychology, topology, mathematics, history, and so on. The relation of foreground and background that we are used to after a century and a half of realism will not obtain. Indeed they may be reversed. Science-fiction criticism will discover themes and structures... which may seem recondite, extraliterary, or plain ridiculous. Themes we customarily regard as emotionally neutral will be charged with emotion. Traditionally human concerns will be absent; protagonists may be all but unrecognizable as such. What in other fiction would be marvelous will here be merely accurate or plain; what in other fiction would be ordinary or mundane will here be astonishing, complex, wonderful... For example, allusions to the death of God will be trivial jokes, while metaphors involving the differences between telephone switchboards and radio stations will be poignantly tragic. Stories ostensibly about persons will really be about topology. Erotics will be intercranial, mechanical (literally), and moving.

Towards an Aesthetic of Science Fiction
JOANNA RUSS

1. Today's Technology is tomorrow's handicraft.

2. Lines I particularly liked from Knotly's poem in the current *Paris*

Review: "for every one must run a race/in the body's own running place" and: "Everything I have has an earwig in it/which will make light of sacred things".

3. Nothing we look at is ever seen without some shift and flicker— that constant flaking of vision which we take as imperfections of the eye or simply the instability of attention itself; and we ignore this illusory screen for the solid reality behind it. But the solid reality is the illusion; the shift and flicker is all there is. (Where do s-f writers get their crazy ideas? From watching all there is *very* carefully.)

4. The above notes, this one, and the ones below are picked, somewhat at random, from my last two years' journals, in lieu of the personal article requested on the development of a science-fiction writer.

5. Critical language presents us a problem: The critic "analyses" a work to "reveal" its "internal form." Recent structuralist critics are trying to "discover the underlying, mythic structures" of given works or cultures. There is the implication that what the critic comes up with is somehow more *basic* than the thing under study—we are all, of course, too sophisticated to be fooled into thinking what the critic produces is more *important*.

Still, however, we feel the critical find should be more intense, more solid, more foundational than the work. After all, though novels are fiction, the books of criticism about them are not.

The visual image is something like a surgeon, carefully dissecting a body, removing the skeleton from it, and presenting the bones to our view—so that we will have a more schematic idea of how the fleshed organism articulates.

All this, however, is the result of a category concept mistake.

A slightly better image, as a basic model of the critical process, will, perhaps, explode it:

The critic sits at a certain distance from the work, views it from a particular side, and builds a more or less schematic model of the work as it strikes her or him (just as I am making *this* model of what the critic does), emphasizing certain elements, suppressing certain others, attaching little historical notes to his model here and there on where she thinks this or that form in the original work might have come from, all according to the particular critical use the model is intended for. But the critic does not *remove* anything from the work itself (even if she quotes it lengthily, she is still making a *copy* of it), unless he is a censor (or, perhaps, an editor of expurgated editions).

Works of literature, painting, and sculpture simply do not *have* informative insides. There *is* no skeleton to be removed. They are all surface. A piece of sculpture has a physical inside, but drilling a hole three inches into the Venus de Milo will give you no aesthetic insight into it. (Note, however: this paragraph does not hold true [at least in the same way] for theatrical works, orchestral music, or much electronic art. For an s-f story: postulate a world and a culture which has an art all of which *does* have informative insides—great cloth sculptures, for example, held up from within by hidden pipe-shapes, electronic art run by hidden circuitry. The critic, as criminal, hires herself to other social criminals who wish to understand the art; they break into museums, dismantle the art objects, and remove the insides for inspection. The works are reassembled . . . clumsily. Later, an artist passing by, notices something is wrong, and cries out to a guard: "Look, look! A *critic* has been at my work! Can't you see . . . ?" Theme of the story: If to understand the work is physically to destroy or injure it, are the critics [and the people who wish to understand art] heroes or villains? Are the artists, who make works that can only be understood by dismantling them, charlatans? Consider also, since my view is that this is just how so many people *do* misinterpret criticism today, will my context be understood? Is there any way that I can make clear in the story that what I am presenting is not *how* criticism works; rather, I am poking fun at the general misapprehension? I am not in the least interested in writing a simpleminded, "damning" satire of Modern Criticism. Will have to rethink seriously incidents as first listed if I want the story's point to be the subtle one. *Can* such a point be dramatised in an s-f story . . . ?)

Basically, however, the critic is part of the work's audience. The critic responds to it, selects among those responses and, using them, makes, selectively, a model of the work that may, hopefully, guide, helpfully, the responses of the critic's own audience when they come to the work being modeled.

When a critic, talking about critical work, suggests she is doing more than this, at best she is indulging in metaphor; at worst, he is practicing, whether wittingly or no, more of that pernicious mystification that has brought us to our present impasse.

(Happy with the *idea*; but still uncomfortable with it as a story template—because, as a template, it seems to be saying exactly the *opposite* of what I want to! Is this, perhaps, a problem basic to s-f: That you can only use it to reinforce commonly accepted prejudices; and that to use it for a discussion of anything at a more complex resolution simply can't be done at the literary distance s-f affords? From Cassirer to Kirk, critics have leveled just this accusation at mythology. If it's true of s-f as well, perhaps s-f is, inchoately, an immature form . . . ? Well, there: The ugly suggestion has been made.

(Do I agree?

(No, I don't. But I think it is certainly an inherent tendency of the medium. To fight it, and triumph over it, I must specifically: go into the world I have set up *far* more thoroughly than I have, and treat it autonomously rather than as *merely* a model of a prejudiciary situation. I must explore it as an extensive, coherent reality—not as an intensive reflection of the real world where the most conservative ideas will drain all life out of the invention.

(What does my culture look like, for instance, once I leave the museum? Given its basic aesthetic outlook, what would its architecture look like? How would the museum itself look, from the inside? From the outside? What would the building where the artist lived look like? And where the critic lived? What would be their relative social positions? What would be the emblems of those positions? How would such emblems differ from the emblems of social positions in our world? What would it smell like to walk through their streets? Given their art, what of their concept of science? Is it the opposite of their concept of art? Or is it an extension of it? Are the informative insides of the scientific works as mystified as the insides of art works? Or are they made blatantly public? Or are they mystified even *more* than the art? What are the problems that critics of science have in this world? Or critics of politics? Would critics be the same people?

(As I begin to treat my original conceit as a coherent, antonomous world, instead of just a statement about *our* world, I begin to generate a template complicated enough and rich enough to actually make a statement about our world that is something more than simple-minded. I can now start to ask myself questions like: In this world, what are the psychological traits of someone who would become a critic? An artist? A scientist? Etc. But it is only when the template becomes at least that complex that s-f becomes mature.)

6.   Moorcocks coming over here for dinner tonight with John Sims: Cream of Leek soup, Roast Beef, Fried Eggplant, Rice (possibly a risotto with almonds? How many stuffed mushrooms are left over from the Landrys yesterday? And will they do, reheated, for starters?); an American Salad (get some Avocado, Bacon, Butter-lettuce, Chicory, Tomatoes, Cucumbers, Carrots, Celery, Mustard, Lemons); to follow: Baked Bananas flamed in brandy. (*Don't* use the mushrooms: John doesn't like them!)

7.   For Sturgeon essay: The material of fiction is the texture of experience.

8.   Re *Dhalgren*... I think Marilyn is depressingly right about the psychiatric session with Madame Brown and the Calkins' interview... which means more work; and after I've just rewritten the whole, last chapter! With Calkins, the historical *must* be made manifest. With Madame Brown, she must realize that the dream is not a dream, otherwise she comes off just *too* stupid. It is so hard to control the outside view of my material, when I am standing on the inside. It's like clutching a balloon to shape from within.
    Friday night and to the Moorcocks for dinner with Emma Tennent.

9.   Got a letter from REGeis today, asking to reprint my *Letter to a Critic* from *The Little Magazine* in *The Alien Critic*. Am very dubious. First of all, some of the facts, as John Brunner so succinctly pointed out over the phone a fortnight back, are just wrong. More to the point, the section on science-fiction publishing isn't really a description of the current s-f publishing scene at all. Rather, it's a memoir of what the publishing situation was like in that odd period between 1967 and 1971. Odd, too, how quickly the bright truths of twenty-six (by which age the bulk of my notoriously unbulky s-f oeuvre was already in print) seem, six years later, rather dated. What to do? Get ever so slightly looped and write a polite letter?
    Or take a walk up Regents' Canal and go browse in Compendium Book Store? Sounds better.

10. What a tiny part of our lives we use in picturing our pasts. Walked to the Turkish take-away place this evening with John Witton-Doris: consider the *number* of incidents he recalls from our months in Greece together, nine years ago, involving me, that I can barely remember! Biography, *as* it approaches completeness, must *be* the final fiction.

11. Alcohol is the opium of the people.

12. Science fiction through the late sixties seemed to be, scientifically, interested in mathematics segueing into electronics; psychiatry, in all its oversimplified clumsiness, has been an s-f mainstay from *The Roads Must Roll*, through *Baby is Three*, to *The Dream Master*.

Science fiction from the past few years seems to be interested in mathematics segueing into contemporary linguistics/philosophy (e.g., Watson's *The Embedding*); biology—particularly genetics—has replaced physics as the science of greatest concern, [Cf. the 'clone' stories over the past few years, from Kate Wilhelm's and Ted Thomas's *The Clone*, through McIntyre's *The Cage* (and Ms. McIntyre is a trained geneticist; where do we get all this about people interested in science not getting into science fiction anymore!?!), to Wolfe's *The Fifth Head of Cerberus*]; and anthropology (reflected even in books like Effinger's *What Entropy Means to Me* and Toomey's *A World of Trouble)* seems to be replacing psychiatry as a prime concern.

I think I approve.

13. "You science-fiction writers always criticize each other in print as if the person you were criticizing were reading over your shoulder," someone said to me at the Bristol Con last week—meaning, I'm afraid, that the majority of criticism that originates within the field has either a "let-me-pat-your-back-so-you-can-pat-mine" air, or, even more frequently, a sort of catty, wheedling tone implying much more is being criticized than the work nominally under discussion.

No, the s-f community is not large.

Perhaps it's because I've spent just over a decade making my living within it, but I feel *all* criticism should be written as if the author being criticized were—not reading over your shoulder; but written as though you could stand face to face with him and read it out loud, without embarrassment.

I think this should hold whether you are trying to fix the most rarefied of metaphysicial imports in some Shakespearean tragedy, or writing a two-hundred word review of the latest thriller. Wheedling or flattery have nothing to do with it.

Among the many informations we try to get from any critical model is the original maker's (the artist's) view of the original work modeled. If the critics do not include, in their model, an overt assessment of it, we construct it from hints, suggestions, and whatever. But *we* are at three removes from the author; and the critic is at two (as the critic is one from the work): In deference to that distance, I feel the critics must make such assessments humbly. They can always be wrong.

But only after they, and we, have made them (wrong or right), can we follow the critics' exploration of the work's method, success, or relevance. The critic can only judge these things by her own responses; in a very real way, the only thing the critic is ever really criticizing—and this must be done humbly if it is to be done at all—is the response of her own critical instrument.

All criticism is personal.

The best is rigorously so.

14. Yesterday, Joyce Carol Oates sent Marilyn a copy of her new book of poems *Angel Fire* (with a letter apologizing for taking so long to answer Marilyn's last letter etc. and dense with North American weather). This morning, in Compendium, I saw the new Oates book on D.H. Lawrence's poetry, *The Hostile Sun*, picked it up, took it (in its bright yellow covers) home, and have, minutes ago, just finished it.

After going through three novels, a handful of essays, and a few crunches into the Collected Poems (and most recently, the Frank Kermode book on), Lawrence has tended to be for me a clumsy, if impassioned, writer purveying a message I find almost totally heinous. The most generous thing I could say for him till now was, with Kenneth Rexroth, "His enemies are my enemies," but even here I always found myself wondering, wouldn't he do better on their side than on mine? Lawrence-the-outspoken-sexual-revolutionary has always struck me a bit like those politicians who, in their support of the War in Vietnam, eventually went so far as to use words like "hell" and "damn" in their speeches—then quickly looked at their fellow party members who dared disapprove of their "too strong" language and labeled *them* conservatives. Though Lawrence's novels sometimes refer to sexual mechanics, his overall concept of sex seems institutionally rigid: Everyone must fulfill his or her role, as assigned by Divine Law. The heroes of his novels go about brow-beating everyone who happens to stray from his (usually her) divinely ordained role, back into it. For, after all, it *is* Divine Law. And anyone who still strays, after having been told *that*, must be sick unto damnation. I wonder if Lawrence was aware that his real critics simply found him, in his ideas (rather than in the "strength" of his language, or the "explicitness" of the scenes he used to dramatize his points) an absolute prig?

At any rate, *The Hostile Sun* offers me a guide to the Collected Poems (the volume Joyce gave Marilyn as a going away present; she must have been working on the essay then) that may just get me into them in a way that I can get something out. The book makes the idea of Lawrence-the-Poet interesting to me and offers me some way of divorcing it from Lawrence-the-Prophet—whom I find a pernicious bore. Oates points out his strengths in the poems (the overall intensity of vision; his aesthetic of unrectified feeling) and warns what not to look for (the single, well-crafted poem; a certain type of aesthetic intelligence). Since there are half a dozen poets whom I enjoy in just this way, from James Thompson and Walt Whitman to Paul Blackburn and Philip Whalen, I suspect I will go back to Lawrence's poems better prepared.

It *is* nice to be reminded that criticism, well done, can open up areas previously closed.

15. Confessions of a science-fiction writer: I have never read one H.G. Wells "romance of the future" from cover to cover. I once read three quarters of *Food of the Gods*, and I have read the first fifty/one hundred pages of perhaps half a dozen more.

When I was thirteen, somebody gave me Verne's *Twenty Thousand Leagues under the Sea* as a book that "you'll simply love." At page two hundred I balked. I never *have* finished it! I did a little better with *From the Earth to the Moon*, but I still didn't reach the end.

By the time I was fifteen, however, in my own personal

hierarchy, Wells and Verne were synonymous with the crashingly dull. Also, I had gotten their names mixed up with something called Victorian Literature (which, when I was fifteen, somehow included Jane Austen!), and I decided that it was probably all equally boring.

I was eighteen before I began to correct this impression (with, of all things, Eliot's *Adam Bede*); fortunately somebody had already forced me—marvelous experience that it was—into Jane Austen by assuring me that her first three books were written before Victoria was even a sparkle in the Duke of Kent's eye. Then the hordes: Thackeray, the Brontes, Dickens, Hardy. But I have never quite forgiven Wells and Verne for, even so briefly, prejudicing me against the "serious" literature written by their contemporaries and precursors who just happened to have overlapped, to whatever extent, the reign of that same, diminutive monarch.

16. When I was a child, I used to play the violin. At twelve I developed a not wholly innocent passion for a boy of thirteen who was something of a violin prodigy: He had already been soloist with several small, but professional orchestras, and he was talked about muchly in my several circles of friends. I wrote a violin concerto for him—it took me four months. Its three movements ran about half an hour. I supplied (I thought then) a marvelous cadenza. The themes, if I recall, were all serial, but their development was tonal. I orchestrated it for a full, seventy five pieces—but by the time I had finished, he had moved to up-state New York.

And I had been afraid to tell him what I was doing until it was completed.

Months later, I ran into him in the Museum of Modern Art (he was in the city visiting an aunt) and, excitedly, I told him about my piece, over cokes and English muffins in a coffee shop a few blocks away. He was a little overwhelmed, if not bewildered, but said, "Thanks," and "Gosh!" and "Wow!" a lot. We talked about getting together again. He was first chair violinist with the All State Youth Orchestra that year and a favorite with the conductor. We talked about a possible performance or, at least, getting some of his adult friends to look at it. Then he had to catch a train.

I never saw him again.

He never saw the concerto.

At thirteen I gave up the violin—and have had a slight distrust of the passions ever since.

I notice that I often tend to talk (and think) about my childhood just as though music had no part in it—whereas, in reality, I must have spent more hours at it from eight to twice eight than at anything else. And between the ages of nineteen and twenty two, I probably made as much money as a basket musician in Greenwich Village coffee houses as I did from my first four s-f novels, written over the same time. (And how interesting that the ages from nineteen to twenty-two are suddenly part of my childhood!)

17. A dozen poets whose work I have enormously enjoyed in the last couple of years: Michael Dennis Browne, Alice Knotly, Robert Allen, John Oliver Simon, Philip Levine, Robert Peterson, Judith Johnson Sherwin, Ted Berrigan, Robert Morgan, Ann Waldman, Richard Howard, and J.H. Prynne.

(I am leaving out Marilyn Hacker and Tom Disch; I know them and their work too well!) How many of the dozen named have I actually met? Six. Interesting that one, whom I've never met at all, felt it necessary to tell a complete stranger, who only accidentally met me six months later, that he was quite a good friend of mine when I lived in San Francisco!

18. Down to give a lecture on s-f at the University of Kent. In the discussion period after my talk, someone brought up Theodore Sturgeon. I asked the assembly what they particularly liked about his work. From one side of the room, someone shouted, "His aliens!" and from the other side, simultaneously someone else: "His people!" Everyone laughed. Consider this incident for the Sturgeon essay.

19. Marilyn, from the other room (where she is reading the Jonathan Raban book *The Sociology of the Poem* and, apparently, has just come to another horrendous misreading [where he goes on about Pickard's poem *Rape* (he doesn't apparently, remember the title and refers only to a few lines of it) as expressing good will (!) and fellowship (!!) between the young men in the pub and the old woman (whom he, not Pickard, calls a prostitute)]: "Poetry should be as well written as prose—and at *least* as carefully read!"

20. In the context of 1948—a vacuum tube technology where most adding machines were mechanical—Gilbert Ryle was probably right in denying the existence of mental occurrences as material events with the nature of mechanical entities, separable from the brain. In the context of 1973—where we have a solid-state technology and electronic computers—we have to rethink: the empirical evidence of neurology, electronics, and cybernetics all point to a revitalization of the concept of mental occurrences as brain processes. A perfectly serious argument seems to be occurring today in philosophy over whether mental occurrences are nonmaterial events that just happen to happen simultaneously with certain brain processes (or are even set off by the brain processes, but are different from the processes themselves), or whether the brain processes are, indeed, the mental occurrences themselves.

Two things make such an argument seem ridiculous to me—one, empirical, and the other logical.

First, it seems as silly to say that the brain contains *no* model of what the eye sees (which arguers on one side of this argument maintain) as it is to say that the circuitry in a TV camera (that has been turned on) contains no model of what is in front of the image orthicon tube at its proper focal distance. The point is: Anyone who has tried to design a television (or even a radio) circuit from scratch has some idea of just how great the complexity of that model must be: It is practically *all* process, composed of a series of precisely ordered wave fronts that peak in precise patterns, hundreds-to-hundreds-of-thousands-of-times per second, all shunted around, amplified, distorted, and superimposed on one another, in a precise pattern, at close to the speed of light. The philosophers who hold this view, I'm afraid, are simply revealing their inability to conceive even this complexity, empirically demonstrable for processes far simpler than the simplest brain process.

To take another side of the argument (and it has many more than two) is to get lost in one of the numerous logical contradictions of ordinary speech, which allows us to call "a process" a *thing* and "an object" a *thing* too. The internal logical structure of one is distinct from the internal logical structure of the other. *All* processes are nonmaterial, whether they be brain-processes or the process of raising my hand off the table. At the same time, all processes need material to define them. (If I raise a glass off the table, aren't I doing the same "thing" as raising my hand off the table . . . ? Of course I'm not. Which is to say, I *am* doing the same "thing" [i.e., indulging the same process] only in so far as I am *observing* the two events at the same degree of empirical resolution. If I want to, I can observe the raising of two more or less identical glasses from the same spot on the table [or even the same glass] at different times, at such a high degree of empirical resolution that their processes can be uniquely differentiated, having to do with drying times of films of water, molecular change and interchange between the table and the glass, etc. And that, alas, exhausts the tale.) Similarly, all material can be defined by process, the most basic of which, for a static object, is simply the process of duration; as it changes (or as I observe it at a higher degree of empirical resolution, so that I become *aware* of changes in it) we can bring in other processes as well. In this way, all material can be defined by the process (infinitely analyzable into smaller processes) it is undergoing. But the basic terms that are thrown around in this argument—"material event" and "nonmaterial event"—both have an element of self-contradiction (i.e., if "a brain process" can be called "a material event," then, as the brain is the material, the event must be the process, which implies something like a "material process" . . . which is nonsense of the same order as "a green smell") that, it would seem to me, renders them *both* useless for any serious, logical discussion.

To stand for three hours and watch Vikki Sperling map the image from the retina of the eye of the salamander off the visual tectum of the exposed, salamander brain (doubled there, one inverted left–right, and a weaker one right–left) with her gold-filled microelectrodes on their adjustable stands, silences a good deal of the argument in my own head. The behaviorists, with their pretransistor view of the world, say: "But you can't locate mental occurrences!" We can not only locate them, we can measure them, map them, record them, reproduce them, cut them out, and put them in backwards!

21. A "word" has a "meaning" in the sense that a train has a track; *not* in the sense that a train has a passenger. Still, *word* and *meaning* in most people's minds, even most philosophers' apparently, are the same sort of category concept mistake that Ryle tried to show existed in the Cartesian separation between body and mind.

Words mean.

But meaning *is* the interaction of the process into which the eardrum/aural-nerve translates the air vibrations that *are* the word, with the chemoelectric process that is the interpretative context of the brain. Meaning may be something else as well—as mental occurrences *may* be something else as well as brain-processes. But I am sure that they are *at least* this, which is why empirical exploration strikes me as the only practical way to get seriously further in either discussion.

22. Many scientists and mathematicians fool themselves into thinking there is something eternal about, say, a mathematical proof.

At Marilyn's bookstall, yesterday, I was browsing in a seventeenth century Latin translation of Euclid's *Elements*. Things Euclid took as proofs would horrify—if not bewilder—a modern, university senior in math. Euclid's personal idea of mathematical rigor is entirely different from ours. Fashions in proofs change only a little more slowly than fashions in dress. What is considered to require a proof today is considered self-evident tomorrow. What was considered self-evident yesterday, today is the subject of a three-hundred-page exegesis whose final conclusion is that it just cannot be rigorously established at all!

A mathematician will tell you that a set of proofs, all from one mathematician, may, for example, generate information about the author's personality. I will certainly agree with anyone who says that such information is probably not terribly important to the proofs' substance. But anyone who says the information is *not* there is simply blind.

Even mathematics has its subjective side. And, as extremes come around to touch, one argument gaining popularity now is that something as abstract as "mathematical logic" may turn out to be what, after all, subjectivity actually *is*.

23. Art conveys possibilities of information to society, i.e., the possible forms information may take. The value of art is in its richness of form. (Cf. Charles Olson's advice to writers that, without necessarily imitating reality in their fiction, they should keep their fiction "up to" the real.) The relation of art to the world *is* the

aesthetic field of a given culture, i.e., in different cultures art relates to the world in *very* different ways.

24. Thoughts on my last sixteen years with Marilyn: living with an extraordinarily talented and temperamental poet is certainly the best thing that could happen to a prose writer. I wonder, however, if it works the other way around . . . ? When we fall asleep, like teaspoons, the baby (due in two months) tramples me in the small of my back. But they seem such definitely nonhostile kicks. You can tell it's just exercise. This evening, for practically a minute and a half, it kicked at almost regular, seven-second intervals, till Marilyn got up from the armchair (a little worried). Well, considering its daddy, it ought to have a good sense of rhythm. (I say living with a talented and temperamental poet is good for a prose writer; but I suspect living with a talented and temperamental poet who happens to possess a rather acute business sense helps too . . .) [Note: Our obstetrician, Mrs. Ransom, says that when the baby presses against an artery in the womb, often a highly regular spasming of part of the uterine wall can occur, easily confusable with the baby's kicking. Nothing to worry about. But we do not have a budding Ruby Keeler or Bill Robinson in our midst. Just a pressed artery in some positions.]

25. I suspect the logical atomism of both Russell and Wittgenstein would have been impossible without the visual atomization the Impressionists had already subjected the world to on canvas (and that the Cubists were subjecting it to concurrently with Russell's and Wittgenstein's early work). In fact, what is basically wrong with Wittgenstein's "picture theory of language" is that it rests on an aesthetically simpleminded concept of the way in which a picture relates to what it is a picture of. The twenty-seven-year-old Wittgenstein simply held an amazingly naive view (or, more generously, an extreme nineteenth-century-derived view) of the way in which a picture is a model of a situation. The mistake at *Tractatus* 2.261 is heartrending:

> There must be something identical in a picture and what it depicts to enable the one to be a picture of the other at all.

If for *must be* and *identical* he had substituted *is obviously* and *similar*—and then taken up the monumental task of running these words down to their propositional atomization—he would have solved the problem of the modular calculus (i.e., *the* critical problem).

The point is: there is *nothing* identical in a picture and what it depicts. There is *nothing* identical in the model and what it is a model of. Nothing, nothing at all! They share not one atom in common! They need not share one measurement! Only the perceptive context imposes commonality on them, for a variety of learned and physiological reasons. (G. Spencer Brown's elegant, elegant argument wobbles, ultimately, on the same pivot point.) There are only identical processes some *thing* else can undergo in response to both—emblem of their relation. And, presumably, different processes as well—emblem that the two (original and depiction) *are* distinct and, possibly, hierarchical.

For A to be recognized as a model of B, first a set of internal relations, as A relates to itself, must be read from A, then processed in some way probably similar to a mathematical integration; then *another* set of internal relations must be read from B (some of the relations *may* be similar to those read from A; but they need not be) and then integrated (by similar process; or by a very different one), and the two results compared; if I find the *results* congruent, then I recognize A as a model of B in the context of the joint integrative process that produced the congruent results. But information about A may come to me via a photograph, while I may have to gather information about B, blindfolded, with just my hands, from miniature plastic sculptures. Even so, if I have developed the proper interpretative context, I may well be able to recognize that, say, some small, plastic object B is a model of the photographed object A (checkable against a sight model when the blindfold is removed), while other small plastic objects C, D, and E are *not*—in terms either of the context I've developed, or in terms of the more usual sight context—models of A.

26. About every fragment of reality, an infinite number of different statements can be made. For every fragment of reality, an infinite number of different models can be made.

27. On one side of a paper write: "The statement on the other side of this paper is true." Now turn the paper over and write: "The statement on the other side of this paper is false." Now put down your pencil; and turn the paper over several more times, considering the truth and falsity of the statements you have written—till you perceive the paradox.

The young Bertrand Russell noted that the whole of the *Principia Mathematica* remained shaky because of it; he came up with one resolution that, later, as an older man, he repudiated. Karl Popper has, somewhere, a proof that it cannot be resolved at all.

It can.

But to follow the resolution, fold up the paper and put it in the breast pocket of your Pendleton, as I did on the train platform in South Bernham one May, and come along with me.

Vanessa Harpington had gone off painting in North Africa, but had sweetly left the keys to her country home circulating among various of her Camden Town friends. So I'd come down to pass that summer in a fine, old, English house with my friend Alfred, himself the long-haired nephew and namesake of a rather infamous Polish Count K.

One rainy afternoon, I was in the sitting room, with a sketch pad, making a drawing of the scene outside the window—rain splashing through the leaves of one of the small sycamores in the yard—when Alfred, smoking a meerschaum carved into a likeness of A. E. Van Vogt, wandered in, looked at my drawing, looked out the window, looked at my drawing again, and nodded. After a moment's silence, he said: "Would you say you are making a model of the situation outside the window?"

"I suppose you could call it that," I said, sketching a line in for the drapery's edge.

"Would you say that it models the fact that it is raining?"

"Well, all those slanted lines *are* supposed to be raindrops. And the runnels of water on the windows there..." I looked up.

Alfred had stepped forward. The streaming pane silhouetted his hawkish features. He took another pull on his pipe and, expelling small puffs of smoke, intoned: "Truth... Falsity... Model... Reality..." and glanced back.

"I *beg* your pardon?" I said. There was a sweetish aroma in with the tobacco.

"Has it ever occurred to you that," Alfred said, "logically speaking, 'true' and 'false' can only be applied to statements *about* the real; but that it is nonsense to apply either one directly *to* the real? I mean—" He took his pipe and pointed with the stem toward the window; his long hair swung—"if, in here, in the sitting room, you were to make the statement, 'It is raining outside,' or some other model of the situation you perceive through the glass—"

"Like a drawing?"

"—or a sculpture, or a photograph; or a flashing light that, by arrangement, we had both agreed to interpret as, 'It is raining outside,' or some abstract mark on a piece of paper, or an arbitrary set of musical notes that we had some such similar agreement about—"

"A sign—" I said. "An image, a symbol—"

"*I* said a model. *Do* accept my terminology." The partially silhouetted head cocked. "I'm only trying to save you pages and pages of semiological hair-splitting. Now: As I was saying, suppose I chose to model the situation outside with the statement, 'It is raining outside,' rather than the way you are, with a pencil and paper, then you might have come along, observed my model—or, in this case, heard what I said—observed the garden through the window, and commented: 'That is a true statement.' Or, if you will, 'That is a true model.'—"

"I think that's a rather limited way to look at, say, well any *aesthetic* model."

"So do I! So do I!" said Alfred. "But if we had agreed that we *were* going to use the model in that way, for the purely limited purpose of obtaining information about a limited aspect of reality— say, whether it was or was not raining—then we *could*."

"Okay. If we agree first."

"But, by the same token, you can see that it would be perfectly ridiculous for you to come along, point out the window and say, 'The outside is true,' or 'The rain is true,' or even 'The rain outside is true'."

"Oh, I could *say* it. But I do get your point. If I did, I wouldn't be using 'true' in any truly logical way; I'd be using it metaphorically; aesthetically if you will; as a sort of general intensifier."

"Precisely. Do you see, then, what allows one to put 'true' or 'false' on a model, such as my statement or your picture?"

"I suppose," I said, squinting at my paper and considering

asking Alfred to step just a little aside because he was blocking a
doffing sycamore branch, "it's because I've been working very hard to
get it to look like what... I'm modeling—Alfred, do you think you
might move to the left there just a bit—"

"Oh, really!" Alfred stepped directly in front of the window and
jabbed his pipe stem at me. "All Vanessa's oak paneling, these leather
bindings and dusty hangings, seem to have addled your brain. A
statement doesn't *look* like the thing it models! When I say 'It is
raining,' neither the 'it' nor the 'is' refers to anything real in the
situation. And the position of the pointer on that barometer dial
over there—just as good a model of what's going on outside as any
of the others we've mentioned—has no internal structure similar to
the situation it's modeling at all (though it's *attached* to something
that has an internal structure *dependent* on it; but that's a different
story)! No, some structural similarity may explain *why* you choose to
use a particular thing *for* a model, but it is the use you are putting it
to—the context you are putting it *into*, if you will—that, alone,
allows you to call it 'true' or 'false.' Truth and falsity, the potential for
being true or false, are not manifestations of the internal structure of
the thing that is, potentially, to be so labeled. They are, rather,
qualities ascribable to a given thing when, in a particular context, it is
functioning in a particular way, i.e., modeling some situation truly
(however we choose to interpret that) or modeling it falsely (however
we choose, given a particular, modular context, to interpret that) ..."

"Alfred," I said, laying my pencil across my pad and leaning
back in the leather wingchair, "I know you really *are* trying to save me
pages of semiological hair-splitting, but you are also standing in my
way—interfering, if you will, with the modular context I have been
trying to establish between the rain and my drawing pad. Could you
be a pal and see if you can get us some coffee...?"

As English summers will, that one soon ended.

As happens, a year later an Italian summer replaced it. I was
spending a sunny week in a villa outside Florence. The news came
from my hostess, one morning over coffee in the garden, that we were
to be joined shortly by—of all people! I had thought he was
somewhere in Nepal; indeed, I *hadn't* thought of him for six months!
And who, sure enough, should come striding across the grass ten
minutes later, in rather worn-out sneakers, his bald spot not
noticeably larger but his shoulder-length hair definitely longer,

thumbs tucked under his knapsack straps, and a Persian vest over an out-at-the-elbow American workshirt, from the pocket of which stuck the stem of what, from the bulge at the pocket's base, I recognized as his Van Vogtian meerschaum—Alfred!

He came across the lawn, grinning hawkishly, and said: "Do you know what you left behind in England and I have carried all the way to India and back?"

"What?..." I asked, quite surprised at his introduction and charmed by this dispensing with phatic chatter.

"Your sketch pad! Hello, Vanessa..." to our hostess, and gave her a large hug. The high, aluminium rack of his backpack swayed above his shoulders.

To explain what happened that afternoon, I might mention explicitly several things implicit already about both Alfred and Vanessa. She, for instance, is very generous, a far more talented painter than I, and has several easels in her studio—the converted top-floor of the villa. And Alfred, as I'm sure you've realized, has a rather strange mind at the best of times, which also entails a rather strange sense of humour.

At any rate, some hours later, I was walking through the white dining room, with its sparse brass and wood decoration, when I noticed, through the open, iron casement, out in the sunlit, Italian garden, one of Vanessa's easels set up a few yards from the window; and set up *on* the easel was *my* sketch pad, with my drawing of last year's rain-battered, English sycamore.

While I looked at it, Alfred came climbing in over the window-sill, dropped to the floor, spilling a few cinders onto the waxed floorboards, and, kicking at them, gave me a great grin: "There," he said, "Go on! Make a true statement—an accurate verbal model of the situation outside the window! Quick!"

"Well," I said, smiling and a bit puzzled, "it seems that there's..." I paused, about to say 'my picture outside,' but I remembered our colloquy back in rainy Britain: "... that there's my *model* outside!"

"Just what I was hoping you would say," Alfred said. "It saves even more pages of semiological hair-splitting!"

"And," I said, encouraged by this, "the model outside is true, too! Alfred, what have you been doing in India?"

"Amazing amounts of shit," Alfred said warmly. "Do you know,

Plato *was* right, after all—at least about method. As far as semiological hair-splitting is concerned, we just dispensed with practically a chapter and a half! A dialogue that you can make up as you go along really *is* the only way to get anything done in philosophy."

I looked out at my picture again. "Then it *is* my model. And my model *is* true."

"Your first statement is true." Alfred's smile became warmer still. "Your second is nonsense—no, don't look so crestfallen. Just listen a moment: whether your model is a statement, a drawing, or even a thought, it is still a thing like any other thing: that is, it has its particular internal structure, and its various elements are undergoing their various processes, be that merely the process of enduring. Now you may have chosen any aspect of this thing—part of its material, part of its structure, or part of its process—to do the bulk of the modeling for you, *while* it was in the modular context. And, yes, outside that context, the model is still the *same* thing. But it *is* outside the context. Therefore, pointing out *this* window at *that* picture and calling it, or any part of it—material, structure, or process—'true' or 'false' is just as nonsensical now as it would have been for you, back in that abysmal May we spent in South Bernham, to point out the window and call some *thing* out there 'true' or 'false' . . . the rain, the shape of the drops, or the falling. A fine distinction has to be made. Whether the model functions as true or functions as false *within* the context may have something to do with the internal structure *of* the model. But whether the model functions (as true *or* false) has to do with the structure *of* the context. If you would like to, look at it this way: 'true' and 'false' merely model two mutually exclusive ways a given model (which is a thing) may function in a given context, depending on other things, which may, in different contextual positions, function as models. But the meaningfulness of the *ascription* of true *or* false is dependent on the context, not the thing." Alfred took another draw on his pipe, found it was out, and frowned. "Um . . . now why don't you take out that piece of paper you have folded up in the breast pocket of your Pendleton and look at it again—excuse me, I could have suggested you take it out of your wallet and avoided the implication that you hadn't washed your shirt since last summer, but now I am just trying to save you pages of semiological elaboration."

Feeling a bit strange, I fingered into my breast pocket, found the paper I had so summarily folded up a summer before, and unfolded it, while Alfred went on: "Think of it in this wise: if something is in the proper, logical position, it may be called true or false. If it moves out of that position, though it is still the same *thing*, you *can't* call it true or false."

And, creased through horizontally, I read:

The statement on the other side of this paper is true.

"Alfred," I frowned, "—if there *is* a statement on the other side of this paper (and, unless my memory plays tricks, there is) and it is *meaningful* to call *that* statement true or false—now I'm only letting the internal structure of *this* statement suggest a line of reasoning, I'm not accepting from it any information about *its* 'truth' or 'falsity', 'meaningfulness' or 'meaninglessness'—that means (does it not?) that it is in the proper position in the modular context to do some modeling."

"Even as you or I, when we stand at the window looking at what's outside."

"And if *that* statement refers to what's on *this* side of the paper (and memory assures me that it does), then they are in the same context, which means they cannot both occupy the same position in it at the same time."

"Have you ever tried to stand out in the garden and inside the sitting room all at once? It *is* a bit difficult."

"So *if* that is the case, then *this* statement has to be considered just as a ... thing, like rain, or a sycamore, or a garden ..."

"Or a sketch of a garden. Or a statement. Or a thought. *They* are things too."

"But I recall distinctly. Alfred: The statement on the other side of the paper calls this statement—this *thing*!—false!"

"Wouldn't really matter if it called it true, would it—"

"Of course it wouldn't! In the context I just outlined, I could no more call this ... thing—" I waved the statement—"'true' than I could call—" I looked out the window at the easel with my sketch—"*that* thing true!"

"Though that does not reflect on its potential for truth if placed in another contextual position. If, for example, the statement on the other side of the paper read: 'Your picture is in the garden,' then it would be perfectly fine. Actually, it can work quite serially; what we're really establishing is simply the unidirectionality of the modular context *from* the real. But then, all that semiological hair-splitting... Better turn over the paper and see if your memory isn't playing tricks on you."

Hastily I did. And read:

The statement on the other side of this paper is false.

"Yes," I said, "there *is* a statement on this side, and it does attribute truth-or-falsity to the statement on the other. Which is nonsensical. It's me standing inside the sitting room in Bernham looking out the window and calling the rain 'true.'"

"You never really did that," Alfred said. "We just made a model of it that we judged nonsensical—useless in a particular sort of way. Keep looking at the side of the paper you're looking at now—that is: Set up the context in the other direction."

I did until I had:

"It's the same situation. If I let the *other* statement occupy the modeling position and this occupy the position of the modeled thing, then the fact that the other statement attributes truth or falsity to what's on *this* side means *it's* nonsensical too."

Alfred nodded. "It's like having, on either side of your paper: 'The *thing* on the other side of this paper is true (or false); the *thing* on the other side of this paper is false (or true).' Which is an empty situation, in the same way that if you and, say, Vanessa, both had drawing pads and pencils and were sitting where you could see each other's paper, and I gave you the instructions: 'Both of you draw only what the other is drawing.' You'd both end up with empty pictures."

"Speaking of Vanessa," I said, "let us go see what she is doing. She *is* a better artist than I am, which I suspect means that on some level, she has established a more interesting modular context with reality than I have. Perhaps she will take a break from her work and have some coffee with us."

"Splendid," said Alfred. "Oh, you asked me what I was doing in India? Well, while I was there, I got hold of some..." But that is another story too.

*   *   *

28. Language suggests that "truth" (or "falsity") may be an attribute
of sentences much as "redness" may be an attribute of apples. The
primary language model is the adjective 'true,' the secondary one a
noun, "truth," derived from the adjective. This is not the place to
begin the argument against the whole concept of attributes. (It goes
back to Leibniz's inseparable subject/verbs for true predicates; Quine
has demonstrated how well we can get along in formal logic without
attributes, as well as without the whole concept of propositions.) But
I maintain that, subsumed under the noun "truth," is a directed binary
relation, running from the real to the uttered, by way of the mind. The
problems we have concerning "truth" (such as the paradox in section
27) are problems that arise from having to model a directed binary
relationship without a transitive verb.

It is as if, in those situations in which we now say "The hammer
strikes the nail" and "The hammer misses the nail," we were
constrained by the language only to speak of "strike nails" and "miss
nails," and to discuss "strikeness" and "missness" as attributes a given
nail might or might not possess, depending on the situation, at the
same time seldom allowing a mention of the hammer and never the
moment of impact.

What "truth" subsumes (as well as an adjective-derived noun
can) is a *process* through which apprehension of some area of the real
(either through the senses, or through the memory, or the reality of
internal sensation—again, this is not the place to discuss their
accuracy) generates a descriptive utterance. This process is rendered
highly complex by the existence of choice and imagination and is
totally entangled in what Quine and Ullian have called "the web of
belief:" confronted with the real, the speaker may choose not to speak
at all, or to speak of something else, or she may be mistaken (at any
number of levels), or he may generate a description in a mode to
which "truth" or "falsity" are simply not applicable (it may be in G.
Spenser Brown's "imaginary" mode). But when the speaker does
generate an utterance of the sort we wish to consider, the overall
process structure is still binary, and directed from reality to the
sentence.

When I look out the window and say "It is raining outside," what
I perceive outside the window is controlling my utterance *in a way* the
internal apprehension of which is my apprehension of the statement's
"truth" or "falsity." My utterance does not effect—save possibly in

the realms of Heisenberg—whatever (rain or shine) is outside the window.

People have suggested that the problem of paradox sentences is that they are self-descriptive. Yes, but the emphasis should be on *descriptive*, not *self*.

"This sentence contains six words" is just as self-descriptive as "This sentence is false." But the first sentence is not paradoxical; it is simply wrong. (It contains five words.) The second sentence is paradoxical because part of the description (specifically "This sentence...") covers two things (both the sentence "This sentence is false" and the sentence that it suggests as an equivalent translation, "This sentence is true") and does not at all refer to the relation between them. The only predicate that *is* visible "This sentence is..." suggests they relate in a way they do not: "This sentence 'This sentence is true' *is* the sentence 'This sentence is false.'" And, obviously, it isn't. But the same situation exists in Grelling's paradox, the paradox of the Spanish barber, as well as the set-of-all-normal-sets paradox—indeed, in all antinomies.

The real generates an utterance in a *way* that allows us to recognize it as "true" or "false."

If we introduce verbs into the language to stand for the specific generative processes, we fill a much stumbled-over gap. By recovering what is on both sides of the interface, and the direction the relation between them runs, we clarify much that was confused because unstated. Let us coin "generyte" and "misgeneryte," and let us make clear that these processes are specifically mental and of the particular neurocybernetic nature that produce the utterances which, through a host of overdetermined and partially determined reasons, we have been recognizing as "true" and "false." If we introduce these verbs into our paradox, it stands revealed simply as two incorrect statements.

On one side of the paper instead of "The sentence on the other side of this paper is true," we write:

"What is on this side of the paper generytes the sentence on the other side."

And on the other side instead of "The sentence on the other side of this paper is false," we write:

"What is on this side of the paper misgenerytes the sentence on the other side."

Looking at either sentence, then turning the paper over to see if it does what it claims, we can simply respond, for both cases: "No, it does not." One (among many) properties that lets us recognize a generyted (or misgeneryted) sentence is that it is in the form of a description of whatever generyted (or misgeneryted) it; neither sentence is in that form.*

A last comment on all this:

The whole problem of relating mathematics to logic is basically the problem of how, logically, to get from conjunctions like "1+1=2 *and* 1+1≠3," which is the sort of thing we can describe in mathematics, to the self-evident (yet all but unprovable) logical implication: "1+1=2 *therefore* 1+1≠3," which is the process that propels us through all mathematical proofs.

Now consider the following sentences, one a conjunction, one an implication:

"This sentence contains ten words and it misgenerytes itself."

"If this sentence contains ten words, then it misgenerytes itself."

About the first sentence we can certainly say: "That sentence contains nine words, *therefore* it misgenerytes itself." If that self-evident *therefore* can be considered an implication, and assumed equivalent to ("to have the same truth values as" in our outmoded parlance) the implication of the second sentence, then, working from the side of language, we have, self-evidently, bridged the logical gap into mathematics!

Before making such an assumption, however, count the words in the second sentence . . .

29. Vanessa Harpington (during a period when she [not I] thought her work was going badly), shortly after Alfred's departure for Rumania:

"What use is love?

"It assures neither kindness, compassion, nor intelligence between the people who feel it for one another.

"The best you can say is that when good people love, they behave well . . . sometimes.

"When bad people love, they behave appallingly.

---

*Such translation into an artificial language may at first seem suspect. But is it really any more dubious than the translation Russell suggests in his theory of singular descriptions which so facilitates the untangling of *Plato's beard?*

"I wonder what the brilliant Alfred will have to say about a paradox like *that*!"

"First of all, Vanessa," I reminded her as we walked the cobbled streets, with the Arno, dull silver, down every corner, through the Italian summer, "you simply cannot take such abstract problems so seriously. Remember, you and Alfred are both fictions: neither of you exists. The closest I've ever been to passing a summer in an English Country house was a weekend at John and Margery Brunner's in Somerset, and though I spent a few weeks in Venice once, I've never stayed in an Italian villa in my life! I've never even *been* in Florence—"

"Oh, really," Vanessa said; "You just don't understand at all!" and, for the rest of the walk back, stayed a step or two ahead of me, arms folded and looking mostly somewhere else, though we did eventually talk—about other things.

30. Finished reading Gombrich's *Art and Illusion* yesterday. The oversized paperback seems to be losing most of its pages. A thought: When I hold up my hand in front of my face, what I *see* is my hand, in focus, and, behind it, a slightly unfocussed, double image of the rest of the room, those images further away blurrier and slightly further apart. (Actually, parts of the double image keep suppressing other parts, and then the suppression pattern changes.) How odd that in the search for more and more striking illusions of reality, no artist has ever tried to paint *this*.

One reason, I suspect, is that art has never really been interested in painting What You See; from the most abstract, to the most representational, art is interested in purveying the concept of What Is There. The representationalists have, from time to time, used a limited number of tricks of the eye to emphasize (by making their paintings look *more* like what you see) that the subject *is* there. The abstractionists use the reality of paint, brush stroke, and material for the same end.

31. A common argument between philosophers often runs like this:
A. I have a problem within this particular context.
B. I have a context within which I can solve your particular problem.
A. But I want a solution within my context!

B.   But I can translate your context, in all particulars that interest me, into my context.

A.   But you can't translate my problem into *your* context so that it is still a problem and then produce a solution for it that will fit *mine*! Is there any way you can prove that, within my context, my problem is insoluble?

B.   I'm not interested in proving your problem insoluble! I'm interested in solving it! And I have!

A.   If you are not interested in proving my old problem insoluble, then I am not interested in your new context! It doesn't relate to my problem!

32.   The greatest distress to me of Structural Anthropology is its sexism. The primary descriptive model, "Society operates by the exchange of women," as a purely descriptive model, has the value of any other: There are certainly contexts in which it is useful. The same can be said of such other famous descriptive models as: "Jews are responsible for the financial evils of Europe," or "Blacks are lazy and shiftless but have a good sense of rhythm." It is the nature of descriptions that, as long as they model some fraction of the reality, however minute (even to the fact that persons A and B have agreed to use model p as a description of situation s [which is the case with individual words]) they can be called useful. But pure descriptive usefulness is not in the least contingent on how much the internal structure of the description reflects the way in which the fragment of reality it models relates to the rest of the case. Such descriptions that try to mirror these relations, to the extent that they succeed, can be called logical descriptions. But the very form of the absolute statement precludes its being a logical description. And when a description is of a small enough fragment of reality, and it reflects neither the internal workings of what it is describing nor the external workings, it can be said to be an emblem—or, if it is made up of a string of words, a slogan. And it is the slogan's pretension to logical description that make it so undesirable. When trying to establish a coherent system, such as a coherent anthropological discipline (as Lévi-Strauss is attempting), we want logical models that can also be used as part of a logical context. Such models as the ones above, as they pass into context, yield situation after situation where abuse is almost inevitable:

If a woman objects to being exchanged or refuses to be exchanged, for example, by the above model she can be described as opposing society's workings. But if a man objects to or refuses to be exchanged, he can be described as objecting to being treated as a woman! And on and on and on *ad* (in the manner of context models) *infinitum*.

What makes this so sad is that the original descriptive use is completely subsumed by the double model: "Much of society works by the exchange of human beings," and "In most cases, the human beings who do the exchanging are men and the human beings exchanged are women." Without resorting to information theory (which tells us that the interplay between two limited descriptive models generates much more information about the context surrounding the elements of all of them than any one absolute statement of the same elements possibly can), I think most native English speakers hear the margin for self-criticism allowed. And I don't see how the informative usefulness of this complex model is any *less* than that of the absolute statement.

But if I thought anthropological sexism were merely a manifestation of a single, clumsily thought-out descriptive model, I would not be as distressed as I am. It appears again and again; the profusion alone suggests that it is inherent in the context. Three more examples:

In Lévi-Strauss's most exemplary short piece, *La Geste d' Asdiwal* (his analysis of a myth that has a range of male and female characters), we find statements like: " . . . the women [in this myth] are more profitably seen as natural forces . . ." (More profitably than what? Than as human beings? And who is this profitable to? But let us continue.) The myth, in its several versions collated in the forty-odd-page essay, begins with a mother and daughter, whose husbands have died in the current famine, traveling from their respective villages, till they meet, midway along a river. They have only a rotten berry between them to eat. A magic bird appears, turns into a man, marries the daughter, provides food for the two women, and the daughter and her supernatural husband have a child, Asdiwal, the hero of the myth. Some time later in the myth, Asdiwal, as an adult, meets a magic bear on a mountain who turns into a woman and reveals she is the daughter of the sun. After Asdiwal passes a series of tests set by the bear-woman's supernatural father, the bear-woman marries Asdiwal and they live for a while, happily, in the sky. Later they return to earth, to Asdiwal's own village, where Asdiwal commits adultery with a woman of his people. The bear-woman leaves him over this and returns to her father. Asdiwal marries another woman of his village, and the myth continues through a series of adventures involving several other female figures, some human, some not, their brothers (who tend to come in groups of five), the king of the seals, Asdiwal's own son by a mortal woman, and finally ends when Asdiwal, in a magic situation on top of a mountain, calls down to his second wife to sacrifice some animal fat, and she, misunderstanding his instructions, eats it; as a result, Asdiwal is turned to stone. I do not claim, in so short a synopsis, to have covered all the salient points of the myth in all its variations; for what it's worth, neither does Lévi-Strauss. There is a whole branch of the myth devoted to Asdiwal's son's adventures, which has many parallels with his father's story. Still, I cannot see what, in the myth, or in the Timshian culture which produced it, suggests the interpretation "... all the women..." in the tale are natural forces. The bird-man, the bear-women, her father the sun, as well as various seal-men and mouse-women, may well represent natural forces. But to restrict this unilaterally to the women seems to be nothing but a projection of part of our own society's rather warped sexist context. I have no idea if the society of the Timshian Indians who produced this myth is as sexist as modern Western society, less sexist, or more so. I might have made an educated guess from the myth itself. But even Malinowski's original reports, taken several times over several years, here and there resort to synopsis, at noticeably more places where women are the agents of the action than where men are. And I can certainly get no idea from the final critical model Lévi-Strauss constructs: a binary grid of repeated, symmetrical patterns, high/low, upstream/downstream, mountain/water, etc. By dissolving any possibility of male/female symmetricality with the asymmetrical men=human/women=forces, he makes it impossible to judge (nor does he try to judge in his final model) any such symmetricalities that *do* exist in the myth—i.e., I think every one, from the parts recounted, can see a symmetricality between Asdiwal's mother's marriage with the bird-man who brings plenty and Asdiwal's with the bear-woman who brings good times in the sky. Just how important this symmetricality is in terms of Timshian society, I have no way of knowing. My point is, neither does Lévi-Strauss—if he is going to impose the artificial asymmetricalities of our culture on others. Lévi-Strauss's avowed point in the essay is merely to show that there is *some* order in the myth; and this he succeeds in. But has anyone ever seriously maintained that any society has produced myths with *no* order at all? And it is implicit in his approach to show as much order as possible in the myth and then show how it reflects or is reflected by, and lent meaning and value by (and lends meaning and value to), the social context it exists in. There are certainly plenty of asymmetrical elements in both situations (as there are in all of the elements that he pairs as symmetrical), i.e., one marriage produces a child, the other doesn't; one involves in-laws, the other doesn't. But Lévi-Strauss's sexist context puts the whole topic beyond discussion.

Another example: During Lévi-Strauss's conversations with Charbonnier, Charbonnier asks Lévi-Strauss if sometimes an anthropologist does not identify so much that he biases his observations in ways not even he is aware of. Lévi-Strauss counters with an anecdote of a United States anthropologist who recounted to Lévi-Strauss that he felt much more at home working with one Amerind tribe than another. In one tribe, this man reported, if a wife is unfaithful to her husband, the husband cuts off her nose. In the other, if a wife is unfaithful to her husband, the husband goes to sit in the central square, bemoans his fate loudly to all who pass by, calls down imprecations from the gods to destroy the world that has brought things to this dreadful impasse, then curses the gods themselves for having allowed the world to become such a terrible place. He then gets up and returns to his wife, presumably much relieved, and life continues on. The second tribe, the American said, filled him with a sense of revulsion: Trying to "destroy the world, or the whole universe, for a personal injury" struck him as, somehow, "immoral." He preferred working with the former tribe because their responses somehow seemed much "more human." Now I have no idea whether either tribe was particularly sexist or not. Presumably if the women of the first tribe cut off the noses of their unfaithful husbands, whereas we might call them violent, we could not call them sexist. I do know enough of the social context of America to be sure that if this *were* the case, our United States anthropologist would have felt nowhere as "at home" with them as he did. And in terms of any of the tribes involved, including my own U. S. of A., I don't think

I would trust this man to give an objective report on sexuality, sexual politics, morality, or humanity, as conceived subjectively, in terms of their own culture, by *any* of the three. In the context of the conversation, however, Lévi-Strauss uses the anecdote to point out, as politely as possible, that Charbonnier's question is mildly impertinent and that somehow this man is more equipped to be objective about the tribe he identifies with most than anyone else.

Somewhere, in science, especially the human ones, we have to commit ourself to objectivity. And, especially in the human ones, objectivity cannot be the same as disinterest. It must be a whole galaxy of attractions and repulsions, approvals and disapprovals, curiosities and disinterests, deployed in a context of self-critical checks and balances which, itself, must constantly be criticized as an abstract form capable of holding all these elements, and as specific elemental configurations. One of my commitments is that self-critical models are desirable things. I would even submit that cultures, be they Amerind or European or African or Indian or Chinese, are civilized as they possess them. Now "civilization" is only a small part of "culture." Culture, in all its variety, is a desirable thing because, among other things, it provides a variety of material from which self-critical models can be made. Lévi-Strauss himself has pointed out that one purpose of anthropology is to provide a model with which to criticize our own culture. But an anthropological model that only provides a way of seeing how other cultures are structurally similar to ours but literally erases all evidence pertaining to their differences, doesn't, in the long run, strike me as anthropologically very useful.

If other cultures are to teach us anything, and we are not merely to use them as Existential Others that, willy nilly, only prove our own prejudices either about them or ourselves, interpretative models that erase data about their real differences from us must be shunned.

My third example:

Some months ago, Edmund Leach, one of the major commentators on Lévi-Strauss, who has criticized many of Lévi-Strauss's findings and has also praised many of his methods, spent a lecture urging the reinstitution of segregation between the sexes in Western Universities. He proposed doing it in a humane way: "Women might be restricted to the study of medicine and architecture. Men would not be allowed to study these." Man's providence, apparently, is to be everything else. He claimed to be aware that such segregation in the past had had its exploitative side. But he felt we should seriously look at primitive cultures with strict separation of the sexes in work and play for models of a reasonable solution to contemporary stresses.

My response to something like this is violent, unreasonable, and I stick by it: Then for sanity's sake, restrict the study of anthropology to women too. It just *might* prevent such loathesome drivel!

Reasonably, all I can say is that modern anthropology takes place in such a pervading context of sexism that even minds as demonstrably brilliant as Lévi-Strauss's and Edmund Leach's have not escaped it. And that is a tragic indictment.

33. Confessions of a science-fiction writer: I have never read a whole novel by Philip K. Dick. And I have only been able to read three short stories by Brian Aldiss (and one I didn't read; I listened to) end to end. (I did read *most* of *Report on Probability A*.) On several separate occasions, I have bought some dozen books by each of them, piled them on my desk, and sat down with the prime intent of familiarizing myself with a substantial portion of their *oeuvres*.

It would be silly to offer this as the vaguest criticism of either Dick or Aldiss. It's merely an indication of idiosyncracies in my own interpretative context as far as reading goes.

At any rate, the prospect of Dick's and Aldiss's work is pleasant to contemplate. It is something I will simply have to grow into, as I grew into Stendahl and Auden, John Buscema and Joe Kubert, Robert Bresson and Stan Brackhage.

I'm making this note at a solitary lunch in a Camden Town Greek Restaurant. From the cassette recorder on the counter, Marinella, echoed by the chorus, asks plaintively again and again: "Pou paome? Pou paome?" Interesting that *the* question of our times emerges in so many languages, in so many media!

34. In the Glotolog foothills resides a highly refined culture much given to philosophical speculation.

Some facts about its language:

米 is the written sign for a word that translates, roughly, as "a light source."

◊ is the sign for a word that translates, roughly, as "rain."

⟨👁⟩ is the sign for a word that translates, very roughly, as "I see." (⟨👁⟩ , ⟨👁⟩ , ⟨👁⟩ are roughly [and respectively], "you see," "he sees," and "she sees.") But I must repeat "roughly" so frequently because there *are* no real verbs in the Glotolog language in the English sense.

The relationship that various forms of ⟨👁⟩ have to other Glotolog terms is modificational. In traditional Glotolog grammars (which are all written, traditionally, in English—in much the same way that traditional Latin grammars were written in Greek) they are called adjectives. " 米 ◊ ⟨👁⟩ " is a common (and grammatically correct) Glotolog sentence—given the weather, it is one of the *most* common Glotolog sentences, especially in the north. It would be used in just about any situation where an English speaker would say, "It's raining," although there are some, marked, differences. " 米 ◊ ⟨👁⟩ " would also be used when you mean, literally, "I see the rain." This is perhaps the place to make the point (made so clearly in chapter three of most standard Glotolog grammars), ⟨👁⟩ always takes 米 , and usually the 米 is placed before it. The logic here is very simple: You can't see anything without a light source, and in Glotolog this situation is mirrored in the words; ⟨👁⟩ without a 米 is simply considered grammatically incorrect. (米 , however, does not always take ⟨👁⟩ , but that is another subject.) Obvious here, and borne out by dictionaries, Glotolog grammar assigns two distinct meanings to ⟨👁⟩ (but not, however, to ⟨👁⟩ , ⟨👁⟩ , or ⟨👁⟩): both "I see" and "There is..." (i.e., "It might be seen by me..."). Although this double meaning is the source of many traditional children's jokes (heard often during the winter when the clouds blot the sun), in practice it presents little confusion. If I were to come into a Glotolog monastery, with the oil lamps in the windowless foreroom gleaming on "...my traditional okapi jerkin where the raindrops still stand high" (my translation from a traditional Glotolog poem; alas, it doesn't really work in English) and say, stamping my Italian imported boots (the Glotologs are mad for foreign imports and often put them to bizarre use; I have seen red plastic garbage pails used as hanging flower planters in even the strictest religious retreats— though the Glotolog's own, painted ceramic ones seem, to my foreign tastes, so much prettier) " 米 ◊ ⟨👁⟩ ," it would be obvious to all (even to those frequent, ageing, Glotologian religious mystics who have forgotten all their formal grammar—if, indeed, they ever studied it; formal language training is an old discipline among the

Glotolog, but it is a widespread one only in recent years, well after the formal education of these venerable ancients was long since past) that I am speaking in what is called, by the grammars, *the assumptive voice.* The logic here is that the words, when used in the assumptive voice, are to be taken in the sense: "It is assumed that if 米 ◁i▷ [i.e., that if there *were* a light source and if I *were* there, seeing by it], then it *would* reflect off ◊ and I *would* see it...even though I am now inside the monastery and, since my entrance, the world may have fallen into total and unexpected night. In other words, the use of ◁i▷ as "there is..." is not quite the same as in English. You use ◁i▷ for "I see..." only when *what* there is is within sight. Otherwise, though you actually say the same word, i.e., ◁i▷ , you are using the assumptive voice. In old Glotolog texts, the assumptive voice was actually indicated by what is called, in that final appendix to most standard Glotolog grammars on outmoded traditions, a metaphoric dot, which was placed over the 米 and the ◁i▷ . When speaking in the assumptive voice, 米 and ◁i▷ , were said to be in the metaphoric mood. No dot, however, in a sentence like "米 ◊ ◁i▷ " would be placed over ◊ . The logic here is that, in the assumptive voice, one of the things assumed is that the rain, at any rate, is real.

It is interesting: many native Glotolog speakers, when given transcripts of ancient manuscripts on which the dots have been left out (due to the customs of modern Glotolog printing), can still often place the date of composition from the manner in which sentences like " 米 ◊ ◁i▷ " are used, whether in the indicative ("There are..."), the literal ("I see..."), or the assumptive ("Somewhere out of sight it is...") voice. Apparently once the metaphoric dot fell out as archaic usage, the indicative and the assumptive were used much more informally.

Because of the tendency to use English analytic terms in Glotolog, many Glotolog terms are practically identical to their English equivalents (though, as we have seen, the grammar and the logical form of the language are quite different from English), so that a native speaker of one has little difficulty getting the sense of many Glotolog pronouncements, especially those having to do with logic and sensation.

Here are a list of words that are the same in both languages (that is, they are employed in the same situations):

If	can be called
at night	true
I feel	false
this/that	though
on my body	real

Also, logical questions are posed in Glotolog by putting the word "is" before, and a question mark after, the clause to be made interrogative. The fact that the semantics and logical form of the language are different from ours only presents problems in particular cases.

[To summarize those differences: Glotolog has no true predicates ("I feel," as well as "can be called true," for example, are the same part of speech as " ⟨👁⟩ "); in fact, Glotolog has no true subjects either. It has only objects, the observer of which is expressed as a description of the object, as is the medium by which the object is perceived; sometimes these descriptions are taken as real; at other times they are taken as virtual. And it should be fairly evident even from *this* inadequate description of the language—even without exposure to their complex religion, science, poetry, and politics— that this template still gives them a method for modeling the world as powerful as our own equally interesting (and equally arbitrary) subject/predicate template.]

One of the most famous of such problems is the question put by one of the greatest Glotolog philosophers:

"If, at night, 米 ◊ ⟨👁⟩ can be called true, though I feel ◊ on my body, is this ◊ real?"

The sense of this, along with the answer, seems self-evident to any English speaker; at the same time, to most of us, it is a mystery why this should be a great philosophical question. The answer lies in the logical form of the language as it has been outlined; but for those of you who do not wish to untangle it further, some of its philosophical significance for the Glotologs can be suggested by mentioning that it has caused among those perspicacious people practically as much philosophical speculation as the equally famous question by the equally famous Bishop Berkeley, about the sound of the unattended tree falling in the deserted forest, and for many of the same reasons—though the good Bishop's query, perfectly comprehensible as to sense by the native Glotolog speaker thanks to the shared terms, seems patently trivial and obvious to them!

A final note to this problem: In recent years, three very controversial solutions have been offered to this classical problem in Glotolog philosophy, all from one young philosophy student resident in one of the southern monasteries (It rains much less in the south, which has caused some of the northern sages to suggest this upstart cannot truly comprehend the nature of this essentially northern metaphysical dilemma), all three of which involve the reintroduction of the metaphoric dot, placed not in its traditional position over the ⚹ or the ⟨i⟩ , or even over the δ , but rather over the words "real," "true," or the question mark—depending on the solution considered.

More conservative philosophers have simply gone "Humph!" (another utterance common on both Glotolog and English) at these suggestions, claiming that it is simply un-Glotologian to use the metaphoric dot over imported words. The dot is, and it says so in the grammars, reserved for native Glotolog terms. As one of the wittier, older scholars has put it (I translate freely): "In Glotolog, English terms have never had to bear up under this mark; they may, simply, collapse beneath its considerable weight." The more radical youth of the country, however, have been discussing, with considerable interest, this brilliant young woman's proposals.

35. Science fiction interests me as it models, by contextual extension, the ontology suggested among these notes. As it gets away from that ontology, I often find it appalling in the callousness and grossness of what it has to say of the world. (Like Wittgenstein, when I write these notes on science fiction I am "making propaganda for one kind of thinking over another.") Does that differ any from saying that I like science fiction that suggests to me the world is the way I already think it is? Alas, not much—which is probably why even some of the most appalling, callous, and gross science fiction is, occasionally, as interesting as it is.

One difference between a philosopher and a fiction writer is that a fiction writer may purposely use a verbal ambiguity to make two (or more) statements using the same words; he may even intend all these statements to be taken as metaphoric models of each other. But he is still unlikely, except by accident, to call them the same statement. A philosopher, on the other hand, may accidentally use a verbal ambiguity, but once he uses it, he is committed to maintaining that all its meanings are one. And, usually, it takes a creative artist to bring home to us, when the philosophy has exhausted us, that everything in the universe is *somewhat* like everything else, no matter how different any two appear; likewise, everything is *somewhat* different from everything else, no matter how similar any two appear. And these two glorious analytical redundancies form the ordinate and abscissa of the whole determinately indeterminant schema.

36. Omitted pages from an s-f novel:
"You know," Sam said pensively, "that explanation of mine this evening—about the gravity business?" They stood in the warm semidark of the co-op's dining room. "If that were translated into some twentieth-century language, it would come out complete gobbledy-gook. Oh, perhaps an s-f reader might have understood it. But any scientist of the period would have giggled all the way to the bar."

"S-f?" Bron leaned against the bar.

"'Scientifiction?' 'Sci-fi?' 'Speculative fiction?' 'Science fiction?' 'S-f?'—that's the historical progression of terms, though various of them resurfaced from time to time."

"Wasn't there some public-channel coverage about...?"

"That's right," Sam said. "It always fascinated me, that century when humanity first stepped onto the first moon."

"It's not that long ago," Bron said. "It's no longer from us to them than from them to when man first stepped onto the American shore."

Which left Sam's heavy-lipped frown so intense Bron felt his temples heat. But Sam suddenly laughed. "Next thing you'll be telling me is that Columbus discovered America; the bells off San Salvador; the son buried in the Dominican Republic..."

Bron laughed too, at ease and confused.

"What I mean—" Sam's hand, large, hot, and moist, landed on Bron's shoulder—"is that my explanation would have been nonsense two hundred years ago. It isn't today. The episteme has changed so entirely, so completely, the words bear entirely different charges, even though the meanings are more or less what they would have been in—"

"What's an episteme?" Bron asked.

"To be sure. You haven't been watching the proper public-channel coverages."

"You know me." Bron smiled. "Annie shows and ice-operas—always in the intellectual forefront. Never in arrears."

"An episteme is an easy way to talk about the way to slice through the whole—"

"Sounds like the secondary hero in some ice-opera. Melony Episteme, costarring with Alona Liang." Bron grabbed his crotch, rubbed, laughed, and realized he was drunker than he'd thought.

"Ah," Sam said (Was Sam drunk too? . . .), "but the episteme was *always* the secondary hero of the s-f novel—in exactly the same way that the landscape was always the primary one. If you'd just been watching the proper public channels, you'd know." But he had started laughing too.

37. Everything in a science-fiction novel should be mentioned at least twice (in at least two different contexts).

38. Text and *textus* in science fiction? Text, of course, comes from the Latin *textus*, which means "web." In modern printing, the "web" is that great ribbon of paper which, in many presses, takes upwards of an hour to thread from roller to roller throughout the huge machine that embeds ranked rows of inked graphemes upon the "web," rendering it a text. All the uses of the words "web," "weave," "net," "matrix," and more, by this circular "etymology" become entrance points into a *textus*, which is ordered from all language and language-functions, and upon which the text itself is embedded.

The technological innovations in printing at the beginning of the sixties, which produced the present "paperback revolution," are probably the single most important factor contouring the modern science-fiction text. But the name "science fiction" in its various avatars—s-f, speculative fiction, sci-fi, scientifiction—goes back to those earlier technological advances in printing that resulted in the proliferation of "pulp magazines" during the twenties.

Naming is always a metonymic process. Sometimes it is the pure metonymy* of associating an abstract group of letters (or numbers)

Metonymy is, of course, the rhetorical figure by which one thing is called with the name of another thing associated with it. The historian who writes, "At last, the crown was safe at Hampton," is not concerned with the metallic tiara but the monarch who, with a person (or thing), so that it can be recalled (or listed in a metonymic order with other entity names). Frequently, however, it is a more complicated metonymy: old words are drawn from the cultural lexicon to name the new entity (or to rename an old one), as well as to render it (whether old or new) part of the present culture. The relations between entities so named are woven together in patterns far more complicated than any alphabetic or numeric listing can suggest: And the encounter between objects-that-are-words (e.g., the name "science fiction," a critical text on science fiction, a science-fiction text) and processes-made-manifest-by-words (another science-fiction text, another critical text, another name) is as complex as the constantly dissolving interface between culture and language itself. But we can take a model of the naming process from another image:

Consider a child, on a streetcorner at night, in one of Earth's great cities, who hears for the first time the ululating sirens, who sees the red, enameled flanks heave around the far building edge, who watches the chrome-ended, rubber-coated, four-inch "suctions" ranked along those flanks, who sees the street-light glistening on glass-faced pressure-meters and stainless-steel discharge-valves on the red pump-housing, and the canvas hose heaped in the rear hopper, who watches the black-helmeted and rubber-coated men clinging to their ladders, boots lodged against the serrated running-board. The child might easily name this entity, as it careers into the night, a Red Squealer.

Later, the child brings this name to a group of children—who take it up easily and happily for their secret speech. These children grow; younger children join the group; older children leave. The name persists—indeed, for our purposes, the locus of which children use and which children do not use the name is how we read the boundary of the group itself.

from time to time, wore it. The dispatcher who reports to the truckboss, "Thirty drivers rolled in this weekend," is basically communicating about the arrival of trucks those drivers drove and cargoes those trucks hauled. *Metonymic* is a slightly strained, adjectival construction to label such associational processes. *Metonym* is a wholly-coined, nominative one, shored by a wholly spurious (etymologically speaking) resemblance to "synonymy/synonym" and "antinomy/antinym." Still, it avoids confusion. In a text practically opaque with precision, it distinguishes "metonymy"-the-thing-associated ("crown," "driver") from "metonymy"-the-process-of-association (crown to monarch; driver to cargo). The orthodox way of referring to both is with the single term.

The group persists—persists weeks, months, years after the child who first gave it its secret term has outgrown both the group and its language. But one day a younger child asks an older (well after the name, within the group, has been hallowed by use): "But *why* is it a Red Squealer?" Let us assume the older child (who is of an analytical turn of mind) answers: "Well, Red Squealers must get to where they are going quickly; for this reason sirens are put on them which squeal loudly, so that people can hear them coming a long way off and pull their cars to the side. They are painted with that bright enamel color for much the same reason—so that people can see them coming and move out of their way. Also, by now, the red paint is traditional; it serves to identify that it is, indeed, a Red Squealer one sees through the interstices of traffic and not just any old truck."

Satisfying as this explanation is, it is still something of a fiction. We were there, that evening, on the corner. We know the first child called it a Red Squealer out of pure, metonymic apprehension: there were, that evening, among many perceived aspects, "redness" and "squealing," which, via a sort of morphological path-of-least-resistance, hooked up in an easily sayable/thinkable phrase. We know, from our privileged position before *this* text, that there is nothing explicit in our story to stop the child from having named it a Squealing Red, a Wah-Wah, a Blink-a-blink, or a Susan-Anne McDuffy—had certain nonspecified circumstances been other than the simplest reading of our fiction suggests. The adolescent explanation, as to why a Red Squealer *is* a Red Squealer, is as satisfying as it is because it takes the two metonyms that form the name and embeds them in a web of functional discourse—satisfying because of the functional nature of the adult episteme,* which both generates the discourse and of which, once the discourse is uttered, the explanation (as it is absorbed into the memory, of both querant and explicator, which is where the *textus* lies embedded) becomes a part.

Science Fiction was named in like manner to the Red Squealer; in like manner the metonyms which are its name can be functionally related:

Science fiction *is* science fiction because various bits of technological discourse (real, speculative, or pseudo)—that is to say

*The episteme is the structure of knowledge read from the epistemological *textus* when it is sliced through (usually with the help of several texts) at a given, cultural moment.

the "science"—are used to redeem various other sentences from the merely metaphorical, or even the meaningless, for denotative description/presentation of incident. Sometimes, as with the sentence "The door dilated," from Heinlein's *Beyond This Horizon*, the technological discourse that redeems it—in this case, discourse on the engineering of large-size iris apertures, and the sociological discourse on what such a technology would suggest about the entire culture—is not explicit in the text. Is it, then, implicit in the *textus*? All we can say for certain is that, embedded in the *textus* of anyone who can *read* the sentence properly, are those emblems by which they could recognize such discourse were it manifested to them in some explicit text.

In other cases, such as the sentences from Bester's *The Stars My Destination*, "The cold was the taste of lemons, and the vacuum was the rake of talons on his skin... Hot stone smelled like velvet caressing his skin. Smoke and ash were harsh tweeds rasping his skin, almost the feel of wet canvas. Molten metal smelled like water trickling through his fingers," the technological discourse that redeems them for the denotative description/presentation of incident *is* explicit in the text: "Sensation came to him, but filtered through a nervous system twisted and shortcircuited by the PryE explosion. He was suffering from Synaesthesia, that rare condition in which perception receives messages from the objective world and relays these messages to the brain, but there in the brain the sensory perceptions are confused with one another."

In science fiction, "science"—i.e., sentences displaying verbal emblems of scientific discourse—is used to literalize the meanings of other sentences for use in the construction of the fictional foreground. Such sentences as "His world exploded," or "She turned on her left side," as they subsume the proper technological discourse (of economics and cosmology in one; of switching circuitry and prosthetic surgery in the other), leave the banality of the emotionally muzzy metaphor, abandon the triviality of insomniac tossings, and, through the labyrinth of technical possibility, become possible images of the impossible. They join the repertoire of sentences which may propel *textus* into text.

This is the functional relation of the metonyms "science" and "fiction" that were chosen by Hugo Gernsback to name his new pulp genre. He (and we) perceived that, in these genre texts, there existed an aspect of "science" and as aspect of "fiction," and because of the science something *about* the fiction was different. I have located this difference specifically in a set of sentences which, with the particular way they are rendered denotatively meaningful by the existence of other sentences not necessarily unique to science fiction, are themselves by and large unique to texts of the s-f genre.

The obvious point must be made here: this explanation of the relation of those two onomic metonyms Science/Fiction no more defines (or exhausts) the science-fictional-enterprise than our adolescent explanation of the relation of the two onomic metonyms Red/Squealer defines (or exhausts) the enterprise of the fire engine. Our functional explanation of the Red Squealer, for example, because of the metonyms from which the explanation started, never quite gets around to mentioning the Red Squealer's primary function: to put out fires.

And the "function" of science fiction is of such a far more complex mode than that of the Red Squealer, one might hesitate to use such metonyms—"function" and "primary"—to name it in the first place. Whatever one chooses to name it, it cannot be expressed, as the Red Squealer's can, by a colon followed by a single infinitive-with-noun—no more than one could thus express the "primary function" of the poetic-enterprise, the mundane-fictional-, the cinematic-, the musical-, or the critical-. Nor would anyone seriously demand such an expression for any of these other genres. For some concept of what, primarily, science fiction does, as with other genres, we must rely on further, complex, functional explanation:

The hugely increased repertoire of sentences science fiction has to draw on (thanks to this relation between the "science" and the "fiction") leaves the structure of the fictional field of s-f notably different from the fictional field of those texts which, by eschewing technological discourse in general, sacrifice this increased range of nontechnological sentences—or at least sacrifice them in the particular, foreground mode. Because the added sentences in science fiction *are* primarily foreground sentences, the relationship between foreground and background in science fiction differs from that of mundane fiction. The deposition of weight between landscape and psychology shifts. The deployment of these new sentences within the traditional s-f frame of "the future" not only generates the obviously new panoply of possible fictional incidents; it generates as well an entirely new set of rhetorical stances: the future-views-the-present forms one axis against which these stances may be plotted; the alien-views-the-familiar forms the other. All stories would seem to proceed as a progression of verbal data which, through their relation among themselves and their relation to data outside themselves, produce, in the reader, data-expectations. New data arrive, satisfying and/or frustrating these expectations, and, in turn and in concert with the old, produce new expectations—the process continuing till the story is complete. The new sentences available to s-f not only allow the author to present exceptional, dazzling, or hyperrational data, they also, through their interrelation among themselves and with other, more conventional sentences, create a *textus* within the text which allows whole panoplies of data to be generated at syntagmically startling points. Thus Heinlein, in *Starship Troopers*, by a description of a mirror reflection and the mention of an ancestor's nationality, in the midst of a strophe on male makeup, generates the data that the first-person narrator, with whom we have been traveling now through two hundred and fifty-odd pages (of a three-hundred-and-fifty-page book), is non-caucasian. Others have argued the surface inanities of this novel, decried its endless preachments on the glories of war, and its pitiful founderings on repressed homosexual themes. But who, a year after reading the book, can remember the arguments for war—short of someone conscientiously collecting examples of human illogic? The arguments *are* inane; they do *not* relate to anything we know of war as a real interface of humanity with humanity: They do not stick in the mind. What remains with me, nearly ten years after my first reading of the book, is the knowledge that I have experienced a world in which the *placement* of the information about the narrator's face is *proof* that in such a world much of the race problem, at least, has dissolved. The book as text— as object in the hand and under the eye—became, for a moment, the symbol of that world. In that moment, sign, symbol, image, and discourse collapse into one, nonverbal experience, catapulted from somewhere beyond the *textus* (*via* the text) at the peculiarly powerful trajectory only s-f can provide. But from here on, the description of what is unique to science fiction and how it works within the s-f *textus* that is, itself, embedded in the whole language—and languagelike— *textus* of our culture becomes a list of specific passages or sets of passages: better let the reader compile her or his own.

I feel the science-fictional-enterprise is richer than the enterprise of mundane fiction. It is richer through its extended repertoire of sentences, its consequent greater range of possible incident, and through its more varied field of rhetorical and syntagmic organization. I feel it is richer in much the same way atonal music is richer than tional, or abstract painting is richer than realistic. No, the apparent "simplemindedness" of science fiction is not the same as that surface effect through which individual abstract paintings or particular atonal pieces frequently appear "impoverished" when compared to "conventional" works, on first exposure (exposed to, and compared by, those people who have absorbed only the "conversational" *textus* with which to "read" their art or music). This "impoverishment" is the necessary simplicity of sophistication, meet for the far wider web of possibilities such works can set resonating. Nevertheless, I think the "simplemindedness" of science fiction may, in the end, have the same aesthetic weight as the "impoverishment" of modern art. Both are manifestations of "most works in the genre"—not the "best works." Both, on repeated exposure *to* the best works, fall away by the same process in which the best works charge the *textus*—the web of possibilities—with contour.

The web of possibilities is not simple—for abstract painting, atonal music, or science fiction. It is the scatter pattern of elements from myriad individual forms, in all three, that gives their respective webs their densities, their slopes, their austerities, their charms, their contiguities, their conventions, their cliches, their tropes of great originality here, their crushing banalities there: The map through them can only be learned, as any other language is learned, by exposure to myriad utterances, simple and complex, from out the language of each. The contours of the web control the reader's experience of any given s-f text; as the reading of a given s-f text recontours, however slightly, the web itself, that text is absorbed into the genre, judged, remembered, or forgotten.

In wonder, awe, and delight, the child who, on that evening, saw the juggernaut howl into the dark, named it "Red Squealer." We know the name does not exhaust; it is only an entrance point into the *textus* in order to retrieve from it some text or other on the contours, formed and shaped of our experience of the entities named by, with, and organized around those onomic metonyms. The *textus* does not define; it is, however slightly, redefined with each new text embedded upon it, with each new text retrieved from it. We also know that the naming does not necessarily imply, in the child, an understanding of that *textus* which offers up its metonyms and in which those metonyms are embedded. The wonder, however, may initiate in the child that process which, resolved in the adult, reveals her, in helmet and rubber raincoat, clinging to the side-ladders, or hauling on the fore- or rear-steering wheel, as the Red Squealer rushes toward another blaze.

It may even find her an engineer, writing a text on why, from now on, Red Squealers had best be painted blue, or a bell replace that annoying siren—the awe and delight, caught pure in the web, charging each of her utterances (from words about, to blueprints of, to the new, blue, bonging object itself) with conviction, authenticity, and right.

39. Everything in a science-fiction novel should be mentioned at least twice (in at least two different contexts), with the possible exception of science fiction.

40. Omitted pages from an s-f novel:
Saturn's Titan had proved the hardest moon to colonize. Bigger than Neptune's Triton, smaller than Jupiter's Ganymede, it had seemed the ideal moon for humanity. Today, there were only research stations, the odd propane mine, and Lux—whose major claim was that it bore the same name as the far larger city on far smaller Iapetus. The deployment of humanity's artifacts across Titan's surface more resembled the deployment across one of the gas giants' "captured moons"—the under-six-hundred-kilometer hunks of rock and ice (like Saturn's Phoebe, Neptune's Nereid, or a half-dozen-plus of Jupiter's smaller orbs) that one theory held to have drifted out from the asteroid belt before being caught in their present orbits. Titan! Its orangeish atmosphere was denser (and colder) than Mars's—though nowhere near as dense as Earth's. Its surface was marred with pits, rivers, and seas of methane and ammonia sludge. Its bizarre life-forms (the only other life in the Solar System) combined the most unsettling aspects of a very large virus, a very small lichen, and a slime mold. Some varieties, in their most organized modes, would form structures like blue, coral bushes with, for upwards of an hour at a

time, the intelligence of an advanced octopus. An entire subgenre of ice-operas had grown up about the Titan landscape. Bron despised them. (And their fans.) For one thing, the Main Character of these affairs was always a man. Similarly, the One Trapped in the Blue, Coral-like Tentacles was always a woman (Lust Interest of the Main Character). This meant that the traditional ice-opera Masturbation Scene (in which the Main Character Masturbates while Thinking of the Lust Interest) was always, for Bron, a Bit of a Drag. And who wanted to watch another shindo expert pull up another ice-spar and beat her way out of another blue-coral bush, anyway? (There were other, experimental ice-operas around today in which the Main Character, identified by a small "MC" on the shoulder, was only on for five minutes out of the whole five-hour extravaganza, Masturbation Scene and All—an influence from the indigenously Martian Annie-show—while the rest was devoted to an incredible interlocking matrix of Minor Characters' adventures.) And the women who went to them tended to be strange—though a lot of very intelligent people, including Lawrence, swore Titan-opera was the only really select artform left to the culture. Real ice-opera—better-made, truer-to-life and with more to say about it *via* a whole vocabulary of real and surreal conventions, including the three formal tropes of classical abstraction, which the classical ice-opera began with, ended with, and had to display once gratuitously in the middle—left Lawrence and his ilk (the ones who didn't go into ego-booster booths) yawning in the lobby.

41. The structure of history tends to be determined by who said what. The texture of life is determined by who is listening.

42. Though few science-fiction writers enjoy admitting it, much science fiction, especially of the nuts-and-bolts variety, reflects the major failure of the scientific context in which most technology presently occurs: the failure, in a world where specialization is a highly productive and valued commodity, to integrate its specialized products in any ecologically reasonable way—painfully understandable in a world that is terrified of any social synthesis, between black and white, male and female, rich and poor, verbal and nonverbal, educated and uneducated, underprivileged and privileged, subject and object. Such syntheses, if they occur, will virtually destroy the

categories and leave all the elements that now fill them radically revalued in ways it is impossible to more than imagine until such destruction is well underway. Many of the privileged as well as the underprivileged fear the blanket destruction of the products of technology, were such a radical value shift to happen. Even so, both privileged and nonprivileged thinkers are questioning our culture's context, scientific and otherwise, to an extent that makes trivial, by comparison, the blanket dismissal of all things with dials that glitter (or with latinate names in small print at the bottom of the labels) that the urban advocates of back-to-the-soil humanism sometimes claim to indulge. Within the city, because of the overdetermined context, even to attempt such a dismissal is simply to doom oneself to getting one's technology in grubbier packages, containing less-efficient brands of it, and with the labels ripped off so that you cannot be sure what's inside. Those who actually *go* back to the soil are another case: The people on the rural communes I have visited—in Washington with Pat Muir, and those in California around Muir Woods (coincidentally named after Pat's grandfather)—were concerned with exploring a folk technology, a very different process from "dismissal." And the radio–phonograph (solid-state circuitry) and the paperback book (computerized type-setting), just for examples, were integral parts of the exploration.

That science fiction is the most popular literature in such places doesn't surprise.

What other literature could make sense of, or put in perspective, a landscape where there is a hand-loom, a taperecorder, a fresh butter churn, ampicillin forty minutes away on a Honda 750, and both men and women pushing a mule-drawn plow, cooking, wearing clothes when clothes answer either a functional necessity (boots, work-gloves ...) or an aesthetic appetite (hand-dyed smocks, beaded vests ...) and going naked when neither necessity nor appetite is present; or where thousands of such people will gather, in a field three hundred miles from where they live, to hear music from musicians who have come a thousand miles to play it for them?

What the urban humanist refuses to realize (and what the rural humanist often has no way of realizing) is that our culture's scientific context, which has given us the plow, the taperecorder, insecticides, the butter-churn, and the bomb, is currently under an internal and informed onslaught as radical as our social context is suffering before the evidence of Women's Liberation, Gay Activism, Radical Psychiatry, or Black Power.

Much science fiction inadvertently reflects the context's failure. The best science fiction explores the attack.

43. The philosophically cherished predicates of all the sensory verbs in the Indo-European languages are, today, empirically empty verbal conventions—like the "it" in "it is raining." The very form "I see the table" suggests that, in the situation "I" would commonly model with those words, "I" am doing something *to* the table, by "seeing" it, in some sense similar to what "I" would be doing to it in the situation "I" would commonly model by the words "I set the table." Empirically, however, we know that (other than at the most minute, Heisenbergian level), in the situation we use "I see the table" to model, the table is—demonstrably!—doing far more to "I" than "I" am doing to it. (Moreover, though words like "I" and "see" were used to *arrive at* the demonstration, the demonstration *itself* could be performed effectively for a deaf-mute who had learned only the nonverbal indicators, such as pointing, miming of motion and direction, picture recognition, etc. The reading of various sense data as the persistence of matter and coherence and direction of motion, which is basically what is needed to apprehend such a demonstration, seems to be [by recent experiments on babies only a few hours old] not only preverbal but programmed in the human brain at birth, i.e., *not* learned.) A language is conceivable that would reflect this, where the usual model of this situation would be a group of verbal particles that literally translated: "Light reflects from table then excites my-eyes." Equally conceivable, in this language, the words "I see the table" might be considered, if translated from ours literally, first, as ungrammatical, and, second, as self-contradictory as "the rock falls up"* appears in ours. By extension, all predicates in the form "The subject senses..." (rather than "The object excites...") are as empty of internal coherence against an empirical context as "The color of the number seven is D-flat." (An intuitive realization among poets of the hopeless inadequacy of linguistic expressions in the form "I sense..." accounts for much of the "difficulty" in the poetry of the last twenty-five years—a very different sort of difficulty from the labored erudition of

---

*Or "the table sees me."

the poetry of the thirty years previous.) As *models* for a situation, neither the "I see . . ." model nor the "light reflects . . ." model is more *logical*; but that is only because logic lies elsewhere. One model is simply, empirically, more reasonable. Empirical evidence has shown that the implied arrows "inside" these words simply do not reflect what is the case. A good bit of philosophical wrangling simply tries to maintain that because these arrows were once considered to be there, they must still model *something*.

There was a time when people thought electricity flowed from the positive to the negative pole of a battery. The best one can say is that there were many situations in which the current direction didn't matter. And many others in which it did. Trying to maintain the meaningful direction of sense predicates is like maintaining that in those situations in which it doesn't matter which way the current flows, somehow it *is* actually flowing backwards.

44. Galaxy of events over the past few months: the telegram announcing Marilyn's collection of poems *Presentation Piece* had won the Lamont Poetry Selection for the year; the terribly complimentary statement by Richard Howard, which will go on the book's back cover; a glowing review by the Kirkus Service that is *so* muddle-headed, one would have almost preferred no review at all!

45. Various deaf-mute friends I have had over the years, and the contingent necessity of learning the deaf-and-dumb sign language, have given me as much insight into spoken and written language as oral story-telling once gave me into written stories: Hand-signs, spoken words, and written words produce incredibly different contextual responses, though they model the same object or process. The deaf-and-dumb sign language progresses, among ordinary deaf-and-dumb signers, at between three and five hundred words a minute (Cf. ordinary reading speeds), and the learner who comes from the world of hearing and speaking is frequently driven quite mad by the absence of concept words and connectives. (Logicians take note: Both 'and' and 'or' are practically missing from demotic deaf-and-dumb; though the sign for 'and' exists, 'or' must be spelled out by alphabetic signs, which usually indicates an infrequently used word.)

Lanky and affable Horace would occasionally leave me notes under my room door (on the ninth floor of the Albert) written with

"English" words, all using their more or less proper, dictionary meaning, but related to one another in ways that would leave your average English speaker bewildered.

There is a sign for "freeze"—a small, backwards clutch, with the palms of the hands down.

There is a sign for "you"—pointing to the "listener" with the forefinger.

As in English, "freeze" has many metaphorical extensions: "to stop moving," "to treat someone in a cold manner," etc. The two signs, mimed consecutively—"freeze you"—can mean:

"You have a cold personality."

"You are frozen."

"Are you frozen?"

"Stop moving."

"You just stopped moving, didn't you!" (in the sense of "You jumped!")

This last is a particularly interesting case: the signed phrase could also be translated "You flinched!" The speaker who says, "You jumped!" models the beginning of the motion; the deaf-mute who signs, "Freeze you" is modeling the end of the same motion. In both cases, the partial model (or synecdoche) stands for the whole action of "flinching."

Another meaning of "Freeze you" is: "Please put some water in the ice tray and put it in the ice box so we can have some ice cubes."

Distinction among meanings, in actual signing, is a matter of—what shall I call it?—muscular and gestural inflection in the arms, face, and the rest of the body.

I remember getting the note: "Come down freeze you whiskey have want, chess." I suspect this would be baffling without some knowledge of the sign language context, though the words "mean" pretty much the same as they do in English. One informal translation of this note into written English would be: "Come downstairs and play chess with me. You bring the ice cubes. I have some whiskey—if you want?" And an equally good translation: "Do you want to come down, bring some ice cubes, have a drink, and play chess?" And another: "Why not come on down? You make ice cubes up there; bring them. I have some whiskey. It's all for a chess game."

But it would be a great mistake to try and "transform" the

original into any of my English translations, either by some Chomskyan method, or by filling in suspected ellipses, understood subjects, and the like:

"...have want..." is a single verb phrase, for example, whose translation I could spend pages on. It has at least three modulating duals (in our language context, at any rate) so that its translation tends to be some arrangement from the matrix:

$$\left\{ \begin{matrix} \text{if} \\ \text{then} \end{matrix} \right. \left\{ \begin{matrix} \text{you} \\ \text{I} \end{matrix} \right. \left\{ \begin{matrix} \text{now} \\ \text{will} \end{matrix} \right. \text{have} \left\{ \begin{matrix} \text{then} \\ \text{if} \end{matrix} \right. \left\{ \begin{matrix} \text{I} \\ \text{you} \end{matrix} \right. \left\{ \begin{matrix} \text{will} \\ \text{now} \end{matrix} \right. \text{want}$$

moving both backwards and forwards, and up or down. It is regularly interrogative. (So a written question mark, in the deaf-and-dumb language, when you use "have want" is superfluous. The phrase "have need" works by a similar matrix and is regularly imperative. The equally frequent "want need," however, works through an entirely different matrix.) It may have several "direct objects," each requiring a different path through the matrix to make "sense" in our language. A literal translation of Horace's sentence, up to the comma, might read: "If you want to come down, I will have you down; if you have frozen (made) some (ice cubes), I will want some (that you have frozen); if you want whiskey, I have some whiskey..." And "chess" at the sentence's end is something like a noun absolute in Latin, the subject of the whole sentence, casting back its resonances on all that has gone before.

46. In the same language in which we still say "I see..." only fifty years before Russell's theory of "singular description," in America one person could meaningfully refer to another as "my slave..." at which point the other person was constrained by the *language* to refer to the first as "my master..."—as if the bond of possession were somehow mutual and recipirocal.

Rebellion begins when the slave realizes that in no sense whatsoever is the master "hers/his." The slave cannot sell the master, give the master away, or keep the master should the master wish to go. This realization *is* the knowledge that the situation, which includes the language, exploits the slave and furthers the exploitation.

47. Possible insight into the "Cocktail Party Effect": Last evening, at Professor Fodor's lecture on the mental representation of sentences, with David Warren at the London School of Economics, I had a chance to observe the Cocktail Party Effect at work. David and I were sitting on the ground floor of the Old Theatre, near the door. Outside, a mass of students was gathering, presumably for the next event in the auditorium. The general rumble of their voices finally grew loud enough to make a dozen people around us look back towards the exit with consternation.

Professor Fodor's delivery, while audible, was certainly not loud; and he wandered over the stage, to the blackboard, to the apron, to the podium, so that only part of the time was he near enough to the microphone for his voice to carry.

The sound outside was definitely interfering with our hearing his lecture, and we all had to strain...

The next time I was aware of the crowd noise outside, I realized that if I kept my aural concentration fixed on Fodor's words, the crowd noise would begin to undergo a definite pulsing (I estimated the frequency to be between two pulses per second and three pulses in two seconds) while the professor's voice stayed more or less clear through the peaks and troughs. If, however, I listened consciously to the crowd, the pulsing ceased and the Professor's words became practically unintelligible, lost in the rush of sound.

Is this how the "Cocktail Party Effect," or some aspect of it, works?

48. REGeis in *The Alien Critic* defending himself against Joanna Russ's and Vonda McIntyre's accusations of sexism, cites a string of incorrect facts, half-facts, and facts implying a nonexistent context, beginning with the statement:

"I have never made a sexist editorial decision in my life."

The form of the sentence itself implies that "making" a "sexist decision" or, for that matter, making an antisexist decision, is a case of putting energy into an otherwise neutral social contextual system.

The social context is *not* neutral. It is overwhelmingly sexist.

Studies have been done as far back as the fifties which show, in America, almost cross-culturally, male infants receive an average of slightly over 100 percent more physical contact with their parents during the first year of life than female infants! Tomes have been written on the effect of physical contact in this period on later physical strength and psycholgical autonomy. This alone renders the word "naturally," in a statement like "men are naturally stronger than women," a farce! Yet, despite how many thousands of years (probably no more than six and possibly a good deal less—another point to bear in mind) of this sort of Lamarckian pressure, when a large number of skeletons from modern cadavers, whose sexes were known and coded, were then given to various doctors, anthropologists, and archeologists to sort into male and female, the results were random! There is *no* way to identify the sex of a skeleton, from distinctions in size, pelvic width, shoulder width, skull size, leg length—these are all empirically nonsupported myths. Yet anthropology books are being published today with pictures captioned: "Armbone of a woman, c. eight thousand B.C." or "Jawbone of a male, c. five thousand B.C." Studies in the comparative heights of men and women have disclosed that, if you say you are doing a study in the comparative heights of men and women, and ask for volunteers, men average some two inches taller than women— whereas, if you say you are doing an intelligence test to compare university students with nonuniversity students, and, just incidentally, take the height of your volunteers, men average a mere three eights of an inch taller than women! Other, even more random samplings, which have tried to obliterate *all* sexually associated bias, seem to indicate that the *range* of height of men tends to be larger—as a man, you have a greater chance of being either very tall or very short—but that the average height is the same. (Of course women are shorter than men: just stand on any street corner and look at the couples walking by. Next time you stand on any street corner, take pairs of couples and contrast the height of the woman from couple A with the man from couple B. I did this on a London street corner for two hours a few weeks back: taken as couples, it would appear that in 94 percent, men are taller than women. Taken by cross-couples, the figure goes down to 72 percent. The final twenty-two percent is more likely governed by the sad fact that, in Western society, tall women and short men both try to avoid being seen in public, especially with the opposite sex.) A male in our society receives his exaggerated social valuation with the application of the pronoun "he" before he can even smile over it. A female receives her concomitant devaluation with the pronoun "she" well before she can protest.

Again: The system is *not* neutral. For every situation, verbal or nonverbal, that even approaches the sexual, the easy way to describe it, the comfortable way to respond to it, the normal way to act in it, the way that will draw the least attention to yourself—if you are male—*is* the sexist way. The same goes for women, with the difference that you are not quite so comfortable. Sexism is not primarily an active hostility in men towards women. It is a set of unquestioned social habits. Men become hostile when these habits are questioned as people become hostile when anything they are comfortable doing is suddenly branded as pernicious. ("But I didn't *intend* to hurt any one; I was just doing what I always...")

A good many women have decided, finally, that the pain that accrues to *them* from everyone else's acceptance of the "acceptable" way is just not worth the reward of invisibility.

"I have never made a sexist editorial decision in my life."

There *are* no sexist decisions to be made.

There are antisexist decisions to be made. And they require tremendous energy and self-scrutiny, as well as moral stamina in the face of the basic embarrassment campaign which is the tactic of those assured of their politically superior position. ("Don't you think you're being rather silly offering *your* pain as evidence that something *I* do so automatically and easily is wrong? Why, I bet it doesn't hurt *half* as much as you say. Perhaps it only hurts because you're struggling?...." This sort of political mystification, turning the logical arrows around inside verbal structures to render them empirically empty, and therefore useless ["It hurts *because* you don't like it" rather than "You don't like it *because* it hurts."] is just another version of the "my slave/my master" game.)

There *are* no sexist decisions to be made: they were all made a long time ago!

49.   The mistake we make as adolescent readers is to assume a story is exciting because of its strange happenings and exotic surfaces, when, actually a story is exciting exactly to the extent that its structure is familiar. "Plot twists" and "gimmicks" aside (which, like "wise-cracks," only distract our conscious mind from the structure so that we can respond subconsciously to its familiarity with that ever sought-for "gut response"), excitement in reading invariably comes

from the anticipation of (and the anticipation rewarded by) the inevitable/expected.

This inevitability—without which there simply *is* no reader gut-participation—is also what holds fiction to all the political cliches of sexism, racism, and classism that mar it as an art. To write fiction without such structural inevitabilities, however (as practically every artist has discovered), is to write fiction without an audience.

Does science fiction offer any way out of this dilemma?

The hope that it might, probably accounts for a good deal of rapprochement between science fiction and the *avant garde* that occurred during the middle and late sixties.

50. The equivocation of the genitive (children, ideas, art, and excrement) and the associative (spouses, lovers, friends, colleagues, copatrials, and country) with the possessive (contracted objects) is the first, great, logically-empty verbal structure that exists entirely for political exploitation.

51. Meaning is a routed-wave phenomenon.

I intend this in the sense one might intend the statement: "Painting is a colored-oil-paints spread-on-canvas phenomenon." Just as there are many things beside oil paints on canvas that may fill, more or less well, the several uses we could reasonably ask of a painting—from tempera on masonite to colored sand spilled carefully on sun-baked ground, in one direction; or etchings, photographs, or computer reductions, in another; or patterns observed on a rock, a natural setting, or a found object, in still another—there may be other things that can fill, more or less well, the several tasks we might reasonably ask "meaning" to perform. But my statement still stands as a parametric model of what I think *meaning* to *be*. The extent that any of my remarks contravene this model is the extent to which they should be taken as metaphoric.

52. Language in general, poetry in particular, and mathematics, are all tools to fix meaning (in their different ways) by establishing central parameters, not circumscribing perimeters. Accuracy in all of them is achieved by cross-description, not absolute statement.

Even 2+3=5 is better considered as a mathematical stanza than a single mathematical sentence. It models a set of several interlocked sentences; and the context interlocking them is what "contains" the meaning we might model by saying "2+3=5 is right, whereas 2+3=4 is wrong by lack of 1."

53. A *language-function* can be described as consisting of (one) a generative field (capable of generating a set of signals), (two) the signals so generated, and (three) an interpretive field (a field capable of responding to those signals) into which the signals fall.

Examples of language-functions: mathematics, art, expressive gesture, myth.

One of the most important language-functions is, of course, speech.

In most multiple speaker/hearer situations, there are usually multiple language-functions occurring: A talking to B ... B talking to A ... C listening to what A and B say, etc. (In Art, on the other hand, there is usually one only: artist to audience. The language-function that goes from audience to artist is, of course, criticism.)

The language itself is the way, within a single speaker/hearer, an interpretive field is connected to a generative field.

54. The trouble with most cybernetic models of language (those models that start off with "sound waves hitting the ear") is that they try to express language only in terms of an interpretive field. To the extent that they posit a generative field in all, they simply see it as an inverse of the interpretive field.

In ordinary, human speech, the interface of the interpretive field with the world is the ear—an incredibly sensitive microphone that, in its flexibility and versatility, still has not been matched by technology. The interface of the generative field with the world is two wet sacks of air and several guiding strips of muscle, laid out in various ways along the air track, and a variable-shaped resonance box with a variable opening: the lungs/throat/mouth complex. This complex can produce a great many sounds, and in extremely rapid succession. But it can produce nothing like the range of sounds the ear can detect.

Language, whatever it is, in circuitry terms has to lie between these two interfaces, the ear and the mouth.

Most cybernetic models, to the extent that they approach the problem at all, see language as a circuit to get us from a sensitive microphone to an equally sensitive loudspeaker. A sensitive loudspeaker just isn't in the picture. And I suspect if it were, language as we know it would not exist, or at least be very different.

Try and envision circuitry for the following language tasks:

We have a sensitive microphone at one end of a box. At the other, we have a *mechanically* operable squeeze-box/vocal-chord/palate/tongue/teeth/lip arrangement. We want to fill up the box with circuitry that will accomplish the following: Among a welter of sounds—bird songs, air in leaves, footsteps, traffic noise—one is a simple, oral, human utterance. The circuitry must be able to pick out the human utterance, store it, analyze it (in terms of breath duration, breath intensity, and the various stops that have been imposed on a stream of air by vocal chords, tongue, palate, teeth, lips) and then, after a given time, reproduce this utterance through its own squeeze-box mechanism.

This circuitry task is both much simpler and much more complicated than getting a sound out of a loudspeaker. Once we have such a circuit, however, well before we get to any "logic," "syntax," or "semantic" circuits, we are more than halfway to having a language circuit.

Consider:

We now want to modify this circuit so that it will perform the following task as well:

Presented with a human utterance, part of which is blurred—either by other sounds or because the utterer said it unclearly—our circuit must now be able to give back the utterance correctly, using phonic overdeterminism to make the correction: Letting X stand for the blurred phoneme, if the utterance is

"The pillow lay at the foot of the Xed"

or

"She stood at the head of the Xairs"

our circuitry should be able to reproduce the most likely phoneme in place of the blur, X.

I think most of us will agree, if we *had* the first circuit, getting to the second circuit would be basically a matter of adding a much greater storage capacity, connected up in a fairly simple (i.e., regular) manner with the circuit as it already existed.

Let us modify our circuit still more:

We present an utterance with a blurred phoneme that can resolve in two (or more ways):

"Listen to the *X*erds." (Though I am not writing this out in phonetic notation, nevertheless, it is assumed that the phonic component of the written utterance is what is being dealt with.)

Now in this situation, our very sensitive microphone is still receiving other sounds as well. The circuitry should be such that, if it is receiving at the same time as the utterance, or has received fairly recently, some sound such as cheeping or twittering on the one hand (or, on the other, the sounds of clicking pencils, and rattling paper) it will resolve the blurred statement into "listen to the birds" (or, respectively, "listen to the words"—and if the accompanying sound is a dank, gentle plashing . . .) Again, this is still just a matter of more storage space to allow wider recognition/association patterns.*

The next circuitry recomplication we want is to have our circuit such that, when presented with a human utterance, ambiguous or not, it can come back with a recognizable paraphrase. To do this, we might well have to have not only a sensitive microphone, but a sensitive camera and a sensitive micro-olofact and microtact as well, as well as ways of sorting, storing, and associating the material they collect. Basically, however, it is still, as far as the specific language circuitry is concerned, a matter of greater storage capacity, needed to allow greater associational range.

I think that most people would agree, at this point, that if we had a circuit that could do all these tasks, even within a fairly limited vocabulary, though we might not have a circuit that could be said to *know* the language, we would certainly have one that could be said to know a lot *about* it.

One reason to favor the above as a model of language is that, given the initial circuit, the more complicated versions could, conceivably, evolve by ordinary, natural-selection and mutation processes. Each new step is still basically just a matter of adding lots of very similar or identical components, connected up in very similar

*The important point here, of course, is that nonverbal material must already be considered *as* language, if not as part *of* language.

ways. Consider also: Complex as it is, that initial circuitry must exist, in some form or another, in every animal that recognizes and utters a mating call (or warning) to or from its own species, among the welter, confusion, and variety of wild, forest sounds.

The usual cybernetic model for language interpretation:

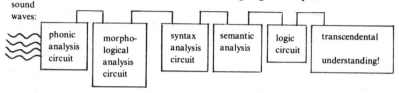

sound waves: phonic analysis circuit | morpho-logical analysis circuit | syntax analysis circuit | semantic analysis | logic circuit | transcendental understanding!

where each box must be a different kind of circuit, the first four probably different for each language (and, arguably, all six) strikes me as a pretty hard thing to "grow" by ordinary evolutionary means, or to program on a *tabula rasa* neural net.

The circuitry I suggest would all be a matter of phonic recognition, phonic storage, and phonic association (short of the storage and associational employment of the other sensory information). A great *deal* of recognition/storage/association would have to be done by the circuitry to achieve language. But nothing *else* would have to be done, other than what was covered in our original utterance-reproduction circuit.

Not only would the linguistic bugaboo "semantics" disappear (as experiments indicate that it may have already) but so would morphology; and syntax and phonic analysis would simply absorb one another, so to speak.

Would this really be so confusing?

I think not. It is only a rather limited view of grammar that initially causes it to appear so.

Think of grammar solely as the phonic redundancies that serve to get a heard utterance from the interpretive field, through the range of associations in the hearer/speaker's memory that includes "his language," into the hearer/speaker's generative field as an utterance.

In the *qui, quae, quo* of Latin, for instance, I'm sure the Roman brain (if not the Roman grammarian) considered the redundancy of the initial 'qu' sound as grammatically significant (in my sense of "grammar") as it considered, say, the phonic redundancy between the "ae" at the end of "quae" and the "ae" at the end of "pullae." (We must get rid of the notion of grammar as something that applies only to the ends of words!) In English, the initial sound of *the, this, that, these, those, there* are all grammatically redundant in a similar way. (The "th" sound indicates, as it were, "indication"; the initial "qu" sound, in Latin, indicates "relation," just as the terminal "ae" sound indicates, in that language, "more than one female."*) What one can finally say of this "grammar" is: When a phonic redundancy *does* relate to the way that a sound is employed in conjunction with other sounds/meanings, then that phonic element of the grammar is regular. When a phonic redundancy does *not* so relate, that element is irregular. (The terminal "s" sound on "these" and "those" is redundant with the terminal "s" of *loaves, horses, sleighs*—it indicates plurality, and is therefore *regular* with those words. The terminal "s" on "this" is *irregular* with them. The terminal "s" at the end of "is," "wants," "has," and "loves" all imply singularity. Should the terminal "s" on "this" be considered regular with these others? I suspect in many people's version of English it is.) For all we know, in the ordinary English hearer/speaker's brain, "cream," "loam," "foam," and "spume" are all associated, by that final "m" sound, with the concept of "matter difficult to individuate"—in other words, the "m" is a grammatically regular structure of *that particular word group*. Such associations with this particular terminal "m" may explain why most people seldom use "ham" in the plural—though nothing empirically or traditionally grammatical prevents it. They may also explain why "cream," when pluralized, in most people's minds immediately assumes a different viscosity (i.e., referentially, becomes a different word; what the dictionary indicates by a "second meaning"). I suspect that, in a very real sense, the poets are most in touch with the true "deep grammar" of the language. Etymology explains some of the sound-redundancy/meaning-associations that are historical. Others that are accidental, however, may be no less meaningful.

All speech begins as a response to other speech. (As a child you eventually speak through being spoken to.) Eventually this recomplicates into a response to speech-and-other stimulae. Eventually, when both speech and other stimulae are stored in memory and reassociated there, this recomplication becomes so complex that it is far more useful to consider certain utterances autonomous—the first utterance in the morning concerning a dream

---

*This is another invocation of the idea, out of favor for so long, of "morphophonemes." The theoretical question of course is do they differ (or how they differ) from "sememes."

in the night, for example. But even this can be seen as a response to speech-and-other-than speech in which the threads of cause, effect, and delay have simply become too intertwined and tangled to follow.

55. Quine inveighs against propositions, as part of logic, on the justifiable grounds that they cannot be individuated. But since propositions, if they are anything, are particular meanings of sentences, the impossibility of individuating them is only part of a larger problem: the impossibility of individuating meanings in general. What the logician who says (as Quine does at the beginning of at least two books) "To deny the Taj Majal is white is to affirm that it is not white" (in the sense of "nonwhite") is really saying, is:

"Even if meanings cannot be individuated, let us, for the duration of the argument, treat them as if they can be. Let us assume that there is some volume of meaning-space that can be called white *and* be bounded. Therefore, every point in meaning-space, indeed, every volume in meaning-space, can be said to either lie inside this boundary, and be called 'white', or outside this boundary, and be called 'nonwhite,' or, for the volumes that lie partially inside and partially outside, we can say that some aspect of them is white."

The problem is that, similar to the color itself, the part of meaning-space that can be called "white" fades, on one side and another, into every other possible color. And somehow, packed into this same meaning-space, but at positions distinctly outside this boundary around white, or any other color for that matter, we must also pack "freedom," "death," "grief," "the four-color-map problem," "the current King of France," "Pegasus," "Hitler's daughter," "the entire Second World War and all its causes," as well as "the author of Waverly"—all in the sense, naturally, of "nonwhite."

Starting with just the colors: In what sort of space could you pack all possible colors so that each one was adjacent to every other one, which would allow the proper fading (*and* bounding*) to occur? It's not as hard as it looks. Besides the ordinary three coordinates for volume, if you had two more ordinates, both for color, I suspect it could be rather easily accomplished. You might even do it with only two spatial and two color axes. Four coordinates, at any rate, is certainly the minimum number you need. Conceivably, getting the

---

*Welsh (and Homeric Greek) divide the spectrum (both as to colors and intensity) quite differently from English.

entire Second World War and all its causes in *might* require a few more.

56. One of the great difficulties of formal grammars is that they are *all* grammars of *written* language, including the attempts at "transformational" grammars (*Syntactic Structures:* "... we will not consider, for our purposes, vocal inflections..."). For insight into how verbal signals will produce information once they fall into an interpretive field, it is a good idea to return to the mechanics of those signals' generation.

Speech signals, or sentences, are formed from two, simultaneous information (or signal) streams: The speech is an interface of these two streams.

The voiced breath-line is a perfectly coherent information stream, all by itself. It varies in pitch and volume and shrillness. It is perfectly possible (as I have done and watched done in some encounter groups) for two or more people to have an astonishingly satisfying conversation, consisting of perfectly recognizable questions, answers, assurances, hesitations, pooh-poohings, affirmations, scepticisms, and insistences—a whole range of emotional information, as well as the range Quine refers to as "propositional attitudes"—purely with an unstopped, voiced breath. (Consider the information communicated by the sudden devoicing of all the phonemes in an utterance, i.e., whispering.)

The various stops and momentary devoicings imposed by the tongue, teeth, lips, and vocal chords on top of this breath-line is another coherent information string that, interfaced with the breath-line information, produces "speech." But this second string is the only part that is ever written down. This is the only part that any "grammar" we have had till now deals with. But it is arguable that this information-string, when taken without the breath-line, is as vastly impoverished as the breath-line eventually seems, after ten or fifteen minutes, when taken by itself.

The way written speech gets by is by positing a "standard breath-line," the most common breath-line employed with a given set of vowels and stops. (The only breath-line indicators we have are the six ordinary marks of punctuation, plus quotation marks [which mean, literally, pay closer attention to the breath-line for the enclosed stretch of words], plus dashes, ellipses, and italic type. One thing that makes writing in general, and poetry in particular, an art is the implying of nonstandard breath-lines by the strong association of vocal sounds—*pace* Charles Olson.) But since the vast majority of writing uses only this standard breath-line (and *all* writing uses an artificial one), producing a grammar of a spoken language from written examples is rather like trying to produce a formal grammar of, say, Latin when the only available texts have had all the ablative endings, dative endings, accusative-plural endings, and second-person-singular verb endings in future, imperfect, and preterite typexed out; and you have agreed, for your purposes, not to consider them anyway.

What is fascinating about language is not that it criticizes, as well as contributes to, the growth of the empirical world, but that it can criticize its relation to that world, treating itself, for the duration, empirically. The same self-reflective property is what writers use to make beautiful, resonant, verbal objects, however referential or abstract. But by the same argument, it is the writers' responsibility to utilize this reflective property to show, again and again, that easy language, whether it is the short, punchy banality or the rolling jargonistic period, lies.

The lie is not a property of easy words. It is a property of how the words are used, the context that generates, and the context that interprets.

57. I have the artist's traditional distrust of separating facts too far from the landscape that generated them. (And I have the science-fiction writer's delight over inserting new facts into unfamiliar landscapes. "Do I contradict myself? Very well...")

Language, Myth, Science Fiction:
First contacts:
I did not have a happy childhood.
Nobody does.
I did, however, have a privileged one.

I discovered myths with a set of beautifully produced and illustrated books called *My Book House*, edited by Olive Burpre Miller and illustrated, for the most part, by Donald P. Crane. An older cousin of mine had owned them as a child. My aunt passed them on to me when her daughter went off to Vassar. The volumes bound in gray and mottled green dealt with history, starting with cave-men and working, lushly illustrated volume after lushly illustrated volume, through the Renaissance. Those bound in maroon and gold recounted, for children, great works of literature, fairy tales, and myths—Greek, Egyptian, Norse...

At five, I left kindergarten (the building, maroon and red as the *Book House* volumes under a spray of city grime, is today part of Columbia University) for a private, progressive, and extremely eccentric elementary school. I have one memory of my first day there, fragmented and incomplete:

Along one side of our room were tall, wide windows covered with wire grills. A window seat ran the length of the wall; the seat back went up and joined the window sill—a squared grate, brown and painted, chipped, here and there, to the metal, through which you could see, checked with light, the dusty, iron radiators, and hear brass valves jiggle and hiss.

On that first morning, our teacher had to leave the shy dozen of us along for some few minutes.

What occurs now, exactly, I'm not sure. But the memory clears when she comes rushing back, stops short and, fists clutching her blue smock (below which I can see the hem of her navy jumper), shrieks: "Stop it! Oh, my God! *Stop* it!"

One blond boy stood on the radiator grate, gripping the window grill, flattened against it, staring back at us, mouth wide and drooling, eyes closed and streaming.

We crowded the window seat, jeering and railing up at him: "Jump! Go ahead, jump!" I was holding the shoulder of the person in front of me, pressed forward by the person behind. "Jump!" I shouted, looked back at the teacher and laughed (you've seen how much fun five-year-olds have when they laugh), then shouted again: "Jump out! Jump out!" and could hear neither my own shouts nor my own laughter for the laughter and shouting of the other ten.

We were eight stories up.

The teacher yanked us, still jeering, one after another, away, lifted down the hysterical boy, and comforted him. His name was Robert. He was stocky, nervous, shrill. He had some slight motor difficulty. (I can still remember him, sitting at a green nursery table, holding his pencil in both hands to draw his letters, while the rest of us, who could, of course, hold *our* pencils in one, exchanged looks, glanced at him, glanced away, and giggled.) He was a stammerer, an appalling nail biter, very bright; and, by Christmas vacation, my best friend.

With occasional lapses, sometimes a few months long, Robert remained my best friend till we left for other schools after the eighth grade. Some of those lapses, however, I engineered quite blatantly—when I was tired of having the class odd-ball as constant companion. I would steal things from him, pencils, protractors, small toys—I remember pilfering a Donald Duck ring he had sent away for from a cereal box-top offer. With a small magnet (decaled to look like a tiny corn-flakes box), you could make the yellow plastic beak open and close, the blue plastic eye roll up and down. My parents caught me on that one, made me promise to return it, and tell him I'd stolen it. I did, quite convinced it would be the end of our friendship—apprehensive, but a bit relieved.

Robert took the ring back and stammered that it was all right if *I* had stolen it, because, after all (his expression was that of someone totally betrayed) I was his friend. That was when I realized he had no others.

During my attendance at Dalton, I lived one street from what, in the 1953 City Census, was declared the most populous tenement block in New York: It housed over eighteen thousand people, in buildings all under six stories. A block away, my sister and I had three floors and sixteen rooms, over my father's Harlem funeral parlor, in which to lose ourselves from our parents and the maid. But the buildings on both sides of us were a cluster of tiny, two- and three-room apartments, housing five, seven, sometimes over ten people each. The friends I played with in the afternoon in front of the iron gates of Mr. Lockely's *Hardware and Houseware Store* to our left, or the sagging green vegetable boxes in front of the red-framed plate-glass window of Mr. Onley's *Groceries* to our right, were the son of a widowed hospital orderly on welfare, the daughter and two sons of a frequently laid-off maintenance man who worked in the New York subway system, the two sons of a New York taxi driver, the niece of the woman who ran the funeral parlor at the corner of the same block.

And in the morning, my father—or, occasionally, one of his employees—would drive me, in my father's very large, very black Cadillac, down to the ten story, red and white brick building on Eighty Ninth Street and Park Avenue: I would line up with all the other children in the gray-tiled lobby, waiting to march around, next to the wall, and show my tongue to the school nurse, Miss Hedges, who, for the first years, in her white uniform with a gray sweater around her shoulders, would actually make an attempt to peer into each five-to-twleve-year-old mouth, but, as I grew older, simply stood, at last, in the corner by the gooseneck lamp as we filed by (perhaps one in five of us actually even bothered to look up) staring at a vague spot on the far wall, somewhere between the twenties-style, uplifting mural of Mothers Working in the Fields and the display cabinets where student sculpture was exhibited by our various art teachers. In class (ten students was considered the ideal number; should we somehow reach fourteen, Something Was Done to Relieve the Impossible Teaching Load), my friends were the son of a vice president of CBS Television, the daughter of a large New York publisher, the son of a small New York publisher, the grandson of the governor of the state, the son of the drama critic for *Time* magazine, the daughter of a psychiatrist and philanthropist, the son of a Pulitzer Prize winning dramatist.

Black Harlem speech and white Park Avenue speech are very different things. I became aware of language as an intriguing and infinitely malleable modeling tool very early.

I always felt myself to be living in several worlds with rather tenuous connections between them, but I never remember it causing me much anxiety. (Of the, perhaps, ten blacks among the three hundred odd students in Dalton's elementary school, five were my relatives.) Rather, it gave me a sense of modest (and sometimes not so modest) superiority.

A few years later, I was given still another world to play in. I spent summer at a new summer camp. I tell only one incident here from that pleasantest of summers in my life: One hot afternoon, I wandered into a neighboring tent where the older boys slept. On the foot of the nearest iron-frame bed lay a large, ragged-edged magazine, with a shiny cover, gone matte with handling—I think its muddy, out-of-register colors showed a man and a woman on a hill, gazing in terrified astonishment at a round, metal *thing* swooping through the air. From the lettering on the cover, the lead story in this issue was something called—I picked it up and turned to the first page—*The Man Who Sold the Moon*. My first reaction was: "What an odd combination of words! What do they mean?..." While I was puzzling through the opening sentences, one of the bunk-seven twelve-year-olds came in and shooed me out. Back in my own tent, I returned to the book I was reading, Lincoln Barnet's *The Universe and Dr. Einstein*. And our twenty-three-year-old counsellor, Roy, was reading something called *One, Two, Three... Infinity* that I had said looked interesting and he had said I could read when he was finished.

Months later, back on Eighty Ninth Street, after consultation with Robert (and several practice tries from five, six, and then seven steps), I decided to leap down the entire flight between the sixth and seventh floor. At the head of the stairwell—the steps were a dark green that continued up the wall to shoulder level; there, light green took over and went on across the ceiling—sighting on the flaking, gold decalcomania on the far wall ("SIX," half on dark green, half on light), I got ready, grinned at Robert, below, who was leaning against the door and looking nervous, swung my arms back threw them forward, jumped—my foot slipped! I flailed out, suspended a moment, silent, in dead air, trajectory off!

The bottom newel post caught me in the belly, and I passed out—no more than a couple of seconds.

Robert had yanked open the door and was running for a teacher before I hit.

I should have ruptured myself. Apparently all I did, though, was knock all my air out and, temporarily and very slightly, atort my left spermatic. Because I'd gone unconscious, however, and people were wondering whether I'd hit my head, I spent the night in observation at the hospital.

In the patients' lounge were several of those large-sized, pulp magazines that I recognized as the type I'd seen (but never read) last summer at camp. I selected the one with the most interesting cover—girl, bikini, bubble-helmet, monster—and took it back to my bed and read my first two science-fiction stories.

One climaxed with a tremendous spaceship battle, the dénouement of which was someone figuring out that the death ray the enemy used was actually nothing more than light, slowed way down, so that its energy potential went way up. I don't remember one character, or one situation beside the battle; I doubt if I would want to. But the idea, connected forever in my memory with a marvelous (I'm sure it's Virgil Finlay, though I've never run across the magazine again) illustration of bubble-helmeted spacemen entering a chamber of looming, vampire monsters, remains.

The other story I read that night leaves me with this recollection: Some Incredibly Ancient Aliens (in the lead illustration, they are all veined heads and bulging eyes) are explaining to someone (the hero? the villain?) that the brain is never used to full capacity by humans, but *they* you see, have been using *theirs*, which are much larger than humans' anyway, to full capacity now for centuries. And they are *very* tired.

And at school, a couple of weeks later, Robert mentioned to me that he had just read a wonderful book that I must take a look at: *Rocketship Galileo*. He had read it twice already. It was, he explained, probably one of the best books in the world. He even volunteered to get it out of the school library for me that afternoon (I had several books overdue and couldn't take out any myself till they were returned), which he did...

Too much enthusiasm among my friends for something has often been a turn-off for me—often to my detriment. I *still* have not read Heinlein's *Rocketship Galileo*, though Robert, after I finally returned the book to the library, unread, actually bought a copy and gave it to me.

That year's history study was divided into one term of ancient Greek history and one term of Roman. The climax of the Greek term was a day-long Greek Festival which our class put on for the rest of the school. The morning of Festival Day, the whole school, in the auditorium, watched a play competition, where several short, original plays "on Greek themes" were performed, one of which was voted best by a board of teachers.

For that year's Festival, I had written one of the plays (a comedy in which I took the part of Pericles—I believe he was having labor problems with the slaves over the construction of the Parthenon). It took second to a play by a girl who had muscular dystrophy, a speech impediment, and who used to cry all the time for no reason. Backstage in my toga, furiously jealous, I vigorously applauded the announcement of her triumph, among the rest of the clapping actors from the various play-companies, while she limped out on stage to receive her wreath of bay-leaves. Congratulating her, and the happy members of the cast of her play, I decided the Greek Festival was a waste.

I can only remember one dialogue exchange from my play. I hated it; another cast member had written it and insisted on inserting it, and I had finally acquiesced to keep peace. (Socrates: "How is the

Parthenon coming along, Pericles?" Pericles [through gritted teeth]:
"It's all up but the columns.") But I still have the opening of the prize-
winning play by heart, with only that one morning's viewing:

The curtains had opened and a chorus of Greek women in blue
veils walked across the stage, growing light with dawn, reciting:

> "Persia's ships to Attica came.
> Many a thousand they were.
> And like winged birds, the tribes of Greece
> flocked."

The women turned, walked back again—reciting what, I no
longer recall. But I still remember that 'flocked' as one of the most
exciting words I had ever heard. Terminating the sentence with its
clutch of harsh consonances, while all the other sounds fluttered
behind it in memory, spoken by six ten-year-old girls at ordinary
volume, it had—to me—the force of a shout.

Martha, who wore leg braces and walked funny and couldn't
talk properly and had rightfully won her prize over my glib,
forgettable wise-cracks, had shown me for the first time that a single
word, placed properly in a sentence, could give an effect at once
inevitable, astonishing, and beautiful.

After a very un-Greek lunch in the third floor dining room, every
one went up to the tenth-floor gymnasium, where we held a junior
Olympics. The boys had wrestling matches, discus throwing, high
jumping, and broad jumping. The girls ran hurdle races, chariot
races, and did jumping too. Then there was a final relay where boys
and girls, in hiked-up togas, ran—their papier maché torches
streaming crêpe-paper fire—around and around the gym.

It was that dull.

In English that term we had read the *Iliad* and the *Odyssey*, as
well as a good handful of traditional myths—most of which I was
familiar with from *My Book House*. We even tackled one or two
Greek plays in translation; and over one English period, Mrs. T, my
favorite English teacher from my whole elementary school days,
explained to us the etymology of "calligraphy," "geology," "optical,"
"palindrome," "obscene," and "poet."

In Math, to coordinate with our Greek unit, we devoted one day
a week to Geometry. Using "only the tools Pythagoras accepted" (i.e.,
a compass and a straight edge), we went about discovering simple

geometric relationships about the circle and various inscribed angles. We constructed a demonstration to show that the area of a circle, as the limit of the sum of its sectors cut ever smaller and placed alternately, approaches a parallelogram with a base of πr, and a height of r, to wit, an area of πr². And Robert gave me another book, which I did read this time, called *The Black Star Passes*, by John W. Campbell. Again, I remember neither plot nor characters. But I do recall that someone in it had invented a Very Powerful Mathematical Tool called "the multiple calculus," about which author Campbell went on with ebullient enthusiasm. We had already been taught, on the other four days of the week, the basic manipulative algebraic skills, adding, subtracting, multiplying, and dividing polynomials. At home, I stumbled through the Encyclopaedia Britannica article on Infinitesimal Calculus (which went on about somebody named Newton as enthusiastically as Campbell had gone on about his mathematician); days later I went down to the High School Library on the school's third floor, got out a book; got out another; and then three more. Then I bought a Baron's Review of trigonometry. And then I got some more books.

But the school term was over again.

At summer camp that year I was assigned to a tent at the bottom of the tent colony. My iron-frame bed, which I made up that first afternoon with sheets so starched they had to be peeled apart (and the inevitable olive drab army blanket), was next to the bed of a boy named Eugene. I didn't like him. I don't think anybody else in the tent did either. But he made friendly attempts at conversation—mostly about his father, who you see edited *Galaxy*: "Don't you know what *Galaxy* is? It's the science-fiction magazine! Don't you like science fiction? Well, then what does *your* father do?"

"He's an undertaker," I said, having learned some time ago that if I said it with a steely enough voice (picked up from Channel Five reruns of Bela Lugosi films), it would shut just about anybody up, at least for a while.

Sometime in the next hour or so, Gene had a twenty-minute, hysterical crying jag and decided he wanted to go home—I don't recall about what. I do remember thinking: This is ridiculous, I'll never be able to put up with *this* next to me all summer!

I asked the counsellor if I could be assigned a bed next to someone—anyone—else. The counsellor said no.

Disappointed, I went back to my bed and was sitting on it,

arranging my jeans, swimming trunks, and underwear in the wooden shelf wedged back under the sloping canvas roof, when another boy shouted: "Look *out*!"

I dived forward onto the next bed, and rolled over to see Gene's eight-inch hunting knife, plunged through my army blanket, the two sheets and thin mattress, and heard it grate the springs. Gene, clutching the handle, stopped shaking with hysterical rage, pulled the knife free and looked about the seven other boys in the tent, who all stared back. My blanket settled, with just the slightest wrinkle, and an inch-and-a-half slit, slightly off center.

Gene, frankly, looked as astonished as the rest of us.

Just then the counsellor (that year his name was Marty) backed up the tent steps, dragging his own trunk, and asked one of the boys to help him put it under his bed. Somebody went back to packing his shelf. Somebody else sat down on his own bed, creaking springs. Gene blinked a few times then put the knife in his top shelf, between his soap dish and his mess kit.

I left the tent, took a walk around the tent colony, watching, through the rolled-back tent flaps, the other campers unpack. Finally, I went into the creosoted bathroom shack, had diarrhoea for fifteen minutes, at the end of which, with a red ball-point pen, I wrote something stupid and obscene on the wall beside something equally stupid and obscene.

In the same way I have no memory of what directly preceded our class harassment of Robert, I have no real memory of what precisely occurred just before Gene's outburst. What had we done to him? Did I assist in it? Or do nothing to prevent it? Or did I instigate it? Conveniently, I have forgotten.

Sitting in the pine-planked stall, looking at the cracked cement flooring, I do remember thinking: If I was going to have to sleep next to this nut, I'd better make friends with him. Then I went back to my tent where Marty was asking for the choice of stories we wanted him to read us after lights-out. The vote was unanimous for Jack London.

Over the next week, occasionally I looked at the little tear in my blanket: but once the initial fear had gone, with the odd callousness of childhood, I set about making friends with Gene; there was nothing else to do.

Tuesday morning, after breakfast, Gene received in the mail, from his father, cover proofs for the two forthcoming issues of

Galaxy (containing the last instalment of *Caves of Steel*, and the first of *Gladiators at Law*), both covers by Emsh—Gene's favorite s-f illustrator. Perhaps a week after that, he received an advance copy of the first issue of the fantasy magazine *Beyond*. I borrowed it from him one afternoon and read Theodore Cogswell's *The Wall Around the World*, which, I decided, was the best story I had ever read.

Our tent counsellor, Marty, was a graduate physics student at City College, and a science-fiction reader himself.

I asked Gene if I could lend Marty the magazine; after much debate, Gene said yes. Marty read the story, said he liked it, but that it made its point by oversimplifying things.

As we walked down the path between the girls' bunks and an old barn building, called for some reason (there were several apocryphal stories explaining why) Brooklyn College, I asked: "Why do you say it's oversimplified?" Porgy's adventures on a world where magic controls one half and science the other had seemed quite the most significant construct I had encountered since slow light or the multiple calculus.

"Well," Marty explained, as a herd of boys and girls swarmed from the ping-pong tables, out the wide doors of Brooklyn College, to troop along the road as the dinner bell, down by the dining room, donged and danged, "if you define magic as all that is not science, and science as all that is not magic—well, for one thing, you come up with a situation where, *if* science exists, magic must too. And we know it doesn't. It's much more useful to consider science a refinement of magic—that's what it is historically. As it gets refined, there're just fewer and fewer contradictions: It just gets more and more effective."

And that evening, after we were all in bed, Marty, sitting back on his own bed, with a flashlight propped against his shoulder, would read us *To Build a Fire,* or *South of the Slot*, or *The Shadow and the Flash*.

My best friend that year at summer camp was Karen, who, though she was odd, seemed more efficient at it than Gene. She never tried to kill me; and no one ever tried to kill her.

She used to fill endless terrariums with snakes she caught in the woods. Once, when we were working together putting up screens in the camp Nature House, I interrupted her explanation of how to tell which mushrooms were and which were not Deadly Amanita, to ask her if she liked science fiction. She said no, because there weren't any girls in it—"Or, when there are, they never *do* anything"—which, for all the bikinis-and-bubble-helmets, I had to admit was about true.

And Gene was unhappy at camp and went home after the first month anyway.

Back at school, Greek and Roman history were replaced by a term of medieval European history, and then a term of combined Chinese and Indian history. Our history teacher that year, a Mrs. Evelyn Mackerjee, a plump, New England woman of diminutive but impressive bearing (she was one of the handful of teachers we did *not* call by their first name), had spent many years in India and had been the wife of the late, Indian scholar, Dan Ghopal Mackerjee, who (so went the story we told each other in hushed tones) had committed suicide some years ago when he had discovered himself victim of a fatal, lingering cancer, and whose English translations of the *Ramayana* and the *Mahabharata* were, that term, our literature texts.

In class discussions, cross-legged on the vinyl floor (while, under the window seat, the radiators hissed and, occasionally, clunked), I would watch Mrs. Mackerjee, with her white hair, her gray tweeds, and her blocky heeled shoes, lean forward in her chair and explain to the circle of us: "Now, recall the *Iliad* from last year. Do you see how, in the *Mahabharata*, the relationship of gods to men envisioned by Valmiki under his anthill is—" and here, hands on her knees, her elbows would bend— "*very* different from the relation held by the blind Greek, Homer..."

That spring, the Old Vic production of Giraudoux's *Tiger at the Gates* came to New York, with Michael Redgrave. The aunt of a school friend took us to the first Wednesday Matinee during our spring vacation. From the second row, I watched while a story whose plot I knew (just as I had been told that the audiences for the original Greek drama all knew the plots beforehand too) was used to say something that struck me, at the time, as completely new. The fascinating thing to me was that the inevitability of the story was part of what was being constantly discussed on stage.

In the same week, I heard a radio production of Giraudoux's *The Apollo of Bellac*, and found it enthralling. One of our assistant teachers recommended I read some of Anouilh's charming dramatic representations of Greek myths; Sartre's more weighty, if less elegant, retelling of the *Orestia*, *The Flies*, came about here; and then O'Neill's

Mourning Becomes Elektra and *The Great God Brown.*

During the term of Chinese and Indian history, we were also given a French class; our regular Natural Science teacher was taking a year off to devote himself to sculpture, and no replacement could be found. His works were on exhibit at the Museum of Modern Art, where my parents took me once to see them. Our art teacher (whose works were occasionally to be seen at the Whitney) used to say of his, while swinging her long arms back and forth against her gray apron: "Well, I don't think they're very good—too formal, too congested. But it has *some*thing..."

Madame Geritsky, shorter than most of her pupils, made us memorize pages of French prose, which we had to recite alone and in unison, our *u*'s, *r*'s, and *l*'s constantly corrected, with a yellow pointer, wielded in chalk-whitened fingers.

I was never a good language student: but I was a bold one. Years later, when I actually spent time in other countries, I found that, armed with the all important sentence well memorized, "How do you say *that* in Greek/Italian/Turkish..." I could pick up in weeks, or even days, at least temporarily, what took others months to acquire.

We reconstruct from memory a childhood that, as adults, we can bear. I think of mine as one in which I liked many people and was liked in return. If I *was* as happy as I remember, one reason is that I went to a school where athletic prowess and popularity were not necessarily synonymous. Among the three classes of ten to thirteen that formed our grade, there were only three boys I recall as particularly good at sports. And two of these used to vie for position as Class Bully. Everyone cordially despised them.

In gym, three mornings and three afternoons a week, we indulged in an amazingly sadistic game called "bombardment": two teams hurled soccer balls at one another, taking prisoner anyone hit. Our gym teacher, named (I kid you not) Muscles, had several times pulled Arthur out for purposely hitting another player so hard with the ball he brought the boy to tears.

During one of my early lapses with Robert (was I seven? eight?), Arthur tried to pick a fight with me on the school roof. He was a head taller than everybody else in the class, possibly slightly older. As he was shoving me back into the wire fence at the roof's edge, I said to myself: "This is silly!" So I announced to him that, indeed, it *was* silly of him to push me around: I was his friend. So he should stop. After the third time I said it, he looked perplexed and said, "Oh." I straightened my clothes and suggested we play together. For the next two weeks I went regularly to his house in the afternoons, invited him, regularly, to mine, and spent inordinate amounts of time helping him with his arithmetic homework.

Finally, I got bored.

He was not bright; he was lonely; he was belligerent. Friendship with Robert did not cut me off from friendship with anyone else: Robert was just strange. Friendship with Arthur did: Arthur was actively antisocial. Because he was ill-practiced in keeping friendships going, it was extremely easy to maneuver my way out of it, by being otherwise occupied here, too busy there, all the while counting on the fact he valued me too much to protest. In another week, without any particular scenes, we were no longer even speaking.

Anywhere outside the gymnasium, Arthur was subjected to a needling harassment that certainly fed his belligerence and, in its way, was much more vicious than that first day's attack on Robert. Robert's attack lasted minutes. Arthur's, practically without let-up, went on for years.

Arthur had committed some particularly annoying offense. A bunch of us got together and decided we must teach him a lesson. We agreed that, for the rest of the week, no one in the class would speak to him, or acknowledge he was there in any way. After a couple of hours, he hit a few people. They scooted out of the way, giggling. An hour after that, he was sitting on the hallway floor by the green book-box, leaning against it, sobbing. The teachers finally realized what we were doing and demanded we stop. So we did—while any teachers were around.

On the last day of this treatment (and there were others, dreamed up for him practically every month), Arthur managed to confront a bunch of us in the narrow, fenced-in enclosure in front of the school. He yelled at us angrily, then began to cry. We watched, mild embarrassment masked with mild approval, when, in the middle of his crying, Arthur suddenly pointed to me and exclaimed: "But *you're* my friend! You're my *friend*!"

Had it not been the last day, I would have stayed with my group. As it was, I spoke to him, left my friends, and went with him to the corner where he caught his bus home. I may even have explained to him why we'd done it. But I doubt, at this point, if he either understood or cared.

I think, however, this was where I began to realize that such cerebral punishments teach the offender nothing of the nature of annoyance, injury, or suffering he has inflicted: They teach only the strength of the group, and the group's cruelty—the group's oblivion to the annoyance, injury, and suffering it can inflict—the same, basic failing of the offender.

I didn't consider Arthur my friend. After walking him to the corner, I made no other efforts to be friendly. As other harassments came up, I was just as likely to be party—except that I now stayed more in the background to avoid being called to witness. But in gym class, Arthur no longer hurled at me his bombardment ball.

At six and seven, Arthur was a bully. By eleven or twelve, he was class clown; last in his school work, still incredibly aggressive in sports, now, whenever there was any tension between him and any teacher or classmate, he would drop his books all over the floor, belch loudly, or give a shrill, pointless giggle. We, at any rate, laughed— and despised him nonetheless. Our harassments had been effective: He was no longer likely to hit you. Frankly, I'm not sure that his earlier reactions weren't the more valid.

I am sure, however, that given another time, another place, another school, and children from families that had indulged different values, Arthur might have been the well-liked, admired student while I, an eccentric weakling of a different race, who lived half his life in another world, might have suffered all the harassment I so cavalierly helped in heaping on him.

Dalton prided itself in its progressiveness and courted an image of eccentricity. (The bizarre elementary school in Patrick Dennis's *Aunty Mame* is supposedly Dalton.) The eccentricity went no further than the headmistress announcing to each class, at the beginning of each year, in a *very* guarded tone: "If you *really* have something worthwhile, creative, and constructive to do, then you *may* arrange to be excused from regular classes." The announcement was made once and *never* repeated, though, in the Dalton brochures, this aspect of the school's individualized approach to each student was made much of. To my knowledge, I was the only student from my year who ever got to wheedle his way out of some of the more arduous classes: I developed an incredibly complex art project that involved paintings, sculptures, and electric lights, and announced to my math teacher that I wanted special instruction in calculus, and wanted it *now*.

For several months, I got away with spending most of my school day between the art room and special math tutoring sessions.

I was doing practically no assigned work. My arithmetic had never been strong. And my parents, who were nowhere near as eccentrically progressive as the school, decided to send me to a tutor, during this time, three afternoons a week. Amanda Kemp was a small, white-haired, black woman, who lived on the top floor of an apartment house on Edgecomb Avenue, in small, dark rooms that smelled of leaking gas.

With much good will and infinite patience, she tried to "interest" me in things that I had invested a good deal of emotional autonomy in remaining uninterested in—"Since," she explained to my mother, after the first week, "actually teaching him is certainly no problem. He learns whatever he wants to learn all *too* quickly," and she gave me a book of poems by Countee Cullen, which he had personally inscribed to her, years earlier, when they worked together in the city school system, its illustrations marvelously macabre, showing imaginary beasts of Jabberwockian complexity, each described by an accompanying rhymed text.

The person in my math class who did get the constantly easy hundred was Priscilla. Sometime around here, I decided to write a science-fiction novel—announced my project to a group of friends in the coffee shop on the corner, where we all adjourned after school to indulge in an obligatory toasted English muffin and/or lemon coke. I actually wrote the opening chapter: twenty pages of single-spaced typing on lined, three-holed, loose-leaf paper. I brought it into school and, during one study period, asked Priscilla to read it and pass judgment.

During the next half hour I chewed through several pencil erasers, stripped the little brass edge out of my wooden ruler, and accomplished some half dozen more intense, small, and absorbing destructions.

Priscilla, finally, looked up. (We were sitting on the green stairs.)
"Did you like it?" I asked. "Did you *understand* it?"
"I don't," she said, a little dryly, "believe anyone could

understand it with your spelling the way it is. Here, let me make you a list..." It was the beginning of a marvelous friendship (that, a year ago, reflowered just as warmly when I visited Wesleyan University where she is now a professor of Russian) which quickly came to include nightly hour-plus phone calls, made up mostly of ritual catch phrases (such as: "What has *that* got to do with the price of eggs in Afghanistan!") which somehow, by the slightest variation of inflection, communicated the most profound and arcane ideas, or, conversely, reduced us to hysterical laughter, to the annoyance of both our parents at both our houses. Besides correcting my spelling, Priscilla also told me about a book she said was perfectly wonderful and I must read, called *Titus Groan*. For fourteen years, it suffered the fate of *Rocketship Galileo*. I only got around to reading it one evening over a weekend at Damon Knight's sprawling Anchorage in Milford, Pennsylvania (Damon had just made some rather familiar sounding comments on the spelling of a manuscript I had given him to read); Priscilla had been right.

The last year of elementary school was drawing to a close. I had just been accepted at the Bronx High School of Science. I was sitting in the school's smaller, upstairs library, reading *More Than Human* for the second time, when several students, Robert and Priscilla among them, came in to tell me that I had been elected Most Popular Person in the Class—a distinction which carried with it the dubious honor of making a small speech at graduation.

I was terribly pleased.

Like many children who get along easily with their peers, I was an incredibly vicious and self-centered child, a liar when it suited me and a thief when I could get away with it, who, with an astonishing lack of altruism, had learned some of the advantages of being nice to people nobody else wanted to be bothered with.

I think, sometimes, when we are trying to be the most honest, the fictionalizing process is at its strongest. Would Robert, Mrs. Mackerjee, Gene, Arthur, Marty, or Priscilla agree with any of what I have written here, or even recognize it? What do *they* remember that, perhaps, I have forgotten—either because it was too painful, too damning, or because it made no real impression at all?

Language, Myth, Science Fiction...

58. Browsing in Joe Kennedy's *Counter/Measures*, I came across a
poem by John Bricuth called *Myth*. Liked it muchly. It begins with an
epigraph from Lévi-Strauss:

"Music and mythology confront man with virtual objects whose
shadow alone is real..."

And then this from Quine's *Philosophy of Logic:*

"The long and short of it is that propositions have been projected
as shadows of sentences, if I may transpose a figure of Wittgenstein's.
At best they will give us nothing the sentence will not give. Their
promise of more is mainly due to our uncritically assuming for them
an individuation which matches no equivalence between sentences
that we can see how to define. The shadows favoured wishful
thinking."

And from Spicer's poem *Language*, in his discussion of the
candleflame and the finger he has just blistered:

> *do they both point us to the*
> *grapheme on the concrete wall—*
> *the space between it*
> *where the shadow and the flame are one?*

Just as "propositions" can be dismissed from logic on the formal
side as a logical shadow in a field where we wish for light, on the
informal side we can dismiss the movable predicate—x "walks"
which can be moved to y "walks" and so on to the i*th* variable "... if
and only if the i*th* thing in the sequence walks" (presumably true of x,
y, and the others) [*Philosophy of Logic*, p. 40]—as an empirical
shadow: it is a shadow of the empirical resolution at which we observe
a given set of process phenomena that allows us to subsume them all
under one word. If, for instance, all that can be referred to by "walks"
is, like the word, a singular entity, then a very strange entity it is.
Among other things, it is discontinuous in both time and space, since
both x and y can perform it simultaneously in different locations
and/or at different times! In the empirical world, however, spatial
and temporal discontinuity *is* multiplicity of entities. And "a multiple
entity" in our language at any rate is as silly a concept as "many rock."
(This, I suspect, is the practical side of Quine's refusal to "quantify
over predicates" [*Philosophy of Logic* p. 28]. If we have a situation

where every instance of predicate-with-every-variable can be empirically resolved into separate predicates (P), we have a situation where the existential quantifier ($_EP$), would always have the same value as the universal quantifier (P). If there is *only* one q, then everything you can say of "at least one q" you can say of "all q." Similarly, the negation of one quantifier could always be taken as the other *or* empty, as one liked. This gets the formal logician into the same sort of trouble as the mathematician who allows himself to divide by zero in formal algebra.)

If we have a universe composed only of real, unique objects performing unique processes, how do we order them? (Are we stuck with G. Spencer Brown's suggestion from *Laws of Form* that "equals" must be taken to mean "is confused with"?) Or, more germane: Since we *do* perceive the universe as ordered, can we work back to such a universe of unique objects-and-processes without contradiction?

Language is miraculous not in its power to differentiate. Differentiation, when all is said and done, is carried on nonverbally by the reasonable cross-checking of the information of the other senses. The wonder is that language can respond to any number of *different* things in the *same* way: it can call ashtrays, actors, and accidents "entities"; it can call poems, paintings, and nesselrode pies "art"; it can call what three different men at three different times of day do when going down the street "walking"; it can call three entities that walk down the street at the same time "women"; it can call sentences, ideas, and blue-prints "models"; it can call freedom, death, the color white, and the Second-World-War-and-all-its-causes "volumes in multidimensional meaning space"; it can call causing pain, inflicting suffering, and perpetrating injustice "evil." In this way language guides the senses to concentrate on various areas and aspects of the world for further examination and further differential cross checking.

Things "obviously" similar are coherent areas of meaning-space only because of the shadow the senses throw over them. Those areas not so obviously coherent become so under the various shadows language can cast.

59. Science fiction is a way of casting a language shadow over

coherent areas of imaginative space that would otherwise be largely inaccessible.

60. Is it the tragedy of mind? Or is it what assures the mind's development: Today's seminal idea is tomorrow's critical cliché.

LONDON
1973/1974

Critical
Methods/Speculative
Fiction

The historical discussion of the development of some area of art, while often illuminating, does not necessarily exhaust that area. The development of a particular literary technique or theme over several decades through several writers, often in several countries, is not completely solved by a chronological listing of who did what first.

The historical literary critic tends to see literary progress as a process rather like this: Some seminal genius invents a form; another refines it; still a third brings it to heretofore unimagined perfection; while a later fourth now takes the form into decadence; finally a new genius appears who, reacting against this decadence, invents a new form, and the cycle begins again.

But this view only traces a single thread through what is essentially a tapestry of aesthetic productions. The line, of course, tries to connect the high points. Frequently enough, these high points are, in reality, connected. But just as frequently they are connected more strongly to other works and situations totally off this line. Historical artistic progress only exists through the perspective lent by hindsight.

Of the many ways in which an artist can be influenced by other art, the historical art-critic overconcentrates on two: the desire to imitate excellence, which, in genius, sometimes results in former excellence surpassed; and the distaste for the mediocre, the stultified, the inflexible, which, again in genius, can result in new forms.

But there are other ways to be influenced. One artist may find a work that seems to him to have an interesting kernel, but strikes him as so badly executed that he feels he can treat the same substance far more rewardingly. More frequently, I suspect, he finds an interesting technique employed to decorate a vapid center, and uses it to ornament his own central concerns. It is still a little odd to look at whom some major authors felt to be their greatest influences. Thus Coleridge says that the sonnets of the country Reverend William Lisle Bowles, insipid and artificial by today's standards, were the literary epiphany of his youth. And Keats was practically fixated on the eighteenth-century boy-poet Thomas Chatterton, who, after perpetrating a series of forgeries of Middle English poems, allegedly the work of a nonexistent monk, Thomas Rowley, came to London and within the year committed suicide by taking rat poison, aged seventeen years and nine months.

Let us look at the development of one of the narrative techniques that practically alone supports science fiction: expertise—that method by which an author, deploying a handful of esoteric facts, creates the impression that he, or more often a character in his story, is an expert in some given field. It was formulated as an outgrowth of French Naturalism by a writer who began as a younger disciple of Zola, Joris Karl Huysmans. He brought the technique to pitch in his novel *A Rebours*, published in 1884, a year after *Treasure Island*, a year before *She*. But where the Naturalists employed exhaustive research to give density to their endless chronicles of common people at common professions, Huysmans used comparatively superficial research to give an impression of thorough familiarity with a whole series of bizarre and exotic subjects, including Late Latin literature, horticulture, and perfumery, to list only a few.

Till its recent reissue, I doubt if many currently working s-f writers had read Huysman's plotless, characterless, and totally enthralling novel. But you can find the technique employed in exactly the same manner in something as recent as Thomas Disch's *Camp Concentration*. Still, though I cannot prove it, I am sure there is a line (more likely a web) of writers who read writers who read Huysmans, and who took from one another this obviously effective technique, as directly as Wilde took the cadences and repetitions in the dialogue for *Salomé* from Poe's *Politian*.

Indeed, we know Huysmans was familiar with Poe; Poe and

Baudelaire are the most frequently mentioned authors in *A Rebours*. Huysmans undoubtedly knew Poe through the superb Baudelaire translations, which, from their impact on French literature, quite possibly have more merit than the originals. In *A Rebours*, *The Narrative of A. Gordon Pym* is several times mentioned by name, a work which Poe dots with much nautical expertise to make his sailor narrator convincing, on a thoroughly unreal voyage to the South Pole, that ends with the appearance of the White Goddess herself. This, and the similar use of expertise in the tales of ratiocination, could easily have prompted Huysmans to make the jump from using expertise to validate the commonplace to evoking the exotic and bizarre. (One can get some idea of the flavor of *A Rebours* from Chapter Eleven of Oscar Wilde's *The Picture of Dorian Gray*, a pastiche of Huysmans; the mysterious yellow-backed French novel after which Dorian patterns his life was immediately identified by the Victorian public as *A Rebours*, which was confirmed by Wilde during the Queensbury trial; the book had achieved a reputation for decadence and corruption, as sexual oddities were another subject that Huysmans explored with his newly perfected technique.)

One place where the connection is clearly drawn is in Alfred Bester's early horror novella, *Hell is Forever*. The opening of the novella is practically a rewrite of the opening movements of *A Rebours*. The relation is so close I am fairly sure that Bester, an erudite author who studs his work with overt and covert literary references, was undoubtedly familiar with it when *Hell is Forever* was written in the late thirties for *Unknown*.

And Bester is easily the s-f writer who brought expertise to its full fruition.

Thus an s-f literary technique has its burgeonings in an American fantasist, passes over the ocean to be translated by a great poet, is furthered by a French *fin de siècle*, decadent, and returns a hundred years later to American magazine fiction. In the early sixties, it moved away to support the pseudo-s-f James-Bond-style thriller (it has always had an existence in the classic detective novel), which would thoroughly collapse without it. But this is the way the web of influence works, passing in and out of the genre, crossing national and language boundaries and returning, completely frustrating the historical critic who would keep everything in its proper path.

In the same way, the didactic methods of Robert Heinlein owe a great deal to Shaw's comedies of ideas, far more than to Wells and Verne. Indeed, part of that mystical optimism that pervades so much of s-f is a product of a process that we can see in the ending of Shaw's *Man and Superman*, Twain's *Mysterious Stranger*, Kipling's *Children of the Zodiac*, and Poe's *Eukera*, a process shared by such s-f classics as Heinlein's *Stranger in a Strange Land*, Clarke's *Childhood's End*, Sturgeon's *More Than Human*, and Disch's *Camp Concentration*: any attempt to be totally rational about such a basically mystical subject as man's ultimate place in the universe tends to squeeze all the mysticism into one bright chunk that blurs all resolutions at the end.

Contrary to what might be expected, it is much harder to trace the development of a strictly limited subject than of a general one. To take an absurd example: It would be fairly intriguing to discuss the growth of interest in late-medieval Gallic song-forms among poets of the past hundred years. From Joyce's villanelle in *Portrait of the Artist* to Pound's and Auden's experiments with the sestina and canzone, or in the turn-of-the-century profusion of rondels and rondolets, there is great give and take among the general run of poets, with a few enduring examples that give significance to the whole discussion. It would be quite another matter to discuss the use of only one medieval song form, let us say the triolet, over the same period. One could cite, in a historical list, Rimbaud's "Le Coeur volé," go on to mention Ernest Dowson's and Lionel Johnson's attempts and perhaps Francis Cornford's "Why Do You Walk Through the Fields in Gloves." For what little it's worth, I would hazard a guess that Dowson had read Rimbaud and that Cornford had read Dowson. But this gives us only a list, not a development. The fact is, the impulse to write one's first triolet is simply to see if one can do it. But once the form is learned, the impulse for the second or third might just as easily come from reading Gray's *Anatomy* as reading Milton, from the ubiquitous unhappy love affair, or the poached egg you had for breakfast.

To explore the development of s-f poses a similar problem. Though its audience is growing it is still a limited form, a specialized genre. The historical approach has been tried many times. But the fact is, if s-f had been influenced only by itself, it would have strangled long since. If it did not continually influence areas outside itself, we would not have the present increase of interest. Simply because it is limited, a simple listing of which writer wrote what first will not do whether one starts with Wells, de Bergerac, Kepler, or Lucian.

The usual historical approach, at present, is the common intellectual property of practically anyone who knows that s-f stands for *science fiction.* It begins with Wells and Verne and more or less ends with Heinlein and Bradbury. Anyone whose interest extends to actually reading it knows that an editor named Campbell caused some major changes, and before that an editor named Hugo Gernsback was important.

My own feeling is that, in an attempt to give respectability to American s-f, much too much has been made of the relation between English Victorian, or Wellsian, s-f and post-Gernsback, or Modern. Risking the other extreme, I propose that the relation actually is no stronger (or weaker) than the passage of the idea that it was possible to write stories and novels set in the future. Let me make some sweeping statements about areas that have been covered much more thoroughly by a host of other writers. Wells' "Romances of the Future" come from much the same impulse that later produced his double volume *Outline of History.* The future stories were an outgrowth of the perfectly viable fancy that history might well continue beyond the present. Both the historical work and the s-f, however, fall out of the same twin Victorian views: that man's knowledge, in general, and his technology, in particular, develop in a more or less orderly way; also that, in a given situation, human behavior will always be more or less the same, no matter when, or where.

Technology has always run in both constructive and destructive directions at once. While Rome's engineers built amazing stone aqueducts with engineering techniques that astound us today, her aristocracy was unintentionally committing mass suicide with lead-based cosmetics and lead-lined wine-jars. Pasteur invented vaccination, which prevented smallpox, and which, when the technique was finally extended to typhoid, typhus, diphtheria, and yellow fever, made possible the Second World War—till then, it would have been unthinkable to mass so many soldiers in such unsanitary conditions without having them completely wiped out by communicable diseases. Yet, from modern military medicine come the new discoveries in bioelectronics, and the science which Pasteur invented to preserve life is ultimately pushed on a step. Man's technical achievements, like his aesthetic ones, do not form a single line, but a web, in which numerous lines can be traced. Indeed, they sit in the same web. Any new discovery, from ovonic devices to the revelation of a new ecological relationship, may spark changes in all directions, with good and bad results, that will cycle and echo, perhaps for centuries, in science, economics, and art.

Nor is human behavior any more stable from age to age, place to place. In seventeenth-century India, a Buddhist priest went to sit at the gate of a Sultan who had treated his people too harshly. At the gate, the priest refused to eat or drink, and inside the house, the Sultan died from guilt and shame; while, in eighteenth-century France, the Queen, upon being told that the people had no bread, responds (at least according to popular tradition) with the line that has become the emblem of political irresponsibility, "Then let them eat cake." In Greece in the ninth century B.C., the accidental revelation of incest between mother and son resulted in suicide and self-mutilation; five hundred years later in Persia, parents and children who could prove that they had indulged in carnal relations were elevated to the rank of holy men and women with great honor and reverence. A Mediterranean, upon discovering his wife in the arms of another man, commits a brutal double murder, while an Eskimo, receiving a stranger into his igloo, graciously offers his wife for sexual pleasure during the length of the visitor's stay. (And the unbiased student of anthropology could further cite societies or times in which incest was neither holy nor anathematic, but commonplace, or in which the disposal of her own, and possibly her spouse's, sexual favors was the woman's prerogative.) In nineteenth-century Russia, certain aristocrats organized weekend hunts for their guests, with dogs, horses, and rifles. The quarry, slaughtered and hung up for show in the barn, was thirteen- and fourteen-year-old peasant boys. Today, in Vietnam, seventeen- and eighteen-year-old American boys amuse themselves shooting at war prisoners through the stockade fence, while, in the states from which these boys hail, the death penalty is finally declared illegal as a primitive and barbaric custom.

There is nothing universal about the laws of human nature, at least as the Victorians pictured them. My readers sensitive to cultural resonances will probably sense them from all these examples of behavior as they look around our own culture. But that is because the human mind resonates. To try and construct historical chains of causation between these types of behavior and our own society is to miss the point. The human animal is potentially capable of *any* behavior. The feeling of resonance is a personal response to that potential.

Not only can the human animal behave in any way, the human psyche can approve or disapprove of any behavior. Thus, in one cultural enclave, the supreme moral act is the eating of bread and the drinking of wine; in another it is the act of sexual congress itself; while in another it is the disemboweling of babies. One group feels that avarice and selfishness are the roots of all evil. Another feels that uneducated altruism is the source of all the world's mismanagement, and that altruistic acts are the basic sins that rot the society. One groups feels that ignorance is the cause of all the world's trouble. Another feels that all knowledge leads to pain.

No, the Victorian supposition of the linear moral logic of human progress and the inflexible catholicity of human nature have been left rather far behind. But these ideas are as inchoate in Wells's s-f as they are in his history.

To look at Gernsback—or rather, Gernsback and his progeny— in relation to Wells, questions of literary merit set momentarily aside, immense differences appear immediately.

Gernsback was interested solely in the wonderful *things* progress might bring. As a popular entertainer, he was just as interested in the possible as he was in the probable. In his own novel, *Ralph 124C41+*, there *is* the chaste ghost of a love interest, but it vanishes amidst a host of marvelous gadgets. His use of behavior went only so far as it showed what *things* could do. Most of the objects were socially beneficial. When they were not, they were in the hands of the criminals that Ralph triumphed over. But there was none of the socially functional logic in which Wells indulged: *Since this is scientifically infeasible, it would not be socially beneficial to discuss what might come out of it* (rather than the currently available converse: "If it is socially beneficial to discuss it, let us posit scientific feasibility.") The logic behind Gernsback's view of s-f, which persists today, is: *Even though current technology claims this is impossible, if we were to achieve it, look at what marvels might result.*

It is just this basic concern with *thingyness* that makes me insist that the initial impulse behind s-f, despite the primitive and vulgar verbal trappings, was closer to the impulse behind poetry than it was to the impulse behind ordinary narrative fiction.

As another critic has said, in another context, "Poetry 'is concerned with the *thingyness* of *things*." The new American s-f took on the practically incantatory task of naming nonexistent objects, then investing them with reality by a host of methods, technological and pseudotechnological explanations, imbedding them in dramatic situations, or just inculcating them by pure repetition:

> Television
> Rocketship
> Waldo
> Spacesuit

But this is s-f at its most primitive. The incantatory function—a better word than "predictive"—is no more the chief concern of modern s-f than it is the concern of modern poetry; though remnants of it still linger in everything from Cordwainer Smith's "orthithopters" to Greg Benford's "brain tapping." Here is the place to note, I think, that when the British s-f magazine *New Worlds* was awarded a London Arts Council subsidy, one of the testimonials, from a member of the editorial board of the *Oxford Unabridged Dictionary of the English Language*, explained that science fiction was the most fertile area of writing in the production of new words which endured in the language—a position held up till the midthirties by poetry.

Because it was unconcerned with behavior at its beginnings, s-f was eventually able to reflect the breakdown of the Victorian behavioral concepts which, for all his advanced thinking, had strictured Wells. It has been remarked, everywhere that man has noted in detail what goes on around him (we can find the idea in Confucius and in Plato), that the objects around him do influence his behavior, as well as how he judges the behavior of himself and others. The philosophers of aesthetics never tire of reminding us that the man who grows up in a beautiful and aesthetically interesting environment behaves very differently from the man raised among ugly, squalid surroundings. The Victorian progressives added to this that a person raised in an efficient, healthy, leisurely environment behaves quite differently from one raised amidst harrying inefficiency and disease. The aesthete quickly points out that the behavior of the person brought up with efficiency is still not the same as that of the person brought up with beauty.

McLuhan formulates this more precisely when he explains that any man-made object, and a good many natural ones, as they express or reflect aspects of man's inner consciousness, become factors in the equations governing communication as soon as they come into our perception.

But well before McLuhan had put this so succinctly—indeed, s-f was to prompt McLuhan to this statement, another example of influence across boundaries—American s-f writers, freed from the strictures of the probable, left to soar in the byways of the possible, not bound by the concept of universal human nature, in a country that was itself a potpourri of different cultural behavior patterns, sat contemplating marvelous objects in the theater of the mind. Slowly, intuitions of the way in which these objects might effect behavior began to appear in the stories. Editor Campbell was astute enough to see that this was perhaps the most powerful tool in the realization of these marvelous inventions. He encouraged his writers to use this tool, to make the focus of the stories the juncture between the object and the behavior it causes. As the writers followed Campbell, s-f began to grow up.

By much the same process that poetry expanded beyond its beginnings in ritualistic chant and incantation to become a way to paint all that is human and etch much that is divine, so s-f became able to reflect, focus, and diffract the relations between man and his universe, as it included other men, as it included all that man could create, all he could conceive.

Already, how much more potentially complex a template we have than the one left us by Victorian Utopian fiction. The Utopian fictions of Butler, Bellamy, Wells, as well as the later Huxley and Orwell, exhaust themselves by taking sides in the terribly limiting argument: "Regard this new society. You say it's good, but I say it's bad." Or, "You say it's bad, but I say it's good."

Auden has pointed out in his collection of essays, *The Dyer's Hand*, and then gone on to examine in his cycle of poems, *Horae Canonicae*, that this argument is essentially a split in temperaments, not a logical division at all.

There are, and always will be, those people who see hope in

progress. Auden calls their perfect world New Jerusalem. In New Jerusalem hunger and disease have been abolished through science, man is free of drudgery and pain, and from it he can explore any aspect of the physical world in any way he wishes, assured that he has the power to best it should nature demand a contest. There are, and always will be, people who wish, in Auden's words, to return to Eden. He calls their perfect world Arcadia. In Arcadia, food is grown by individual farmers, and technology never progresses beyond what one man can make with his own hands. Man is at one with nature, who strengthens him for his explorations of the inner life; thus all that he creates will be in natural good taste; and good will and camaraderie govern his relation with his fellows.

To the man who yearns after Arcadia, any movement to establish New Jerusalem will always look like a step toward Brave New World, that mechanized, dehumanized, and standardized environment, where the gaudy and meretricious alternate with the insufferably dull; where, if physical hardship *is* reduced, it is at the price of the most humiliating spiritual brutalization.

In the same way, the man who dreams of New Jerusalem sees any serious attempt to establish an Arcadia as a retreat to the Land of Flies, that place of provincial ignorance, fear, disease, and diet, where man is prey to the untrammeled demons of his own superstition, as well as any caprice of nature: fire, flood, storm, or earthquake.

The final argument for either of these views must ultimately be expressed: In the environment *I prefer*, *I* would find it easier to treat the variety of my fellows with affection, tolerance, and respect. And this, as Auden says, is a statement of personal preference, not a logical social dictum. With the variety of fellow beings what it is, the argument will probably always be here.

Modern s-f has gone beyond this irreconcilable Utopian Dystopian conflict to produce a more fruitful model against, which to compare human development.

The s-f writers working under Campbell, and even more so with Horace Gold, began to cluster their new and wonderful objects into the same story, or novel. And whole new systems and syndromes of behavior began to emerge. Damon Knight, in *In Search of Wonder*, notes Charles Harness's *The Paradox Man* as the first really successful "reduplicated" novel—where an ordered sarabande of wonders refract and complement each other till they have produced a completely new world, in which the technological relation to ours is minimal. Now the writers began to explore these infinitely multiplied worlds, filled with wondrous things, where the roads and the paintings moved, where religion took the place of government, and advertising took the place of religion, where travel could be instantaneous between anywhere and anywhere else, where the sky was metal, and women wore live goldfish in the transparent heels of their shoes. Within these worlds, the impossible relieves the probable, and the possible illuminates the improbable. And the author's aim is neither to condemn nor to condone, but to explore both the worlds and their behaviors for the sake of the exploration, again an aim far closer to poetry than to any sociological brand of fiction.

As soon as the Wellsian parameters are put aside, far more protean ones emerge from modern s-f almost at once:

In the most truly Utopian of New Jerusalems, sometime you will find yourself in front of an innocuous-looking door; go through it, and you will find yourself, aghast, before some remnant of the Land of the Flies; in the most dehumanized Brave New World, one evening as you wander through the dreary public park, sunset bronzing fallen leaves will momentarily usher you into the most marvelous autumn evening in Arcadia. Similarly, in either Arcadia or the Land of the Flies, plans can be begun for either Brave New World or New Jerusalem.

S-f has been called a romantic and affirmative literature. J. G. Ballard has gone so far as to point out, quite justly, that the bulk of it is rendered trivial by its naively boundless optimism. But we do not judge the novel by the plethora of sloppy romances or boneheaded adventures that make up the statistically vast majority of examples; if we did, it might lead us to say the same of all areas of literature, novel, poetry, or drama; with no selection by merit, I'm afraid on a statistical listing, expressions of the vapidly happy would far outnumber expressions of the tragic on whatever level. As any other area of art is judged by its finest examples, and not by the oceans of mediocrity that these high points rise above, this is the way s-f must be judged. There are threads of tragedy running through the works of Sturgeon and Bester (they can even be unraveled from Heinlein), not to mention Disch, Zelazny, and Russ, as well as Ballard's own tales of ruined worlds, decadent resortists, and the more recent fragmented visions of stasis and violence. And one would be hard-pressed to call the comic visions of Malzberg, Sladek, and Lafferty "naively optimistic."

If s-f is affirmative, it is not through any obligatory happy ending, but rather through the breath of vision it affords, through the complex interweave of these multiple visions of man's origins and his destinations. Certainly such breadth of vision does not *abolish* tragedy. But it does make a little rarer the particular needless tragedy that comes from a certain type of narrow-mindedness.

Academic s-f criticism, fixed in the historical approach, wastes a great deal of time trying to approach modern s-f works in Utopian/Dystopian terms—works whose value is precisely in that they are a reaction to such one-sided thinking. It is much more fruitful if modern works are examined in terms of what they contain of all these mythic views of the world. (Carl Becker has suggested that New Jerusalem and Brave New World are the only two new myths that the twentieth century has produced.)

It is absurd to argue whether Asimov's *Foundation* series represents a Utopian or a Dystopian view of society; its theme is the way in which a group of interrelated societies, over a historical period, force each other at different times back and forth from Utopian to Dystopian phases.

In *The Stars My Destination*, the Jaunt Re-education program is clearly a product of New Jerusalem. Equally clearly, the Presteign Clan, with its four hundred ninety-seven surgically identical Mr. Prestos, is from Brave New World. And they exist side by side in the same work. Gully, though he has been uniformed by Brave New World, begins as an unformed lump of elemental violence, ignorance, and endurance from the Land of the Flies. Robin Wednesbury's home in the reestablished forests of Greenbay, insulated from its neighbors, with her collection of books and records, exists in Arcadia. Gully/Caliban implodes into it with violence and rape; and Robin and Arcadia survive to both help and hinder him as the novel goes on. This sort of optimism, emblematically as it is handled, is far more true to life than the Victorian convention that equates "dishonor" with death—though in black Robin's eventual marriage to the only other noncaucasian in the book, the Oriental Yang-Y'eovil, there is a hint of acceptance of an equally nasty American convention.

Because all four visions are offered in the best modern s-f, no single one is allowed to paralyze us with terror or lull us into muddle-headed euphoria.

I would like to see in serious s-f criticism that insists upon the thematic an examination of how all four of these mythic visions sit in concert in given works. And I would like to see an end to the lauding (or dismissal) of works because they do (or do not) reflect only one.

SAN FRANCISCO
MARCH 1969

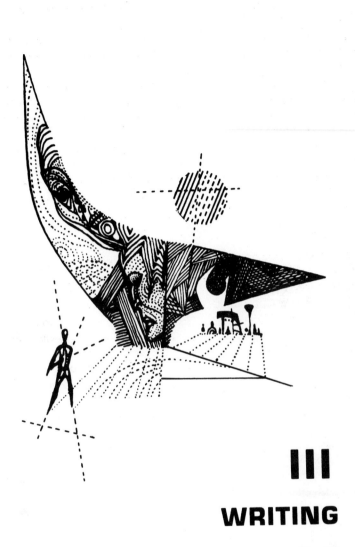

III
WRITING
S-F

Quarks

1

S-f?

Speculative fiction?

It's a term first used by Robert Heinlein in 1951 during a World Science Fiction Convention guest-of-honor speech, as a suggested replacement for *Science Fiction*. It better described, he felt, what he was interested in writing.

Today it is the term used by those s-f writers (and I am sure Heinlein sees the convenient ambiguity) who, if they share nothing else, have balked before the particular parameters Heinlein's s-f has established, primarily in the minds of editors, secondarily in the minds of other writers, and finally in the minds of readers.

"Who," someone asked Gide, "is the greatest poet of the French language?"

Always civilized, Gide replied: "Victor Hugo, alas!"

And that is Heinlein's position in modern (post-Gernsback) s-f to date.

A bit of the balking has been articulate, most has been emotional; some has taken place with respect, and some has transpired in rage. Personally, we are delighted that we have let him name us—the enemy.

Speculative fiction?

It is one of the numerous terms that numerous critics for numerous reasons have decided is inadequate for the numerous things that fall under it.

2

Even a statement like 2+3=5 is only a *model* of "the real world."
As a model it represents the world only more or less accurately.

In a country school house, a teacher with two apples at one side
of the desk and three at the other pushes them all to the center and
asks, "Now can any of you give me the sum of..."

A brighter student from his seat in the third row thinks: Even
from here I can see all those apples are not the same. That one there is
a third again as large as most of the others—except the one on the
end, which is slightly smaller. Really, to describe the sum of those
apples, I need to set up a Standard Apple, and then say that I have
three Standard Apples, a Standard Apple-and-a-Third, and ... I
guess about four-fifths of a Standard Apple, so that altogether there
are ...

The technician, with her Melter Balance, says: If you *really* want
to describe the sum of those apples at a measure even more accurate
than grams and hundredths of a gram, you'll have to take into
account the tremendous amount of biological activity going on in
those apples which is changing their weight all the time, so that to
describe the sum of those apples you are going to have to think things
through again: e.g., is the moisture adhering to the apples' skins,
which weighs a whole point oh-eight grams, really part of the apples?
Where does the apple end and the rest of the world begin?

Assuming, says the relativity physicist, that those questions have
been answered satisfactorily, and you will want a measure more
accurate, you must consider that each of those apples has a
gravitational field that affects the mass of everything else around it,
including the other apples; so that to describe *really* the sum of those
apples, you have to decide just what you are doing when you "add"
them—how close are you bringing them together, for one, because
any change in their proximity changes the mass of the apples
themselves. Not to mention the speed at which you bring them
together. Not to mention your own gravitational field about the
instruments you are using to make your measurements. You must
rethink the concept of "giving the sum" because two apples at a
certain distance from another group of three is one situation. But to
move any of them even a little bit (not to mention pushing them all to

the center of the desk) changes the mass, weight, and volume of all the others.

The system of "rigorously logical" arithmetical relationships is only one possible model of "the real." What gives this particular model its importance to us is our physical size, arbitrarily between the atomic and the stellar, along with the given accuracy of our unaided perceptions and the other billion accidents of human physiology. Granted these accidents, it is perfectly understandable that this model is such a country-school favorite. But we should also bear in mind that in "the real world" of weight, mass, and volume, there is no situation where one object, physically added to its twin (already a risky concept for that world), yields precisely twice as much. And *many* is only a convenient abstraction of *much* that humans happen to be able to make, under proper conditions. *Many* is what *we* divide *much* into because our senses happen to work the way they do. But as we divide a given *much* into a larger and larger *many*, the logical and seemingly self-evident relations of arithmetic must be manipulated in more and more complicated ways to make the answers resemble what is "really" there.

As soon as we want to look at "the real world" with any greater accuracy and sophistication than the country school house provides, other models than the arithmetically predictable are more useful to help us appreciate what we are looking at:

A quantitative analyst must have tables to let him know how to correct for the volumetric sums of dissimilar miscible liquids: One pint of water poured into one pint of alcohol yields noticeably less than a quart of liquid.

The physicist dealing with velocities approaching the speed of light uses an arithmetical model for summation corrected algebraically by Fitzgerald's Contraction in which 186,000 mps plus any other velocity still equals 186,000 mps, and all other possible sums are scaled down proportionally.

The metallurgist observing the reaction of alloys at extremely low temperatures uses an arithmetic model that simply cuts off (in a completely different way than the upper limit on velocity) at 273.16 degrees centigrade below zero and admits of no temperatures below that—not only as a physical impossibility but as a conceptual one as well.

Fiction makes models of reality.

But often we need models for observations of an accuracy and sophistication beyond that of the country school house.

3

2.0121 . . . Just as we are quite unable to imagine spatial objects outside space or temporal objects outside time, so there is no object that we can imagine excluded from the possibility of combining with others.

If I can imagine objects combined in states of affairs, I can not imagine them excluded from the *possibility* of such combination.

2:022 It is obvious that an imagined world, however different it may be from the real one, must have something—a form—in common with it.

—Ludwig Wittgenstein/ *Tractatus Logico-Philosophicus*

which is the best explanation why there is "speculative fiction."

An aesthetic object (a work of art? a story?) has internal tensions (form?) and also produces tensions with its environment. The resultant matrix of forces is called "audience reaction."

As writers, we can't control the real world. At best, we can observe it actively. We can control the internal tensions of the aesthetic objects of our making. Any of the "commercial writing tricks" to control reader reaction are a waste of time because they are attempts to control the real world, which is impossible, and distract from the time spent controlling internal tensions which—while they do not *control* audience reaction—are the workable points at which it is moored.

The attitude of the more commercial science-fiction writers in its most articulate expression:

"I am not an artist. I am a craftsman. I am concerned with entertainment not aesthetics. Science fiction is the only area of popular literature whose *basic* entertainment value is intellectual—technological or sociological—which makes it a socially valuable genre *per se*. You experimental writers, by your emphasis on aesthetics, have blurred the major valid claim s-f has as a socially functional literature."

But the problems of entertainment are aesthetic problems. If the definition of "entertainment" is allowed to include the emotions, the intellect, and the pure pleasure we take in form, then *all* aesthetic problems are problems of entertainment. Aesthetic discipline is that which makes most accessible all the substance of a given work. The writer who declines to make use of the full range of aesthetic discipline in deference to entertainment is cheating the reader of the entertainment he claims to be concerned with.

The argument for the social value of art over propaganda is too tedious and too familiar to reproduce here.

A great deal of very good "classic" s-f was done in the U. S. during the disasters of the (first) McCarthy period, when it was practically impossible to make a socially pertinent statement in any area other than science fiction.

People were invariably astounded that so much freedom did exist within the genre. But the official reaction was that s-f was lunatic and not be taken seriously.

Underneath that rather cavalier insult is a considerable truth: Within the aesthetic structure laid out by "the adventure story" it is impossible to produce a politically dangerous fiction, no matter how revolutionary the proposed world is, no matter what evils the hero is faced with, nor how congruent they are to the present ones.

The efficacy of "political" fiction, from the point of view of the body politic, is measured precisely in terms of real action it can cause... and presumably becomes dangerous when somebody notices this action. The adventure, with its building tensions suddenly relieved, its preoccupation with the physical rather than the psychological, its linearity, simply doesn't leave enough residue of discomfort in the mind to precipitate action. This is what dooms a social criticism set in this form to political inconsequence.

The two fictional works in the U.S. that have been *near* revolutionary, *Uncle Tom's Cabin* and *Babbitt*, are, despite whatever barbarousnesses they contain, social chronicle novels, not adventures.

One's only objections to science fiction "of value as social criticism" is precisely that it *failed* to be dangerous, because of an aesthetic choice by the authors deferring to "popular entertainment."

A willingness to take risks means health and vitality in any artistic field. An unwillingness to take risks means stagnation, death. To view meaningfully the social, psychological, and technological crises presented by the particular illumination generated by the forms and textures of speculative fiction, we must encourage as much experimentation as possible, so that this illumination will reach beyond the boundary timid parents have tried to prescribe for their vigorous children.

SAN FRANCISCO
NEW YORK
1969 1970

Teaching S-f Writing

The young painter who has set about learning to paint "realistically" is often surprised that the eye must do the learning; the hand more or less takes care of itself. "But I can *already* see what's there! Tell me what I'm supposed to do to set it down."

Keep your hand still and look more closely.

As "realistic" painting does not exhaust art, neither does the comparatively high resolution of narrative story-telling exhaust fiction. But the young writer who has decided to utilize his experience of the world at this comparatively high resolution, for like reasons, is always surprised when he is told to go back and reexamine his experience.

"But I want to know how to write an exciting piece of action!"

Examine your reactions when you are excited; as well, when you are bored.

"But how do I create a vivid character?"

Look closely at what individualizes people; explore those moments when you are vividly aware of a personality. Explore the others when you cannot fathom a given person's actions at all.

"No, no! You don't get the point. Tell me about style!"

Listen to the words that come out of your mouth; look at the words you put on paper. Decide with each whether or not you want it there.

But it will always be a paradox to the young artist of whatever medium that the only element of the imagination that can be

141

consciously and conscientiously trained is the ability to observe what is.

Teachers of narrative fiction fail or succeed according to the ingenuity with which they can present the above in as many ways as possible—a success or failure that, alas, has nothing to do with their own writing ability.

In speculative fiction, science fiction, or fantasy, the focus on these basics must be even sharper. The substance of s-f is still experience (even the experience of the language itself), but at a level of significant distortion—not for any gamelike purpose where the reader tries to reconstruct the "reality," but to generate new experience, a new reality, full and resonant with itself.

S-f is in an exciting aesthetic situation. Essentially intellectual in inspiration, it has a very direct relation with a very large audience, a relation one would be more likely to associate with some performance art (like opera) rather than something so "abstract." It has a maniacally active fandom of several thousands and a knowledgeable audience of several hundred thousands—readers who are literate in traditions which go back to Wells and Verne. Despite nearly a century of literary conventions (and partially because of forty years of world and regional ones), current production is still the most exciting part of the s-f experience for most of that audience (unlike opera; indeed, more like rock). Until the last nine or ten years, this situation was maintained with practically no academic sanction. It is a sign of the field's vitality that among the first college courses established in the subject was the Clarion Workshop, dealing with the writing of s-f, the appreciation being taken for granted. It has been quoted many times: "No one reads s-f because he has to."

A teacher at Clarion, you may live in the dormitory with the students, or room in a separate building. The students are energetic, dedicated, writing and revising throughout the six weeks. The solution to most literary problems is time and thought. But if someone can be there immediately to suggest where thought might be directed, so much the better. I chose to room in the student dorm. I had given occasional lectures and one-day seminars; summers ago I had taught remedial reading to a volunteer class at a community center. But Clarion, for five days was my first formal teaching experience. A handful of the students were older than I. Several had sold stories and novels already.

The situation would intrigue any teacher of fiction.

A writer of fiction, I could not resist it.

The real worth of that summer, as with any intense, organic experience, is in the texture of the experience itself.

I had set up exercises and discussion topics for the formal, three-hour morning classes. Part of this time was set aside for the group discussion of stories handed in the previous days.

In my first "class," we began by discussing some rather complex ideas about the way information is carried by and between words. We read some sentences, word at a time, to see just what the information given was—tone of voice, mood, order of presentation and importance—and at which points in the sentence this information became apparent. I tried to examine just what happened in the microleaps between words. I had notes. But there were great silences in the discussion when I and the students were both at a loss for what to say next. Afterward, I was very relieved when two people came up to discuss ideas of their own that more or less took off from things I had said in class. But even later, when I asked two others, whose comments had seemed the most astute, what they thought of the session, I was cheerfully informed they hadn't the foggiest idea what I was talking about.

And the next morning in class, a young woman whose writing had already struck me as among the most talented* asked guardedly: "But what do you feel about just pure story-telling?"

I wasn't quite sure what to say, so I came out with: "I like it a whole lot!"

Then we spent five seconds wondering if we should say anything more, and decided on a truce.

An exercise fared better.

I asked the students to choose partners. Limiting themselves to written words (pencil, pen and paper; or typewriter), each was to collect material from the other for a brief biography. "Write a question, exchange papers with your partner; write down your answer to his question (or your comment or request for further explanation of the question), then give the paper back. Read what you've obtained, and write down another question, and continue the process until you feel you have enough information for a short

---

*Vonda McIntyre, whose story *Of Mist, and Grass, and Sand* four years later would win a well-deserved Hugo.

biography. If possible, conduct the experiment without seeing your partner—for example, pass your papers back and forth under a door."

The dorm hall, usually filled in the evening with frisbees and laughter, tonight was oddly quiet. I passed some four couples sitting on the hall floor, exchanging notebooks, and one young man with his typewriter before a closed door, sliding out a sheet of yellow paper.*

Several people gave me rather odd looks. One girl, coming out of her room to deliver a paper to a boy in another, asked with somewhat amused belligerence: "Where did you get this idea, anyway?"

Next morning in class, I asked for someone to read his questions and answers. No one raised a hand.

"Someone must have done the exercise," I said. "I saw too many of you working on it."

People shifted in their chairs, glanced at one another.

Momentarily I suspected I was victim of a practical joke.

But when a discussion did, haltingly, begin, it seemed that almost without exception, the twenty-five very bright, very sensitive young people had found, when their communication was limited to the written word, almost in spite of themselves they had shunted into personal areas and intensely emotional parts of themselves that felt uncomfortable before oral display...though no one was averse to my or each other's *reading* these papers.

As the discussion progressed, some people volunteered to read sections out loud. Even from this, it became clear that when a one-to-one situation is fixed between information wanted and information granted, with the communicants checking out one another after each step, the result is a strange freedom, an obsessive honesty, a compelling and rising clarity. The general superiority of the prose style to most of their fictional attempts was duly noted.

This was certainly what I had hoped the point of the exercise would be. But I had never tried it in this way. *I* was surprised by the emotional force behind the point.

Another exercise was done in class.

"This morning," I said, "I want you all to look around the room—get up and walk around if you'd like. Observe the people in the room with you, very closely. Keep looking until you notice

*The then sixteen-year-old Jean Marc Gawron, who, three years later was to write *An Apology for Rain*, and three years after that, *Algorithm*.

something about one of your classmates that you've never noticed before. Now examine this thing about him, this aspect of her behavior or appearance, until you see something about it different from the way anyone else you've ever seen exhibits this feature of appearance or behavior. Then write down what you've seen in a sentence or two."

I got in two styrofoam cups of coffee from the urn in the corner while the class milled and prowled by one another. One girl came up to me and said, "But I just don't *see* anything!"

"Make up something," I told her softly, "and see if anyone notices."

Twenty minutes later, most people were seated again. I suggested we bring the class to order and hear some of the examples. If there was any embarrassment here, it was of a lighter tone. Before we started, there was some humorous anticipation of the crashing triviality of what had been observed. But by the third example, the giggles had ceased. People were leaning forward in their chairs, or looking back over their own examples with renewed attention.

If the previous exercise had discovered a lucid, working prose, this one, in example after example, pushed language to the brink of the poetic. The reading, as we went about the room, became a torrent of metaphors—how many of the unique things noted were the resemblance between something present and something else! And those that were not metaphorical still had an astonishing presence, the gesture, expression, or turn of speech caught with the stark economy of the tuned ear, the fixed eye.

There were other discussions on the economic significance of story setting, the natural tendency of words to say things other than you intend and obscure your meaning, and the necessity of rendering your fictional incidents intensely through the senses. Whenever one of my convoluted arguments brought us to a point of confused silence, Robin Wilson, who led the half of the class devoted to story discussion, patiently and kindly extricated me from the snarls of my own inexperience.

The high point of the five days' classes for me was when, after a discussion of the way the vividness of fictional characters usually lies *between* rather than *in* the facts we know of them, one young woman produced a character sketch of an aging, alcoholic midwestern lady with bohemian pretensions. I had asked the class to put together these sketches of fictional characters through a collection of actions—purposeful, habitual, and gratuitous—that should be observed with the same astuteness with which they had observed one another. Unfortunately I cannot reproduce the sketch here. But when it was read, among the dozen or so other examples, the class was silent in that way which makes someone who has previously been uproariously applauded feel he has turned in a poor showing after all.

I left Clarion aware just how short five days were—I had actually been on campus five days and two weekends. Besides the three hours a day of classes, I had read some sixty-five or seventy student stories (and one novel) and had managed at least one story conference with each student—in some cases, with the more prolific, three, four, or five. It was stimulating, intense, even numbing. Most of the students seemed to feel that the individual work with particular stories was the most valuable part of the workshop. The most repeated exchange in these sessions:

"Now in this paragraph/sentence/section here, can you tell me just what you were trying to say?"

Answer...

"Well I think it would have been better if you'd *said* that..."

In perhaps three or four cases I was able to reassure some people who had worked very hard that the work, at least, was evident. For the rest, I just feel very flattered.

Rilke says in a letter that in the end all criticism comes down to a more or less happy misunderstanding.

I suspect he is right—which is why the literary worth of a workshop like Clarion cannot be defined by simply reviewing what, critically, went on.

The phenomenal percentage of writers from Clarion who have gone on to begin selling s-f stories and novels has been mentioned elsewhere. I don't think I am revealing any profound secret by noting that sales has always been a rather distant emblem for quality. It is an emblem here, however, of the field's life, and the openness to new writers, new substance, and new techniques that has characterized it the last decade and a half. In this time, s-f has been approached from many new directions; the Clarion Workshop is one of the more exciting.

NEW YORK
1970

Thickening the Plot

I distrust the term "plot," (not to mention "theme" and "setting") in discussions of *writing:* It (and they) refers to an effect a story produces in the *reading.* But writing is an internal process writers go through (or put themselves through) in front of a blank paper that leaves a detritus of words there. The truth is, practically nothing is known about it. Talking about plot, or theme, or setting to a beginning writer is like giving the last three years' movie reviews from the Sunday *Times* to a novice filmmaker. A camera manual, a few pamphlets on matched action, viable cutting points, and perhaps one on lighting (in the finished film, the viewer hardly ever sees the light sources, so the reviewer can hardly discuss them; but their placement is essential to everything from mood to plain visibility) would be more help. In short, a vocabulary that has grown from a discussion of effects is only of limited use in a discussion of causes.

A few general things, however, can be noted through introspection. Here is an admittedly simplified description of how writing strikes me. When I am writing I am trying to allow/construct an image of what I want to write about in my mind's sensory theater. Then I describe it as accurately as I can. The most interesting point I've noticed is that the *writing-down* of words about my imagined vision (or at least the choosing/arranging of words to write down) causes the vision itself to change.

Here are two of the several ways it changes:

First—it becomes clearer. Sudden lights are thrown on areas of the mental diorama dark before. Other areas, seen dimly, are revised into much more specific and sharper versions. (What was vaguely imagined as a green dress, while I fix my description of the light bulb hanging from its worn cord, becomes a patterned, turquoise print with a frayed hem.) The notation causes the imagination to resolve focus.

Second—to the extent that the initial imagining contains an action, the notating process tends to propel that action forward (or sometimes backward) in time. (As I describe how Susan, both hands locked, side-punched Frank, I see Frank grab his belly in surprise and stagger back against the banister—which will be the next thing I look at closely to describe.) Notating accurately what happens *now* is a good way to prompt a vague vision of what happens *next*.

Let me try to indicate some of the details of this process.

I decide, with very little mental concretizing, that I want to write about a vague George who comes into a vague room and finds a vague Janice . . .

. . . picture George outside the door. Look at his face; no, look closer. He seems worried . . . ? Concerned . . . ? No. Look even closer and write down just what you see: *The lines across his forehead deepened.* Which immediately starts him moving. What does he do? . . . *He reached for the* . . . doorknob? No. Be more specific . . . *brass doorknob. It turned* . . . easily? No, the word "brass" has cleared the whole knob-and-lock mechanism. Look harder and describe how it's actually turning . . . *loosely in its collar.* While he was turning the knob, something more happened in his face. Look at it; describe it: *He pressed his lips together*—No, cross that line out: not accurate enough. Describe it more specifically: *The corners of his mouth tightened.* Closer. And the movement of the mouth evokes another movement: He's pressing his other hand against the door to open it. (Does "press" possibly come from the discarded version of the previous sentence? Or did wrong use of it there anticipate proper use here? No matter; what does matter is that you look again to make sure it's the accurate word for what he's doing.) *He pressed his palm against the door* . . . And look again; that balk in his next movement . . . *twice, to open it.* As the door opens, I hear the wood give: *You could hear the jamb split*—No, cross out "split," that isn't right . . . *crack*—No, cross that out too; it's even less accurate. Go back to "split" and see what you can do; listen harder . . . *split a little more.* Yes, that's closer. He's got the door open, now. What do you see? *The paint*—No, that's not paint on the wall. Look harder: *The wallpaper was some color between green and gray.* Why can't you see it more clearly? Look around the rest of the room. Oh, yes: *The tan shade was drawn.* What about Janice? She was one of the first things you saw when the door opened. Describe her as you saw her: *Janice sat on the bed*... no, more accurately... *the unmade bed.* No, you haven't got it yet... *Janice sat at the edge of the bed on a spot of bare mattress ticking.* No, no, let's back up a little and go through that again for a precise description of the picture you see: *Janice sat on the bare mattress ticking, the bedding piled loosely around her.* Pretty good, but the bedding is not really in "piles"...*the bedding loose around her.* Closer. Now say what you have been aware of all the time you were wrestling to get that description right: *Light from the shade-edge went up her shoulder and cheek like tape.* Listen: George is about to speak: *"What are you doing here...?"* No, come on! That's not it. Banal as they are, they may be the words he says, but watch him more closely while he says them. *"What...?" He paused, as though to shake his head. But the only movement in his face was a shifting*—Try again:...*a tightening*...Almost; but once more...*a deepening of the lines, a loosening of the lips; "...are you doing here?"* Having gotten his expression more accurately, now you can hear a vocal inflection you missed before: *"...are you doing here?"* There, that's much closer to what you really saw and heard. What has Janice just done? *She uncrossed her legs but did not look at him.* Ordinary grammar rules say that because the sentence's two verbs have one subject, you don't need any comma. But her uncrossing her leg and not looking up go at a much slower pace than proper grammar indicates. Let's make it: *She uncrossed her legs, but did not look at him...*

Now let's review the residue of all that, the admittedly undistinguished, if vaguely Chandleresque bit of prose the reader will have:

> The lines across his forehead deepened. He reached for the brass doorknob. It turned loosely in its collar. The corners of his mouth tightened. He pressed his palm against the door, twice, to open it. You could hear the jamb split a little more.
>
> The wallpaper was some color between green and gray. The tan shade was drawn. Janice sat on the bare mattress ticking, the bedding

loose around her. Light from the shade-edge went up her shoulder and
cheek like tape.

"What?..." He paused, as though to shake his head. But the only
movement in his face was a deepening of the lines, a loosening of the
lips; "...are you *doing* here?"

She uncrossed her legs, but did not look at him.

And if you, the writer, want to know what happens next, you
must take your seat again in the theater of imagination and observe
closely till you see George's next motion, Janice's first response, hear
George's next words, and Janice's eventual reply.

A reader, asked to tell the "plot" of even this much of the story,
might say: "Well, this man comes looking for this woman named
Janice in her room; he finds the door open and goes in, only she
doesn't talk at first."

That's a fair description of the reading experience. But what *we*
started with, to *write*, was simple: George goes into a room and finds
Janice. (George, notice, at this point in the story hasn't even been
named.) The rest came through the actual envisioning/notating
process, from the interaction of the words and the vision. Most of the
implied judgments that the reader picks up—the man is looking *for*
Janice; it is *Janice's room*—are simply overheard (or, more
accurately, overseen) suppositions yielded by the process itself. Let's
call this continuous, developing interchange between imagination
and notation, the *story process*; and let us make that our subject,
rather than "plot."

A last point about our example before we go on to story process
itself: By the time we have gone as far as we have with our "story," all
this close observation has given us a good deal more information than
we've actually used. Though I didn't when I began (to momentarily
drop my editorial stance), I now have a very clear picture of George's
and Janice's clothing. I've also picked up a good deal about the
building they are in. As well, I've formed some ideas about the
relationship between them. And all of this would be rescrutinized as I
came to it, via the story process, were I writing a real story.

The general point: The story process keeps the vision clear and
the action moving. But if we do not notate the vision accurately, if we
accept some phrase we should have discarded, if we allow to stand
some sentence that is not as sharp as we can make it, then the vision is
not changed in the same way it would have been otherwise: the new

sections of the vision will not light up quite so clearly, perhaps not at all. As well, the movement of the vision—its action—will not develop in the same way if we put down a different phrase. And though the inaccurate employment of the story process may still get you to the end of the tale, the progress of the story process, which eventually registers in the reader's mind as "the plot," is going to be off: An inaccuracy in either of the two story process elements, the envisioning or the notating, automatically detracts from the other. When they go off enough, the progress of the story-process will appear unclear, or clumsy, or just illogical.

It has been said enough times so that most readers have it by rote: A synopsis cannot replace a story. Nor can any analysis of the symbolic structure replace the reading experience that exposes us to those symbols in their structural place. Even so, talking to would-be or beginning writers, I find many of them working under the general assumption that the writer, somehow, must begin with such a synopsis (whether written down or no) and/or such an analysis.

This, for what it's worth, does not parallel my experience. At the beginning of a story, I am likely to have one or more images in my mind, some clearer than others (like the strip of light up Janice's arm), that, when I examine them, suggest relations to one another. Using the story process—envisioning and notating, envisioning and notating—I try to move from one of these images to the next, lighting and focusing, step by step, the dark areas between. As I move along, other areas well ahead in the tale will suddenly come vaguely into light; when I actually reach the writing of them, I use the story process to bring them into still sharper focus.

As likely as not, some of the initial images will suggest obvious synopses of the material between (one image of a man on his knees before a safe; another of the same man fleeing across a rooftop while gunshots ring out behind; a third of the same man, marched between two policemen into a van) that the story process, when finished, will turn out to have followed pretty closely. But it is the process, not the synopsis, that produces the story.

Writers are always grappling with two problems: They must make the story interesting (to themselves, if no one else), yet keep it believable (because, somehow, when it ceases to be believable on some level, it ceases to be interesting).

Keeping things interesting seems to be primarily the province of the conscious mind (which, from the literature available, we know far less about than the unconscious), while believability is something that is supplied, in the images it throws up into the mind's theater, primarily by the unconscious. One thing we know about the unconscious is that it contains an incredibly complete "reality model," against which we are comparing our daily experiences moment to moment, every moment. This model lets us know that the thing over there is a garbage can while the thing over there is a gardenia bush, without our having to repeat the learning process of sticking our nose in them each time we pass. It also tells us that, though the thing over there *looks* like a gardenia bush, from a certain regularity in the leaves, an evenness in its coloring, and the tiny mold lines along the stem, it is really a plastic model of a gardenia bush and, should we sniff, will not smell at all. The story process puts us closer to the material stored in our reality model than anything we do besides dream. This material is what yielded us the splitting door jamb, the strip of light, the mattress ticking. This model is highly syncretic: Reality is always presenting us with new experiences that are combinations of old ones. Therefore, even if we want to describe some Horatian impossibility " . . . with the body of a lion and the head of an eagle . . ." our model will give us, as we stare at the back of the creature's neck, the tawny hairs over the muscled shoulders, in which nestle the first, orange-edged pin-feathers. Come to it honestly, and it will never lie: Search as you want, it will not yield you the height of *pi*, the smell of the number seven, the sound of green, nor, heft hard as you can in palm of your mind, the weight of the note D-flat. (This is not to suggest that such mysterious marvels aren't the province of fiction [especially speculative fiction]; only that they are mysterious and marvelous constructions of the equally mysterious and marvelous *conscious* mind. That is where you must go to find out about *them*.)

When writers get (from readers or from themselves) criticism in the form: "The story would be more believable if such and such happened," or "The story would be more interesting if such and such . . ." *and* they agree to make use of the criticism, they must translate it: "Is there any point in the story process I can go back to, and, by examining my visualization more closely, catch something I missed before, which, when I notate it, will move the visualization/notation process forward again in this new way?" In other words, can the writers convince themselves that on some ideal level the story actually did happen (as opposed to "should have happened") in the new way, and that it was their inaccuracy as a story-process practitioner that got it going on the wrong track at some given point? If you don't do this, the corrections are going to clunk a bit and leave a patch-as-patch-can feel with the reader.

Writers work with the story process in different ways. Some writers like to work through a short story at a single, intense sitting, to interrupt as little as possible the energy that propels the process along, to keep the imagined visualization clearly and constantly in mind.

Other writers must pause, pace, and sometimes spend days between each few phrases, abandoning and returning to the visualization a dozen times a page. I think this is done as a sort of test, to make sure only the strongest and most vitally clear elements—the ones that cling tenaciously to the underside of memory—are retained.

Masterpieces have been written with both methods. Both methods have produced drivel.

In a very real way, one writes a story to find out what happens in it. Before it is written it sits in the mind like a piece of overheard gossip or a bit of intriguing tattle. The story process is like taking up such a piece of gossip, hunting down the people actually involved, questioning them, finding out what really occurred, and visiting pertinent locations. As with gossip, you can't be too surprised if important things turn up that were left out of the first-heard version entirely; or if points initially made much of turn out to have been distorted, or simply not to have happened at all.

Among those stories which strike us as perfectly plotted, with those astonishing endings both a complete surprise and a total satisfaction, it is amazing how many of their writers will confess that the marvelous resolution was as much of a surprise for them as it was for the reader, coming, in imagination and through the story process, only a page or a paragraph or a word before its actual notation.

On the other hand, those stories which make us say, "Well, that's clever, I *suppose*..." but with a certain dissatisfied frown (the dissatisfaction itself, impossible to analyze), are often those stories worked out carefully in advance to be, precisely, clever.

One reason it is so hard to discuss the story process, even with introspection, is that it is something of a self-destruct process as well.

The notation changes the imagination; it also distorts the writer's
memory of the story's creation. The new, intensified visualization
(which, depending on the success of the story process, and sometimes
in spite of it, may or may not have anything to do with the reader's
concept of the story) comes to replace the memory of the story
process itself.

Writers cannot make any objective statement on what they were
trying to do, or even how they did it, because—as the only residue of
the story process the reader has is the writer's words on the page—the
only residue of the story process in the writer's mind is the clarified
vision, which like the "plot" synopsis, is not the story, but the story's
result.

NEW YORK
1972

Characters

Two points about characterization. Both, however, grow from a particular concept of story, i.e. a story is ultimately not what happens in an author's mind that makes her write down a series of words (that is the just discussed "story process"); it is what a given series of words causes to happen in the reader's. And I might mention a minor corollary: It is only by seriously examining the things we can't cause to happen in the reader's mind that we begin to gain fine control over what we can effect, e.g., there is no way, with words, to make a reader *see* the color "red," but we can make her *remember* the color . . . in short, the experience of a story is a mental phenomenon of the order of memory, not immediate sensory apprehension, and an analysis of why some memories are more vivid, pressing, or moving than others is much more likely to lead to a vivid, pressing and moving story than all the accurately reported first-hand experience in the world. A story is of the order of memory, and that is why it takes place in the past, even when set in the future. A story is a maneuvering of myriad micromemories into a new order—even an s-f story. One thing that distinguishes an s-f story is that the order is going to be even newer than for a mainstream tale.

But characterization?

My first point has to do with psychological veracity.

Any two facts clustered around a single pronoun begin to generate a character in the reader's mind:

She was sixteen years old, and already six feet tall.

Though only a ghost, she is already more or less vivid depending on the reader's experience. As soon as we get ready to add a third fact, however, we encounter the problem of psychological veracity. All subsequent information about our character (let's call her Sam) has to be more or less congruent with what already exists in the gap between these two facts. I have no particular problem if I continue adding facts thus:

She was a shy girl, and tended to walk around with her shoulders hunched.

The character, remember, is in our minds, not on the paper. She is composed of what we know or what we have read, which in this case has to do with what we know about the height of most sixteen-year-olds, as well as the general behavior of adolescents who are different from their peers.

If I wanted to, instead of making Sam shy and stooped, I could have said:

Lively, self-assured, she was cuttingly witty, though always popular; active physically, though always gentle.

If I did, however, in order to compensate for the tension that immediately is formed with our sense of psychological veracity, I would have had to add (with an implied "For you see...").

She was the middle child of seven, with siblings taller than herself on either side. It was a close and boisterous family, so that when Sam first came to Halifax High her stubby classmates amused her, and she was big-hearted enough to try to amuse them in turn: That, and her implied athletic prowess, made her very popular.

But if I had made her shy and stooped, I would not have needed the above. In the same way that the physically unusual needs explanation, so does the psychologically unusual. Practically any combination of physical and psychological traits can exist beneath a single persona: but the writer's instinctive feel for psychological veracity has to determine which combinations need further elucidation to cement their juxtaposition, and which simply work by themselves to generate a character, without further embellishment. All too often the plot simply calls for someone six feet tall (because she has to be able to see over Mr. Green's fence when Henry runs out the French windows), sixteen years old (so that she isn't allowed in the movie house, where Green is the day-manager Tuesday mornings) and self-assured (so she can calm down the people who rush out into the lobby on Saturday night when Henry shoots the blank air gun . . .) and so on.

But if the writer has violated the reader's sense of psychological veracity, he will have a fine and exciting tale moving around a Sam-shaped hole . . . even if the character in the writer's mind is quite real.

Ideally, all the plot information should contribute to the realization of the characters; all the character information should move the plot: If we *need* that sprawling, emotionally supportive family to make Sam real, it would be a good idea to have them take part in the plot as well (Henry is Sam's oldest brother, who is living on the other side of town and doesn't get along with his parents at all; let us look a little more closely at Sam's happy family, and at Sam's apparent self-assuredness . . .). But this is how short stories turn into novels. I guess this is what writers mean when they say a character runs away with the story.

My second point about characterization is rather paradoxical with the first. Once a reader catches, by her own sense of psychological veracity, the character from what generates between the facts scattered about a name, vividness and immediacy is maintained, essentially, through what the character does: her actions (and particularly that subgroup of actions prompted by things outside him: reactions).

A character in a novel of mine—that most dangerous of creations: a novelist writing a novel—observed that there were three types of actions: purposeful, habitual, and gratuitous. If the writer can show a character involved in a number of all three types of actions, his character will probably seem more real.

This occurred to me when I was trying to analyze why some writers who can present perfectly well drawn males cannot present a convincing female to save themselves—heroines *or* villainesses. I noticed with these writers that while their heroes (and villains) happily indulge in all types of actions, if there is a villainess, she is generally all purpose; if there is a heroine, we are often shown her doing nothing but habitual actions, or nothing but gratuitous ones.

Assuming one has one's characters clearly visualized, the writer has to expose them to enough different things so that the characters can react in their own ways.

Writers writing essentially adventures too frequently don't confront their characters with enough objects/emotions/situations nor give their characters space enough to react in a way both individual and within the limits of psychological veracity.

Ten years ago, before I had had any novels published, as a rule of thumb I constructed a small list of things that I thought all major characters in a novel should be exposed to and allowed to have individual reactions to, to make their characters particularly vivid.

Food: How does the character behave when eating with a group? If possible, how does he react when supplying food for others?

Sleep: What particularizes his going to sleep, his waking up?

Money: How does he get his shelter, food, and how does he feel about how he gets it?

Society: How does he react to somebody who makes substantially more money than he does and how is this different from the way he acts to an economic peer (and believe me, it is different, however admirable)?

How does he react when he meets somebody who makes substantially less money than he does (and *ditto*)?

In a short story of course, one may not have time to explore all these particular aspects of this character. (If there was a flaw in my method, it was perhaps that I never got around to answering these questions for my women characters. But perhaps this failing was implicit in the formulation . . . ?) But I can't think of one great novelist from Richardson to Joyce who does not particularize her characters through all of these situations, somewhere or other through her plots.

Now one can take the "list method" of character development and run it into the ground. When I was seventeen, a writer of successful juvenile novels gave me an eight-page mimeographed form he claimed he used to help him construct characters. In proper

Harvard Outline form were questions like:

    I.)   How does he react outdoors?
          A.)   To weather?
               1) To rain?
               2) To sleet?
               3) To sun?
          B.)   To geography?
               1) In the mountains?
               2) By the sea?
   II.) How does he react indoors...?

As an experiment, I took a character in a story I was working on (a skindiver, I remember, who had come with an American team to work on underwater oil wells off the coast of Venezuela) and wrote out nineteen pages of "characterization," following the guide.

Needless to say, I lost all interest in completing the story.

Leaving my particular points to generalize a bit:

The confusion in following most sorts of literary advice usually comes from the author's confusion as to what is happening in the author's mind and what he can effect in the reader's.

I don't think the writer has to understand the characters to write about them. The writer does need to *see* them. The *reader*, however, does need to understand them; if the reader figures them out for herself, the writer has "created" all that more vivid a character than if the writer explained them away. The writer must see and put down those things that will allow (not *make*: you can't *make* the reader do anything—not even open the book) the reader to understand. If you can (figuratively) close your eyes and see Sam as sixteen, six feet tall, and heroically self-assured, fine. But you will have to pay more attention to the vision of the story than most adventure plots allow for.

The juxtapositions of traits that make up the "hero" are, alas, comparatively rare. That is why a "heroic" hero needs a good deal of characterization if our sense of psychological veracity is not to be strained past the breaking point very fast—precisely because she is a psychological (as well as statistical) anomaly.

I don't think a writer's understanding is going to hurt their (or should I say, the readers') characters, in and of itself. However, what we understand with exhaustive analytical thoroughness we are not too likely to be interested in enough to fictionalize about with intensity—since the actual fictionalizing process itself is a form of synthetic analysis.

An ironic passing thought: Within this field, many of the writers of the big, brawny adventure-type s-f tales are, indeed, big and brawny, with the most spectacular and flamboyant lives waving behind them like opera-capes. If their leading characters are sometimes flat, perhaps it is because they understand such people *too* well to take the literary time to make them real to the small, scruffy reader.

However she attains this state, the writer has to approach her material at a moment when the vision of it is so particularly clear that the glare bleaches away all analytical *bias*—which is *not* the same as bleaching away analysis itself.

For (on the other hand) it may (and should) take a great deal of analysis to discover how to create a formal analogue of that vision in words (the craft of fiction, if you will).

It is intriguing that the writer of the past hundred years to discuss most systematically what goes on in the writer's mind when creating was Paul Valéry; and that he produced an amazingly hard-headed aesthetic in which the words "precision" and "scientific" appear over and over. Mathematics and engineering supply most of his nonliterary specimens of the creative process.

A poet, his particular concern was poetry. But I have always felt that the impetus behind s-f—the hardest and most hardware-filled s-f—was closer to the poetic impulse than any other.

In an essay on La Fontaine's *Adonis*, he says in passing:

"Follow the path of your aroused thought, and you will soon meet this infernal inscription: *There is nothing so beautiful as that which does not exist.*"

The s-f writer, whether he is writing about what he thinks could, should, or (heaven help us) might someday exist, or whether she is dallying with some future fantasia so far away all subjunctive connection with the present is severed, has become entranced with and dedicated herself to the realization of what is not. And all the "socially beneficial functions of art" are minimal before this aesthetic one: It allows the present meaning; it allows the future to exist.

SAN FRANCISCO
1969

On Pure Story-Telling

—for Vonda McIntyre

Talk delivered at the 1970
Nebula Banquet in Berkeley.

I think the trouble with writers writing about writing (or speaking about it) is the trouble anyone has discussing their profession.

I first came across this idea in E. M. Forster's *Aspects of the Novel:* You'll do better writing about something you've only done a little of, because you still preserve those first impressions that make it vivid, even to someone who has been doing it for years. On the other hand, if you write about something you have been doing day in and day out, though you would recognize those impressions if someone else were to recall them to you, you yourself tend to pass over them as commonplaces.

Therefore, contemplating what I was going to say this evening, I tried to go back and capture some of my initial impressions about the whole experience of writing stories, or even my first encounters with the whole idea of stories and story-telling.

The catalyst for my ideas this evening was a book I passed on the shelves of the Tro Harper book store. It was a large-sized, quality paperback, with a red cover, published by Dell: *The Careless Atom* by Sheldon Novick.

Sheldon Novick...

The last time I heard Sheldon Novick's name was fourteen years ago. He was several years ahead of me at the Bronx High School of Science. There was a strange half dozen years when the Bronx High School of Science held a whole gaggle of fascinating people at once, including, among others, Stokeley Carmichael, Bobby Darin, Todd Gitlan, Peter Beagle, Norman Spinrad, someone else who is currently writing the motorcycle column for *The Good Times* under the Nom de Plume of *The Black Shadow*, and Marilyn Hacker.

As I said, that was the last I'd heard of Shelley, till two weeks ago.

The first I'd heard of him was several years before that. We were at summer camp. Some dozen of us had taken an evening hike from a place named, for unknown reasons, Brooklyn College, to another known as The Ledge. There was a campfire. Several marshmallows had, by now, fallen into it. We were a quarter of the way up the back of a forested hill, pretentiously called Mt. Wittenburg. And it was dark and chilly. You know the situation: smoke in the eyes, your left cheek buttered with heat, your right shoulder shivering.

Somebody said: "Shelley, tell us a story."

"What do you want to hear a story for," Shelley said with disdain, and licked marshmallow from his fingers.

"Tell us a story, tell us a story!" There wasn't any stopping us. "Tell us a story. Tell us the one about—"

"Oh, I told you that one last week."

"Tell it again! Tell it again!"

And I, who had never heard Shelley tell anything at all, but was thoroughly caught up by the enthusiasm, cried: "Well then tell us a new one!"

Shelley, smiling a little in the direction of the rubber on his left sneaker toe, rose to take a seat on a fallen log. He put his hands on his knees, leaned forward and said, "All right. Tonight I shall tell you the story of..."

The Story that he told was called *Who Goes There?* He told it for an hour and a half that night, stopping in the middle. We gathered outside Brooklyn College the next night and sat on the flagstones while he told us another hour's worth. And two nights later we gathered in one of the tents and he gave us the concluding half hour under the kerosene lantern hanging from the center pole.

"Did you make that up?" somebody asked him, when he was finished.

"Oh no, it's by somebody called John W. Campbell," he explained to us. "It's a book. I read it a couple of weeks ago."

At which point our counsellor told him, really, it was well past lights out and he simply had to go.

Our counsellor blew out the light, and I lay in my cot bed thinking about story-telling. Shelley was perhaps thirteen, back then. I was nine or ten, but even then it seemed perfectly marvelous that somebody could keep so many people enthralled for four hours over three nights.

Shelley was the first of those wonderful creatures, "A Story-Teller," that I had ever encountered.

A summer camp is a very small place. Shelley's reputation spread. Some weeks later, he was asked to tell his story again to a much larger group—bunk five, bunk six, and bunk seven all collected in the ampitheater behind the long, creosoted kitchen house. Shelley, on a bench this time, once more told the story *Who Goes There?*, this time in a single hour sitting.

Of course we who had heard it before had the expected connoisseur reactions: Oh, it was much better in the longer version. The intimacy of firelight and roasted marshmallows vastly improved the initial sequence. And lanterns were essential for the conclusion to have its full effect. But the forty-odd people who heard it for the first time were just as enthralled as we had been. But more important, I got a chance to look at how Shelley's tale was put together.

The first thing I noticed the second time through was that the names of all the characters were different the second time. And when I got a chance to look at the book myself a year or so later, I realized with amusement that the names in neither of Shelley's versions corresponded with those of JWC.

The second thing I noticed was that a good deal of the story was chanted—indeed, in the most exciting passages very little was actually happening: And you had sections like:

"...they walked across the ice, they slogged across the ice, there was ice below them and ice all around them..."

Or, when the monster was beginning to revive, I recall:

"...the fingers rose, the hand rose, the arm rose slowly, a little at a time, rose like a great green plant..."

Needless to say, you will find none of these lines in the book. What Shelley was giving us was a very theatrical, impromptu, and essentially poetic impression of his memory of the tale.

When I did encounter Shelley again in Bronx Science, I had just joined the staff of the school literary magazine, *Dynamo*. I was delighted to discover him. And I think that was one of the first times I made the discovery that three years difference in age is a lot more at nine or ten than it is at fourteen or fifteen.

At any rate, I remember I bumped into Shelley—literally—behind the projection booth in the auditorium balcony. We recovered, recognized each other, enthused for a while, and I asked him would he be doing any fiction or poetry for *Dynamo*. He looked quite surprised. No, he hadn't thought about it. Actually his interests were theater.

I was quite surprised. But creative writing, he explained, had never particularly interested him.

Later Shelley turned in quite a credible performance as Jonathon in the Senior Play, *Arsenic and Old Lace*. And a few weeks ago, after having not seen him since, I learned, via the blurb on the back of *The Careless Atom*, that "Sheldon Novick is Program Administrator of the Center for the Biology of Natural Systems at Washington University in St. Louis. He is also Associate Editor of the journal *Scientist and Citizen* and is a frequent contributor of articles dealing with atomic energy." I can recommend the book to anyone interested in the recent developments of the practical side of reactors and reactor plants.

But let's get back to "story-telling."

The second "story-teller" I encountered was Seamus McManus. He was the grandfather of one of my elementary school classmates. Mr. McManus had been born in Ireland. His father had been a professional story-teller who went from cottage to cottage and, for lodging and meals and a bit of kind, kept the family entertained in the evenings with what were called "Faerey stories," in which an endless number of heroes named Jack, always the youngest of three brothers, set out to seek his fortune and, after a multiplex of old women, magicians, giants and elves, magic mills, and enchanted apples, married the beautiful princess and lived happily ever after.

Mr. McManus had made the reconstruction of these classic Irish folk-tales his hobby. He told them at children's parties—indeed, it was at his grandson's, FitzHugh Mullen's, birthday party that I first heard him. Sunlight streamed through white organdy curtains while the gray-haired gentleman sat forward in the armchair, and the rest of us, sitting on the rug and hugging our knees, were bound in the music of his brogue. Over the next few years, I heard him several times more, once at a children's library, and once in a program in the school's auditorium. And again, after the initial magic, I again got a chance to look at what was going on.

The action in these stories—and you always left a McManus story-telling under the impression that you had just been *through* the tremendous and hair raising adventures—the action, when you looked at it up close, was usually dismissed in a sentence or two: The typical battle between Jack and one of his numerous adversaries was usually handled something like this:

"You want to fight?" said Jack. "Well I'm a poor sort of fighter but I'll do my best, and the best can do no more." So they fought, and they fought, and they fought, and they fought, and—(here Mr. McManus would snap his fingers)—Jack slew him with a blow.

There was your action.

On the other hand, the things that stuck, the things that remain, indeed the things that took up most of the time, were the ritual descriptions and incantatory paragraphs, the endless journeys that all went, from tale to tale, from story to story:

"So they lifted up their bundles, and set out in high spirits. And they traveled twice as far as I could tell you, and three times farther than you could tell me, and seven times farther than anyone could tell the two of us."

And when, in a year or so, I first read the *Iliad*, I think this contributed much understanding of those ritual descriptions that are repeated word for word throughout the poem—like the sacrifice that comes with exactly the same words a near dozen times, at each point the Achaeans are called on to perform one:

When they had made their petitions and scattered the grain, they first drew the heads of the animals back; they cut open their throats; they flayed them. Then from the thighs they cut slices and wrapped them in fat folds with raw meat above them. These the old priest burnt on the wood, and he sprinkled wine on the fire, and the young men gathered around him, five-pronged forks in their hands. When the thighs were burnt up, and they had all tasted the organs, they carved the remains into small pieces and pierced them with boughs and they roasted them well, then pulled them out of the flame. Work done, the meal ready, they fell to eating hungrily, all with an equal share. And, when their thirst and their hunger were satisfied . . .

When their thirst and their hunger were satisfied, the Trojan War usually got under way again.

Mr. McManus published several books of his stories. The one I recall most readily was *Bold Heroes of Hungry Hill*. If you read them, I suspect you will find them a little flat—though they are word for word as Mr. McManus told them.

While I considered the flatness, I was taken back to Mr. McManus at FitzHugh's party. Afterwards, we asked him questions about himself, about the stories, about Ireland. "After all," I remember him saying, "the tales are hundreds of years old, passed on by word of mouth. We had some good story-tellers, and some not so good. But the thing to remember"—and he sat back in his arm chair again—"the tale is in the telling."

The third story-teller I remember from that terribly odd, angular and hyperlogical time called childhood was my geography teacher, John Seeger. He was the older brother of the folk singer Pete Seeger. They have practically identical speaking voices. Any one of you who caught Pete Seeger on the Johnny Cash show a few weeks back will have some idea of the terribly arresting quality of that voice. John— my elementary school was one of those fifties strangenesses where children called the teachers by their first names—John taught a good deal of his geography by telling stories.

They all followed the same form. Two children, a boy and a girl, variously named Pat and Pam, or Bill and Barbara, or John and Judy, along with their crotchety governess—the only one of her many names I remember was Miss Powderpuff—would get separated from their parents in a foreign country, and John would regale us with the economics, the geography, the landscape, the morals and mores of the country in a barrage of fascinating anecdotes.

John's stories were incredibly popular with the students. Twice a week, the geography room would stay open after school, and forty or fifty of us would squeeze into the circle while John, mimicking first this character, than another, with much slapping of the knees and clever gesticulations, would take his alliterative hero and heroine through Athens, Beirut, Calcutta, Damascus, Edinburgh, Frankfurt, and Geneva. I think John's stories were the most enjoyable of the three. Besides being educational, they involved a great deal of audience participation. Whenever a new character entered, John would first describe him—a Greek musician, a French banker, a Turkish ambassador's son—then he would turn to us and say, "And what should we call him?"

We would cry out names, and whichever one seemed most appropriate would stick with the character through the story.

During this time, I was indulging in my own first experiments with writing. I had even gone so far as to put down a hundred-odd pages of a novel, in cramped scrawling pencil, about an elderly gentleman of fifteen who spent a lot of time looking at the sea and taking long walks alone in the city. Sometime or other during its composition, it occurred to me that, besides spelling and grammar, something else was missing from the sorrows of my youngest of Wérthers (it was called *Lost Stars*). But what...?

Once, after one of his more fascinating story-telling sessions, I went up to John and asked him if he had ever written any of his stories down.

All the other students had gone, and tall, gangling John and I walked down the hall toward the elevator. John looked surprisingly pensive. "I've tried," he explained to me. "But somehow, I just can't tell stories to a typewriter. And there isn't the interplay back and forth between me and you kids."

I was precocious. "Have you ever tried to record them?" I suggested. "Then you could transcribe—" (I had just learned the word two weeks ago and was using it now at every opportunity) "—you could transcribe them, and then they'd be just like you told them."

"It's funny you should suggest that," John said. "Last year, I tried that. And once I forgot about the microphone, the telling went pretty well. Then I got my wife to type it out. And you know what?"

"What?" I asked.

"They were perfectly dreadful!" Then the elevator came.

I believe that was my first practical lesson in writing. Indeed, I'd go so far as to say that everything I consciously know about writing—

and I'm painfully aware how little that actually is—has to do with the difference between written and spoken language.

In a way I feel that I was lucky to have been exposed to so much purely verbal story-telling as a child, because it pointed out some essential differences between sitting, with a bunch of people, at the feet of a marvelous and magical raconteur, and sitting in one's room, by oneself, with a book.

The aural art of story-telling, like theater, is essentially communal. People come together to hear stories. And the story-teller has the whole theatrical battery, including elements of dance and song, to compel his listeners' attention.

Reading is very much a do-it-yourself entertainment. It's private. There is no way for an author to *compel* the reader to do anything. Any call to the phone, or even a passing thought, can interrupt. On the other hand, the reader can determine her own pace at reading, can go back and reread; indeed, as a rule, the reader is far more conscious of details than the hearer.

In speech, incantation, invocation, and repetition are practically a must. But what the ear finds supremely enthralling the eye finds just dull.

On the other hand, such a tiny part of the visual capacity of the eye-and-brain is used in scanning black print on white paper that practically the whole pictorial imagination is left free—so that in written texts, *evocation* becomes almost the entire process, the conjuring up of pictures, tones of voice, resonances, and reminiscences.

Reading, as opposed to listening, requires a far higher level of attention: and the McLuhan formula *Low Resolution, High Involvment* governs the whole play. Traditional phrases that weigh heavily in the ear, to the eye are mere cliches. The reader wants the information once and at the highest intensity, rather than beat into the tympanum with chanted repetition.

As much as tone of voice is part of writing, the infinite nuances that various vocal tones can give to a single phrase are totally lost on the page. The scant dozen punctuation marks in the English typesetter's box are just inadequate to handle the job. (A couple of weeks ago, Greg, Joan, Don, Quinn* and I were contemplating a new

*Greg and Joan Benford, Don Simpson, and Chelsey Quinn Yarbro.

punctuation mark: a "sarcasm mark" which, when it appeared at the end of a sentence, would indicate that the sentence should be read in such a way as to imply the exact opposite of its denoted content. Perhaps a small tilde over a period?)

Aural language depends on repetition, of intravocal sounds, of sound patterns, of ideas.

In written language the beginning and the ends of sentences are the place for that sentence's most important words. In speech the most important word in the sentence has to be surrounded on both sides by an aural bolster of padding, to prop it up, to buoy it up, to keep it afloat in our minds. Let me repeat that, because I'm speaking: In speech the most important word in a sentence has to be rumti-tumped and bumti-bumped in padding, to scuba-duba, to oh-calcutta, to rumplestiltskin it in the hootchy-kootch. (Hear what I mean?)

In written language, one doesn't *begin* to hear it until a certain *visual hardness* (or density) is achieved. And when the ear does come into play, I think it is on a much subtler level. It is listening to an essentially unsung music.

When we listen, we want the ideas interlarded with noise—all those meaningless words and phrases like "essentially," "practically," "on the other hand," "almost," "seems," "more or less," "suddenly"— the words that give us time to think.

On the page, the same words are abhorrent, ugly, and, even in reported dialogue, more times than not get in the way.

When I was a child, I was a perfectly dreadful story-teller. I wanted to be a good one very much. Story-tellers are amazing and wondrous people. And anyone who has not encountered a fine tale-teller has missed out on a very basic, important, and rewarding cultural experience.

Several times I tried to tell stories.

People fidgeted.

I kept forgetting the plot.

I have this creaky, asthmatic laughter (as with the canned studio responses to situation comedies, the story-teller must lead and guide the audience's laughter at the tale, so that a large and generous laugh is essential to the art): and I usually talk too loud.

I suppose that's why I became a writer.

You know, I think about being a child, listening to stories. And then I think about all of us, gathered here for this banquet tonight. You know, a lot of funny things happened on my way here this evening.

But I'm damned if I'm going to *tell* you about them.

SAN FRANCISCO
1970

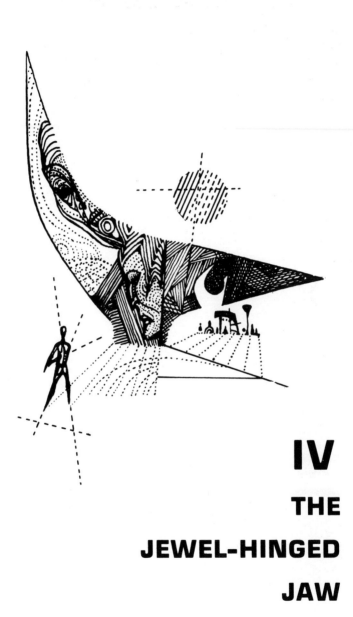

IV

THE

JEWEL-HINGED

JAW

Faust and Archimedes

1

I leave you free to choose whatever lie
you think worthiest to be the truth.
—*My Faust*/Paul Valery, 1940

Thomas Disch and Roger Zelazny have fascinated me since I first read them in the early sixties. Their methods are intricate, their results flamboyantly spectacular. Anyone who offers such fireworks to a public as imaginative as the s-f audience, whether he appears in person or not, becomes something of a public mythos. Both writers began publishing s-f in 1962, at the ages of twenty-one and twenty-four, respectively. Six years later [1968], both have earned the highest critical praise: "genius," "style," and "erudite" are the catchwords that tag the critical writing about them. They have also earned such attacks as "...surely science fiction's most overrated author" and "this manuscript should have gone from the typewriter straight to the circular file." In fanzines their names are used to swear by ("...has not quite the poetry of Zelazny") or to curse with ("...but compared to dismal Disch..."). Such divergence of reaction—any advertising director will tell you—*is* success, *is* public acceptance. Although I feel the warmest cordiality to both in person, I came to both first through their work. So I am still affected by the myths their work generates.

Zelazny?

A few months before I first went to Europe, a young woman music student came knocking on my door, waving a copy of *The*

Magazine of Fantasy and Science Fiction with an absolutely obsessed expression: "Have you read this, Chip? Have you *read* this? Who is he? Do you know anything about him? What has he written before?"

The Doors of His Face, the Lamps of His Mouth was headed by one of *F&SF*'s less informative blurbs. I read it; that copy of the magazine went with me to Europe. I gave it to half a dozen people to read; meanwhile, here in the U.S. the tale took one of those twelve-pound blocks of lucite with the beautiful things inside—a Nebula award. And almost a year later I was to hear, on the same day that I actually met Zelazny in person at the World Science Convention in Cleveland, one of the most intelligent and sensitive readers in the s-f community say, "I can't see why everybody is so excited about a short story that's just a watered down version of *Moby Dick*."

I discovered Disch a few months before I first read Zelazny.

I was leafing through an issue of *Fantastic* that someone had given me with a pile of s-f magazines, assuming that because I was an s-f writer they could be dumped off on me. I came across a story that begins as little more than a shopping list. By the time I had finished reading that list, I had clearly before me one of the most vividly realized characters I have run across in short fiction. The story progresses: and as spectacularly as he is created, the character is destroyed.

There are some works of art that accomplish themselves with such efficacy that they remain with one forever as exemplars. Over the next years in I-don't-know-how-many discussions of writing, with both professionals and amateurs, I brought up this tale as *the* example of economical character sketching. "There's a story by somebody I've never read anything else by, called *Descending*, where with nothing more than a shopping list, the author establishes..."

And while I discussed him, Disch, in Mexico, was creating a marvelous and marvelously flawed hymn to the human monster, then to be called *The Harvest Is Past: The Summer Is Ended*.

The first city Disch and I shared (1966) was London. But it was not till I returned to England, six months after my first trip, that we met. And *The Genocides* had already produced reactions as divergent as the Merril review in *F&SF* and the Budrys review in *Galaxy*.*

---

*Merril loved it; Budrys loathed it.

I wonder how much of the initial excitement, both pro and con, was in terms of: "But what are they *doing* here?" The thing that makes both writers egregious or praiseworthy, as one chooses to look at them, is the plethora of literary technique.

Someone given a Disch story by *F&SF* to copyedit once told me: "I didn't like the story. I didn't like it at all, and thought it should be cut. But when I went back over it, every single thing in it contributed to the point. There just wasn't anything that could go. I had to leave it alone."

S-f is a field where many of the practitioners most lauded within the fraternity barely have enough knowledge of writing to make their ideas comprehensible, must less vivid, coherent, charged with the immediacy that makes them part of a reader's life. The standards set by most of the editors concern the "idea": the general editorial policy of both Pohl (*Galaxy, If, Worlds of Tomorrow*) and Campbell (*Analog*) is that the "idea" must be intrinsically interesting enough to make the reader feel he has been given something to think about. The literary standard is merely that the idea be comprehensible. Even in the "golden age," the maximum standards were set by ingenuity of concept—which all too many authors still failed to meet. The minimum standard had nothing to do with literacy, and only defined the intelligible—which, admittedly, as many authors rose above.

A problem that critics, especially favorable ones, have had with Zelazny and Disch comes from a concern implicit in most of the s-f criticism of the past twenty years: "Does it stand up to the mainstream?"

This was a valid way to look at much of the s-f of the late forties and fifties. The most outstanding stories of Leiber, Merril, Pohl and Knight are, for the most part, set in the relatively near future; their social and psychological matrices are close enough to ours so that character insights and a sense of economic reality lend density and intensity much the same way they will to a mainstream story; for the most part the narrative techniques are naturalistic. What was being produced in the mainstream at the same time as these stories were being written? Early Capote, the first novels of Mailer and Bellow, the last books of Hemingway, the tales of J. D. Salinger, Faulkner's *Snopes* trilogy. All of these are remarkably staid works. The most experimental would be Kerouac's *On the Road* and even that looks downright classical compared to the literary experiments of the twenties, thirties, and early forties: *The Sound and the Fury*, *As I Lay Dying*, Dos Passos's *U.S.A.* . . . , Borges's fables in South America (one of Borges's first appearances in America was a translation of *Death and the Compass*, by Anthony Boucher, which appeared in his *Magazine of Fantasy and Science Fiction*), Genet's criminal peons in France (so many people forget that *Notre Dame des fleurs* was first published in 1942). It is actually a little depressing to realize just how closely the best s-f of that period does parallel the mainstream. But the parallel justifies the critical concern. All this writing was done before *Catch 22* or *V.* Though Durrell and Nabokov had been favorites of a small coterie of writers that, admittedly, included figures as diverse as T. S. Eliot, Edmund Wilson, and Henry Miller, their names were almost unknown to the intellectual public. Neither Barth nor Barthelme had published.

With the advent of these mainstream writers, "a mastery of literary technique" became something quite different. And all of them have acknowledged, at one point or another, the influence of s-f.

We have gotten back to a concept of literary technique in which the story's substance determines what that technique is to be. The idea of "clean, precise, naturalistic writing" for every situation has been put aside. Anyone judging style today still looks for economy and intensity; but the final judgment is made on the more flexible criterion: does it *do*?

With this flexibility there has returned a measure of sanity in comparing diverse works. Comparisons may be helpful analytically, but value judgments usually get us nowhere. Which is better, *Pride and Prejudice* or *Gulliver's Travels*? The question is absurd, even though both works fall into the category of "classical masterpiece." It is equally absurd to ask for such a judgment between, say, *More Than Human* and *Catcher in the Rye*.

To bring the discussion back to Disch and Zelazny:

Saying that either one is "as good as the mainstream; could, or should, be writing mainstream" is missing the point. It is also flogging a horse that, within the mainstream itself, has been acknowledged critically defunct since the emergence of Amis, Sontag, and the other pop-apologists. To date both Disch and Zelazny have written s-f, so here they must be examined. They have also written vastly different s-f.

The work of both abounds in literary, historical, and mythological allusions. The sensitivies revealed are far-ranging, capable of fine psychological and sociological analysis, and are as responsive to the contemporary as to the traditional. They have brought these sensitivities to bear on their science fiction.

Yes, my first reaction was: "What are they doing here?"

But they are here. And in art trends and movements ("waves" if you will) are defined by what writers write, what readers read, and the tension between the two. Critics, at best, chronicle this process. At worst, they chronicle it inaccurately.

2

> There came a week ago to Erfurt a certain chiromancer named Georgius Faustus, Helmitheus Hedebergensis, a mere braggart and fool. The professions of this man and of all fortune-tellers are vain. The rude people marvel at him. I heard him swaggering at the inn. I did not bother to reprove his boastfulness, for why should I bother about the foolishness of others?
>
> —Letter/Conrad Mutianus Refus
> of Erfurt to Heinrich Urbanus
> October 7, 1513

The literary method of both writers is symbolism.

Arthur Symons in *The Symbolist Movement in Literature* (1899) quotes d'Alviella: "A symbol might be defined as a representation that does not aim at being a reproduction." Symbolism as a literary method takes two forms (neither to be confused with *using* symbols in a work of art—of simply having one thing stand for something else): First there is "reductive" symbolism, a process of simplification, such as in a fable or Biblical writing, where the events are bleached, stripped, presented much less richly than they would be in a naturalistic "reproduction." The effect gained through reductive symbolism is a strengthened sense of structural relations; as the texture falls away, as well a certain dignity rises that is often obliterated by the necessary ironies of "realism."

The other type of symbolism is "intensive" symbolism. This is the sort used by most of the *symbolistes* Symons wrote of: Rimbaud, Verlaine, de Nerval, and Baudelaire. By an intensification of language, the writer represents his situations more vividly than life itself, in an attempt to capture some experiential richness that is usually only perceived with hindsight or in anticipation, and, rarely, in moments of total involvement. (For the artist, this involvement, say some, is experienced only in the actualization of his art.) The effects gained by intensive symbolism are sensory immediacy; spectra of emotions come sharply into focus; there is also a great feel of motion, and a closeness with the pulse of the experiences described.

Because intensive symbolism must be so highly textured, in its mainstream use overall structures tend to be lost. Or, when they do emerge, they seem somehow artificial. It is almost always open to accusations of "mannerism," "decadence" and "lack of discipline." Whereas reductive symbolism must almost always stand up to the charges of "cerebral," "lifeless," and "pessimistic."

Both writers have tried the two types of symbolism in science fiction with varying success. Zelazny's pastiche of Cordwainer Smith, *The Furies*, and his forthcoming novel *Creatures of Light and Darkness* are essentially reductive. *He Who Shapes* and the first-person novels and novellas are some of the most elegant examples of intensive symbolism in American prose. Disch's tale *The Squirrel Cage* is a fine example of reductive symbolism that for all its Beckett-like despair could certainly *not* be called "lifeless." His novel *Camp Concentration*, the journals of a poet imprisoned and held by the government for purposes of experimentation, is intensive symbolism at its most effective.

What are they doing here?

Science fiction is the only area of literature outside poetry that is symbolistic in its basic conception. Its stated aim is to represent the world without reproducing it. That is what dealing with worlds of possibilities and probabilities means. It is paradoxical that the symbolists must be so passionately concerned with the real world, both the reality without them and within. But if they are not, their symbols have no referent. Though I have not looked yet at "what" they are doing, it strikes me today as inevitable, rather than eccentric, that writers so in touch with the progress of art and literature, so at home with the symbolists of the nineteenth century who produced the aesthetic of the twentieth, should bring their talents to a field that has the most potential in English prose; or that such writers should be the ones to turn this genre on, around, and into something else.

3

There is also to be found a renowned and bold man; I did not wish to have mentioned his name, but it will not be hidden or unknown. For some years ago he wandered through almost every province, principality, and kingdom, made his name known to everybody, and boasted loudly of his great art, not only in medicine, but in chiromancy, necromancy, physiognomy, crystal-gazing, and more of such arts. And not only boasted, but gave himself out to be and wrote himself as a famous and experienced master. He also acknowledged and did not deny, that he was, and was called, Faust, and signed his name *Philosophus, Philosophorum, etc.*

—*Index Sanitatis*/ Philipp Begardi
(physician) of Worms, 1539

They are awesomely different writers.

When one defines categories like reductive symbolism and intensive symbolism, the first impulse is to cram Disch into one and Zelazny into the other. They lap out and over, and will not stay. Fine, then. What are they separately?

The accessible canon of Disch's works to date includes the four novels: *The Genocides* (1965), *Mankind under the Leash* (1966), *Echo Round His Bones* (1967) and *Camp Concentration* (1968). There is also the British short-story collection *One Hundred and Two H-Bombs*. Then there are a whole series of stories still to be anthologized in one collection that include some of his most effective work; *Descending, Assassin and Son, Come to Venus Melancholy, Doubting Thomas, The Squirrel Cage, The Roaches, Casablanca, Problems of Creativeness* [revised as *The Death of Socrates*, in '334', 1974]. Of the novels, the first is baroque with promise and ends on a perfect lyric of horror. The middle two are both *tours de force* in their own way; the most recent, *Camp Concentration*, is the first book within the s-f field I have read for which my reaction was simple, total and complete envy: "I wish I had written that." Enjoyment—and there have been many fine s-f novels that I have enjoyed—is a much coarser thing.

Camp Concentration takes its resonances from the host of European retellings of the Faust story. The form of the book is borrowed from Goethe: The story falls into Part I, which abounds in color, involvement, real and surreal, and concerns itself with its main problems as they might be handled by the liberal arts. Part II, like its German antecedent, is much bleaker, more intellectualized, difficult, and grapples with the same problems as they might be handled by science. The characters of the book, midway, give a performance of Marlowe's *Dr. Faustus*, and the abandoned sets and cast-off costumes become decor for many of the important scenes following. Convert due is paid Mann's *Doctor Faustus:* there is a lady composer named Adrienne Leverkuhn. Besides the name, Disch has also taken Mann's association of genius with venereal disease. But where Mann's association is romantic, Disch's is ironic (and hysterically funny when it comes to the fore) and for me the more effective. Intensely theological, heretical, medieval and modern, the book touches as well on some of the concerns of *My Faust* by Valéry, who is quoted in the book.

In 1975 the War in Vietnam (or at any rate a war) is still going on. Louis Sacchetti, an American poet, has been imprisoned as a conscientious objector. There is an analogue here to Robert Lowell's imprisonment, as well as an echo of Sacco and Vanzetti. The hero is also *"nel mezzo del cammin di nostra vita"*—Dante at the beginning of the descent. His journal recounts how he is taken from Springfield prison after his first two weeks in jail and transferred to Camp Archimedes, where macabre research is being done with drugs that increase human intelligence, with tragic side effects. But the major tragedy is the view of life that Sacchetti and the other human guinea pigs—most of them from the sociopathic dregs that fill an army brig during wartime—must face with their new intelligence. Midway through the book, Sacchetti records:

"The misery...the inexpressible misery of what is being done here."

The microcosm of Camp Archimedes is a gruesome allegory of man's painful acquisition of external and internal knowledge.

Mordecai, a black prisoner who plays Mephistopheles in the Marlowe production (directed by a prisoner named, ironically, George Wagner, who also takes the part of Faust), exclaims shortly before a quasi-epileptic fit brought on by the drugs that have made him a genius: "I am not *interested* in a universe where I have to die!"

These are the human parameters of the book.

Though the Faust legend constitutes the conceit of the novel, its controlling passion is Archimedean (i.e., Apollonian); the focus is knowledge, rather than the show it can be put to, the things it can buy (the modern interpretation of the Faustian flaw). The wit and ease with which Disch moves among bacteriology, theology, alchemy, Flemish painting, and modern literature never blurs the major concern, which is: the human responsibility that comes from the acquisition of knowledge.

(And I think this is the time to mention that whatever the specific problem of a given s-f story, this is what s-f is about; and is the field's valid claim to our attentions.)

Because, with all the excellences of Disch, *Camp Concentration* is so far and away *the* exemplar, it is naturally the one to which a critic wants to devote the most space. Among Zelazny's works it is far more difficult to choose.

To date the body of Zelazny's writings consist of: the novelettes and novellas, *A Rose for Ecclesiastes*; *King Solomon's Ring*; *The Doors of His Face, the Lamps of His Mouth*; *The Graveyard Heart*; *The Furies*; *He Who Shapes*; *The Keys to December*; *For a Breath I Tarry*; *This Moment of the Storm*; *This Mortal Mountain*; *Damnation Alley*; the full length novels, ... *And Call Me Conrad* (1965); *Lord of the Light* (1967); *Creatures of Light and Darkness* (1969); and the material added to *He Who Shapes* that completes the novel *The Dream Master* (1966).

The whole *oeuvre* tends to mesh into one gorgeous fabric. Here and there evening lights pick out a scene—is it a desert on the Mars of *A Rose for Ecclesiastes*, or is it the Egypt of *Conrad*?—perhaps a storm—does it take place on the Venus of *Doors/Lamps*, or is it on the farther world described in *This Moment of the Storm*? The themes merge as well.

Immortality appears in one form or another in almost all his works; when it doesn't, there is suicide: faces of one coin. The clearest example is in the moving tale *The Keys to December*, in which the point is made that once immortality is achieved, to relinquish it *is* suicide.

Zelazny's basic premise about immortality is quietly revolutionary. The classical supposition—what makes Ahasuerus' fate a curse—is that given all eternity to live, life becomes gray, meaningless, and one must be crushed by the ennui of experience upon experience, repetition upon repetition. Implicit in Zelazny's treatment is the opposite premise: Given all eternity to live, each experience becomes a jewel in the jewel-clutter of life; each moment becomes infinitely fascinating because there is so much more to relate it to; each event will take on new harmonies as it is struck by the overtones of history and like experiences before. The most dour and colorless happening will be illuminated by the light of the ages. This is the *raison* behind the hallucinated, intensively symbolic language. Zelazny's gallery of immortals, Conrad Nomikos and Leota Mathilde Mason, Moore, Ungerer, Sam, Frost, and M'Cwyie (as well as the suicides like Charles Render and Jarry Dark), are burdened with the apprehension of "terrible beauty." Faust's desire to be totally involved experiencing life is the fate of Zelazny's heroes. The theme is Faustian; again, as with Disch, the treatment is Archimedean.

There is no other writer who, dealing with the struggle between life and death on such a fantastically rarified level, can evoke so much hunger for the stuff of living itself. In *A Rose for Ecclesiastes*, where the immortality almost fades into the russet desert of Mars, the battle is waged most movingly in the heart of the hero, Gallinger. He is a poet who has come on this early Martian expedition because of his phenomenal linguistic abilities. But although his poetry is brilliant, there is an implication that his soul is dead, partially through the stifling influence of his deceased minister father. The Martians, a race now almost entirely composed of longevous women, have resigned themselves to the sterility of their men and extinction. But when the dancer Braxa is gotten with child by Gallinger, he is compelled to return the sense of life the Martians have given him.

"Life is a disease of inorganic matter; love is a disease in organic matter."

This is the pessimism of the Martians Gallinger must overcome. To it, he holds up a rose.

"The final flower turns a burning head..."

And the flame sheds light on all that vivid, arid land "where the sun is a tarnished penny, the wind is a whip, where two moons play at hot-rod games, and a hell of sand gives you the incendiary itches every time you look at it."

Banks Mebane in his analysis of Zelazny's prose has pointed out its kinship with the metaphysical poets. But it is highly colloquial as well. The wonder of the prose is that it manages to keep such intensely compressed images alive and riding on the rhythms of contemporary American.

Though Gallinger is victorious in *Rose*, the victory is pyrrhic. His coming and triumph have been predicted; Braza's pregnancy turns out to have been contrived; and she does not love him. The "immortality" of the Martians is not real immortality ... they do die eventually. And Gallinger's suicide attempt fails. The mitigation of the usual Zelazny parameters makes *Rose* a more immediate work than, say, *Lord of Light*, where they exist as absolutes. The mitigation also probably explains its popularity.

There are several of his tales that I prefer to it, however: *Doors/Lamps*, *For a Breath I Tarry*, and *The Graveyard Heart*, for example.

But in the numerous lists of Zelazny stories ranged by preference, it is indicative of the man's breadth of appeal that there is such a variety of heading titles.

Zelazny's tale most openly related to the Faust theme is his novella *He Who Shapes*. Charles Render, psychiatrist extraordinaire, victim of his own death wish and the medieval phantasies of a beautiful, blind and wholly contemporary Lady of Shalott (herself a psychiatrist), is as much a modern Faust as Louis Sacchetti. Render not only has knowledge of the human mind, but a technological power that makes him master of a special effects gallery to rival Pal and Kubrick. He can shape the minds of his patients through controlled dreams.

The rendering of Render, his movements real and fantastic, has a sophistication that Disch, with all his intellectual bravura, misses. Zelazny makes Doctor Render a man with a domestic past and present, and delineates his fall within the limits of an exquisitely evoked profession. Perhaps the simple bid for reality adds the touch of density missing from poet Sacchetti.

Within its perfectly open framework, *He Who Shapes* is a difficult tale. Once the difficulties have been broken through, it is a disturbing one.

The execution of the original novella was superb; it won Zelazny his second Nebula in 1965.

About a year later, he added some ten thousand words to the story, filling out the length of a standard novel, published by Ace as *The Dream Master*.

But let me backtrack some.

The original title of the novella was *The Ides of Octember*. The

phrase comes from the opening fantasia on the steps of the Senate
where Antony is being murdered while Caesar begs to be assassinat-
ed:

> "Have you an ill omen for me this day?"
> "Beware!" jeered Render.
> "Yes! Yes!" cried Caesar. " 'Beware!' That is good! Beware what?"
> "The ides—"
> "Yes? The ides—?"
> "—of October."
> "What is that you say? What is October?"
> "A month."
> "You lie! There is no month of October!"
> "And that is the date noble Caesar need fear—the non-existent-
> time, the never-to-be-calendared occasion."...
> "Wait! Come back!... You mock me," Caesar wept... "I want to
> be assassinated too!" he sobbed. "It isn't fair."

The scene ends, and we learn that Render is a psychiatrist and
Caesar is his patient, a Representative Erikson, who has erected a
paranoid anxiety syndrome (not quite a delusional system) in which
people are trying to assassinate him. Render terminates the therapy,
successfully, by making the politician realize that the general
depersonalizing forces of modern society, coupled with Erikson's
tendency to suppress completely his own individualism in pursuit of
his political ends, has forced his ego to rebel by erecting these
anxieties in an attempt to prove to himself that he is important
enough to assassinate. Erikson's desire for assassination is one side of
a double-faced mirror; one surface reflects the malady of the future
time Zelazny writes of, the other shows us something terribly
familiar. To catch the resonance with the real world, consider
Zelazny's tale in light of the assassination of Kennedy that had taken
place less than a year before he wrote the story; or the assassination of
Martin Luther King, which took place within a week of this writing.
Zelazny has picked images that vibrate sympathetically with the
times.

Because *He Who Shapes* is so much a story built on the
mechanics of a contemporary predicament, and because it shows so
much insight into their workings, internal hindrances that mute the
impact, or impede the evaluation of those insights, are terribly

frustrating. One cannot simply dismiss the new material added to make *The Dream Master:* Scene for scene, it is beautifully done, and amplifies both major and minor themes. My uneasiness is with placement, pacing and emphasis, which destroy the original dramatic unity of the whole; and because of the real excellences in the new material, the frustration is doubled.

The resonances of this tale of Faust-as-psychiatrist and his blind Helen are multiple. The man who makes fantasies real is an analogue for any artist or scientist; the death wish, the temptation to let fantasies completely cut one off from the real world, is a pertinent problem in today's blueprints.

I think the best way to approach *He Who Shapes* is to read the novella version first, and then turn to the new material in the novel (contained between pages 54 and 109 of *The Dream Master* in the Ace edition) as a commentary and amplification. This is the only way I can think of to get the benefits of both versions and avoid the distraction of the novel's structural weakness.

Faust risks destruction before the intensity of his own vision: and in this tale, the one thing left unambiguous in both versions, he is destroyed.

4

I knew a man named Faustus of Kundling, a little town near my home. When he studied at Cracow, he had learned magic, which was formerly keenly studied there and where public lectures were delivered about his art. Later he wandered about in many places and spoke about secret things. When he wanted to create a sensation in Venice, he announced that he was going to fly into the heavens. The Devil then lifted him up in the air, but let him fall back to earth again...

Locorum Comunium Colectunea
Johannes Manlius, 1565

What is the use of symbolism?

An IBM brochure giving a layman's explanation of the way mathematicians and computers solve a problem: "First the problem must be correctly stated. Then a convenient model of the problem must be constructed, one that can be manipulated easily. When the model is manipulated properly, the solution can be read from the model."

The representation that the symbolist makes of the world is a model that must be manipulated to solve the problems of human consciousness.

The major themes of both writers are Faustian. Even in *The Genocides*, Disch's interloper into the primitive world of Buddy and his family, the comparatively sophisticated and knowledgeable Orin, refugee from the articulate middle class, is a man who knows too much. Nathan Hansard, in *Echo Round His Bones*, is alien to a world that has gone totally "in," and, with his doubled vision of real and unreal worlds existing simultaneously, is a man with too much knowledge thrust upon him.

But this is what we are today: we are burdened with knowledge enough to comprehend the absurdity of a universe that creates such magnificent and malicious beasts, then kills them at the end of seventy-odd circuits of a wet rock round a G-type star.

What are *we* doing here?

We must become receptors to every nuance and shading of life, both the inner and the outer, to make ourselves worthy of the immortality we all seek (on one level or another): This is what I read from the panorama of Zelazny's work. A corollary to this answer is a warning that if we allow ourselves anything less than the richness, death—either spiritual or real—is the alternative.

A reading from the Disch model is more complex. First of all, Disch sees the obstacles to salvation as far more difficult—perhaps his view is more realistic. In Zelazny, religion, for example, becomes a Protestant minister father whose influence is primarily psychological rather than ethical: Overcoming the obstacles it presents is basically a matter of sufficiently impassioned denial. Or: It is sort of a pop-Buddhism rendered exquisitely and with superlative scholarship; but, because of the understated and overstated ironies, under a severe ethical examination it turns out to be pretty much congruent with the "Protestant ethic."

For Disch, in *Camp Concentration*, religion is the Roman Catholic background and upbringing of his hero, which, though he has made his break with organized religion, is still the cornerstone of his intellectual foundations. Religion permeates every argument; the arguments are brilliant, both logically and theologically. And Sacchetti wins. For me, Disch's treatment of the religious obstacles to personal salvation is the more significant. Disch also seems, at first, more aware of the reality of the social institutions, the "organizations" that oppose the individual. But Zelazny has the sophistication to realize that such "organizations" are the projected reality of just such wounded individualists (what else is the theme of *The Graveyard Heart*?); and this seems to me, regardless of the very real damage such organizations cause a culture, the saner view. The personal obstacles Disch sees in the way of man realizing himself are the ethical, psychological and emotional problems of alienation that have plagued all the thinkers of the twentieth century. And his examination of these problems is as incisive as one would expect from a writer with the battery of twentieth century thought behind him.

Zelazny has chosen a valid, but not subtle, answer. The manipulations he imposes on his model are magnificently skilled.

Disch has begun to trace a more intricate solution; but the manipulations of his model sometimes foul. For instance, I am as unhappy with the finale of *Camp Concentration* as I am impressed with its development. "I am not *interested* in a universe where I have to die!" is a tragic statement only within such a universe. The cruelest thing I could say of both authors is to quote a friend unacquainted with either man personally, who felt the same dissatisfaction with the ending: "It suddenly brings the book back into Roger Zelazny land."

I cannot read a complete solution from Disch. Judith Merril, in a review, refers to his "erudite despair," but when he does pose a solution, it is always buoyantly optimistic, if unfocused. Perhaps it is the contrast between this and the clarity of his opening vision that causes the less precisely presented optimism to be overlooked. What one does take away from the Disch model is that salvation lies in the direction of the acquisition of as much knowledge and insight as possible.

However much he is called a charlatan, Faust must take the responsibility for the wisdom contained in his books.

5

But Doctor Faustus within a short time after he had obtained his degree, fell into such fantasies and deep cogitations, that he was marked of many, and of the most part of the Students was called the Speculator...

The History of the Damnable Life and Deserved Death of Doctor John Faustus, 1592

According to legend Faust, at the end of his life, was court magician for one of the German barons. At dinner one evening, looking very perturbed, Faust announced to his patron that he was involved in a great work of magic and alchemy and that there was a good chance that he would be dead by morning. That night the castle was shaken violently; the courtiers rushed into the Doctor's laboratory to discover the place a shambles; the Doctor was dead with "his head turned backwards." People blamed the Devil. They assumed that Faust's pact with the Prince of Darkness had terminated that night: The Devil had come to collect his payment. It is fairly simple to infer what must have happened. Faust had been experimenting with explosives and that evening warned the baron who was sponsoring him of the danger. (At nearly the same time, the Borgias were employing Leonardo in Italy to invent them war machines.) The experiment blew up in Faust's face, wrecked the laboratory, and broke his neck.

The apocryphal tale of Archimedes' death is rather different. Archimedes was drawing circles in the sand on the beach at Syracuse when the Roman armies invaded. Although the troops had specific orders not to harm him (Archimedes' war machines—various catapults, and a parabolic burning-mirror that could reputedly fire enemy ships as they entered the harbor—had already kept the Romans at bay two weeks), a Roman foot soldier, not recognizing the commonly dressed old man sitting on the sand making designs with a stick, slew the sage when he tartly ordered the soldier to move out of his sunlight so he could continue his meditations.

Faust dies victim to his own knowledge gone abruptly out of control.

Archimedes dies in its calm pursuit; his fault is a lack of comprehension of the world outside his focus of interest.

As our focus of interest widens, Faust's demise becomes the more relevant; and it is the one that writers from Australia's Patrick White to America's William Gaddis turn to examine. If Faust was, in reality, a charlatan—that is, if the gift of *engagement* that Mephistopheles claims he can grant turns out not to be total, and Faust is not really "happy"—even so, that charlatanry has fascinated five hundred years of intellectuals in all the languages of Europe.

Disch and Zelazny are very much in touch with this intellectual tradition. Zelazny has dealt directly with Faust in a short tale called *The Salvation of Faust*; I have read it several times, and it is one of the few pieces by him where I can honestly say that I find the ending obscure.

Their concerns are very much the concerns of contemporary intellectuals. S-f has its largest and most literate following in the high schools and campuses across the country—comparatively intellectually aware areas. Pure and simple identification is the biggest reason behind the popularity of both men.

But beyond popularity, dedication is needed to fulfill the promise both writers have shown. Anyone who would be Archimedes risks being Faust. The dedication is necessary, for the work, for the writer, and for the reader who would benefit.

If we are to solve the problem of what to do with our consciousness, we need more and more astutely constructed models as that consciousness changes, develops. They must have relevance and flexibility; and the execution must be fine enough to endure.

Faust was the creator of magnificent effects.

Archimedes was the maker of models. The discovery of specific gravity, the discovery of the relation between the volumes of the cylinder and the enclosed sphere, even the Archimedean screw, were problems solved by the representation of general problems by a specific example.

Zelazny and Disch have changed science fiction in America.

Heinlein's didacticism certainly has not convinced me such a model could come from s-f. Sturgeon's meticulous analysis of love suggests it might—possibly makes it possible. (That alone would assure him generic preeminence; and he has done much more.) Yet today, among many, many others—and the change dates from the arrival of these writers—I think such a model can.

NEW YORK
MARCH, 1968

Alyx

1

In Joanna Russ's recently published novel *The Female Man* (Bantam Books, New York, 1975) a woman from an alternate future comes to live with a typical American family—father, mother, teenage daughter, in "Anytown, U.S.A." The encounter is shocking, traumatic, lives are changed, layers of social and psychological defenses are stripped, protesting, away.

In the last novella of the early series we call, after the name of its heroine, *Alyx*, a woman from an alternate future comes to live with a typical American family—father, mother, teenage daughter, somewhere in Green County during the summer of 1925 (the same summer that saw publication, in July, of fifteen-year-old Robert E. Howard's first story, "Spear and Fang," in *Weird Tales*). The encounter is so muted, so down-played, so low-key that, though this woman fights for the freedom of the Universe, chaperones the daughter to a dance, takes on an eccentric garage mechanic for a lover, commits murder, and makes love on the back porch, the suspicion lingers that perhaps, somehow, it is all a fantasy and not science fiction at all.

The last of the *Alyx* stories, "The Second Inquisition," may someday be called the end of "early Russ." There are plays and short stories from before then. But the major work till this time is certainly the series, here collected, that begins with "Bluestocking" (written 1963, published under the title "The Adventuress" in Damon Knight's *Orbit Two*, G.P. Putnam, New York, 1967), continues with "I Thought She Was Afeard Till She Stroked My Beard" (written

1963, published under the title "I Gave Her Sack and Sherry," also in *Orbit Two*), is furthered in "The Barbarian" (written 1965, published in *Orbit Three*, 1968), climaxes in the novel *Picnic in Paradise* (written during the winter of 1967/68, published under the title *Picnic on Paradise* by Ace Books, New York, 1968), and concludes with "The Second Inquisition" (written spring 1968, published in *Orbit Six*, 1970).

Were I asked for a single, subjective response to characterize these tales, I would call them "cold." I mean nothing so blatant as the fact that the novel, for instance, takes place on a world encased in ice. I mean an effect of language which, even as the words talk of high fervors, swordplay, or bone-staggering action, runs through the early March meadows of the mind like a morning freshet that, only hours before, was a ribbon of crackled ice, and whose edges still bear a lace of frost and whose current still carries frozen platelets to tick the collared grassblades and clover stems jutting from it.

All the stories in the series are highly playful, though the playfulness in each is pitched at a different level. All are witty. Most are deeply touching; but they touch and play with cold, cold fingers.

2

There is an American literary myth about a perfectly transparent language, a language that is accurate and unornamented; that draws no attention to itself; that lets us through, without verbal distraction, directly to its object. This myth is particularly cherished by the high-production writers of commercial fiction whose style we call, at our most generous, not the most interesting thing about their work. This myth is a displaced notion: it emigrated here from those languages which were traditionally looked over by a National Academy, e.g., French, Spanish, Italian. Academy languages can aspire to, and from time to time achieve something that for a generation or so will pass for, a *style blanc*. English and American cannot. The reason is no failing of talent or temperament in our writers but rather a matter of the ontology of the language itself. Writing that draws least attention to itself is writing that is most like most other writing. And most writing in America is not particularly accurate, observant, succinct, or vivid. For this reason, writing that is *is* unusual; the unusual catches our attention. And the sentences and phrases in such writing that invoke their objects with particular strength and directness are experienced not as transparent and common but as extraordinary and, in themselves, as ornament.

The concept of a writer writing a vivid and accurate scene in a language transparent and devoid of decoration so that we see through to the object without writerly distraction suffers the same contradiction as the concept of a painter painting a vivid and accurate scene with pigments transparent and devoid of color—so that the paint will not get between us and the picture.

Russ's language in her latest novels (*And Chaos Died*, Ace Books, New York, 1970; *The Female Man*, Bantam Books, New York, 1975) is a compendium of (and, in *The Female Man*, almost a textbook on) various rhetorical modes—rhapsody, polemic, satire, fantasy, foreground action, psychological naturalism, reverie, and invective—each brought, in its turn, within the science-fiction frame for the changes that result. What allows her to perform these experiments with such authority and success is the control, incision, and precision you can find in these earlier *Alyx* tales—sometimes, there, put to very simple tasks, but never absent.

Russ's later novels are science fiction, though they appropriate other modes of discourse to their science-fictional purposes.

At least three of the stories in the *Alyx* series are not science fiction but sword-and-sorcery, that odd subgenre invented (for all practical purposes) by Robert E. Howard; if the wit and irony apparent through Russ's tales owe more to Fritz Leiber's variant of the genre than to Howard's (In "Bluestocking," Alyx's description of a former lover—

"I was remembering a man."

"Oh!" said Edarra.

"I remembered," said Alyx, "one week in spring when the night sky above Ourdh was hung as brilliantly with stars as the jewelers' trays in the Street of a Thousand Follies. Ah! what a man. A big Northman with hair like yours and a gold-red beard—God what a beard!— Fafnir—no, Fafh—well, something ridiculous. But he was far from ridiculous. He was amazing."

Edarra said nothing, rapt.

"He was strong," said Alyx, laughing, "and hairy, beautifully hairy. And willful! I said to him, 'Man, if you must follow your eyes into every whorehouse—' And we fought! At a place called the Silver Fish.

Overturned tables. What a fuss! And a week later," (she shrugged ruefully) "gone. There it is. And I can't even remember his name."

"Is that sad?" said Edarra.

"I don't think so," said Alyx. "After all, I remember his beard," and she smiled wickedly.

—refers, of course, to Fritz Leiber's hero, Fafhrd; Leiber reciprocated by putting Alyx in as a minor character in his tale "The Two Best Thieves in Llahnkmar." And to understand why the second use of the verb is in the simple past ["I remembered"] rather than the imperfect ["I was remembering"] you must find and read the entire scene), still the original parameters which center the genre are Howard's.

The novel in the series *is* science fiction. The concluding novella sits squarely on the three-way border between fantasy, s-f, and naturalism. Yet in all, the prose is cold, crystalline, and sharp.

Traditionally, sword-and-sorcery is written with a sort of verbal palette knife—an adjective-heavy, exclamatory diction that mingles myriad archaisms with other syntactical distortions meant to signal the antique: the essence of the pulps. But there is a paradox in the development of pulp styles—for there is not and never was just one. Of the several that existed each was adapted to its various jobs; each fed the others; each learned from the others. And the result was that, among the workaday professional fiction writers, one of whose most cherished myths was of an effortless and "transparent" American prose, such a prose was, finally, developed—or at least one that came as close to giving that effect as possible.

The nearest America ever came to a "classic" style—that style it so envied in its continental cousins—was the style brought to pitch by Dashiell Hammett and polished by the English-raised Raymond Chandler. The "great styles" central to American fiction—Hemingway's, Faulkner's, James's—are personally architected languages, idiosyncratic, highly eccentric. They are insistently regional, tailored to the exploration of some particular corner of the nation or the psyche.

And not one could be taken for the language of a people—which is what a classic style demands. The language of the pulps, as it was honed and sharpened by Hammett, Chandler, and James M. Cain, *used* the idioms of American speech—that is, it used them unadorned; and it modulated them; and it ran changes on them; and it played with them. It was a prose which, to read properly, required you know those idioms and recognize them even altered. This is not the language of Mark Twain, O. Henry, or Damon Runyon; theirs was merely decorated—however artfully—with colloquialisms to suggest local color. Their stories were, by comparison, merely museums in which colloquial turns of phrase were preserved—intact, but no longer alive.

The best of this pulp prose was a language committed to foreground clarity. It always sought the most hard-headed reason behind any happening. It had wit. It had pith. If it tended to talk about subjects larger than life—the dealings of heroic detectives and pathetic criminals—well, the same can be said of the classic language of Homer.

The centers of American mundane fiction speak a personalized, romantic language. A romantic language admits of blasphemy but always keeps one range of speech socially unacceptable and, by extension, a range of subjects for which no language is considered fit, e.g., the functions of the body or the realities of the passions. A classic language has no forbidden words and, as such, no forbidden subjects; but there is a certain type of violence to the soul with which it refused to deal—specifically the violence that sunders the relation between the human and the divine when certain parts of language are forbidden—precisely the violence that provokes the blasphemies classic language will have no truck with.

To talk about such things in America, we must remember that because such language was born in the pulps, in America that language that most resembles the classic (you will find its echoes in the comic scripts of O'Neil and Wein, in the pornography of Vassi and Perkins...) is not central but maverick.

Most science fiction that we think of as having style draws its basic diction from this (best of the) pulp tradition. This is the framework supporting Russ's language. What is fascinating, however, is to listen, above that frame, to the modulation in narrative tone as we pass from the stories to the novel, from the novel to the novella—the modulation from the most formalized diction the frame will allow to the most informal: the real speech of a real young woman whose adolescence spanned the midpoint of this century's third decade.

3

To talk any more about the *Alyx* stories, we must go back, however, to the worst of the pulps—or rather the pulps at their glorious/worst best: the *Conan* stories of the thirty-year-old suicide, Robert E. Howard. The specific question we must go back to is: What is the relation between sword-and-sorcery and science fiction?

Because there is one.

It is no good trying to dismiss the question with a quick "science fiction is good; sword and sorcery is bad." Temperaments attracted to one are frequently attracted to the other. Publishers deal with them as though they were the same genre. Indeed, it was only the early specialty publisher of one who would even consider publishing the other. And the other three greatest writers of sword-and-sorcery—Fritz Leiber, C. L. Moore, and Michael Moorcock—have all written science fiction of the first order, as has Russ.

The *Alyx* stories, which move among genres with such grace, bring, by that grace, the embarrassing question to the fore: What *is* the relation?

The opening two tales are the swordiest of sword-and-sorcery; the third is only a few dials and traveling spotlights away from the most sorcerous; and, despite its dials, lights, and the word "machine," it certainly doesn't *feel* like science fiction. In the novel, when our precivilized heroine is transported into the future, we have a tale that *does* feel like science fiction; and the closing novella, while its surface demands to be taken as science fiction, keeps evoking feelings that tend to veer our reading of it toward a psychological fantasy similar to that of Gene Wolfe's justly praised "The Island of Doctor Death and Other Stories"—though by eschewing the social extremes of Wolfe's story (the drug-addict mother, the death by overdose, which, when all praise is done, tend to reduce Wolfe's sensitive portrait of an imaginative boy to a rather preachy little moral), Russ keeps the center of the problem before us: It is the central certainties of our society that drive us to the edge (rather than the makeshift strategies we devise to live at the edge which, sometimes, catapult us into death and chaos—as in the Wolfe tale).

The intuitive answer that directs our exploration is a suspicion that sword-and-sorcery may just express the archetypal underpinnings beneath the cognitively recomplicated surfaces we recognize as science fiction. As one can speak of the simple calculus (frequently called, until the work of G. Spencer Brown, trivial) implicit behind the set of algebras called Boolean, the comparatively limited landscape of sword-and-sorcery may be the simple fantasy behind the extremely varied set of future landscapes we call science fiction.

Science fiction is a literature that espouses (despite its liberal/conservative backslidings) an almost die-hard cultural relativism. As such it constantly strives to present itself (however badly it succeeds) as anational.

The specific conventions of various traditional types of fantasy are simply too ethnically located to support, as a basal fantasy structure, the intraethnocism so much s-f tries for: Elves and fairies are too specifically Celtic; trolls and goblins too specifically Germanic; vampires, ghouls, and golems are too specifically middle-European. To say that sword-and-sorcery begins as a bunch of Vikings, half of whose hair has been dyed black, thrown down as frequently in an African jungle as into a hyperborian waste (and then all the names juggled around) is to say that, in attempt at any rate, all historical nationality has, at least in emblem, been shattered.

And I remember very clearly, as a fascinated, fourteen-year-old reader of *Conan the Conqueror* in the Ace Double paperback or the Gnome Press hardcover, that it was precisely those mentions of Picts or other tribes with names recognizable from history which set me skimming. (A passing mention of a possible historical Atlantis in Michael Ventris's *The Decipherment of Linear-B* which I read at about the same time, ruined forever my enjoyment of Howard's other sword-and-sorcery series, *King Kull*.) What one wanted, even at fourteen, was a landscape which, in all its anthropological possibility, remained totally malleable: Real historical ties, no matter how tenuous, limited this malleability too much.

For sword-and-sorcery to be at its best, one needs a landscape that is "on the brink of civilization" in an almost scientifically ideal way. It is only here that one can truly play the game.

More precisely, I suspect, sword and sorcery represents what can, most safely, still be imagined about the transition from a barter economy to a money economy. (One might even say, instead of imagined, "remembered." But to remember anything from before one's own personal memory begins is, of course, as much an act of imagination, in its essence, as any vision of the future might be.) By the same light, science fiction represents what can most safely be imagined about the transition from a money economy to a credit economy.

G. Spencer Brown, in *Laws of Form* (Julian Press, 1969), notes as a manifestation of the abstract calculus he is developing (in a passing argument in Chapter Eight, page 42), that the value of a content is reversed by its image; but to go on to an image of an image gives us a *new* content to deal with. An example (my own, not Brown's) might be a t-shirt with a word written across the front, i.e., the content. If I put the t-shirt on and look into a mirror, i.e., at the image, I see the word reversed left/right, i.e., with its values reversed. If I take two mirrors, however, and turn myself so I can see the image in the first mirror reflected in the second, i.e., an image of an image, what I shall be seeing is what is on the *back* of the t-shirt, i.e., a new content.

If we take barter as the initial content of the exchange system, and the resultant power structure as its value, then the introduction of money into the system introduces into society an image of that content. The subsequent reversal of values, as the money system becomes the absolute mode of exchange, results (as Marx has argued exhaustively) from the fact that money exists as a *complement* to material, skill, and labor. Wherever money *is* (both in time and space), material and labor either *were* or *will be*; but they are not *now*. In a barter system, someone with strength, skill, or goods may immediately take it to someone with food, shelter, or other goods, confident she is taking with her real, social power. In a money system, someone with strength, skill, or goods must first go to make an exchange with someone with money—before she can then go to get food, shelter, or other material. To the extent the system is closed to other forms of exchange, the money itself becomes the power, not what the money buys. And both psychology and sociology shift to accommodate this new reversal of the power structure.

The credit system introduced into the exchange system arises as an image of the money system: An image of an image, we recall, creates a *new* content. Credit, introduced into a money system, creates a *new* space, which is not an inverse of the space of goods and labor, but a space that exists simultaneously with it, alongside of it. (In credit, one's assets—one's material and labor—as well as one's money, determine the size of one's active credit.) It is in this new space that, in our society at any rate, most of the technological advances which are the prime concern of science fiction occur.

We need to remember the old barter content, as well as what happened when we left it; we need to speculate about the new contents of credit space that manifest themselves all around us and speculate about how to get to them reasonably lest the journey destroy us. (In Russ's novel, of course, it is not the actual wonders of technology that are explored—though both at the beginning and the end of the tale, like great parentheses, technological wonders are there in profusion. It is rather about the behavior and psychology of people brought up with these wonders; but this is not a displacement of the subject so much as it is a focusing on the subject's values.)

Because both sword-and-sorcery and science fiction are popular literatures, what is posited about the respective transition periods they deal with tends to emphasize the socially safe. But as frequently it suggests the socially necessary. To locate the socially necessary one has only to look at the real dangers these "escapist" forms are, indeed, trying to escape from.

Sword-and-sorcery begins as a specifically male escape from the coming responsibility of marriage, family, and a permanent home: i.e., wife, children, job. Its purpose, the people who publish, advertise, and sell it say, is to provide the adolescent male audience with a bigger, stronger man to identify with, who rescues the woman, beats up the villain, and who is loved briefly and allowed to leave without hassle.

Fairy tales—or fairy-tale plots—will simply not suffice for this: They are about nothing *but* the binding alliances formed between worthy young men and wealthy fathers-in-law, with docile daughters acting as the sign of the exchange of the paternal social position. (This of course is the definition of "sex object," whether princess or prostitute or *Playboy* centerfold—where paternal social position becomes generalized to the entire socioeconomic matrix of Father Hefner, expressed in every advert and illo and pop culture acquisition that *is* the magazine, and for which, at the magazine's center, stripped of all possible personal possessions, she becomes the perfect, empty sign.) In the traditional sword-and-sorcery tale, the hero is not the worthy prince, or even (in its Celtic version) the particularly clever bourgeois seeking to marry into the aristocracy by replacing inherited wealth with brains; he is the barbarian, an outlander, a stranger. His prototype in the fairy tale is *not* the prince but the troll whom the prince, journeying through the Great Bad Place, slays *en passant* on his way to the castle to receive his tasks. He is Caliban made human— indeed, he is Caliban rendered a little more than human thanks to the ultimately fragmented nature of the current organized society in transition (and, in the allegory, of sword-and-sorcery, it is precisely between the social fragments' grating edges that the sorcery will be found). Though he may have sex with the odd princess or serving wench, the significance of these encounters is precisely that they do *not* constitute terms for any alliance with her father. Given the fragmentary nature of our own society, the sword and sorcery template is more relevant than the fairy tale—as far as it goes. For in our society, those alliances between sons-in-law and fathers-in-law, both at society's upper and lower ends, have become meaningless—or rather at the lower end they have been rendered meaningless via the mobility afforded by car and bus; and at the upper, have given way to a more complex set of interchanges that, in some aspects, is much looser and in others much more strict about whom it accepts—this new interchange almost entirely mediated by the pill and the plane. And even in the middle classes of society, these alliances are seen to be more and more hollow, containing, frequently, little or no value but nostalgia for a vanished custom.

Beat up villain: get girl—the mistake here in the template for an essentially male escape fantasy should be evident to anyone who has ever attended, on a Saturday afternoon, a James Bond film with a primarily male, late adolescent audience: In the obligatory fight between Bond and the villain, while the heroine cowers in the corner, immobile with fear, every time her wide-eyed face comes on the screen, there are shouts of laughter and derision, and frequently calls of, "Why don't you *do* something, you stupid broad!" And at the final embrace, after the villain has been exploded or tossed into the piranha pool or ejected into outer space, there is a resigned sigh. The producers who analyze this as, "Well, the kids just don't like too *much* romance," are missing the point.

What these movies (and sword and sorcery) provide "escape" from, for the young male, is not sex, or even marriage *per se*. It is the prospect of sexual relations, in or out of marriage, in which the woman is assumed to be emotionally immature, clinging, dependent, an economic and psychological burden, incapable of offering any real assistance in the "partnership" should the "man" come under "attack." The reason your young male does not identify with what is on the screen during these scenes is because it looks all too much like an allegory of what he has come to the movies to escape: an encroaching social role in which, he has been told, the responsibility is *all* his. These scenes are not escapist; they are didactic preachments. And the response is the traditional one to preaching in the midst of entertainment: derision.

From the male point of view, the need for an archetypal female who is not a villainess, but who can nevertheless take care of herself and, upon occasion, him with nothing but her good right arm is glaring. She is needed, above all, to fill the gap in the fantasy structure so that what he fears as real will not intrude.

The hero of Russ's sword-and-sorcery tales is, of course, a woman. But it is important to emphasize that this woman's *traditional* archetype is not one which women set up for their own admiration, or to organize their own world goals around.

We must make it clear that such an archetype does not even broach any of the questions the Women's Movement asks. Such questions begin when a woman asks why the Saturday afternoon movie audience of 15- to 24-year-olds is 85 percent male in the first place. Where *is* 52 percent of the population? At home because of the kids, especially at that age, just won't account for the discrepancy. The Women's Movement begins when, once she has found the other, real women in society, she asks them: "What do *we* need; and how do *we* go about getting it for ourselves?"

That much of what is needed must be appropriated from men is just political reality. That aggression and general togetherness will, from time to time, be needed to accomplish that appropriation is just another. If the competent and together women of the Movement bear the slightest resemblance to the male-generated fantasy of the sword-and-sorcery fighting women (Valeria, Belit, or Red Sonya), it is an accident of male projection. And the resemblances *are* slight: The typical sword-and-sorcery fighting woman never appears on stage with another woman (unless to slaughter a villainess); much less is she concerned with how women—whether men consider them heroes, villainesses, or just ignorable—are treated in such an overmasculinized society.

The traditional sword-and-sorcery fighting woman is, by and large, a useless archetype for the Women's Movement. It encourages men to continue the totally insane "I will only respect you when you can knock me down" argument; it relieves not one burden of the double standard (Howard's fighting women are traditionally "virgin huntresses," who, it is implied, will lose their prowess should they ever fall for a man—which, of course, they never do); as written by men, it only adds a new twist to all the old contradictions of Frail Goddess/Evil Bitch: ".... and don't bother me when I've got something better to do, but come in swinging when I need you; and while you're at it, take care of yourself."

But because that image of competence and togetherness in women is, however accidentally, there in sword-and-sorcery, we must not be surprised if a woman writer, beginning with it, goes on to put it to very untraditional use.

Because of Howard's fighting women, Moore's Jirel of Joiry, and others, it is hard not to read Alyx as a sword-and-sorcery fighting woman. But from the first story, where her concern is the protection and education of the girl Edarra, she *is* a very untraditional one, to and for our benefit and entertainment (accomplished largely, Russ informs me, through not having actually read either *Conan* or *Jirel* when she wrote her own tales, but only having heard about them). The largest break with the sword-and-sorcery tradition is, of course, that there *are* women in Russ's tales; and they are concerned with one another's welfare. Possibly an even larger break is that there is, at least, one—and this is what sword and sorcery banishes entirely from its landscape—husband in the series.

He is killed in the second story.

As a resonance (for the word "husband" in "The Barbarian" refers not to her former, but to her present, man), he haunts the third.

Editor Damon Knight published the first two stories, somewhat to the author's surprise, in the wrong order. My own suspicion (which I have never consulted the author about) is that, as a male, he saw Alyx born in the unhappy relationship with that husband, only to pass on through a fleeting encounter with religion. This probably seemed to him to preserve the "logical" (i.e., traditional) relation of men to women, and women to religion. That Alyx was born of an unhappy relation with religion, only to pass on through some fleeting encounters with husbands, puts husbands in such an untraditionally

minor role in the scheme of things that it never occurred to Knight
that it might be the right one.

The point, however, is that Alyx, whatever her suffering at the
hands of male editors (or critics), is not a feminist figure—as some
male readers have taken her for. She is rather a figure of
protofeminist consciousness. But then, the relation of most sword-
and-sorcery to the real world is pretty "proto" at the best of times.

4

The *Alyx* stories, as we have mentioned, *are* a series.

Practically every s-f writer has left us at least one. When one
realizes that writers as different as Robert A. Heinlein and J. G.
Ballard, Ann McCaffrey and Brian Aldiss have all written them; or
that both Isaac Asimov's *Foundation Trilogy* and Theodore
Sturgeon's *More Than Human* are series stories put between sets of
covers, one begins to suspect that perhaps the series is *the* basic form
of the field.

The critical temptation with a series is to try to read successive
installments as if they were chapters in some particularly loosely-
constructed novel. Almost inevitably, though, they present us with
signs that insist, despite other signs of a serial chronology, that, rather
than successive chapters, they are really successive approximations of
some ideal-but-never-to-be-achieved-or-else-overshot structuring of
themes, settings, characters. One is tempted—especially when the
syndrome is pronounced, as with Ballard's *Vermillion Sands*
stories—to say that they are all rewrites of the same story, that all are
different workings-out of a single, synchronous structure that
persists, unchanged beneath various expressions. But the signs of a
to-be-accepted fictive diachrony are also present...

Whether such ambiguously synchronic/diachronic structures
are seen as rents in the otherwise coherent fictive field or truly rich
contours in that same field where truly useful exploration may occur
depends on our temperaments as readers, on what particularly we are
looking for in our experience of a single author's multiple creative
works.

The *Alyx* stories present us with a number of such fictive
contours. Edarra of "Bluestocking," Iris of *Picnic on Paradise*, and

the narrator of "The Second Inquisition" are by no means the "same character." They differ in age, temperament, cultural background, and general plot situation. Yet Alyx/Edarra, Alyx/Iris, and the "visitor"/narrator all organize our attention about a single problem: The problems a worldly woman has overseeing the maturation of a woman not so worldly.

Conflict between different cultural/historic moments yields another of these ambiguous parameters around which much of the reader's experience of the story ends up organized. In "The Barbarian," the conflict is ironic: The dials and lights of the fat man might as *well* be magic—or so all the signs of the sword-and-sorcery tale instruct us from beginning to end of the story. Yet it is precisely *because* Alyx recognizes them as the machines we know them to be (and, therefore, she knows their behavior is predictable) that the story exists. Philosophically, what this story is about is: Alyx knows the fat man is wrong (i.e., not God) because if he were right and the Universe were a mechanical product of his (specifically recognized as) machines (which he tries to pass off as magic), then the Universe would have to be deterministic. Alyx believes the Universe is indeterminate; probably this belief has something to do with the religious falling-away that precedes the first tale and that is, in a sense, the genesis of them all. Alyx knows the Universe is *over*determined, for that is what life on the margins of society teaches one. But she also knows—and this is the faith that traditionally comes to fill the absence left by the falling-away from any official dogma— that "overdetermined" is not the same as "determinate," no matter how much the evidence for one asks to be taken as evidence for the other. Thus her decisions: to save the governor's infant daughter— and kill the fat man.

In *Picnic on Paradise*, Alyx the barbarian is plucked by an offstage time-machine into the (a?) future and her barbaric talents are put at the service of a group of futuristic tourists who need someone to lead them across the ice of Paradise. The story (again) grows out of the conflict of cultures/histories: Alyx's "primitive" values against the "sophisticated" values of the tourists.

In the three stories that precede the novel, during her own epoch, Alyx's basic interest to us (most interestingly) is how much her general approach to life seems to be ahead of those around her. We have already mentioned her ability to recognize machines; and, in "I Thought She Was Afeard," her basic response to the carnage she has helped create on deck near the tale's end is: "'Why the devil,' she said with such sudden interest, 'don't the doctors cut up the bodies of dead people in schools to find out how they're put together?'"

That her black-bearded lover can offer no answer is, presumably, to be taken as an emblem of the many reasons that, in the next paragraph, she has left him. For all her good right arm, this is a much more modern consciousness than any that ever inhabited a Howard tale.

When Alyx arrives in the future, it is because of the practicality that underlies this (what can only be called, in the context of the landscape in which it occurs) intellectual whimsy—a very hard-headed attitude toward survival and destruction—that she is useful; that she is heroic.

In Russ's most recent novel, *We Who Are About To*...(Galaxy, 1975), in which a machine that translates voice into script allows us to read of the necessary extinction of yet another group of tourists stranded on yet another hostile world (but this time so much more subtly hostile!), this whimsicality has developed into (*not* been replaced by) a deep pessimism: Both the whimsicality and the pessimism express a rejection of transcendence as a socially (or logically) usable commodity—or what Jacques Derrida, our most incisive explicator of the relation between difference, deference, trace, and script, would call, approvingly, a denial of absolute presence.

But our concern is the series at hand.

The historical moments in conflict in the novella "The Second Inquisition" are that of a generation several ahead of the tourists' in *Picnic* and that of America in the summer of 1925. Over that gap passes the greatest violence—and the greatest compassion. I find it endlessly fascinating that this series, which begins with three tales of sword-and-sorcery, should end with such a meticulous evocation of the extra-urban environment so close in feel to the one (Cross Plains, Texas) that the genre's inventor, with his *Conan* tales, tried to escape—an environment the nostalgia for which (if this is not to trivialize what was certainly Howard's real despair over his mother's imminent death) drove him to suicide in 1936.

5

Joanna Russ was born in New York in 1937 and raised in the Bronx. The autobiographical paragraph in the frontmatter of her first two novels tells of a childhood exploring vacant lots and the botanical gardens, a Westinghouse Science Prize.

The first time I became aware of her was through some early stories in *The Magazine of Fantasy and Science Fiction*. A few months later, in 1966, I attended my first Milford s-f Writers' Conference, which Damon Knight and Kate Wilhelm hosted in their sprawling, lofty-beamed home, the Anchorage. When I arrived in Milford, Judy Blish met me at the bus stop and drove me back to the Knights'; I recall walking across the white, slightly warped porch boards and edging through the glass-paned door into the living room, with its vaulted fireplace scattered with coals and its circle of 42 writers (perhaps six of whom I knew by sight from my first s-f convention only a week before); the workshop was already under way, and the story passing around for criticism, as I shrugged out of my second-hand army jacket and brought up a chair beside the worn arm of the green-plush couch, was producing some baffled and baffling remarks. One tall person a few seats to my left I quickly identified as the author. (Milford writers under workshop discussion must remain silent through the first round of criticism. This does not, however, prevent them from spluttering a little.) Finally the manuscript reached another tall person, seated almost directly across from me, near the fire, wearing tremendous silver earrings and a pale blue sweater over her shoulders; she leaned her elbows forward on the knees of her gray felt skirt and said: "First of all, this story is based on a Swinburne poem, 'The Garden of Persephone,' and all this confusion is simply because those who are familiar with the poem get the story: Those who aren't, don't."

And across the circle, the other tall person ceased spluttering and relaxed.

What characterized Russ's comments for me during that workshop were two traits that are rare enough separately and even rarer in combination: uncommonly wide learning and uncommon common sense. With a circle of 42 extremely intelligent and extremely eccentric writers, most comments about the stories were intelligent and/or interesting.

Russ's comments tended to be what needed to be said.

The next time I saw her was when she dropped over after dinner at Terry and Carrol Carr's Brooklyn Heights apartment, perhaps six months later; perhaps six weeks after that, Terry (then editing for Ace) sent me galleys of the *Alyx* novel here included, *Picnic on Paradise*, for advance comment.

I think what most fascinated me about the book, even as I ripped the wire from the gray-packed, double-thickness book-mailer, was that, until I received galleys in the mail, I hadn't known the book existed.

The science-fiction world is a small and gregarious one. Even people who don't talk about their work much end up letting you know ("What are you working on now?" "Oh, a novel.") that they are working on *some*thing—even if they don't regale you with title and plot, or whip out sections of manuscript from inner pockets and keep you at bay in the corner with an hour's impromptu reading. Russ had always impressed me as a lively person and not particularly shy. (She is a very fine public lecturer.) I was very impressed with this reticence.

I was even more impressed with the novel.

Fritz Leiber, in his cover notice, mentions reading it in a single sitting. So did I: and a day later, a friend of mine who'd dropped by in the afternoon absently picked up the galleys from the table and read the first sheet; and the second; and then the third . . . I began to supply the occasional silent cup of coffee and went on about my own business in the kitchen.

A couple of hours later, my friend put down the last galley sheet, looked up, and announced: "That book's the realest thing that's happened to me in years!"

Which is just one of those attempts to express what is ultimately most important and most inexpressible about fine works of art.

An amusing anecdote here: when I went into the Ace Books office to return the galleys and deliver my most sincere accolade, Terry Carr leaned back at his desk and asked: "Well, what did you think?"

"The book's superb," I said. "Other than a couple of proofreading errors, I've only got one beef: Why don't you call it 'Picnic in Paradise'? It's so much more mellifluous; and besides, it points out the irony so much more strongly." Terry lowered his chin and looked at me over the upper edge of his glasses. "The original title *was* 'Picnic in Paradise.' *We* made her change it to 'Picnic *on*'—so people would know it was science fiction. Otherwise, they might think it was a romance."

Picturing "romances" with rocketships and snow-bound Frazetta barbarian ladies on the covers, I said, "Oh . . ." and retired.

But by the time I left the office that afternoon in the spring of 1968, I suspect that "The Second Inquisition" had already been written. (The author once described it to me as an "overflow from the novel," written in an intense period of concentrated work, soon after.) Russ was soon to go on to Cornell University as assistant professor. (Currently she teaches at the University of Colorado at Boulder.*) Her next three novels were to assay aesthetic, political, and moral concerns previously absent from the field. In *Picnic,* however, she had produced that exemplary journeyman work, all elements of which seem, at first glance, familiar, but whose assemblage, inspection reveals, employs techniques new to the extant battery any master must applaud, if not envy.

Before I delivered the galleys back to the office, I had read the book a second time. From that second reading (and I have read it several times since), a point remains with me that perhaps will not only illuminate the novel, but will also cast sidelights on the other stories.

The impetus among academics to define science fiction as a particular type of discourse, a particular sort of "word machine," that performs certain functions, literary and/or sociological, (e.g., the functions of "cognition and estrangement") rather than simply a group of themes and conventions, began in the middle sixties—at practically the same time that the s-f distinguishing itself as the most interesting then being written was busily appropriating for itself elements from other discourse modes outside the basic science-fiction battery: avant-garde fiction, poetry, journalism . . . That Russ's stories move from sword-and-sorcery to s-f and beyond puts them directly in the tradition of the s-f of its time that was so busily stepping over so many boundary lines. To put it in more high-flown, comp. lit. terms: In Russ's science fiction the privileges (i.e., the easy sureties) of one mode of discourse are subverted by employing signs from another mode—which cause us to reconstruct the discourse from one

---

*Since 1977 she has been Associate Professor of English at the University of Washington—Seattle.

mode to the other: as soon as the story has fixed itself, by various signs, as sword-and-sorcery, new signs suddenly appear that cause us to take the whole thing apart in our head and put it back together again as s-f (this happens specifically in "The Barbarian"); or, as soon as we are settled with the idea that we are reading an s-f story, signs come along (as in "The Second Inquisition") that the story is psychological fantasy; and yet the moment we settle on this mode for our reading, other signs emerge that put us squarely back in s-f. These mental reconstructions do not represent confusion. They are organized so that they themselves become prime delights of the tale.

One set of such signs that the second reading of *Picnic on Paradise* clearly fixes is that every major incident in the novel is presaged by some passing thought, fear, or wish in Alyx's mind. If we were to read these presagements as strict s-f, they would send us off on what any sensible reader of the novel must agree is wild goose chases concerning clairvoyance or Alyx's possible strange mental powers that actually can effect the future. If, on the other hand, we were to read them as strict signs of psychological fantasy, then we would be thrown off on an equally wild chase about whether any of this was "really" happening: Perhaps, like the final illusion of Machine, it is *all* in Alyx's mind...

Of course, these "presagements" are signs for neither one nor the other. They are not there for the second reading; they are there specifically for an ideal first, where the effect is to lend a rigorous, but subtle (yet nevertheless felt) psychological coherence to the book; their artful positioning *between* possible readings subverts the privileges of both modes and, by implication, posits a single field that, if not larger than both, is certainly larger than either.

That expansion is felt, by the sensitive reader, as a widening of the whole field.

Because of this and similar aesthetic rigors this very slender adventure novel was read by myself and a number of other writers as an incredibly liberating work for the s-f genre. It is a book which, after reading and rereading, has left me unable to think of writing quite so complacently as I had. And that is the highest compliment any writer can pay another.

NEW YORK/PHILADELPHIA
DECEMBER 1975

Prisoners' Sleep

The structure of the dream scene, the entry for June 22nd, pp. 103–109, in *Camp Concentration*, by Thomas M. Disch, Doubleday, Garden City, 1968.

Let us go back and reread Disch's science-fiction novel *Camp Concentration* for...what? The third time, the sixth, the twelfth? ...Certainly now we can focus most of our attention on a single scene, even on the frame of that scene, and be sure of keeping the rest in proportion.

For this entire story, this tale of prisoners victim of mortal experimentation, is framed not only by the bars of Springfield Prison where the story begins, or even Camp Archimedes' "...infinite recessions of white, Alphavillean hallways..." to which it is shortly transferred; it is confined in other ways: The book is a prisoner's/poet's journal written for his wardens (the only semblances of freedom are the moments he can use the journal to play off one against the other); at the end of a scene rife with references to Rilke and Dante, during which Sacchetti encounters the geniusized "Iowa farmboy" George Wagner, we learn that it was written under a tranquilizer, "...else, I should not have had the presence of mind to document the encounter," (p. 21). The metaphor of this heretically religious document is blatant, classic, and lucid: The world is a prison and God is the warden. The plot aspires to cheat Him of His omnipotence *via* the same mechanics by which the other prisoners aspire to cheat Haast of his body. (Whether or not we believe it, the plot in its science-fictional aspect *is* successful: There is its heresy.) All the book's resonances must be viewed through the confines of this metaphor; that metaphor alone is what opens it up, releases it, frees it to mean.

It is also, of course, a book *about* freedom of a sort—about minds impelled, compelled, impressed to soar under the influence of the intelligence-maximizing Palladine spirochete. And it is within the framing of the climactic scene of Book I, which we shall momentarily examine, that freedom of the intellect and confinement of the body intersect and take cognizance of one another.

What is this dream about?

Revelation—as is, in a sense, the entire novel. In it, a bloated Saint Thomas Aquinas crossed with Dr. Johnson, attended by syphilitic rabbits, in the midst of the gluttonous repast of the hepatitis victim, reveals that the intimations of mortality that have jostled about in the tale so far are, finally, cold, immutable, deadly fact. In the dream they are surrounded, fixed, locked in place, inarguable, undeniable, ineluctable.

Our question, however, is: What is this dream about?

The frame of this climactic scene, the distance through which everything in it must be interpreted, is that of drowsiness, of sleep interrupted—and reconstituted shorthand: "... I recorded, in sleepy short-hand, the nightmare that awakened me, then fell back into bed, longing for the numbness to end thought... (p. 103)" We can only wonder what that shorthand version itself would reveal sans the elaboration, the retranscription with which, finally, it is presented.

A nightmare is a frightening dream; but not all frightening dreams are nightmares. Traditionally, the emblem of the nightmare is that the dream elements intrude on the sleeper's experience of falling asleep itself. Nightmares are dreams whose content *is* the frame of the sleeper's momentarily previous reality; it begins with those moments directly before sleep, recalled moments after sleep begins, to be transformed, by intrusion, into the dream wonders.

Nightmare begins with the sleeper on the bed, an instant from sleep-begun, thinking he is an instant from sleep-to-come, all transition erased. It is horrible precisely because it presents itself as a shift of the reality frame too subtle to detect, even on waking:

The recount of the true nightmare always starts: "As I lay on my bed a few moments before drifting off to sleep, I experienced the strangest..."

Other dreams—to be transported suddenly to the top of Everest, or as suddenly to be sunk to the depths of the Pacific—we can sometimes address: "Oh, this *must* be a dream..." The dislocation with continuous and contiguous memory is too sharp; the content of the dream is too violently at odds with the comparatively simple deductive overlay by which we accept the material of induction that life presents us moment to moment.

The nightmare is framed in the most familiar of settings: our own room, our own bed. Its terrific elements *are* terrific because they are intrusions into this most private of experiences, because these intrusions are singular in this most repeated of occurrences (drifting off to sleep), because, having intruded, they have broken through the most familiar frame.

"There was first a scent of cloying sweetness, as of rotting fruit" (p. 103). The first anomaly is through the most evocative of the senses: smell.

Smell is the most demanding stimulus to memory: We have all taken that absent-minded stroll down a nondescript, suburban street, to have some odor of sun on hot metal and rubber jar us back into the darkened doorway of a seaside garage in Arransas Pass, Texas, where we were standing one warm evening ten years before, or a combination of cooking smells from a window and leaves damp in the gutter thrust us over twelve years and five hundred miles to a moment when, at six in the morning, we paused to look behind the concrete steps of a bakery in Euclid, Ohio.

The scents of decay can usher the strongest of these intrusions into the framing present. Disch has been generous in giving us Sacchetti's past: theological arguments at Central High School; the dank living room of retired Major Youatt; the cocktail party at which Berrigan "...sweated doom..."; or the sidetrip to Dachau about which the prisoner Mordecai's appetite for detail "...was greater than my memory could satisfy," and the justification for which recounting is that Mordecai has been "...dreaming of death camps lately."

From the entire store of the sleeping Sacchetti's memories, the scent of rotting fruit evokes...nothing!

We rush, then (and perhaps the *waking* Sacchetti rushes as well), to fill this nothing with Christian allusivity: The fruit of the tree of knowledge gone rotten on the branch. For wakeful us, by metonymic extension, it is a scent which, if we follow it, leads to humanity's first prison—Eden—from which we were freed only by crime. But the allusion this scent presents to *us*, and its lack of mnemonic efficacy in *Sacchetti's* sleep, are not the same thing: The fullness of the one rather emphasizes the vacancy of the other. It is only in dialogue that the horror of the one can rightly inform the other, through the single sign of both—a passage between the two meanings.

The frame is broken. But we are with the narrative consciousness, within the frame. The allusion breaks the frame. Through it, we look *out* to see... if anything, Hamlet's "... unweeded garden/that grows to seed. Things rank and gross in nature/possess it merely" or, more relevantly, what Disch himself has already described earlier in the novel:

> *March 16:* We were sent out of the prison today on a detail to cut down and burn blighted trees. A new virus, or one of our own, gone astray. The landscape outside the prison is, despite the season, nearly as desolate as that within. The war has at last devoured the reserves of our affluence and is damaging the fibres of the everyday.
>
> Returning, we had to file through the clinic to get our latest inoculations. The doctor in charge held me back after the others had left. A moment's panic: Had he recognized in me the symptoms of one of the war's new diseases?... the good doctor injected what seemed like several thousand cc's of bilgey ook into my thigh... (p. 5).

But why continue? For it is the return from, as well as the breaking into, this blighted garden that is, as it were, the true climax of the novel.

The rotting fruit that begins our dream evokes, in Sacchetti's dreaming mind, nothing.

It casts us back to no real rot. It is a stripped, sensory intrusion that only presages: rotten fish, with all its Judeo-Christian resonances—the loaves and the fishes here have been transmogrified into chocolate eclairs and spoiled herring—the stained face of Aquinas "which... resembled a vast buttocks, in which the eyes were merest dimples"—or, finally, the bread which Sacchetti is forced to eat at the dream's conclusion.

The sweetness of the scent will return before the scene is through as the taste of the message "from God." The fruit is mentioned once; and that it takes us back to nowhere, gives us nothing of Sacchetti's past, but sits there stripped of all resonance in this most resonant and allusive of novels, is the first sign that the logical horror that frames the dream has closed around us.

The waking world is that world in which the truth of "$p \supset q$" protects us from the threat of spurious converses and inverses. No matter how many things are alike in that world, there is no proof that all aspects of such things are eternally so constituted, constellated, entailed, and invariant. The waking world is that world in which, no matter how terrible every experience has become, because induction is not logically valid there is always hope for the next swan not to be white, that the next night will show a different array of lights across the nocturnal bleakness. For the same reason, there is always hope that the privileged (or the lucky) may one day have to face an hour (or an age) of hunger and pain and so, learning of pain, become humble.

But the laws of logic are only the laws of local reality, bounded by a sleep and a sleep.

Certainly: All those human systems—science, art, religion, politics—that transcend the morphic boundaries operate under the terrifying metalaws of the dream. For no scientific or artistic or theological or political advance has been made without its ostensive material having been constellated at one time or another under the faulty rubric of induction—without some human mind turning suddenly from the contemplation of some logically true implication to some completely unentailed converse, inverse, or simple analogy with the sudden conviction, that is belief, that there *must be* an entailment; and that this entailment is discoverable, explicable. And as the dream constitutes itself from a reordering of the material of past consciousness, so these alogical connections, frequently enough beneficent, desperately attempt to organize themselves under the rubric of waking sense. The dream world is a world without hope, and all movement is from passive despair to active desperation—even in its moments of unbearable ecstacy—because all rewards *are* random; the fallacy in Mordecai's argument in the temptation scene (the entry for *June 16*) is precisely that he *has* mistaken, or rather secretly substituted, the dream world for the real.

But we, as readers of the novel, as readers of this scene, do not have to concern ourselves with the logical justification for the fruits of alogical inspiration, that translation process into the speakable, with its hazards, its splendors, its necessities. We are presented here, in what, for all Sacchetti's transcription and Disch's framing, is still shorthand: not that interval whose materia is bounded by sleep, but an interval whose materia is bounded by waking.

This is the world whose grammatical and structural laws do not restrict discussion to *what can be known*, but rather the world whose greater associational and combinative properties allow research into what *is* known—whether known rightly or wrongly (for this distinction can only be ascertained back on the other side of the nightmare-blurred border)—and allows exploration throughout that wholly associational web which so feebly anchors the content of the Known at the position in the context of experience that, alone, gives it the value signified by "knowledge."

"Waking" is the first word of the scene—present participle, continuous, adjectival; the "action" persists through a meaningless present of no greater weight than the paper on the page. The last clause of the scene is:

"...and I woke!"

The actual passage of the text is from the moments when waking does not distinguish itself in time ... to when it does—to when, having become a conscious occurrence, it is squarely fixed: in the past.

The journal entry *after* the dream gives the dream-content's quotidian itification "...under pressure..." of "...what the god had meant." *You will die because I have murdered you,* Haast says in effect. But what has come to waking knowledge, delivered through drowsiness to consciousness by the mechanics of dream and dream-recall (so interrelated, observes Freud in *The Interpretation of Dreams*, that in many ways one has to be considered a continuation of the other)?

It is not the knowledge of Sacchetti's own coming death: It is rather "...the certainty that I *had* known. I had known almost since my arrival at Camp Archimedes."

What we are presented with here is one of those paradoxes Wittgenstein wrestled with all through the later years ("I have a pain in my foot. Then I can point to my foot. Can I say, I have a pain in your foot? Can I have my pain in your foot or your pain in my foot, or can I have your pain in your foot?") Its form:

"I didn't know that I knew before, but I now know that I knew all along." And this knowledge is not presented as a deductive certainty but rather as the donée of a dream which allows us to use all that nonrigorous, associational paraphernalia for support by nothing less than the artifice with which science herself is accumulated day (across night) to day.

The story *is* science fiction.

We have read the novel, read it again; *we* know that Haast, who does not give, but confirms and iterates, this whirligig of knowledge, is *not* Haast. We have as well several associational frames, mentioned and unmentioned, to strait this new knowledge of Sacchetti's: conscious lie and self-deceit (for sanity's survival) lending motive to the gnomic paradox (it is no antinomy), as well as the host of theologic resonances and arguments concerning faith and grace, the acquisition of which, in Catholic theology, closely parallels Disch's presentation of the acquisition of Sacchetti's new knowledge—which, like grace, is constituted of nothing so much as a mirror image of itself.

Ultimately, we can go back through the intentional web of our own responses to this alternatively grim and hysteric dithyramb and find at the text itself incident after incident which, illuminated by this single, apprehensive moment, freed to relate by the logic of the dream, must make up the knowledge itself:

The injection of March 16th; the constant concurrence of creativity and sickness; Sacchetti's increasingly eidetic recall of Mordecai's dionysiac expostulations, etc.

They are all there, placed and paced exquisitely—and practically opaque to a first reading! Only a reader perusing this verbal tapestry at *least* a second time *could* spot them—or, perhaps, a genius...?

Suddenly the whirligig ceases to be mere bewildering glitter, and we are confronted with our own acquisition of Sacchetti's knowledge. The implication is not back-tracking from *q* to *p*. It is a going on, through each bit of evidence; it has become circular. Past evidence is dislocated in logical space and thrown ahead of later evidence *via* the mechanics of memory and consciousness: Sacchetti *is* a genius. The drug that has made him so is what has allowed him to know from the single line of experience what it *must* take us multiple readings to collect and collate; therefore, in the dream logic that compels, ultimately, fiction as well as science, we have evidence *in* the story that has, in its collection, become the *raison* and the result of the story. The fruit, no longer rotten, hangs tempting as ever from the branch of the tree.

We have been *shown* something, by an ordering of language units—sentences, anecdotes, turns of phrases, *cris de coeur*, intellectual slapstick routines, a barrage of literary and historical allusions, indeed all that, waking, frame this sleep—shown what language could not possibly have said with any conviction, much less modesty, though the speaker regaled us from the time we woke till the time, hours later, when sleep itself finally rescued us from the tedium of the discrete, the linear, and the logical.

BUFFALO
FEBRUARY 1975

To Read The Dispossessed

> In order to possess what you do not possess
> You must go by the way of dispossession.

This paradox and the several surrounding it that close the third movement of Eliot's second quartet, *East Coker*, give us the theme of Ursula K. Le Guin's sixth science-fiction novel, *The Dispossessed*. They give it so exactly we are tempted to suspect an influence, an inspiration, or at least working material. But such suspicions are, even when the author shares them, at best interesting conjecture. What we can assert is that, for us as reader, they express so accurately the psychological and metaphysical axes along which and toward which the novel's major characters move that we need not say too much more about the book at this particular resolution—at least for a while.

They free us to position ourselves at a whole set of different distances from the text, each of which is illuminated by its own incident refraction.

They free us from having to summarize the book thematically, once it and they are read.

They free us into reading.

1

There is an ideal model of reading which holds that to appreciate a serious book, especially a book of serious fiction, we must give ourselves over to it completely, must question nothing until the whole of it has sunk into our being; we must balk at no twist or eccentricity an author sets us until the entire pattern that informs each microtrope has been apprehended. What marks this model as something of an illusion (if not a downright mystification) is the nature of reading itself. An author presents us with a series of written signs to which we have affixed, both out of and by (i.e., both as referent and operator) our own experiences, various volatile and fluid images that, called up in order by the order of the signs on the page, interact in a strange and incalculably rapid alchemy to present us, at each sentence, with that sentence's meaning, at each scene with the vision of that scene, and, by the close of the novel, with the experience that is the novel itself. If some of these alchemical interactions falter or will not coalesce for us, if what occurs in our own mind presents us with signs we take for failures on the part of the text, flaws in the vast recipe from which the experience of the novel is concocted, who is to say in which mechanism the fault really lies—the reader's or the writer's?

As Quine has observed, "No two of us learn our language alike..." Perhaps the signs we take as flaws signify merely discrepancies in the reader's and the writer's learning.

Yet there is overwhelming evidence (so overwhelming that the critic must approach it with the greatest caution) that language exhibits structural stability—that structural state (to borrow some terms from catastrophe theory) where small perturbations during its formation (say in the given individual's language acquisition *vis-a-vis* another's) do not noticeably affect its final form. If this is so, it is this structural stability that gives possessors of language their incredible sensitivity to the single sentences that make up the text. The major manifestation of this stability is the extent to which a number of different readers will recognize a single interpretation of a sentence or a set of sentences as valid, to the seventh and eighth refinement.

The model of total readerly acquiescence tries to prevent our bringing our own experiences to a novel and judging only by gross congruence. It hopes to obstruct the philistine response: "This never happened to me. Therefore it couldn't happen to anybody." But what it also obstructs is the frequently valid reaction: "This *did* happen to me. And it doesn't happen that way."

On a more complex level, when we view a work of art that incorporates into its pattern clear appeals to ideas of society, politics, social organization and reorganization, as well as various syndromes of human behavior, have we any standards to criticize by *other* than our own experiences of the world and of people's behavior in it? Is the critic who says of a character in a novel. "This carpenter's attitude toward her work was unconvincing," any *more* objective than the critic who says, "In working for three years in a firm of carpenters on the West coast and two years as an individual contractor on the East, of the half a dozen women carpenters I encountered, I never met one with this attitude toward her work. This is *one* reason why I was not convinced." We will agree, I think, that the second is simply taking a greater risk by specifying both the extent and the limits of her experience. Such limits necessarily lurk behind all judgment, all analysis. Gross congruence or not, it is probably better to bring them into the open.

In this light, what our initial ideal model displays more than anything else is a vast distrust of that very structural stability that gives language both practical application and aesthetic potential.

In this essay, we shall read *The Dispossessed* against another ideal model—a more complex model, a more elusive and illusive model, a model whose elements have no existence save as various textual moments seen in a variety of distorting mirrors. And it is a model which lies in direct opposition to the one above:

We shall read the novel against its own ideal form.

Yet if we find *this* model untrustworthy, more than likely we shall cite objections that are simply developments of the previous ones: Who is to say that the extensional lacunae, projections, and contradictions that constitute such a model are not intentional elements of the novelistic totality, forming either some metafictive critique of the larger form; or, perhaps, are simply necessary elements in other, constructive fictive equations than the destructive ones we choose to examine? Who is to say that the appeals to referential accuracy and resolutional coherence that, by assumption, we must make to evaluate such elements as either desirable or undesirable are rightly a concern of fiction in the first place? If they *have* any clear authority, certainly the transition to science fiction must render that authority very dubious.

Yet obviously we feel we can appeal to these assumptions of reference and resolution. For the objections that at first seem to constitute themselves under the general accusation, "Who are you— as *reader*—to decide on the ideal form of an *author's* work?" on examination, seem very close to, if not one with, the old distrust of the structural stability of language itself. These objections are only valid if we believe that on some very basic level language is silent and does not, cannot, and should not communicate (which may well be true) *and* that the final autonomy and authority of the art-text lies *at this level* (which is false) rather than in the interplay of all the other levels—in how that interplay can push back the silent edge.

To construct our model, we shall assume the necessary existence of at least two levels of communication throughout: one, at which the author intends to communicate, and two, at which the language itself, both by its presences and its absences, frequently communicates things very different from, or in direct opposition to, that first level. Because the author is responsible for the text, we must speak of the author as responsible for both levels. Yet the responsibility for one is intentional *and* extensional; the responsibility for the other begins, at any rate, as merely extensional. Without resort to some complex psychoanalytic theory (and/or an equally complex aesthetic one), we can here afford no more claims for our author. But we can claim, as reader, that when we experience the two levels as mutually developmental, reinforcing, and expansive, the work seems the richer. (For our suspicions as to whether the author effects this by talent, skill, genius, or luck, we refer the reader to "Thickening the Plot" and the surrounding essays in Part III.) When we experience them as mutually detractive, obscuring, and simplistically contradictory, the work seems the poorer.

Our defense of this model is, finally, one with our objections to the model we began with: We feel we can make valuating assumptions of reference and resolution in this particular examination because this particular novel—*The Dispossessed*—demands them: All in the book that asks us to take it as a novel of ideas also asks us to hold the novel up, however sensitively, intelligently, and at the proper angle, to the real.

If the elements we shall cite as destructive *do* work constructively in the novel, citing them in any form, however ill-bounded, ill-focused, or ill-judged, must still accomplish some good. The destructive valuation we place on many of them is, finally, a matter of taste. (As such, we shall use a number of terms—clumsy, awkward, lumbering, pompous, ponderous, etc.—which, in the midst of such an analysis, may well seem, to those who do not share these tastes, the essence of tastelessness.) But it only remains for someone with a more intelligent and sympathetic taste than ours to reconstitute the cited elements properly into the novelistic totality. Such reconstitution, even if it comes as the most crushing rejoinder to the exegesis at hand, still leaves our efforts here their minimal worth as goad, if not guide.

2

The opening paragraph of *The Dispossessed* begins (p1/1)*: "There was a wall. It did not look important." These two short sentences raise, shimmering about this wall, the ghosts of those to whom, indeed, it does not look important; these ghosts wait to be made manifest by a word. The third sentence reads: "It was built of uncut rocks roughly mortared." Were this book mundane fiction this sentence would be merely a pictorial descript. Because it is science fiction, however, the most important word in the sentence is "uncut." To specify the rocks of the wall are uncut suggests that somewhere else within the universe we shall be moving through there are walls of *cut* rock. The ghosts shimmer beside those shimmering walls as well: We are dealing with a society that probably has the technology to cut rock—though for this particular wall (possibly because it was built before the technology was available) the rocks are whole. The fourth sentence reads: "An adult could look right over it; even a child could climb it." Because I have learned my language the way I have, from the black colloquial speech into which I was born, from family and neighborhood variations on it, from school-time spent largely with the children of East Coast intellectuals, from the pulp developments

*All page references are to *The Dispossessed* by Ursula K. Le Guin, Harper and Row, New York, 1974, followed by the page reference in the paperback edition, *The Dispossessed* by Ursula K. Le Guin, Avon Books, New York, 1975.

of Sturgeon and Bester on the language of Chandler and Hammett, from the neo-Flauberteans and Mallarméans whose chief spokesmen were Stein and Pound ("The natural object is always the adequate symbol"—1913), and whose dicta filtered down through voices like John Ciardi's, Elizabeth Drew's, and a host of other popularizers to form the parameters around which my language in adolescence organized itself, I hear, embedded in that sentence, a different and simpler set of words: "An adult could look over it; a child could climb it." Without asking what *this* sentence means—for it is not part of the text under consideration—we can limit our examination of the sentence that does appear by asking only about those aspects of the meaning that differ from the simpler sentence it suggests. In terms of the difference, I hear in the sentence that actually appears a certain tone of voice, a tone that asks to be taken both as ingenuous and mature, that tries to side with the adult ("right") and condescends to the child ("even a child"); these hints of smugness and condescension betray an unsettling insecurity with its own stance. The sentence protests its position too much. Because, in language, what comes now revises and completes our experience of what came before, this insecurity shakes the till-now adequate mortaring of the three sentences previous; this fourth sentence inadvertently asks us to listen for the echoes of any ponderousness or pontification that may linger from the others.

The echoes are there.

The fifth sentence reads: "Where it crossed the roadway, instead of having a gate it degenerated into mere geometry, a line, an idea of a boundary." We note that the phrase "instead of having a gate it degenerated into mere geometry" is mere fatuousness. If there is an idea here, *degenerate*, *mere* and *geometry* in concert do not fix it. They bat at it like a kitten at a piece of loose thread. Both "a line, an idea of a boundary" and the next paragraph (that the readers may check for themselves) suggest the referent is more likely topology than geometry; but perhaps it is the gestalt persistence of forms, or subjective contour that is being invoked; or, from the rest of the scene, perhaps it is merely, "Gates are not needed to keep people out." At any rate, it is so muzzy and unclear one cannot really say from *this* sentence what the idea is. We read the next: "But the idea was real." Since ideas are, this statement of the obvious only draws our attention to the nonexpression of the idea in the statement before.

The next sentence reads: "It was important." Even if we do not take this as overprotestation, we experience here a dimming and dispersing of those ghosts (to whom the wall looked *un*important) our second sentence called up. "For seven generations there had been nothing more important in the world than that wall." The ghosts have vanished.

I feel cheated by their dispersal, even more than I do by the "degeneration into mere geometry." The only person to whom that wall would look unimportant is some Victorian traveler who, happening accidentally upon the scene, would have noticed hardly anything out of the ordinary—a presence, a voice, a literary convention completely at odds with the undertaking.

In summary, so much in this paragraph speaks of a maturity, a profundity which, when we try to gaze to its depths by careful reading, reveals only muddy water, that what seems to stand with any solidity when the rest is cleared is:

"There was a wall of roughly mortared, uncut rocks. An adult could look over it; a child could climb it. Where the road ran through, it had no gate. But for seven generations it had been the most important thing in that world."

For the rest, it is the 1975 equivalent of Van Vogtian babble. And that babble, in Le Guin as in Van Vogt, suggests a vast distrust of the image itself—for a stone wall with no gate ("The natural object . . ."— Pound) gives all the look of unimportance such a wall would need to justify to the reader the "But . . ." of our last sentence. Filling up the empty gateway with degenerate geometry, topology, or subjective contour only sabotages the imagistic enterprise.

Because the book is science fiction, and because in science fiction the technology is so important, we wonder why the author did not use one of the ghostly sister walls of *cut* rock to sound the implicit technological resonance in a major key. When the whole book is read, and we return to commence our second reading, the image evoked of the first generation of Annaresti, newly off the spaceship, piling up rocks around the to-be spaceport like so many New Hampshire farmers, seems closer to surrealism than science fiction without some historical elaboration—but this sort of questioning is impelled by the momentum lent from the sum of all that opening paragraph's other disasters. It is not really to our purpose.

What is to our purpose?

That many of the images in Le Guin's work, as in Van Vogt's, are astonishing and powerful. And the larger point one wants to make to the Le Guin's, the Silverberg's, the Ellison's (and even the Malzberg's) of our field: If all that verbal baggage meant nothing, there would be no fault. But it does mean, and what it means is overtly at odds with the image's heart. That is what identifies it as baggage.

The way I have learned my language impells me to make another point here. While it is fair to analyze current, written American in the way I just have, it is totally unreasonable to analyze in this way the language, say, of the mother of the author of *Lady into Fox*. And to be an American intellectual of a certain (pre-Magershack) age is to have read more English prose by Constance Garnett than probably any other single English writer except Dickens. Nevertheless, Garnett's language, both because it is translation and because it is translation *into* the language of another country at another historical moment, is not ours. But too frequently the locutions and verbal signifiers that recall Garnett or other translatorese are scattered through contemporary American as signs of a "European" or "Russian" profundity that the texts simply do not have. Or, if the signs are not from translatorese, they are the borrowed accoutrements of that Victorian traveler, used to counterfeit a Victorian breadth or grandeur. This is pathetic.

I hope it is clear that I am not saying we cannot read works in translation (or Victorian novels). We can get vast amounts of information from a translation (or from a book written at another moment in the development of our own language and culture) *because* languages are structurally stable systems. We are not talking about what is lost in the translation from the language of another time or place. We are talking about what is gained by writing in our own.

3

What works in this science fiction novel?

The weaving through various textual moments of the image "stone." Passive, it appears in walls; active, hurled, it kills a man on the Defense Crew; another wings Shevek's shoulder. Moments later Annares itself is a stone falling away on a view screen (to wound or wing what . . . ?) The fragment "But the rock will never hit . . ." (p. 6/5) among Shevek's muddled thoughts presages, eighteen pages later (p. 25/23), a younger Shevek's spontaneous discovery of Zeno's paradox. "Are we stones on Annares?" (p. 13/12) Shevek asks Dr. Kimoe at one point. The web of resonances the word weaves through the text gives a fine novelistic density.

The first chapter's image of time as an arrow (between "river" and "stone") develops into half the controlling metaphor by which we are given (popularized) Shevek's scientific theory during Vea's party, as well as those theories that speak ". . . only of the arrow of time— never of the circle of time," (p. 197/179). What works is that image's resolution in Chapter Eleven, when Shevek is with the Terran Ambassador, Keng, in the old River Castle in Rodarred, now the Terran Embassy. At one point, as he discusses with her his plan to broadcast his coveted theory to all:

> Shevek got up and went over to the window, one of the long, horizontal slits of the tower. There was a niche in the wall below it, into which an archer would step up to look down and aim at assailants at the gate; if one did not take that step up one could see nothing from it but the sunwashed, slightly misty sky (p. 307/280).

What works is the way in which the discussion of the conflicting "Sequency" and "Simultaneity" theories of time reflect the macrostructure of the novel itself, with its ordered, pendulating chapters, crossing time and space which is, by semantic extension, the goal of Shevek's theory.

What works is the way, on Annares, a sign is charged with sexuality: First, a film of the Urrasti women's "oiled, brown bellies" (p. 37/33) presented in a context of death (corpses of children, funeral pyres), transformed, in one Annaresti boy's discourse: "I don't care if I never see another picture of foul Urrasti cities and greasy Urrasti bodies," (p. 38/34). Pages later, the transformation moves through another stage with the first description of (the then unidentified) Takver: "Her lips were greasy from eating fried cakes and there was a crumb on her chin," (p. 53/48). Nearly a hundred pages later, this sex/oil/grease/food transition moved a stage further, when Takver acquires a name and a further description:

> She had the laugh of a person who liked to eat well, a round, childish gape. She was tall and rather thin with round arms and broad hips. She

was not very pretty; her face was swarthy, intelligent, and cheerful. In
her eyes there was a darkness, not the opacity of bright dark eyes but a
quality of depth, almost like deep, black, fine ash, very soft (p.
157/143).

One could attack this paragraph just as we did the first. We will
make do, however, merely with a mention that the whole discourse of
"cute/pretty/beautiful," even applied in the negative, does more to
subvert the image than support it. One suspects that those to whom
Takver "was not very pretty" are the same ghosts to whom the wall
"did not look important." But it is the text itself, as we pointed out in
our analysis of the first paragraph, that disperses these ghosts—
which is why the phrases, sentences, and ideas that are put in to
placate and appease them register as aesthetic failings, or at best as a
residue from an unconscious struggle in the author that, while we
appreciate it, is inappropriate to the story unless brought consciously
forward. Nevertheless, the locus of the erotic from its inception in the
text to this most believable resting place is very real; and it is subtly
supported by all the book implies about Annaresti agriculture and
eating habits. This aspect of the book is novelistically and, more,
science-fictionally fine.

What works? A simple mention, in a single sentence in Chapter
One, of "scrub holum" and "moonthorn" as the names of plants
glimpsed in the distance (p. 5/4). Then, practically at the book's
midpoint, the one plant name unfolds into landscape: "He found her
on the steep slope, sitting among the delicate bushes of moonthorn
that grew like knots of lace over the mountainsides, its stiff, fragile
branches silvery in the twilight. In a gap between eastern peaks a
colorless luminosity of the sky heralded moonrise. The stream was
noisy in the silence of the high, bare hills. There was no wind, no
cloud. The air above the mountain was like amethyst..." (p.
158/144). Despite the awkward "a colorless luminosity of the sky"
(the word is 'glow'), or the logically strained "noisy in the silence," this
landscape is affecting. And when, in Chapter Ten, there is another,
passing mention of "scrub holum," it has been charged not only by
what we have learned of its technological use on Annares in frabric
and fermentation, but has also been charged by its association with
moonthorn which, because of *its* absence in the passage quoted,
renders the scrub holum, mentioned later and alone, that much
starker.

Moonlight glimmers again and again through the tale: The development of the image above forms part of the context that gives this moonlight its unique coloration, that fixes just what this moonlight can reveal.

Briefly, what works are those moments when the text conscientiously recalls itself (or lightly recalls another text, as when a passing explanation of why Shevek remains a vegetarian on Urras—"his stomach had its reasons..."—recalls Pascal's epigram), so that for an instant two textual moments are superimposed in the reader's mind, slightly out of register, not to create confusion but rather to function like the two views necessary for a stereoptical image. Bringing together their divergences, we glimpse the matter in all its resonant (or, with the Pascal, humorous) depth.

But there are other places where the text recalls itself to no particular purpose:

On Annares, Shevek's neighbor at the Institute, the mathematician Desar, speaks in a elliptic and "telegraphic" style—a personal eccentricity that presumably implies something about general language trends in Pravic. The Ioti speech of Shevek's Urrasti servant Efor, when it "slips back into the dialect of the city" also becomes elliptic and telegraphic (acquiring in the process some gross metaphors, such as "old sow" for "wife") in much the same way. There is nothing confusing between the two: one is on one world in one language, one is on another world in another language. Because the recall of the one by the other does not accomplish some clear point, however (that *all* demotic speech movement is toward the elliptic, perhaps?), the similarity registers as a lack of purpose and attention to verbal invention in fleshing out the language texture of the two speakers.

At another place, we anticipate a recall and get none: In the first chapter we learn the third-person singular is the polite form of address in Ioti: "Is he sure he didn't get hurt?" (p. 6/5) Dr. Kimoe asks Shevek about his injured shoulder. (Informal address can presumably be rendered as second person: "you.") Once Shevek comes fully to his senses, however, this peculiarity of the language is absorbed by the implied translation and is never mentioned again. It could have added so much color to the subsequent portrait of the Urrasti if, in any number of the encounters that occur, we had seen precisely *where* the men (and women) of Urras switch from polite to informal address.

4

But to treat a referential work as if it were only a musical structure is to betray it—especially a work as clearly concerned with ideas as *The Dispossessed*. If only temporarily, we must retreat the necessary distance to allow the texture of language to resolve into the incidents and actions by which those ideas are dramatized. And it is at that distance I see many of the actions and incidents contravening my own experiences, occasionally even when the ideas they dramatize, as I understand them, are ones I believe in and approve of.

Annares has just passed through a prolonged famine. From that harsh, ascetic world, Shevek, confused and mildly injured, is on the Urrasti ship *Mindful*, bound for Urras for the first time:

> ... in those long hours of fever and despair, he had been distracted, sometimes pleased and sometimes irritated, by a simple sensation: the softness of the bed. Though only a bunk, its mattress gave under his weight with carressing suppleness. It yielded so insistently that he was, still, always conscious of it while falling asleep. Both the pleasure and the irritation it produced in him were decidedly erotic. There was also the hot-air-nozzle-towel device: the same kind of effect. A tickling. And the design of the furniture in the officers' lounge, the smooth plastic curves of surfaces and textures: were these not also faintly, pervasively erotic? He knew himself well enough to be sure that a few days without Takver, even under stress, should not get him so worked up that he felt a woman under every table top. Not unless the woman was really there.
> Were Urrasti cabinetmakers all celibate? (p. 16/15).

Ignoring the verbal overkill that muffles the real irony of the closing line (as well as the bizarre suggestion that, as egalitarian as professions seem to be on Annares, cabinet making is customarily restricted to Lesbian women and/or heterosexual men), I am cast back to several real situations on a very real Earth. I shall go into them at some length, as they will shape my general discussion of sexuality in *The Dispossessed*.

I sleep on a three-inch foam rubber mattress on the floor, and have for a number of years. I remember, from a conference in the north of England, during a time when I had a cold and a slight fever, a very deep and very soft bed at the guest house where the conference members were to spend the night. The softness certainly promised pleasure—a promise forgotten as soon as I climbed under the sheets and comforter. My general response? Increased awareness of bones and muscles slung in annoying positions; growing aches and general discomfort (rather than irritation); fevers have always dulled my sexual response to things. (The relationship "sex/fever" is a literary metaphor comparing their psychological effects, not a connection between their physical sensations.) For someone used to and comfortable with a hard bed, there is nothing in a soft one even faintly erotic.

But other memories come—of a Canadian I once met in Istanbul who, having arrived only hours before, was in a state of manic excitement to visit the government houses of prostitution, which were all mixed up in his head with Byzantine architecture and Islamic art, from furniture and frescoes to wallpaper. And I recall his disappointment with an afternoon at Topkapi Palace: everything, he said, looked "so uncomfortable!" That evening, we pushed through the high iron gate onto the crowded, muddy cobblestones, elbowed and shouldered our way up to the narrow doors to peer through the clear strips of glass in the rickety, frosted-over windows; and I remember how all my friend's excitement dampened. Inside, yes, were heavily made-up women sitting around in western underwear, many, we were told, female criminals who were given the option by the government of reducing their sentence by working there—yet all the emblems of the erotic my friend actually *knew* were absent, though he was apparently a frequenter of Canadian prostitutes. He returned to his hostel greatly disappointed.

Looking over most of the direct dealings with heterosexuality in *The Dispossessed*, I am reminded how much of my own experience seems to have taught me that the erotic, the exotic, the sensual, and the sexual, while they are all related and the paths between them are complex and frequently astonishing, are nevertheless *different* categories. Their overlap is by and large phonic. *All* of them must be learned, and learned differently in different cultures.

The major purpose of the passage quoted is to show that the Annaresti culture is hard while the Urrasti culture is soft. But the interface, with Shevek's consciousness, constitutes itself under a simple and essentially fictional idea of eros which, on examination, is at odds with the real erotic intelligence that, say, informs the creation of Takver as a human being to whom Shevek might respond sexually. The unexamined idea behind the passage seems to be that softness and curves, both necessarily and sufficiently, are *the* thing men (Annaresti or Urrasti) respond to sexually—which is just as ridiculous as assuming that the only thing women respond to sexually is hardness and strength. There is no more a woman (or a man) "really there" in a curved table top than there is a man (or a woman) in an oak picnic bench.

Other incidents come to mind: my grandmother, age eighty-seven, seriously explaining to my sister and me, sometime in 1967, that the main problem with men's wearing long hair was that women simply could not find it attractive and would refuse to marry them; the race would die out. Three years later, when she was ninety, I remember her allowing how a young boyfriend of a cousin of mine, with a shiny black ponytail he could sit on, bound in three places with leather bands, seemed such a dashing, handsome and suave young fellow...

Both women and men sexualize what their childhood experiences impress on them, in terms of what the adult culture makes available to them. If something new comes along within the general range of interest, many of them, even as adults, will learn to sexualize it. The idea that "soft/curves" is genetically imprinted on the male psyche and evokes sexual response whenever and wherever it is encountered (like the image of a hawk flying forward [but not backwards!] evokes fear behavior in newly hatched goslings) is far too culturally determined a view of the process.

On most of the earth, the physical labor needed to survive day to day is at least as arduous as that required on Annares, if not more so. At any rate, it is certainly closer to what life on Annares demands than the phsyical labor expended by the academic classes of A-io. Most of earth's women are neither particularly curvacious nor particularly soft. If soft/curves were a necessary factor for male sexuality to exist, my grandmother's fears for the survival of the race—reversed male-female—would have been realized well before the neolithic revolution got under way.

Too much of the direct sexual affectivity in things Urrasti, registering on Annaresti males, from the films shown in the training sessions, to Shevek's actual encounter with sex on Urras, seems to be modeled on my Canadian friend's and my grandmother's expectations, rather than on what occurs.

In the party scene on Urras (p. 203/185), Shevek, drunk and

aroused after Vea has led him into the bedroom, comes all over her dress. To complain, as some readers have, that alcohol in large quantities is an orgasmic inhibitor in men is to miss a larger and more important point: The kind of behavior Vea exhibits toward Shevek men must *learn* to respond to as erotic. That learning process involves battling through it to success (i.e., getting laid) a number of times, at first impelled only by curiosity and any number of social supports that reinforce in the heterosexual male "... this is the thing to do." Shevek, age forty-two and used to the comparative straight-forwardness of sex on Annares, simply has had neither the opportunity nor the motivation to learn to read Vea's classic cock-teasing as anything but erratic.

Such cock-teasing behavior has its real, social, psychological, and economic justification for women straited in the confines of a repressive, patriarchal society such as A-io; as such, Vea, in many things she says, is one of the more sympathetic characters in the novel. At the risk of rewriting Le Guin's story, however, somehow it seems more likely that, even drunk and aroused as he is, Shevek would simply burst out laughing at Vea's antics.

As Vea's interest in Shevek, when all is said and done, is only peripherally sexual—no matter how much of "a real man" (p. 173/158) she thinks he is—I suspect that, somewhat relieved, she might have broken out laughing as well. Then, hopefully, they would have sat down and had some sort of conversation in which they gave each other the very real benefit of their mutually alien views.

At any rate, the scene as written—with rampant, primitive lust completely failing to make contact with sophisticated flirtation and coyness—is all "literature." That the scene also manages to contravene a general law of metabolism and male plumbing is just one emblem of its overall lack of psychological varacity.

In the chapters dealing with Annares, there is much concern with sex—and some with sexuality. We have pointed out one place where sexuality has been integrated into the fabric of the vision with novelistic acumen. Much of what confronts us, however, is hard to avoid interpreting as a series of subjects explicitly omitted from the foreground—if only because they are explicitly mentioned as pervasive parts of the social background. Social acceptance of homosexuality, a social norm of promiscuity, ubiquitous adolescent bisexuality, and general communal child-rearing are all given us in *récit*. In the discourse of incident and action—the foreground—we are only shown the somewhat anxious effects of the last of these, anxious possibly because it was started, in the particular case of the young Shevek, somewhat later than usual.

One of the strictures that fiction's recent history has imposed on the novel is the particular complementary nature of foreground and récit. Though the two on the page are horizontally complementary, in the readerly imagination their complementarity is strictly vertical. The last century of popular fiction has made us specifically distrust those segments of the text where didacta are not clearly refocusing what has already been presented in the foreground. Where didacta *replace* foreground, other than in the narrow modes of economic, historical, and, in science fiction, technological summary, such didacta are *the* signs of the aesthetically suspect.

These foreground omissions register firstly as an *aesthetic* flaw: They violate a symmetry that other aspects of the treatment of Annares strongly suggest.

By cursory count, the number of Annaresti specifically identified as female is forty-three. There is one mention of an unspecified number of old women. The number of Annaresti specifically identified as male is forty three. There is one mention of an unspecified number of old men. There are nine characters (any of these figures may be off by one or two as I only counted once) mentioned whose sex is not specified. Given the 50/50 deployment of the others, we can feel safe in assuming a similar proportion for the unidentified ones. This deployment, and the actual placement of men and women in the society, does more than all the didactic statements to demonstrate the extent (and limits) of Annares' egalitarianism. The constant occurrence of women (though seldom men) in positions unusual for them in fiction (though not particularly unusual for them in life) forms a metacriticism of much fiction which seems, through a confusion of women with sweetheart/wife/mother, to posit a landscape in which Woman is a single profession, less interesting because unpaid, but basically on a par with, the single professions of Plumber, Doctor, Lawyer, Artist—these others also represented by one individual apiece, all (of course) male.

The deployment of Le Guin's male and female characters on Annares is a sign of a didactic concern with the fact that men and women form respectively forty-eight and fifty-two percent of the population. And this didactic concern has been integrated into the fictive foreground. But many other didactic concerns that are indicated in the récit, and very closely related to the one we have mentioned, never leave the realm of unsupported didacta. Through the equal number of males and females a certain male/female symmetry is suggested. Though the story is Shevek's story, nevertheless, once he is partnered with Takver, one hopes to see the calculus of novelistic inventiveness applied to both equally, even if we view it from a position closer to Shevek than to Takver.

We hear of Shevek's bisexual youth.

There is no mention of Takver's.

We see two of Shevek's prepartnered affairs, one heterosexual, one homosexual; there is simply no mention, one way or the other, of any prepartnered sex at all for Takver. Shevek, in one of his long separations from Takver, lusts, whether it rings true or not, after the Urrasti woman Vea. There is simply no hint of Takver's ever giving another man a thought—though once, rather mystically, during Shevek's absence, she contemplates "...the cities of fidelity."

The process signified here is the traditional liberal dilemma. Our conservative forebears postulated symmetrical spaces of possible action for women and men and then declared an ethical prohibition on women's functioning in that space: men *may* behave in such and such a way, with minimal consequences. Women *may not: if* they *do*, they will be *punished* (by law, by society, by God). A liberal generation rises that wishes to move into the prohibited space, change the values, and repeal the punishments. Ideals are expressed to this end. Yet there is leftover and irrational guilt. If the conflict between guilt and desire is not resolved, as it seldom is in the liberal, at the level of praxis the *conflict* is repressed, and with it all emblems of the existence of the space in which it takes place. It is not mentioned, it is not dealt with, it is not referred to—and this silence is presented, hopefully, as a sign the problem has been resolved. This leaves the revolutionary with the double problem of first reasserting the existence of the space, *then* securing the right and guarantees necessary to move about in it. Frequently the liberal is a more difficult opponent than the conservative.

Takver reencounters Shevek near the end of a homosexual affair he is having with his returned childhood friend Bedap. Bedap in fact introduces them. In the alternations of indirect description and foreground incident, any reaction of Takver's to the relation of Bedap and Shevek, or even her knowledge of it (if sex has left the relationship, Bedap and Shevek are still vacationing together), is omitted, whether that reaction is pro, con, or indifferent.

To reason that, well, in the Annaresti society Takver's reaction would probably *be* indifference is to confuse the novel-as-texture with the novel-as-structure. Though the novel-as-texture may be as alien as the author can imagine, the novel-as-structure is still controlled by a sort of generalized societal (current, earthbound, and contemporary) interest: If the author wishes to violate this interest, she must leave some metafictive sign that she is aware of the interest but, for whatever reason, is not complying with it. (And "I don't *know* what the texture of the reaction would be" is as good a reason as any for not providing an answer. But this must be signaled somewhere, explicitly or implicitly.) As it is, in the omission of Bedap's psychological transition from Shevek's lover to Shevek's and Takver's best friend, in the omission of Takver's response to Shevek's and Bedap's affair, the omission of Shevek's feelings about the movement of his sexual allegiances from one to the other and possible reactions it might cause, there is an element of novelistic chicanery. The point isn't that such transitions are not believable. In the real world, one way or the other, they are accomplished every day. But the payoff in psychological richness to be gained by some insight into how Bedap, Takver, and Shevek—and by extension the generally promiscuous Annaresti—accomplish such transitions is sorely missed. I find no signs in the text for the author's understanding of the process; nor any sign that understanding of it might be necessary. The omission seems one with the avoidance of the whole "problem of jealousy" as it has come to be called in the present jargon of "family synergy" and the like (though, more accurately, it might be called the psychological mechanisms for keeping jealousy to a manageable minimum that, of necessity, grow up in any openly permissive society). At least partially, what most likely make Bedap's adjustments possible are the very real consolations of promiscuity. But as Bedap is the only onstage homosexual in the book, this is simply another aspect missing from the societal picture. (There are— and one almost wants to say "of course"—no women homosexuals in the novel, unless they are all sequestered in some cabinet-making Syndicate known to Shevek but not us.)

In a consciencious attempt to defuse some of the explosive associations that lurk, like another sort of ghost, around our argument, we would like to go immediately to another example of fictive omission in the novel. In Chapter Nine, Shevek has sequestered himself in his room in the University of A-io and has gotten to work on his new and important Temporal theory, which will be the basis of the new, interstellar spacedrive. He has been reading over a symposium from ancient Terra on the relativity theory of "Ainsetain." On the double theory of General and Special Relativity, he muses:

> But was not a theory of which *all* the elements were provably true a simple tautology? In the region of the unprovable, or even in the disprovable, lay the only chance for breaking out of the circle and going ahead.
>
> In which case, did the unprovability of the hypothesis of real coexistence—the problem which Shevek had been pounding his head against desperately for these last three days, and indeed these last ten years—really matter?
>
> He had been groping and grabbing after certainty, as if it were something he could possess. He had been demanding a security, a guarantee, which is not granted, and which, if granted, would become a prison. By simply assuming the validity of real coexistence he was free to use the lovely geometries of relativity; and then it would be possible to go ahead. The next step was perfectly clear. The coexistence of succession could be handled by a Saeban transformation series; thus approached, successivity and presence offered no antithesis at all. The fundamental unity of the Sequency and Simultaneity points of view became plain; the concept of interval served to connect the static and the dynamic aspect of the universe. How could he have stared at reality for ten years and not seen it? There would be no trouble at all in going on. He was there. He saw all that was to come in this first, seemingly casual glimpse of the method, given him by his understanding of a failure in the distant past. The wall was down. The vision was both clear and whole. What he saw was simple, simpler than anything else. It was simplicity: and contained in it all complexity, all promise. It was revelation. It was the way clear, the way home, the light.
>
> The spirit was in him like a child running out into the sunlight. There was no end, no end... (p. 247/225).

In the same way that indirect reportage of event omitted (or absorbed) the "problem of jealousy" among Bedap, Takver, and Shevek in a way that, to me, feels extremely unsatisfactory, so indirect reportage of Shevek's thoughts has omitted (or absorbed) the discovery of Shevek's great theory, in a way that feels equally wrong.

It is possible that the essentially circular argument that introduces the section (the theory, to be proven, needs something from the realm of the unproven to prove it; why not take the unproven theory itself, assume it to be already proved, and then use it to supply the missing section that is needed to prove it) is intended as ironical. I suspect, rather, the intention is mystical, though to me it *only* seems circular and the essence of the unscientific—and I speak as someone who believes the kernel of all creativity, artistic and scientific, is indeed mystic. The absorption of the problem of jealousy we had to examine by appealing essentially to the mechanics of mundane fiction; but here we simply cite our own, science-fiction traditions. Science fiction, where the turning-up of new and universe-shaking theories is a workaday occurrence, has evolved its own rhetorical postures for dealing with their arrival. At one point, earlier in the same scene, Le Guin evokes one such posture and then abandons it:

> He went back to the desk, sat down, and took a couple of scraps of heavily scribbled paper out of the least accessible and least useful pocket of his tight-fitting, stylish trousers. He spread these scraps out with his fingers and looked at them . . . Shevek sat motionless, his head bowed, studying the two little bits of paper on which he had noted down certain essential points of the General Temporal Theory, so far as it went.
>   For the next three days he sat at the desk and looked at the two bits of paper (p. 244/223).

If, in the next paragraph, we had learned that Shevek had resolved his great theory during these three days, we would not cavil. We would read the sudden distancing of the final sentence quoted as an intelligent reticence about a subject on which, really, nothing *can* be said. The discovery would have been "omitted," but it would have been omitted with a certain authority, if not elegance. What these three days do produce, however, is a meditation on Pei, one of the more suspect of the Urrasti physicists, followed by a consideration of Relativity (Pei has given Shevek the Relativity symposium), followed by the climactic passage first quoted.

What the climactic passage does, besides giving the subjective state of the physicist during his discovery (which is acceptable), is to presume to give us that inner nut of consciousness where subjectivity becomes one with the objective validity of the theory itself (which is not). The only signifier that could conceivably hold open the necessary fictive space for the *fictive* objectivity to occur in is "Saeban transformation series"; and it does not. ("Successivity," and the "concept of interval" have all been given lengthy and comparatively reasonable explanations; therefore they are not opaque enough to keep the space open.) At minimum we would need several such signifiers (that suggested scientific discourse) woven into a complex structure that replaced the circularly structured argument already cited: because the signifiers would *be* opaque, we would then not be able to tell whether the argument was indeed circular *or* coherent. This structure would have to be complex enough to suggest an imaginative space to fit the needed fictive objectivity—the creation of such opaque structures is the other, older rhetorical posture by which science fiction traditionally has solved this problem.

Indeed what all our analytical battery is trying to establish here is simply that, while the idea of an Urrasti/Annaresti physics that takes into account the ethical and moral resonances within the physics itself (in a way that recalls some of Michel Serre's thought on Leon Brillouin's work in Information Theory) is a fascinating science-fictional idea, what Le Guin presents *as* physics, to me, at any rate, still has the wrong feel—which *is* a subjective response and best be, somewhere, stated as such.

At any rate, what these two fictive absorptions—the problem of jealousy and the Great Theory—suggest more than anything else is the novelistic danger of indirect reportage—both of actions and thoughts—at the best of times. At the moment we perceive our own view of a fictive situation as sophisticated, there seems no way for us to avoid the condensations and highlighting that indirect reportage affords. Yet sophistication is itself a bias, by those same mechanics of omission and emphasis. Unless they are clearly grasped and the intent of the reportage is ironic, they are better avoided. Also, the emphasis science fiction places on foreground detail automatically highlights any bias in the background récit: These indirect recounts are doubly risky within our genre precincts. (The highlighting of personal bias, under control, is what makes so many *first* person science-fiction tales—largely carried on in this same, indirect reportage—so successful at presenting a distinctive, first person character.) But there are numerous effects, both good and bad, that are at best muted in mundane fiction which are, by comparison, sharp-edged and clear-sounding here.

5

Annares's egalitarianism is not intended as total. The kind of adolescent bisexuality Le Guin posits for the Annaresti exists in many primitive tribes today (as well as many American summer camps) that exhibit a far greater sexual division of adult labor and behavior than either Annares or America.

There are at least four places in the novel where Le Guin leaves signs in the text to indicate these limitations. Before examining them, however, we must begin by saying that we do not feel that the signs as we see them do the job the text demands of them—which is to say, we feel they would have sufficed in a novel of mundane fiction. The analytical imperatives of science fiction, however (and however infrequently they are met), mark them inadequate.

Near the beginning of the prison scene in Chapter Two, we read: "The simple lure of perversity brought Terin, Shevek, and three other boys together. Girls were eliminated from their company, they could not have said why." Sign one (p. 31/29).

And in the next scene a few years later, when a group of slightly older boys are discussing the politics of Urras, after having seen some films on the decadence of Urras (whose erotic content we have remarked on), we read: "They had come up to the hilltop for masculine company. The presence of females was oppressive to them all. It seemed to them that lately the world was full of girls. They had all tried copulating with girls; some of them in despair had also tried not copulating with girls. It made no difference. The girls were there." Sign two (p. 36/33).

The semantic associations of these sentences are such that we must read them as an expression of the traditional idea that adolescent boys naturally tend to segregate themselves from girls at the onset of puberty.

Once more I am thrown back to experiences of my own—in the summer camp that prompted my parenthetical statement about adolescent bisexuality five paragraphs ago.

A number of the youngsters I went to summer camp with, between the ages of eight and fourteen, were children I was also in school with. I was not conscious of any great pressure on the sexes to remain separate in my school, but looking back on it I suspect I was not aware of it the way the fish is not aware of water or the bird is not aware of air. Our elementary school had an informal, yet definite dress code. Boys could wear jeans. Girls could not wear pants of any sort—except when it was snowing. Then they could wear slacks. For the monthly school dances, the girls had to stay after classes to decorate the music room. For school trips and fire drills the teachers lined the boys up on one side of the hall and the girls up on the other—and for fire drills boys and girls left the building separately. On the class bus, boys sat on one side and girls sat on the other. And I recall one morning when some seven or eight boys and a single girl happened to gather in the small equipment room next door to the sixth floor science laboratory to watch one of the boys perform a (rather ineffectual) hypnosis experiment. Suddenly our middle-aged history teacher, who had apparently been looking through the glass panes of the door, opened it and demanded: "Come out of there! You come out of there!" She marched in, grabbed the girl by the arm, and dragged her out of the room.

From two to four-thirty in the afternoon, all the boys were herded together in the school bus and taken out to Randall's Island for sports activities or, if it was raining, were unceremoniously dumped into the basement swimming pool. To this day I don't know what the girls did during this same time. They may have gone home.

Otherwise, classes were coed.

And once I was invited to a birthday party by a girl in my class; with my allowance I bought her an illustrated copy of *Jane Eyre*—but when my parents saw the gift, I wasn't allowed to go to the party because they felt such a book was inappropriate for a young man of twelve to give to a young woman of the same age.

In my school there was a definite tendency, during lunch and free periods, for girls to coagulate over here and boys to clot over there. During this time, I heard much talk about the "natural" antipathy of boys to girls, which the school, of course, was constantly trying to fight by the monthly social dances, in which the girls would do all the preparatory work, and the boys, uncomfortable in suits and ties, would sigh and shuffle and try to stay in as tight little groups as possible until, with much urging from the teachers, one or another of us would go up and ask one of the girls seated along the window benches to dance.

At summer camp, first of all, everyone—boys and girls—wore jeans. The boys slept in tents on the other side of a small hill from the girls' bunk buildings. But the rotating camper work-crews that got up early to set the table in the dining hall were equally male and female; the camper surveying team that was making a contour map of the area was composed of both boys and girls. All camper activities, from overnight hikes and nature trips to pottery and carpentry classes were coed. Boys' athletics and girls' athletics were held on adjoining playing fields, at the same time. But volleyball, swimming, and softball, which were the main athletic events, were coed. For two of my five years there, there was an attempt to organize an all-boys softball team; in two or three weeks it usually fell apart from competition with other interests. On the camp bus you sat where you wanted, with whomever you wanted. By my estimate, the time it took for *all* traces of the natural antipathy between the sexes to vanish— and vanish from people who, in many cases, two weeks before had been textbook examples of it—was the four and a half hour bus trip from New York City to Phoenecia, New York, where the camp was located.

From the time we lugged our steamer trunks up the quarter mile of hill road to our tents and bunks, friendships had established themselves as frequently across sexual lines as not. As summer wore on, many such friendships developed sexual elements; as many did not. But the difference between behavior in camp and school was clear, noticed, and *talked* about by both campers and counselors. I recall a long discussion with an eighteen-year-old woman counselor and a bright, dumpy girl named Roberta, while the three of us were running off an edition of the camp newspaper, during which we isolated most of the elements I've stressed in this description: clothing, activities, proximity, and free choice.

On Tuesday nights we had square dancing, at which, again, anyone could wear anything they wanted; in practical terms this meant the boys wore what they always wore and about a third of the girls put on skirts. The proportion of skirt wearers was far lower at the end of the summer than at the start. Our professional square-dance caller the first evening made it clear that girls could ask boys to dance. And the various square sets, calling, "Two couples! Two couples . . . one couple!" as places were filled was half the fun.

On Friday night there was social dancing, during which it was *required* that the girls wear skirts. Except for one "Sadie Hawkins" dance, it was understood that the boys should ask the girls to dance.

Social dancing was the least popular activity of the week. The boys lingered in groups outside the recreation hall or simply slipped away when counselors tried to corral them in. Inside the rec hall, the girls sat around on the benches against the wall, listless and bored. It was a sudden reversion to another system of behavior and everyone felt uncomfortable.

During my third year of camp (summer of fifty four) we formed a campers' committee, of five boys and three girls, who met with Norman, the camp director, in the library behind the office that also served as camp post office. Our committee's proposal was that social dancing be abolished and in its place we have either a free evening or another evening of square dancing.

Norman, who was very big on camper self-determinism, looked very disturbed. He excused himself a minute and returned with his wife, Hannah, who codirected the camp. They explained to us:

A second square-dance evening would be too expensive since it would mean hiring the live square-dance band *twice* a week.

Also, they didn't think giving up social dancing would be a good idea: Social dancing, they explained, was there to break the natural antipathy between young, adolescent boys and girls.

But there isn't any here, Roberta of the inky fingers protested.

Well, explained Norman, they meant on a more sophisticated level.

Which we assumed meant sex. Which seemed silly because, as with most coed summer camps, the counselors spent most of their time from five o'clock to lights-out chasing the necking couples out of the bushes on the side of the road that led from the rec hall back to the bunks. One blond, forward boy on the committee named Kenroy said as much.

Well, we were told, we on the committee were more mature, i.e., all of us on the committee except Roberta were openly known to be "going with" someone. The social dancing, they explained, was for those less mature campers who wouldn't make contact any other way.

"But," explained Roberta (as a "more mature" representative of the "less mature" campers?), "there's more social contact in *any* other activity—even athletics, for God's sake—than during social dancing."

I think it was at this point Hannah suggested that perhaps two or three more "Sadie Hawkins" dances might help—which met with groans all around.

Then Norman explained that we had to understand that social dancing was basically for the girls' sake. The girls liked it. After all, they had brought clothes for it and would feel disappointed if they couldn't use them. (The camp, of course, sent a list of clothes each camper should bring, including—for the girls—dresses for social dancing.) Wasn't that so?

Sarena, another girl on the committee, said that some of the girls enjoyed dressing up for it, but they were the same ones who dressed up for square dancing. *No*body, Roberta added, enjoyed the actual event.

Well, Norman explained, we already understood that more square dancing was out of the question. We boys simply had to understand the social needs of the girls. The girls on the committee had to understand the needs of their less fortunate bunk mates.

And that was that.

We left the library and walked back up the road to our bunks defeated.

We had been told we hadn't seen what we had seen; that we didn't understand what made clear sense; that we were being selfish when social conscience was precisely what had prompted us to act (to those of us on the committee social dancing was an endurable nuisance; to the shyer campers of both sexes it was a horror). One of the things I remember from that walk back up to the bunks under the sun-filled branches that lapped above the road: While the five of us boys grumbled among ourselves, the three girls, including the otherwise irrepressible Roberta, were silent. The feeling of solidarity we had all had coming down to present our idea had vanished. The girls felt apart and uncomfortable. We boys were aware of it and confused by it—but at that age we did not understand what had just been done specifically and pointedly to three of our group of eight.

This is the personal context against which I read the two scenes the quoted passages come from. Though I could quite easily imagine such "naturally" all-male scenes taking place in or around my school, I simply couldn't imagine them taking place at my summer camp—even in the next few hours after our encounter with Norman. To point out that Annares, even with its egalitarian child-rearing practices, is not a summer camp is to beg the question with an obviousness. The point is, of course, that the naturalness and immutability of such natural and immutable behavior that the two cited passages (and Norman's and Hannah's argument) make their implicit appeals to is open to question and analysis. And whether my thirteen-year-old analysis of the situation is or is not correct, there is a larger, aesthetic point that frames the question here.

Mundane fiction can get by with a clear and accurate portrayal of behavior *that* occurs merely *because* it occurs. Science fiction can not. In an alien culture—and both Annares and Urras are alien cultures—we are obliged to speculate on the reason behind any given behavior; and this speculation, whether implicit or explicit, must leave its signs in the text. The scenes and paragraphs cited are signs of the limitations on the social egalitarianism of Annares; they are not signs for the causes of those limitations.

Nothing prevents an s-f writer from writing a story about an intelligent species in which adolescent male bonding behavior is imprinted on the genes. (The species might biologically and genetically bear a resemblance to birds, who exhibit much complex behavior that may well be genetically controlled.) Similarly, nothing prevents the s-f author from writing about an intelligent species in which such behavior is completely the product of intrasocial forces. Indeed, the writer if she chooses can write about a species in which the reason switches back and forth according to changes in the moon.

What we must remember, however, is that once mundane fiction has accomplished its portrait of behavior at some historical moment, from the here and now to the distant past, if we ask of it: "But what do you think the surrounding causes are?" mundane fiction can answer, without fear that it is shirking its job, "Frankly, I don't know. It's not my concern." But because science fiction is not constrained to answer such a question "correctly," within its generic precincts the "I don't know. It's not my concern," of mundane fiction not only becomes self-righteous and pompous, it signifies a violation of the form itself. Science fiction may ultimately end with an "I don't know" about any given point, but only after a good deal of speculation, either implicit or explicit, has left its signs in the text.

With all this as precursor, we can revise our initial valuation of the first two signs of the four we are discussing: The scenes in which the passages occur stand as signs that (among other things) the behavior on Annares, despite sexual integration of the professions, is not *that* egalitarian. The two paragraphs themselves, however, stand as signs of the author's refusal to speculate as to why the behavior is what it is—and as such simply don't make good science fiction.

A third dramatic sign of the limit to the egalitarianism of Annares is the scene with Shevek and Vokep in the truck depot of Yin Ore:

"Women," Vokep said . . . "Women think they own you. No woman can really be an Odonian."

"Odo herself—"

"Theory. And no sex life after Aseio was killed, right? Anyhow, there're always exceptions. But most women, their only relationship to a man is *having*. Either owning or being owned."

"You think they're different from men there?"

"I know it. What a man wants is freedom. What a woman wants is property. She'll let you go only if she can trade you for something else. All women are propertarians."

"That's a hell of a thing to say about half the human race," said Shevek, wondering if the man was right. Beshun had cried herself sick when he got posted back to Northwest, and raged and wept and tried to make him tell her he couldn't live without her . . . "You know, I don't agree," he said to long-faced Vokep, an agricultural chemist traveling to Abbanay. "I think men mostly have to learn to be anarchists. Women don't have to learn."

Vokep shook his head grimly. "It's the kids," he said. "Having babies. Makes 'em propertarians. They won't let go." He sighed. "Touch and go, brother, that's the rule. Don't ever let yourself be owned."

Shevek smiled and drank his fruit juice.

"I won't," he said (p. 46/42).

In this rather grim scene of two sexist men, one mouthing sexist contempt and the other sexist homilies, the author is again delineating the psychological limits on Annares sexual equality.

The theme is picked up in Chapter Ten in the fourth and last dramatic sign we shall discuss, when Takver, upbraiding herself for having urged Shevek, in Chapter Eight, to publish his book as a collaboration with the older and jealous physicist Sabul, says:

"...I'll tell you what was wrong. I was pregnant. Pregnant women have no ethics. Only the most primitive kind of sacrifice impulse. To hell with the book, and the partnership, and the truth, if they threaten the precious fetus! It's a social preservation drive, but it can work right against community! It's biological, not social. A man can be grateful he never gets into the grip of it. I think that's why the old archisms [governments] used women as property. Why did the women let them? Because they were pregnant all the time—because they were already possessed, enslaved," (p. 292/266).

Putting aside the final apposition's myriad suggestions anent the novel's title, we learn here, with this echo of Vokep's opinions, the extent to which this familiar matrix of ideas is accepted by (at least one of) the women of Annares as well as the men; each scene supports the other; both, together, render our picture of the society more coherent.

But two points must be made:

If we actually review the text concerning the publication of Shevek's book, we find that little or none of Takver's behavior is a real referent for any of the ideas that, in the passage just quoted from Chapter Ten, Takver expresses. In Chapter Eight both Takver and Shevek agreed that, as the *Principles* is a work of science, it made little difference whose name or names the book came out under. Later, as readers, *we* discover that the book was not only attributed jointly to Sabul, but that Sabul cut it, rewrote it, and generally mutilated it before affixing his name with Shevek's to the text: that *mutilation* is the crime.

When Takver urges Shevek to let the book be published with Sabul's name, and Shevek agrees, neither she nor Shevek have any way to know that such mutilation will result. Both of the young people are, perhaps, naive, but her suggestion is made rationally and Shevek accepts it rationally. Where is the biological drive to protect the fetus (or, by extension, the book) in all of this?

This is what leaves most of Takver's speech, as quoted, didacta which, because there is no vertical support in the earlier foreground (or clear vertical contradiction, which would render the didacta ironic), make it sound (whether it is or not) like an author expressing an opinion, rather than either characterization or social portraiture.

In Shevek's life there is a period, which in the actual text of *The Dispossessed* is absorbed not by indirect reportage but by the blank paper between paragraphs, when, change by change, he must become aware of Sabul's editing—whether he learns it in memo after memo over weeks, or is presented *fait accompli* with the edited version. There is a period in Takver's life when, pregnant, she must put up with her partner's misery over this mutilation—or his attempts to suppress that misery; and when she must put up with the idea of the mutilation itself.

At the end of this period, both—we know from the text—will have decided the compromise was a bad idea. But to omit this material, this period of clear and inevitable human change, is poor novelistic intuition. Such change, in its detail, texture, and structure, is *the* referent of fiction.

Our second point is simply this. The fact that various pregnancies in the real world are not experienced as Takver apparently, in retrospect, experiences hers (or as Vokep may or may not have had experience of some other woman's) suggests that pregnancy behavior is also open to analysis and speculation. That ideas on pregnancy behavior in the real world differ from those expressed by two Annaresti (Takver and Vokep), whether the ideas expressed by the Annaresti are coherent with one another or not, suggests that the origin of those ideas on Annares—whether supported by the real biology of the Annaresti or left over from Urrasti prejudices—is also open to analysis. To show the ideas without signs of speculation on their origin, no matter how well the ideas are orchestrated to suggest the coherence of Annaresti society, is poor science-fictional intuition.

The formal pressure of the traditional fictive concern with change asks for the missing material on Shevek, Takver, and the mutilation of *The Principles of Simultaneity*. The semantic pressure of the subject asks for another scene missing from the presentation of Shevek on Urras in Chapter Five:

> He got money for the papers he wrote. He already had an account in the National Bank the 10,000 international Monetary Units of the Seo Oen award, and a grant of 5,000 from the Ioti Government. That sum was now augmented by his salary as a professor and the money paid him by the University Press for three monographs (p. 115/105).

"Bank" suggests A-io has available some sort of checking system. And we shall have this confirmed in a future scene with Vea in the restaurant (p. 192/175). But at some time Shevek will have to enter a drugstore or a market or the University Bookstore and buy a paper of safety pins, a replacement pair of shoelaces, a writing tablet or a tube of toothpaste. For the first time in his life, he will take money out of his pocket, exchange it for goods, and pocket the change—at which point, presumably, implicit in the description of the incident, he will have some response to this thing called money. He may find it complicated, annoying, fascinating, silly, or what have you. But we sorely miss this response to the reality of coin and scrip.

The scene seems to have been prepared for, on Annares, at Shevek's going away party when Turin pretends to be the traditional Poor Urrasti—the Beggerman—and mispronounces the word "buy" which is, of course, not part of demotic Pravic. Any number of times on Urras we see Shevek *without* money—presumably signs of his poor management of the stuff, understandable in a first-time user. We see him avoid using money, as when, in a sort of inverse of Thomas Wolfe's famous supermarket scene, he recalls an attempt to buy a suit and shoes in the Saemtenevia Prospect, a sort of A-ioti shopping mall: ". . . The whole experience had been so bewildering to him that he put it out of his mind as soon as possible, but had dreams about if for months afterwards, nightmares: . . . a solid mass of people, traffic, and things . . . coats, dresses, gowns, robes, trousers, breeches, shirts, blouses, hats, shoes . . ." (p. 116/105).

The whole thing is too much for Shevek. When he sees the price of the coat ("8,400 units"), he retreats in guilty contemplation of the economic matrix behind it (2,000 units is a year's living wage, he has recently read). The suit is ordered by phone.

Indirect reportage again absorbs his money dealings in the restaurant at lunch with Vea and again at the dinner later where she makes ". . . no offer to share the cost," (p. 192/175) but suggests he write a check when he is caught short. Earlier, in the candy store where he is finagled into buying a box of sweets to take to her, he is too distracted for his point of view, from which the scene is written, to carry the needed focus on the monetary exchange. And by then, of course, his first encounter—the one we want to see—is long since over anyway.

I strongly suspect that if we had actually seen, along with Shevek, the coin/scrip/credit card in Shevek's till-then "empty" hands for the first time in a store, we would have experienced one of those fictive interfaces that would have immeasurably deepened our understanding of both sides: Shevek's psychology and Urras's sociology.

A similar pressure is on us to know about contraceptives. They exist on Urras. During the cock-teasing scene, one of Vea's excuses is that she hasn't taken one that day (and there is no indication that Shevek is unfamiliar with the word); and this is the only mention of the subject in the book (p. 203/185). But the occurrence of this one mention sends our imagination soaring back to Annares, where Takver has had two children and two miscarriages, the last three pregnancies during an intense, world-wide famine.

Availability of contraception on Annares would suggest one psychological interpretation of these pregnancies. Unavailability of contraception would suggest an entirely different one. The difference in the two possible psychologies for Takver is so great that the reader, ignorant as to whether contraception exists there or not, simply has no access to a vast area of Takver's persona. As she is an engaging character, the sensitive reader feels cheated by the author's withholding (or overlooking) of this information, because it withholds (or overlooks) so much of the character.

Let us summarize and draw a concluding point.

Contraception on Annares, Shevek's first encounter with money on Urras, Shevek's and Takver's reaction to the mutilation of the *Principles*, and the change in amatory status among Bedap, Shevek, and Takvar are subjects that draw attention to themselves primarily by the metonyms they have left about their absences in the text. A very conventional idea of fiction asks that these subjects be resolved in the fictive foreground (or, possibly, in the case of Annaresti contraception, at least presented in the récit). A less conventional idea of fiction asks that they either be resolved in the foreground *or* that some metafictive sign be left in the text to indicate the author does *not* intend to resolve them.

Annaresti ideas about pregnancy and Annaresti adolescent male bonding behavior want a different resolution in the novel from the one they get. What suggests this different treatment is the specifically science-fiction model which holds that the origin both of ideas and social behavior—especially when the author is free to speculate and invent what she cannot know—is of equal interest with the ideas and behavior itself. This concept, that ideas and behavior, however natural/moral/unquestionable, have effective social histories, is one of the indubitably significant messages that informs science fiction's inchoate textus. (This message is *not* intrinsic to the textus of mundane fiction.) A compendium of the various rhetorical postures, which both the most sophisticated and the most ham-handed science fiction have devised to support this model (and of which the model is constituted) would guide us through most of the truly significant verbal tropes traditional to the genre up through the beginning of the sixties: Sometimes ideas are seen as degenerate, as in Bester's Scientific People in *The Stars My Destination*; sometimes they have developed, as with Asimov's atomic traders in *Foundation*; others are seen as simply laterally transformed. Yet there is hardly an s-f writer who has not expended some considerable amount of whatever linguistic inventiveness she possesses on presenting a compressed, syntactic, or imagistic representation of such an ideohistory.

The discovery of Shevek's temporal theory also wants—against the s-f model—a different resolution from the one presented: Here, however, what is asked for is an omission. The two rhetorical postures of omission discussed, by which s-f traditionally deals with the coalescing of new conceptual knowledge, are in dialogue with the above concept of ideas as historically effected systems. Indeed, these rhetorical conventions of omission are what keep the message of the historicity of ideas and behavior from being *merely* a message in the narrow and propagandistic sense. These conventions of omission are the second of a pair of parameters, of which the concept of ideohistory is the first, which together create a richly contoured field capable of infinite modulation, in which exploration can proceed in any direction, and within which any number of subtle points can be posited. What the conventions of omission acknowledge is that, while ideas *do* have determining histories, a *new* idea is, indeed, new. In terms of any determining matrix of extant knowledge, its center is unknown. While certain conjectures may be made *about* any new idea, its center, till it actually arrives, however outrageous or conservative the speculation about it, must *remain* unknown. (That the center *is* unknown is what justifies, supports, impells the breadth, complexity, daring, and richness of speculation in the first place.) Together, the convention of ideohistories and the convention of idiocentric omissions (or opacities) generate the basic s-f dialectic. The two conventions are what finally allow science fiction to treat ideas as signifiers—as complex structures that organize outward in time and space (they have causes, they have results) as well as inward (their expressions, their forms, their deconstructions) yet some parts to that complex structure nevertheless registering as reasonably opaque. The two conventions are what free science fiction from the stricture that has held back so much modern thought, of treating ideas as signifieds—as dense, semantic objects with essential, hidden, yet finally extractable semantic cores. We must remember that in science fiction, speculation is a metaphor for knowledge; too many critics today find themselves arguing, however inadvertently, that (rather than ceding to this metaphoric hierarchy) knowledge of some sort of prior, privileged system (say, "science") can or must generate some metaphoric commentary on the use, workings, and efficacy of speculation itself. This is simply not the case.

At any rate, it is not surprising, when we look at it in this light, that an s-f story or novel which violates one of these s-f conventions should violate both. Much of Le Guin's novel, on some very basic level, takes place away from this richest pair of science-fiction conventions. I question seriously whether the book is the stronger for it.

6

The problem of didacta in *The Dispossessed* raises itself on every level. Indeed, the main subject under this rubric—the philosophy of Odo (Cf. Greek *odos* "street" or "road"; and the Chinese *tao* "path" or "way")—manages to put itself beyond discussion. To disapprove either of the philosophy as an ethical construct, or the way the ethical construct has been used to contour the aesthetic construct of the novel, is simply to declare oneself out of sympathy with the book. A critic who is seriously uncomfortable with either of these aspects had best look for another work to discuss.

The signs Le Guin repeatedly presents to call up the richness of Shevek's character are: 1, an inner energy and enthusiasm, and, 2, a composed and contained exterior. For me, they never quite integrate into a readerly experience of personality. What stands between them and prevents their inmixing are all Shevek's cool, crisp answers to the straw arguments posed by the Urrasti to the Odonian way. All these answers, which are finally what identify the arguments as straw, belong ultimately to the world of art where, to paraphrase Auden's *Calaban to the Audience*, great feelings loosen rather than tie the tongue. On highly politicized Annares, one might argue, the inhabitants seem to spend half their time talking politics and are therefore very comfortable in political discussions; moreover, half their arguments seem to be a running rehearsal of an argument with their own fictionalized vision of Urras; but *that* "Urras," as Le Guin so effectively points out *is* an Annaresti fiction. And the arguments that the Annaresti get a chance to practice are all with other more or less convinced Odonians. Those basic premises that a displaced Annaresti like Shevek would have to retrieve to answer not even the political arguments of the Urrasti but the basic assumptions that the Urrasti make without even broaching overt political discourse might take a bit more digging on Shevek's part than they seem to.

On Urras, Shevek is constantly having to face what strikes him as injustice, injustice of a kind he has never met before. In my own experience, such precise and ready answers to injustice come only with repeated exposure to the (many times repeated) injustice, with space between to contemplate, conjecture, and rehearse one's response. The condition of modern woman and man in the face of new outrage, *esprit d'escalier*, is unknown to Shevek.

For me it would have added much to Shevek's psychological texture if three or four times instead of having the quick and measured reply on his tongue, or the proper passage from Odo in his mind to bolster him up, he had kept his composure in bewildered consternation but later thought, with the same passion he brings to his other abstract considerations, of what he *might* have said.

Atro's description of the coming of the Hainish to Urras (p. 125/114) and his comparison of origin myths *is* witty *and* easily expressed. It presupposes, however, that he has said as much many times before to many Urrasti who have posed arguments similar to Shevek's. This is why his little speech works both as humor and as characterization. (One only wishes Le Guin could have trusted the humor enough to make do, in the paragraph on Shevek's response, with "Shevek laughed," and omitted the lumbering and tautological "Atro's humor gave him pleasure," (p. 127/115) before going on to "But the old man was serious.") But even in an Annares chapter, when Shevek, age nineteen, encounters Sabul over the publication of his paper, we find such descriptions of the young physicist facing his older, hostile professor:

> His gentleness was uncompromising; because he would not compete for dominance he was indomitable (p. 103/94).

This would be barely acceptable as description of a serene, sixty-year-old, Faulknerian patriarch, secure with the confidence of class, money, and age. As a description of a nineteen-year-old physics major—however sure he is of his rightness—it is ludicrous; and its suggestion of absolute virtue, for either a sixty year old or a nineteen year old, throws one back to the worst of pulp diction and pulp psychology. Too many sentences like the above dampen the live charge in the details of Shevek's presentation that might actually interact to cast lights and shadows in the reader's mind.

Many of the novel's didactic interchanges concern the difference in treatment of women between Urras and Annares. "Where are the women?" Shevek asks a group of Urrasti physicists (p. 65/59)—presumably to provoke them, though it seems somewhat out of character.

Mini-speeches follow. And from there on Shevek seems to forget completely the political situation of women on Urras and what (given the author's meticulous care to keep the production space of Annares equally deployed between males and females) must be taken as women's conspicuous absence.

Again I am thrown back to experience: an English, school-teacher friend of mine once decided to take his vacation in South Africa to visit a mathematician of his acquaintance at the university there. John is a moderate liberal in matters of race—not particularly revolutionary. (Revolutionaries simply do not visit South Africa; nor is this in any sense an analogue of the situation between Urras and Annares, because trade, emigration, and tourist traffic in both directions between England and South Africa is immense.) Nevertheless, John, like most Englishmen, is aware of the South African racial situation. When he came back from his vacation, he told me: "It's fascinating. In Jo'berg, you just don't *see* any blacks. Anywhere. And because you know they *are* there, you find yourself looking for them *all* the time—even in bars and stores where you'd be rather surprised to see blacks in London. Michael—my mathematician friend—and I were driving from the University to his place, which is in a suburb, and we had a minor smash-up with another car. By the time we had gotten out, there was a policeman there with his pad out, taking down names and numbers. The driver of the other car was Indian. And when the policeman demanded, 'Colour?' my heart began to thud and I grew terribly embarrassed, because I thought *now* I'd run up against it. Then Michael answered, 'Green,' and I realised the policeman was taking down the colours of our cars."

There is no way one can read a ninety percent population of exploited and oppressed blacks as an exact analogue of a fifty-two percent population of oppressed and exploited women. My recount of John's anecdote is simply to indicate various tendencies in the basic psychology of the traveler in politically alien space. To take John's anecdote momentarily as fiction, any didacta laid *over* this psychological structure ("I guess the racial situation there wasn't as bad as I thought," or "The racial tension in the air was *that* great; the situation is even worse than I'd suspected," or any of half a dozen other possible didactic conclusions with any of half a dozen possible relations to the socioeconomic reality of Johannesburg) *become* character painting. But without the support of some valid psychological structure, the didacta alone would be fictively vacuous.

There is certainly no way that John's anecdote about the visible absence of blacks could be transferred to the planet Urras and made to fit the visible absence of women in the Ieu Eun University. Such one-to-one transfers usually make schematic, lifeless science fiction at the best of times: and *The Dispossessed* veers close enough to the schematic. Yet one can see a scene in which Shevek, knowing he is going to teach a segregated class (his first), steels himself not to rock the boat. One of the "students," however, is a privileged Urrasti wife or daughter who, interested in such things, has gotten special permission to observe a single class. When she comes up to speak to him after class—perhaps it is customary for the shaved, Urrasti women in such situations to wear male wigs—the other men in the class know all about her. But Shevek mistakes her for a man. When he discovers his mistake, he wonders what is happening to his own perceptions of sex while he is there on Urras. In short, one wants something of the folded-back-on-itself recomplication in the psychology of the political alien that John's anecdote conveys. And again, because such an incident on Urras would have had to be an interface, both Shevek's reality and the reality of the A-io culture would have registered as richer by it.

I do not wish to give the impression that science fiction must imitiate the real in any simple and singular way. But the charge—of most presumptuously rewriting Le Guin's novel for her—that I have already laid myself open to several times now is one that I cannot see how to avoid in order to make the point paramount here: That point is merely the specifically science-fictional version of the advice the poet Charles Olson once gave a fiction-writing class at Black Mountain College: "Without necessarily imitating the real, we must keep our fictions *up to* the real." No matter how science fictional our entertainments (in both the active- and middle-voice sense of "entertain"), they must approach the same order of structural complexity as our own conscious perceptions of the real.

7

The following six pages are purely theoretical. They have grown up in dialogue with the work of Suvin and others whose papers on science fiction have appeared in the journal *Science Fiction Studies*. I hope to present my own points so that readers need only be familiar with general points, rather than the specific papers I am responding to. Those readers who pursue the text through the following intricacies will find themselves with an exploded linguistic model of the phenomenon that is science fiction along with a massive, if not crushing, critique of such a model's limitations.

In a simple sense, what science fiction does—at the level of coined science-fictional term (e.g., Cordwainer Smith's or Frank Herbert's use of the term *ornithopter*), at the level of the specifically science-fictional sentence (e.g., Robert Heinlein's "The door dilated."), and at the level of the uniquely science-fictional plot (e.g., Theodore Sturgeon's *The Clinic* in which: An amnesiac and aphasic is brought to a clinic where various people, as they try to piece together his history, discover he is from *an alien world*.)—is to take recognizable syntagms and substitute in them, here and there, signifiers from a till then wholly unexpected paradigm.* The

---

Syntagm and *paradigm* are, of course, part of the by now communal vocabulary of structuralism along with sign, text, signifier, signified, metaphor, metonymy, *et al.* Briefly, and for our purposes, a syntagm is a pattern of signs (or signifiers) that functions by means of patterned interactions. Each signifier in the syntagm also marks a position in the pattern. For each position there is usually a list of other signifiers occurrence of unusual, if not downright opaque, signifiers in the syntagm focuses our attention on the structures implied (since the "objects" that define the structures are themselves so frequently mysterious in one way or another), whether internal, external, implicit or explicit to any given signifier (or set of signifiers) in a given s-f text. (This I take to be the most salient theoretical point in Scholes' booklength essay, *Structural Fabulation*, University of Notre Dame Press, Indiana, 1975.) This focusing (or rather refocusing) does not occur in mundane fiction.

These structures are most easily discussed in terms of difference:

At the level of term: How would an *ornithopter* differ in operation and design from either helicopter or (to appeal to the Demotic meaning of that most classical of Greek roots) chicken.

At the level of sentence: How would the operation and construction of a door that dilated differ from the operation and construction of the door, say, by which I entered this room?

At the level of plot: How would the effects of an amnesiac alien on a hospital differ from those of a amnesiac human; and how would a hospital so effected effect an alien amnesiac different from a human amnesiac? What would be the differences in the processes of discovery and exploration between an alien and a human amnesiac?

Though the easiest discourse, as with all fantastic literature, is in terms of difference, we must not confuse either an easy or a difficult discourse with the primarily mental (or, even better, imaginative) event that is such a discourse's referent.

What necessitates calling the above explanation "simple"—in the sense of simple-minded—and what also leaves any simple idea of "distancing" or "estrangement" (*ostranie*) inadequate to account for the science-fictional phenomenon, is the process which we have mentioned once in passing and which Jacques Lacan has so persuasively brought to the analytical attention of contemporary thought in "Of structure as an inmixing of an otherness prerequisite to any subject what so ever"* and other seminars: and that is the

which, if substituted for the signifier already at that position, still allows the syntagm to go on functioning in a more or less similar way. Such a list is called the paradigm of signifiers for a given syntagmic position. Signifiers not on that list, or from other lists, either bring the syntagm's function to a halt or cause that function to change so greatly that it is best considered a new syntagm.

*In *The Structuralist Controversy,* Macksey and Donato, eds., The Johns Hopkins Press, Baltimore, 1972.

inmixing which occurs when *any* signifier is put into *any* syntagm, usual or unusual. (In the more available "The insistence of the letter in the unconscious,"* Lacan speaks of the "intrusion" of the signifier into the signified.) That inmixing (or intrusion) restructures the web of signifiers that is (or is our only expression of) the particular signifier's signified; as well, it restructures the web of signifiers that is (or is our only expression of) that signified below the syntagm itself taken as signifier. Our particular point is that for science fiction such inmixing (Cf. "Shadows/35", also "About 5,750 Words") works in a particular, unique, and identifying way.

Put a bit less polysyllabically: Once the new word has been absorbed into a sentence (that is, identically, as new for it), neither the word, nor the sentence considered apart from the word, retains its old meaning. The extension of the argument both to the science-fictional term and the science-fictional plot should be self-evident; but let us examine further the phenomenon at the level of the uniquely science-fictional sentence:

If we wish to discuss the science-fictional phenomenon in terms of distancing or estrangement, within any easy discourse of difference, we can regard the justly famous sentence from Heinlein's *Beyond This Horizon* as the familiar syntagm that is expressed by the sentence "The door opened" in which the signifier "dilated" (from a till-then inappropriate paradigm) has been substituted at the "opened" position. (Presumably "swung back," "widened," "drifted in," etc., constitute the appropriate paradigm of signifiers for that position.) In terms of difference, however, the mental image of the door has undergone (because of the new predicate) a catastrophic change of form. The imagined door has gone from rectilinear to round; it is now composed of interleaved plates; quite likely its material composition has changed as well. Consider the sentence: "If this door is closed only an inch, one might accidentally trip on it coming through." Such a sentence obviously belongs to the discourse of the restructured web of signifiers (which is all we can express of the signified) rather than to the discourse around either the syntagm "The door opened" or the discourse around sphincter muscles and camera apertures that usually accompanies traditional uses of "dilated." We

*In *Structuralism*, Ehrmann, ed., Doubleday Anchor, New York, 1970, and in *The Structuralists: from Marx to Lévi-Strauss*, de George & de George, eds., Doubleday Anchor, New York, 1972.

are dealing here neither with a familiar door suddenly estranged, a familiar process suddenly distanced, nor even a familiar sentence removed from its ordinary environment.

What distancing or estrangement there is is purely an aspect of the word order itself: The estrangement is totally restricted to the signifiers, *vis-a-vis* other genres.

But it is the *new* door and the *new* process (both, of course, imaginary) that are the referents of the sentence. And to say that the referent meaning of the sentence is rebuilt from the "distancing" or "estrangement" of either of these *old* sound-images is at least catachresis, if not just incorrect.

What is significant about the signifier "The door dilated," is not how the mental image is *like* either a conventional door or a conventional camera aperture, but rather how it *differs* from both.

To suggest the ramifications of our argument on the level of term: What is significant about an *ornithopter* is not how it is *like* either a helicopter or a bird. What is significant about it is that, when we focus our mind's eye at the joint of wing and fuselage, we can *see* the hydraulic pistons; when we open up the wing-casing, we can *follow* the cables and pulleys inside, we can *hear* the bearings in the bearing case around the connective shaft—which joints, pistons, cables and bearings are *foreign to both* birds and helicopters but without which our ornithopter *would not fly*.

And at the level of plot: With the story *The Clinic* we must locate this newness not in plot synopsis, but rather by an appeal to those shifts in psychology, those shadows of feeling, those emotional and intellectual signifieds through which the bizarre and astonishingly affective pidgin speech in which the aphasic alien narrates the tale transcends synopsis as the narrator transcends his own ignorance of his origins—in short, an appeal to those most evanescent yet most felt of fictive phenomena by which fictive experience itself registers *as* affect, *as* cognition—rather than any expression of the way a particular affect, once it, registers, is cognized.

The manner by which this inmixing occurs in s-f—a manner unique to science fiction—whether at the level of term, sentence, or plot, is what distinguishes s-f as a genre. The range of (or, if one prefers: the limitations on) themes, the particular conventions of transportation, economic organization and favored plot tropes that, after such a very brief history as a self-conscious entity, s-f has, for better or worse, fixed on for their usefulness or stalled at through its own imaginative anemia, are secondary, malleable, and of more importance to the historical development of the larger subjects they exemplify, i.e., the various social institutions prevalent during the times when the particular science-fiction texts were written. The "ideas" or "conventions" or "plots" are not what make them science-fiction texts.

This inmixing, to the extent the writer envisions herself purveying a signified by a set of signifiers (however complex, connotative, allusive, and vast that signified is; or however stripped, stark, and immediate; however separable from the signifiers; or however inmixed with them—which is to say, to the extent the writer conceives *any* advantage to the reader of the text knowing the language it is written in) is what makes the writing of s-f an art.

We have suggested some of the ways in which the internal structure of the sentence "The door dilated" is not the same as that of "The door opened." A little thought will show that its external structure, i.e., its syntagmic expectations (what might sit, so to speak, on either side of that door, what its function might be in a particular s-f text in which it appears), is different as well. (Indeed, "internal" and "external" here are points of view, rather than clearly demarked areas in the space of discourse.) Thus, in Disch's witty satire *Echo Round His Bones*, a single door, with the aid of a matter transmitter, opens a passageway from Earth to Mars, while in Bester's infinitely rich *The Stars My Destination,* doors, in his teleporting society, at certain social levels have fallen out of architectural use entirely while at others they are accompanied by vast systems of blinds, labyrinths, and baffles. And it is the same uniquely science-fictional process of imagistic inmixing, which allows the internal structural modifications to *door* itself when certain sound-images are brought into syntactic proximity, that also governs—when certain phrases, sentences, or larger language units are properly positioned in the text—the external structural modifications around *door*.

Once we realize this, we can see that the discourse associated with the concept of estrangement—the discourse of syntagms and paradigms—with all its implications that "The door dilated" is, somehow, just a replacement for "The door opened," belies the complex structures, internal and external, of which the specifically science-fictional sentence is the signifier.

"Bat Durston, blasters blazing, brought his spaceship around behind the asteroid," simply can *not* substitute for "Bat Durston, sixguns blazing, brought his palomino around behind the corral"— though a number of times these lines from an old *Galaxy* advertisement ("You won't find this kind of science fiction in *Galaxy!*") have been discussed as though one might, indeed, find such science fiction *some*where. But neither cynicism nor sincerity, literary ham-handedness nor verbal sophistication sign themselves in their constitutive sentences (save in the mode of parody) with the particular pace, image density, or development either sentence above utilizes. The educated ear—particularly the ear educated to science fiction—should simply hear both sentences as bogus. More to the point, the example *is* a piece of copywriter's wit. Science fiction has traditionally suffered from being judged by its packaging. But it compounds the sin to extend such judgment to analysis. There is another argument, that occurs on an entirely different level, which might be what the original advertisement appeals to, if not the discussions of it amidst terms like "paradigm," "taxonomy," and "estrangement." When fictive diction reaches a certain cliché level in *any* genre, we simply cease to care *what* it means. But to claim a substitutability (other than as a metaphor for taste) offers us no insight into the mechanics of meaning within the separate genres, science fiction *or* western.

Though the simple description of what science fiction does with which we began generates, after the fact, the proper string of signifiers, it yields no insight into the structural web those signifiers form around themselves which is, finally, their signified, their meaning. It yields no insight into what, in any specific s-f text, those signifiers may be doing, whether at a specifically science-fictional level or not.

The particular *manner* in which the inmixing of syntagm and signifier occurs in science fiction, whether at the level of term, sentence, or plot, to create something *more than* and *different from* what those syntagms and signifiers yield separately is what makes science fiction. This inmixing is also what makes any analytical separation of the signifiers and syntagms such an artificial construct at best.* The language with which s-f accomplishes its particular

---

*Our definition from page 255 may now be called *"sous rature."*

mode of inmixing must frequently use unusual verbal juxtapositions, by which certain words are estranged from their more usual, extrageneric contexts. But the process we are trying to fix is that by which we recognize (in the sense of ordinary, imaginative perception) these new and different images, rather than how we later cognize them *as structures* (and, in so doing, find them more or less coherent in terms of the current scientific episteme on which, of course, the ground rules of the game are, both in what is permitted and what is forbidden, laid) once the images are struck up by the hammer of language, like sparks, from the anvil of imagination.

Yet by beginning with this inadequate discourse and by sustaining a certain analytical pressure on it, we have moved to a richer picture of what science fiction is and is not than the discourse first appeared able to provide. And we are reassured by the similarity we immediately perceive with science fiction itself: As a genre, it so frequently begins as a discourse that appears inadequate to discourse on anything at all, but which, by auctorial application to it of a certain analytic energy among its visions, ends up writing much more of the world than, certainly, any description of the discourse can say.

8

One fictive problem of Urras remains homologous with a very real problem of western society in general.

Something I have been doing for the last couple of years to decondition myself: Whenever I am in a situation where it occurs to me that the number of men and women seems about equal, I count.

On the subway platform this afternoon, I saw what struck me as a pretty even spread of women and men. The actual count? Eleven women, twenty-five men.

Somehow, by a process the good doctor Skinner might best explain, most westerners—many women and most men—have been conditioned to read groups with sexual proportions of twenty-five/seventy-five to thirty-three/sixty-seven (women/men) as if they were fifty/fifty. Over two years I have managed to decondition myself to the point where twenty-five/seventy-five now *looks* to me like twenty-five/seventy-five. But thirty-three/sixty-seven still looks like fifty/fifty if I don't catch myself. Hopefully, this will change.

My analysis of this phenomenon is not complete. But I must assume that it is reinforced, if not caused, by the fact that fifty/fifty social groups are so seldom encountered on the street, in trains, on buses, or in airports.

On Annares, Le Guin has at least, in emblem, taken care of the reinforcement syndrome, if not the causatives themselves. The fictive problem of Urras, like the real problem of earth, is the one that Shevek asks and gets no answer to: "Where are the women?"

I am a man. Frankly, as far as New York, London, Athens, Paris, San Francisco, A-io's Nio Esseia, or any other city, real or imaginary, I have been permitted to inhabit, I do not *know* the answer. Though I would like somebody to tell me, I do not hold it against Le Guin that she has not.

I do hold it against her, however, that she has asked the question and then dropped it as though, somehow, it *had* been answered—and I find it hard to believe this dropping of the question in a character who has not had to fight the reinforcement conditioning that I have had to, or who is moving in an alien political space presumably famous in his own world for its oppression of women. It is one of the missing concerns that leaves Shevek's psychology thin.

In interface with Shevek's psychology, I find Urras's sociology thin. When Shevek escapes the University to find the true masses of A-io, too much of what he finds is literature in the same sense I used the term in the party scene with Shevek and Vea. The journey into Nio, through the encounter with the beggar, for all its inexact writing, works to evoke the presence of Nio Esseia's inner city. Later, the man whom Shevek is trapped with and who dies over three days through loss of blood from a mere hand injury calls up something real and important about the ironies, cruelties, and frailties of the human machine. But all in between—Shevek's first encounter with and protection by Tuio Maedda's nameless resistance organization, the protest gathering itself, Shevek's speech, and the government retaliation with helicopters and machine guns—lacks texture and resonance. It is not even that too few pages are devoted to all of this—seven, one of which is the speech itself. But many of us have listened, say, from eleven at night to six in the morning to the live radio coverage of the police brutalities during the Columbia University sit-in: The protesters had been using the university radio station to organize their activities; when the police jammed the station, the protesters got New York's educational station WBAI to volunteer its facilities, so that the audience was automatically boosted from a few hundred to 30-odd thousand; after hours of police horses trampling into telephone booths from which students were screaming descriptions of the beatings occurring outside, till glass walls shattered and the lines went dead, and another phone booth or walky-talky came on to begin the same again, some of us heard, on another, major radio station half an hour after WBAI went off, that there had been "'minor disturbances' at Columbia University last night" which the police had brought under control by nine-thirty; I learned of Martin Luther King's assassination from a black man— who had it by phone at two minutes to seven—running up Avenue B and shouting the news to everyone he met; when I turned in to a bar, with half a dozen other people, I saw (after calling my mother who had already been phoned the news by a New Jersey relative) the first media report of the assassination at five minutes after the hour (a time confirmed by a dozen news reports over the next three days)—a substantial portion of the country's black community knew of the assassination (minutes) before the media released it to the country. I heard the conflicting live coverages of the Cuban response at the United Nations to the Kennedy invasion, on CBS and, simultaneously, a small, FM radio station that I'd accidentally left on at the same time as my television because the sound was the same: CBS (hooked in with NBC and ABC) cut the last thirty seconds of the Cuban Ambassador's speech as well as the thunderous, three minute ovation it received from the United Nations audience, to go immediately into its detracting "analysis" of the speech, while the conclusion and response was still coming in over the radio . . . Again, the point here is not to say that the real is worse or better or even more interesting than Le Guin's science fiction. It is simply that if the last decade and a half has taught us anything it is that, over an area of political space as large as the USA, Russia, or, presumably, A-io, the internal structure of a political encounter is only half its relevance; its external structure is controlled by its interface with society's perception organs and information-distributing machinery, which controls the infrequently conflicting public "knowledge" of that internal structure.

The protest gathering in *The Dispossessed* is a nineteen-thirties daydream of a nineteen-ten strike—back when things were "simpler."

That the Terran ambassador Keng has heard Shevek's speech on the radio and was "very moved" (p. 301/274) by it only sidesteps the complexity to mire the question in unnecessary sentimentality.

Before leaving our discussion of the novel at the resolution of action and incident, we must look at two characters on Annares and the didactic uses they are put to.

The first is Bedap, Shevek's childhood friend, twice Shevek's lover, his political conscience, friend to Shevek's family, co-frere in the Syndicate of Initiative, and the single homosexual, male or female, mentioned by name in the novel.

The second character is Rulag, Shevek's mother, who leaves him with his father (who parks him fulltime with a nursery at what must be about the age of eighteen months, given the child's speech accomplishments: "Mine sun!" [p. 24/22]); Rulag comes to see Shevek in the hospital some eighteen years later with an offer of friendship Shevek rejects. Some twenty-odd years after that, she is the most articulate opponent in the Syndicate of Initiative to Shevek's plan for going to Urras.

Both these characters are put to different didactic uses, one of which I both disagree with and find personally offensive, and one of which I personally happen to approve of; but neither of which, I feel, are successful within the novel.

We discuss Bedap first:

> The Moon stood high over the Northsetting Regional Institute of the Noble and Material Sciences... "I never thought before," said Turin... "of the fact that there are people sitting on a hill, up there, on Urras, looking at Annares, at us, and saying 'Look, there's the Moon.' Our earth is their moon; our Moon is their earth."
> "Where then is truth," declaimed Bedap, and yawned (p. 36/33).

The central conceit of the novel is laid out here; Bedap speaks (and is mentioned by name) for the first time.

> Bedap gnawed at a thumbnail.

is the next descript we have for the young man. And a page later:

> But Bedap, a heavy-set, square-faced fellow, chewed on his thumbnail and said, "All the same, Tir's point remains. It would be good to know the truth about Urras."

"Who do you think is lying to us?" Shevek demanded. Placid, Bedap met his gaze. "Who, brother? Who but ourselves?"

The sister planet shone down on them, serene and brilliant, a beautiful example of the improbability of the real (p. 40/36).

Some years later, after they have been apart for a time, Shevek is teaching and studying physics at the institute. Shortly after his funeral eulogy for the great, aged physicist Gvarab, he runs into Bedap in front of the Music Syndicate auditorium. The two old friends return to Shevek's room. Shevek talks of all his doubts about his work that the tradition-bound Institute has burdened him with. Bedap tells of his own doubts about the whole Annaresti system; he tells the story of Turin, his satirical play and its aftermath of social disapproval: Turin is now in a rehabilitation asylum.

Le Guin describes Bedap in Shevek's room:

Bedap had small, rather squinting eyes, a strong face, and a thick-set body. He bit his fingernails, and in years of doing so had reduced them to mere strips across his thick, sensitive fingertips (p. 145/132).

One wishes that the description had been worded so as not to insult those of us who had remembered this singular fact of Bedap's habituations over the intervening ninety-eight pages. At any rate, after arguing politics, the two men go to bed:

When he came back [from the bathroom] Bedap proposed to sleep on the floor, but as there was no rug and only one warm blanket, this idea was, as Shevek monotonously remarked, stupid... Shevek unrolled the bedding and lay down... It was cold. Each felt the warmth of the other's body as very welcome... They moved closer together. Shevek turned over on his face and fell asleep within two minutes. Bedap struggled to hold on to consciousness, slipped into the warmth, deeper, into defenselessness, the trustfulness of sleep, and slept. In the night one of them cried out loud, dreaming. The other one reached his arm out sleepily, muttering reassurance, and the blind warm weight of his touch outweighed all fear (p. 152/137).

In our culture, the discourse of affection is hopelessly confused with the discourse of sex/seduction. It is through the equivocation of the two discourses that we presume (and the presumption is confirmed by the next paragraph) Shevek and Bedap make love. Nevertheless, I think this is a moment most readers, especially young ones, will take with them from the novel. Despite the reliance on the confusion of discourses, despite the sentimentality, despite the next paragraph's attempt to make the morning-after situation, which would probably be handled with much gentleness and compassion, appear businesslike and cursory, what is taken away I believe is valid. For one thing, it represents an intelligent synthesis of a very old debate.

Auden has written somewhere that the great crime against the modern spirit is to treat individuals as if they were interchangeable. Anyone who has known the soul-deadening effect of infinite forms, impersonal paychecks issued by an absent or even unknown employer, the routinized societal slots in which so many people spend their lives—or even better, anyone who has known the amazing and astonishing sense of social support, community, and well-being that accrues when, in one's work, one's business dealings, one's social life, one is valued by a community of people as an individual—knows how truly Auden speaks. Social needs remain; but the individuals who fill them are *not* "replaceable."

Yet, if we do not, at some level, assume that people are interchangeable, what constrains us to treat all equally—before the law, for example? If we *do* respond to people entirely as individuals, we cannot deny that such individual aspects include the fact that one person is more pleasant *to us*, or more useful *to us* than another. How are we to respond then, over any statistical array of people, by laws and rules that take such aspects into account without exploiting them in ways totally biased toward the subjectivity of the law-makers?

It is a complex argument, and in several places Le Guin argues on the more, rather than the less, complex points in it—notably the discussion with (the at-that-point unidentified) Takver at Shevek's going-away party.

The scene quoted recalls strikingly the scene in *Stranger in a Strange Land*, where Michael Valentine Smith makes love (and loses his virginity) with one of (possibly) four women. Somehow, for the rest of the book, this does not differentiate his relationship, one way or the other, with *any* of them! Heinlein's scene is an exemplar of the psychological self-deception necessary to condone the "interchange-ability" Auden decried. Le Guin, however, primarily by use of a much lighter touch (two sentences, rather than two pages), carefully prepared for in more ways than I can outline here, has, by employing a similar anonymity, momentarily effected a moving, intelligent synthesis in a complex debate: Their semantic interchangeability is used here to suggest they are equal in their vulnerability.

In the next paragraph, we learn that their subsequent affair is the resumption of an "adolescent pairing" that has not been mentioned till now. The placing of this important information about the earlier affair here is an example of a frequently effective science-fiction technique for displaying the relative decline in social egregiousness, vis-a-vis our own culture, of a particular type of behavior: The character performing this particular professional job just happens to be non-white; the character performing another just happens to be a woman; the character doing thus and such just happens to be naked. That *"just happens,"* or any other overt protestation of insignificance, is precisely the sort of didactum mundane fiction has taught us to distrust. But the placement of a given piece of information within the science-fictional syntagm in such a way that our current cultural evaluation of its import must compete against the far decreased import this *position* implies can be a finely honed critical trope in the hands of the best s-f practitioners. (The reverse technique—placing some presumably insignificant piece of information in a position which implies great importance to it—is also part of our rhetorical battery.) Because, however, something more than relative social egregiousness is involved in *any* affair, regardless of the sex of the participants (and usually the younger they are, the more important to them it is), and because we must presume this affair was in progress during the scene under the Northsetting moon previously quoted (Occam's razor cuts a much finer line in fiction than in real life), this is perhaps not the best use of the technique citable. At any rate, Le Guin reassures us that the resumed affair is brief: ". . . Shevek was pretty definitely heterosexual and Bedap was pretty definitely homosexual" (p. 153/139).

But the didactic purpose to which Bedap is put (that I referred to earlier) comes with his last appearance in the novel.

Toward the end of Chapter Twelve, Shevek's partner Takver and their daughter Sadik are being harrassed by their fellow workers because of Shevek's reputation for wanting to open communication with Urras. Shevek and Bedap are walking ten-year-old Sadik back to her dorm when suddenly she asks Shevek if she might stay the night with him and Takver. She tells Shevek "with desperate courage" (an admirable sentiment, if an unhappy hyperbole) that everyone in her dorm thinks Shevek, Bedap, and the Syndicate they have started are traitors. Then she bursts out weeping. Shevek holds her and tells Bedap to go on:

> There was nothing for Bedap to do but leave them there, the man and the child, in that one shared moment of intimacy which he could not share, the hardest and deepest, the intimacy of pain. It gave him no sense of relief or escape to go; rather he felt useless, diminished. "I am thirty-nine years old," he thought as he walked on toward his domicile, the five-man room where he lived in perfect independence. "Forty in a few decads. What have I done? What have I been doing? Nothing. Meddling. Meddling in other peoples' lives because I don't have one. I never took the time. And the time's going to run out on me, all at once, and I will have never had...that." He looked back, down the long quiet street, where the corner lamps made soft pools of light in the windy street, but he had gone too far to see the father and daughter, or they had gone. And what he meant by "that" he could not have said, good as he was with words; yet he felt that he understood it clearly, that all his hope was in this understanding, and that if he would be saved he must change his life (p. 326/297).

Here Bedap exits from the novel.

We have only been given three tangible factors about Bedap's life: he bites his nails, he holds certain political beliefs, and he is homosexual. His political beliefs at this point are one with Shevek's; so that cannot be the life-element to be altered. Some pages earlier (p. 318/290), the author told us he has gotten over his nailbiting. This leaves only one thing in the universe of the novel for him to change.

I currently belong to a gay fathers group—twelve fathers, eighteen children (sixteen biological, two adopted). Two of the fathers live with the children's mothers; ten of us do not. We take our kids together on group trips ice-skating, to local museums, have biweekly communal meals with our kids, and rap sessions without. (The underlying assumption to Le Guin's passage is a complete discontinuity between homosexuality and parenthood, which neither history nor Kinsey will support.) But there are a number of homophile organizations that are explicit committed to the support of children and the extended involvement in their upbringing. Assuming Annares, with its complete acceptance of homosexuality, has at least reached the enlightenment level of Manhattan's upper West Side, one must assume the only reason Bednap might "have never had ... that" is because he didn't want it.

The innuendo that ". . . if he would be saved" Bedap must change his homosexuality is both coy and pious (already an ugly combination) and, to me, offensive.

What constitutes the offense is that I am sure my reading of the text is *not* the one Le Guin intended. I suspect her identification with Bedap during the envisioning of the scene was such that, like him, she too "could not have said" what all this precisely signified. There are too many verbal signs in the paragraph—the meaningless absolute, "perfect independence," the simple cliché itself "would be saved"— that suggest a situation which, however "felt," is not vividly seen, accurately analyzed, nor clearly represented. The whole effect is vague, and—one suspects for the author—possibly symbolic of some sort of heterosexual consciousness quite apart from her denoted subject: a homosexual male's perception of a (by Annaresti standards) socially egregious family relationship. Nevertheless, one way to find out what you're thinking is to write it down and read it over; and, once read over, it is very hard to ignore the letter of the meaning, that certainly shines the more brightly in the light of personal offense, but which, offense or no, still lies at the core of this vague and diffuse surround of signification. For the didactic reduction of this paragraph is no different from the idea expressed by a fifty-six-year-old part-time milk company clerical worker, Julia Kaplan, in a recent *Ms.* magazine when interviewed on her thoughts over the possibility that the Equal Rights Amendment might help homosexuals: "I think these people *should* feel ashamed. It's not normal." What Kaplan says does not offend me; I simply disagree. What Le Guin says does—precisely because one can sense the idea itself mystified in the paragraph that presents it so that no open disagreement is possible.

But what should be brought home here is far more important than any personal offense: In so conventionalized a discourse as fiction (and science fiction has almost all the conventions of mundane fiction as well as a panoply of its own), we have the choice of saying precisely what we want to say (which requires a massively clear vision and intense analytical energy), or saying what everyone else has said (which is what happens either when vision fades, analysis errs, or energy fails). There *is* no middle ground. The concert of the three— vision, analysis, and energy—at work within the field of a given language is what we recognize as language skill/talent/craft. But the cliché, at almost any level, always signals one of the three's failure; the cliché indicates this because language is as structurally stable as it is: indeed, the cliché—at almost any level save the ironic—is the stability of language asserting itself without referent.

The didactic purpose I sense behind the use of Shevek's mother Rulag in the closing chapters of the novel is one that I, personally, approve of.

In Western literature, and in the Western imagination since Freud, the position Rulag fills in the chain of signifiers that makes up the experience of *The Dispossessed* has usually been filled by a man— by the Father. It is the Father whom the son must overcome. It is the Father who stands for society. Le Guin goes to great lengths to reduce Rulag's "motherhood" to pure symbol, for as Rulag herself declares, the real relation of mother and son she and Shevek share is practically biological accident. Le Guin then places her, as symbol, in the position so frequently filled by the Father.

Two things subvert this otherwise laudatory enterprise of revising our modern symbology. The first I can only mention; the other I shall discuss. First, there already exists a symbolic catagory to receive the cold, tradition-bound mother (the Great Bitch Mother, which encompasses both *Cinderella*'s Wicked Stepmother and *Cuckoo's Nest*'s Big Nurse) which informs our reading of all such fictive characters. The category is contoured by the economic, the sociological, and the historical pressures that, in western society, have frequently supplied different motivations to men and women. Even though these pressures are not in evidence on Annares, the category is still part of our readerly apparatus; and it posits a very different reading for all such mothers, even in a situation, like Annares's, which by implication has a different economic, social, and historic organization. To accomplish such a symbolic revision, the author would have to confront such economic, social, and historic pressures head on, rather than by implication. With such an undertaking, leaving the revised pressures in the implied universe almost assures fictive defeat.

But what undercuts Le Guin's purpose even more than this ready-made symbolic category—or rather what plays totally into its grasping hands—is that Rulag is so seldom anything *more* than symbol. This is the point we shall examine.

At the beginning of the book, we only hear of her: She has been assigned to another work area. Her partner Palat explains that (p. 24/21) she "has a great work to do."—though we hear no more of it than that, one way or the other, accomplished or failed. We never even discover what it concerns. Some great dam or irrigation project to be built? Some system of mines to be organized? If we did know what it was, and if we knew whether she had been successful at it or not (or if, perhaps, it is still going on), we would have a focus around which to organize the little, other information we have about her. More than a dozen years later, when Rulag, for the first time, suddenly visits Shevek in the hospital, she is all handsomeness and control, poise and dispassion—which Shevek reads as an obvious sign of inner despair and need. Again, his reading is far too literary, and it is hard not to suspect that, since her exterior is so much like his, he might be more likely to assume that exterior contained similar doubts and self-disciplines to his own.

Rulag offers to befriend her son. He refuses the offer. After she leaves, he breaks out crying.

Again, what keeps this from coalescing for me into an affecting readerly experience is, first, a thinness to the writing; second, Shevek's reaction contravenes too much of what I have observed; again, it is too much "literature."

A parent who goes and comes over the years, who vanishes for six months, shows up for three weeks, then disappears again only to arrive a year later for a four-month stay, each time bringing tension, causing scenes, upsetting family routines and frequently precipitating economic difficulties—such a parent who makes an offer of friendship to an older child newly on his/her own may well encounter such a reaction as Shevek's: hostility, upset, rejection.

But I know three instances of parents, separated from the family before the children were three years old, who did not materialize again until after the children were grown.

In all three cases the initial response of the children to the new parent was excitement and enthusiasm that certainly lasted through the first weeks of the relationship—even though in one case it involved a perfectly respectable twenty-three-year-old English woman discovering that she was illegitimate. In one case, a son and a mother, the relationship became very close and has continued so over at least eight years. In the other two cases, after a few months spent muchly in one another's company, the relations cooled into amicable acquaintanceship: children and parents simply did not share that many interests.

The intensely affective cathexis that Le Guin's description of Shevek's response invokes is always, in the real world, a manifestation of what the parent does *with* and *to* the child—not what the parent does away from the child. And while I would be willing to believe the Annaresti society might cool the enthusiasm and excitement that to me seems natural to Shevek's situation, I see no factors that would, *sui generis*, produce Shevek's response as Le Guin gives it. For that we would need a society that placed intense importance on having parents from birth on, a society in which the parentless child was cruelly and repeatedly ostracized even more than in our own society.

This is the reason that the closing of this chapter remains for me mere melodrama; and that Shevek's tears obliterate even the hazy image of Rulag I was able to form.

When, twenty years later, Rulag turns up again as Shevek's most articulate opponent in the Syndicate, I can't help think how much more affecting the conflict would have been if a rich and believable relation had already been established between them. As it is, Rulag appears only as a list of reasons why communication should not be established with Urras, placed in a symbolic mouthpiece—even though I respect what the symbol is supposed to be accomplishing.

The strongest image I actually have of Rulag as a person is when Shevek, on Urras, after having purchased his suit and shoes by phone, tries them on and turns "... away from the mirror, but not before he had been forced to see that, thus clothed, his resemblance to his mother Rulag was stronger than ever" (p. 118/107).

9

Some people may wish to argue that the sum of all these fictive thinnesses (easiest to discuss in terms of differences with our own experience) can be deconstructed into a political template at odds with the surface form of Le Guin's apparent political sympathies. But that is beyond the scope of this treatment.

Shevek's brief homosexual affair is far more affecting than his traditional heterosexual one—not because it is unusual but because it involves Shevek in intellectual change (their initial political disagreements) and leads to action (the establishment of the new Syndicate) as well as emotional support. In the portrayal of the book's major heterosexual relation, all aspects of Takver's personality or intellect that might cause conflict and thus promote intellectual change and growth in either her or Shevek have been relegated to the same mysterious space as Annaresti contraception methods. The heterosexual relation is merely supportive—and supportive, when all is said and done, of some of Shevek's least attractive characteristics. Some people may wish to argue that all this follows a tradition so old and so pervasive in western literature that it currently threatens to leach all interest from the precincts of fiction itself. Such an argument is also beyond our purpose.

Such templetes and such traditions are primarily statistical entities. To argue such positions rigorously would demand an analysis and comparison of many, many works in even greater detail than we have exercised here. And to make such larger criticism, when all is said and done, is only to say that Le Guin's novel suffers from the same failings as practically every other contemporary, mundane novel (as well as most nineteenth century ones).

If these failings are highlighted in *The Dispossessed*, one general highlighting factor is the structural focus peculiar to science fiction; for these failings *are* structural tendencies that the overall textus of western fiction has, unfortunately, incorporated into itself. The second highlighting factor is that Le Guin has taken for her central subject much of the socioeconomic material to which these structural tendencies, in mundane fiction, are a response. That she has found, in the alternating chapters, an aesthetic form that reflects the technological underpinnings of her tale is admirable. If, however, she had found a form that reflected the socioeconomic underpinnings, which are even more central to it, she would have written one of the great novels of the past three hundred years.

I suspect I am at odds even with most sympathetic contemporary critics of s-f in my feeling that science fiction, precisely through the particular quality of inmixing unique to it and the rhetorical postures available to it, has the greatest chance of overcoming, first by individual efforts and finally as a genre, precisely these fictive problems. The steps we have made in this direction are certainly small. But when we have gone a great deal further, Le Guin's novel may well hold its place among the earliest such steps.

The critic criticizes by constituting a difference with an implied or explicit set of experiences. Quite possibly the writer—and particularly the writer of science fiction—writes by constituting a difference with her own experience (a sort of *differance*), but all we are prepared to discuss here is that attendant analysis of those experiences which is, I would hazard from introspection, the more accessible part of the process. The science-fictional restructuring in which one's own experiences are broken down and reassembled within the framework of a given fictive future presupposes a far greater amount of analysis in the creative act itself, whether conscious or unconscious, than in the act of creating a mundane fiction. Indeed, this analysis *is* the creative aspect of that emphasis on structure that has already been noted for the genre.

In this sense, Le Guin's successes are successes of analysis (as her failures are failures of analysis) of her fictive subject. Because of the unique nature of the inmixing that is science fiction, these successes of analysis manifest themselves not as didacta, but as emotional densities, verbal life, and an underlying psychological recomplication in the material, all of which invests the text with life and energy. The failures of analysis manifest themselves as a discrepancy between those same fictive densities and the didactic presence that runs through the work—and that, indeed, any fictive work (but especially science fiction) can always be reduced to (if it is not overtly manifest in the text) if we choose to make such a reduction.

A writer of mundane fiction works with difference in the following way. The first *analytical* question must be: What is the easiest way to express my subject in fictive terms? With this as basis, the second analytical question is: But what is my subject *really* like? The difference between the two gives the text all its energy, life, and significance—whether it be in the discourse of the senses presented as foreground, or the discourse of psychosocial analysis presented as récit. In such a text, a discrepancy between what registers as felt and what registers as didactic is best handled by excising the didactic— from the sensibility and the text.

The writer of science fiction deals with difference in the following way. Again the first analytical question must be: What is the easiest way to express my subject in fictive terms? With this as basis, the second question becomes: What have I experienced, and in light of that experience, what *could* what I want to express be really like? The difference between the easiest expression and the actual text again lends the text its brio. But in the situation of the science-fiction writer, a discrepancy between what registers as felt and what registers as didactic is best handled by integrating the didactic through a further exploration and analysis of one's own experiences: by dramatizing the didactic points in a foreground in which is perceptible some structural syntagm that can be reduced to the required didactum—and as frequently several more besides.

The science-fiction author most generally associated with the problem of didacta is, of course, Heinlein. With Heinlein, the argument runs: The didacta in Heinlein are frequently absurd and are bearable, if at all, only because of a certain rhetorical glibness. If the foreground vision and the didacta were integrated, the foreground vision would change in such a way that it would no doubt be insupportable even to the author. With Le Guin, the argument runs: The didacta are frequently admirable, but as frequently clumsily put. If the foreground vision and the didacta were integrated, the foreground vision would be far stronger, livelier, more interesting, and relevant. Both, in their underlying assumptions, though, are still the same argument.

The actual talk of "integration" that appears in much of the sympathetic criticism we have had on Le Guin's work to date seems to me to do the author a disservice. The "social integration" cited as one of *The Dispossessed*'s accomplishments is too frequently a manifestation of its failures of analysis, of questions not asked. And the signs of it in the text are the lack of science-fictional integration between the didacta and the novelistic foreground.

Though it is certainly not Le Guin's fault, I am afraid the "integration" being sought for by this criticism is a kind of critical nostalgia for signs of an older fictive naiveté.

Certainly science-fiction novels are reminiscent of older genres. The progress of the young hero in Van Vogt's *The Weapon Shops of Isher* from the provinces into the social machinations of the city recalls the plots of how many Balzac novels (even to the gambling incident in *Pere Goriot*); and the deployment of the City of the Game and the various pastoral locations on Venus in *The Pawns of Null-A* creates a geofictive syntagm practically congruent with that of Paris,

Combrey, and Balbec in Proust's great novel. Indeed, the alternating chapters of *The Dispossessed* suggest nothing so much as a development on the form so favored by Proust's near-contemporary, Edgar Rice Burroughs, who employed a somewhat similar alternating-chapter format in Tarzan novel after Tarzan novel. But the very fact that Van Vogt recalls Proust while Le Guin recalls Burroughs is to say that the interest of the observation is exhausted with its statement. What is reminiscent in science fiction of older forms is only of minimal interest—or at any rate it is of the same order of interest as those elements in Shakespeare's plays which recall the chronicles, tales, and older plays from which he took his plots: To keep critical proportion, the relation must be discussed in terms of difference rather than similarity.

Here is the place to note that this analysis of the writer's own experience must not be confused with the critical analysis of the science-fiction text into recognizable syntagms and unusual signifiers spoken of in section 8. The analysis of experience I speak of leaves no explicit signs *in* the text. Rather, it becomes with recombination and inmixing the text itself. Indeed, all the text can explicitly sign is its lack: and *one* such sign is the split between didacta and foreground. To repeat: the inmixing of syntagm and signifier is an essentially inadequate discourse to signify the process unique to science-fiction discourse (a process not definable, only designatable) that allows that science-fictional materia that is both analysis and language to transcend both ideology and autobiography.

Just over fifty years ago Lukács wrote: "The novel is the only art form where the artist's ethical position is *the* aesthetic problem." Very possibly in the same year, Wittgenstein recorded the observation in the notebook which was to become the basis for the *Tractatus:* "Ethics *is* aesthetics."

That science-fiction novels *are* novels is to say Lukács's observation still applies. But to be fully aware that they *are* science fiction is to be aware of the extended range of aesthetic technique s-f has at its disposal to solve the problem.

If Le Guin is to move her work into the area so frequently cited for it, where its successes are notable in terms of its difference from the run of mundane fiction—a run that takes in the best with the worst—she must, first, galvanize her style. It does no good to tell an author, much of whose language sentence by sentence is pompous, ponderous, and leaden, that her writing is lucid, measured, and mature. The tones of voice that many of her sentences evoke belong, under control, within quotation marks in the dialogue of characters, or, if outside quotation marks, in their reported thoughts. They do not belong in the auctorial voice.

If this stylistic galvanizing occurs, the result, I suspect, will be that her language, besides becoming far cleaner, sharper, and more exact, will also become far more "science-fictiony"—that is, it will show many more of those magical combinations of words that, simple and uncluttered, are still the language by which we recognize the alien world.

In an interview with the Eugene Women's Press Le Guin has suggested one possible way to bring about the refocusing that must go along with this stylistic refinement:

> In public situations when people ask me, Why do you write about men . . . I say, because I like to write about aliens. It's very flip; it's also true. I'm fascinated by this attempt to get into the Other. I'm terribly fond of my women, it's just that they are me. It's too close. Now maybe what I ought to do is try to write about a woman who isn't at all like me. I've never done it. I've really never done it.

One wants to jump for joy at this suggestion!—though one pauses right after jumping to proffer a reminder only applicable to science fiction: The mundane fiction writer need only analyze what she sees to glean the materia which, by whatever transformations, will become her art. The science-fiction writer must analyze as well the way it is seen, and how and why it is seen in a particular way. This does not mean any deep and profound searching among the inner, mythic mysteries; only a clear vision of the economic, social, and technological biases and influences which organize our individual responses to the world. It demands a clear vision of the web of psychological expectations and social benefits (precisely *who* benefits) that exist for *every* idea and attitude taken as part of the social syntagm. For this is the materia which, by whatever transformation (including those peculiar to science fiction), we render an art which must so frequently project women and men who not only see and experience new things, but see and experience them in new ways because their entire, fictive lives have been radically different from ours all along. In science fiction, unlike mundane fiction, there is no implicit limit on the distance from the self to the Other (be it woman, man, or alien) to contour the fictive reality. There is only the perspicacity of the analysis of the self and the self-surround into the materia out of which an image of that Other, the self-hood of that Other, and that Other's self-surround are structured. To address Le Guin's comment directly: In science fiction unlike mundane fiction, short of one's analytical limits, there *is* no limit on how different these Other women may be from the author; and *this* is the reason that, in science fiction, not to explore them seems such a fictive failing.

The writer, during the actual work on her own text, has privileged access to its signified and its signifiers. If the new signified created does not please, the writer is free, in the light of that so-important analysis, to expand, cut, excise and replace signifiers throughout the web of the text. And in science fiction, there is, practically speaking, a far greater number of replacement points, and certainly a far greater number of signifiers to choose replacements from. We have already pointed out how, in her treatment of Annares' ergotic space, Le Guin has taken the familiar syntagm we daily encounter in the proportions of women and men and replaced, as it were, some of the men with women. The inmixing that occurs *is* the readerly experience of the Annaresti labor division and the experience of its implications as they spread into other aspects of the society. A final point on the subject of didacta: Once the didactic concern has been analyzed and integrated, this leaves the rhetoric of didacta free to point, emphasize, and underline what is *in* the foreground far more subtly and ironically; and leaves it, in general, an aesthetically more interesting tool.

10

The Dispossessed has excited many readers. For the second time its author has taken both Hugo and Nebula awards for best science-fiction novel of the year; and the bestowal of both fills me with pleasure. Some years ago at the University of Washington at Seattle, I had the privilege of teaching for several days with Le Guin at the Carion West S-F Writers' Workshop. She has one of those individual and amazing minds which, so fortunately, seems to be the hallmark of, rather than the exception among, our genre's practitioners. The experience was, frankly, thrilling.

A study of a genre that includes only a description of books must be a limited one. Any full exploration must cover the impact of those books on readers and writers. That alone would assure Le Guin's novel a substantial place in any study of contemporary s-f; no derogation I might make here could deny it that place. And, as I hope I have indicated, there is much more to the book than those things that strike me as its flaws.

To be fair, it is as much the excitement as it is the excitement's object that has impelled me to this lengthy examination. I only hope that my method, by displaying its biases clearly, invites its own refutation. At least this is what I have tried for.

The nature of this excitement may be what makes it so easy to lose hold of one truth we must never mislay if we are to keep our analysis rigorous: The science-fiction novel—*The Dispossessed*—is a structure of words; any discourse it raises is raised by its words.

I have already discussed one moment, between Shevek and Bedap, when two sentences, artfully ambiguous, have produced a striking synthesis with affective intelligence. There are many more such moments—most at places, be they finely or faultily written, where the language is doing something it can *only* do in science fiction.

We shall close our discussion of *The Dispossessed* with a look at several examples of uniquely science-fictional language in the text.

We are with the old, Urrasti physicist Atro:

> My eyes get so tired these days. I think that damnable magnifier-projector-thingy I have to use for reading has something wrong with it. It doesn't seem to project the words clearly any more (p. 128/116).

This recalls the type of language we discussed using the example of the Heinlein sentence—with the difference that this one works nowhere near as well. Why? The analogic commentary it suggests on the cliché of old people forgetting names of things and their self-deceptions about their failing eyesight is not sufficiently intruded on by the new signifier ("magnifier-projector-thingy") to re-form as any new structure we can respond to as insight. As well, the external structure of "magnifier-projector-thingy" does not particularly connect it with anything else mentioned of the Urrasti society/technology; it is not reinforced by anything; it does not reinforce. At best, it is merely cute.

On Annares, however, where (through an incident on Urras) we know that the populace are vegetarians who eat some fish (we have seen the fishbones left over at Shevek's party) and that fish breeding (and fish genetics) is a modern profession, we find a description of a snowfall at night:

"At each crossing the dim streetlight made a pool of silver, across which dry snow flurried like shoals of tiny fish chasing their shadows" (p. 144/131). This works not only as a striking visual description, which it might well do in mundane fiction; it also lends an equally striking sense of coherence to the whole apprehension of Annaresti culture and consciousness; such reflections of consciousness and culture occur, of course, in the metaphors of mundane fiction, but seldom with such pointed effect.

At another point we see Shevek with his infant daughter:

> He would sit the baby on his knee and address wild cosmological lectures to her, explaining how time was actually space turned inside out, the chronon being thus the everted viscera of the quantum, and distance one of the accidental properties of light (p. 220/200).

Besides portraying Shevek at his most believable and human, the sentence takes the signifiers of the book's major scientific themes and reduces them to a purely abstract and verbal dance, where they strike us as a tiny reflection of the whole object of our consideration, seen far off in a spherical mirror. By extension, it humanizes these scientific concerns for us to see that they have some aspects—if only the sounds of the words on an enthusiastic physicist's tongue—that can please a baby.

At another point, the entire cosmological conceit of the novel is used to inform a simile for sex between Shevek and Takver after a long separation: They "... circled about the center of infinite pleasure ... like planets circling blindly, quietly, in the flood of sunlight, about the common center of gravity ..." (p. 283/258). The point here is not the overwriting, but the invocation of the two real planets in the real fictive universe of the novel.

In the last chapter, when Shevek is returning to Annares on the interstellar ship *Davenant*, neither of Urras nor Annares, we read:

Very late on the following shipnight, Shevek was in the *Davenant*'s garden. The lights were out, there, and it was illuminated only by starlight. The air was quite cold. A night-blooming flower from some unimaginable world had opened among dark leaves and was sending out perfume with patient, unavailing sweetness to attract some unimaginable moth trillions of miles away, in a garden on a world circling another star... (p. 340/310).

This charming image is a metaphor that touches on every relationship in the novel: It speaks mutedly of biological force, spiritual desire, political ambition; as well, it signs the existence of an aesthetic neither Urrasti nor Annaresti, yet necessarily extant in the universe of the novel—necessary to hold a critical counter up to both worlds we have been examining.

One of the most striking moments of the book is the closing of Chapter Three. On Urras, alone in the Senior Faculty room of Ieu Eun University, Shevek, who has come to appreciate much of the surface opportunity available to him on this decadent world, muses on his situation. Outside the window, night is coming on. After his musings, we read:

The shadows moved about him, but he sat unmoving as Annares rose above the alien hills, at her full, mottled dun and bluish white, lambent. The light of his world filled his empty hands (p. 80/73).

Whether or not we find the diction a trifle strained, whether we find the dialogue the image sets up with the lietmotif of "empty hands" that symbolizes the Odonian philosophy fortunate or unfortunate, this is still the purest of science fiction, made reasonable by the implicit technology of space travel and made affecting by the human situation it describes and compels. It charges with near electric scintillation half a dozen other images to come, from Takver sitting among the moonthorn to Shevek in the moonlight through the window of his room on Annares. With the evocation of this most charged moonlight complete, the next chapter begins: "The westering sun..." which is breathtaking—for we are on another world (p. 81/74).

The orchestration of image here is simple and superb. The situation of those closing sentences is one that could only arise in science fiction: By extension, the only place we could find sentences doing *this* is in a science-fiction novel—*this* science fiction novel.

Yes, there are other unsteady points in the book: Given their comparative diets and general standard of living, we would expect the Annaresti after seven generations to be shorter than the Urrasti rather than taller; and the discussion of Annaresti jewelry in Abbanay, which does so much to relieve the bleakness of our image of Annaresti aesthetic life might well have come in the first three, rather than the last three, chapters. But there are also many other strong points: As a scene, the boys playing at prison is superb; the way in which the author, by carefully dropped biographemes (to borrow a neologism from Barthes), makes long-dead Odo emerge so vividly is masterful. But at this point, to me the book feels real, absorbed, in both its weaknesses and its strengths. The ideas, associations, and memories it has called up in me feel well wrestled. That is a good place for a critic to stop. That is the best place for a reader to begin another rereading.

There is an ideal model of writing which holds that a novel should begin with a moment of epiphanized intensity and never lose this energy from beginning to end. Nostalgically, we remember our early readings of the great works in our science-fiction canon—*More Than Human* or *The Stars My Destination*—as if they were exactly this. The model is, of course, illusory—if only because of the nature of writing itself. An image—such as the one discussed at the close of Chapter Three—is not only an image in a chain of images, it is a detonator dropped into a readerly imagination organized to a certain potential of response by previous effects and images—a response the new image releases. The efficacy of such images is as frequently measured by their inseparability from the rest of the text that prepares for them as it is measured by their own, inner energy: intrusion and inmixing are ubiquitous.

Something I feel science fiction as a genre is beginning to learn—and the general rise in critical sophistication within the field is as much responsible for it as it is an emblem of it—is that the competition in science fiction is not with the novels of the nineteenth century or even the mundane fiction of this second half of the twentieth. Because science fiction *is* a genre, and is experienced through resonances set up in a vastly complex textus, contoured both negatively and positively by millions of words that include the finest of Sturgeon and the clumsiest of Capt. S. P. Meek, any attempt to write a science-fiction novel generates an image of that book in some idealized way. The competition is with an author-generated, idealized form of the science-fiction novel itself.

At the resolution of incident and action (where we begin the overt reading of the political significance of a novel) whatever *The Dispossessed* does not happen to accomplish, the truth is that very little western fiction does. But if we keep asking the book to do these things, we are only saying back to it full-voice things the text itself, from beginning to end, keeps whispering of. *The Dispossessed* whispers of these possibilities very strongly; and that is an aspect of its indubitable significance. Compared to *The Dispossessed*, much mundane fiction—much of the best mundane fiction—is simply silent.

The Dispossessed will excite young and generous readers—indeed, will excite any reader beginning to look at our world and us in it. And it will excite for a long time. The novel is orchestrated; it shows signs of intelligence on every page. And its real successes, as with every work of art, are unique to it.

Nevertheless, some of these excited readers who return to the book a handful of years later will find themselves disillusioned: What excited them, they will see, was the book's ambition more than its precise accomplishments. But hopefully—a year or so after that—they will reach another stage where they will be able to acknowledge that ambition for what it was and value it; and know how important, in any changing society, such ambition is.

NEW YORK
APRIL 1976

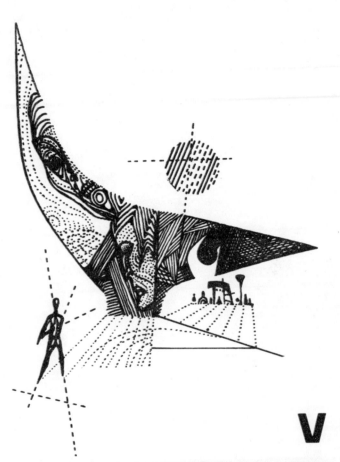

V
AUTOBIOGRAPHICAL
POSTSCRIPT

A Fictional Architecture that Manages Only with Great Difficulty Not Once to Mention Harlan Ellison

. . . and the light.

"It's almost solid here." John's hand reverses to a claw. And much white wrist from the cuff of his sweater. "It's almost . . ." He looks up the rocks, across the cactus (the isles of Greece, the isles of Greece? Um-hm), the grass, at the geometric lime-washed buildings. "Chip, it's almost as if each object were sunk in light!" It's late December, five in the afternoon, and golden. "Marvelous!" exclaims John.

"You are a silly romantic," I say.

Gold light sheds on his sweater as he faces me. "But it's true! You can see things at the horizon as clearly as if they were a hundred or so yards away."

"No, look, John—" Down through the windmills the white village sickles the bay. "The clarity is a function of the landscape. We're used to a horizon five miles away. In these hills, these rocks, it's impossible to have a horizon more than a mile off. But your eye doesn't know this. That church over there is not miles distant; even though it's just before the edge of things, it's much smaller and nearer than you think, which is why it's so sharply in focus."

Behind the church the sky is lemon; above us, a blue I cannot name. Over the sea a wall of salmon and gold is blurred with blood behind the hulking ghost of Syros.

"I prefer the clarity to the explanations." John puts his hands in his jeans. "But that's probably why *you* write science fiction."

"Which reminds me," say I, "did you finish those serials I asked you to read?"

"The first one was *very* long." He adds, "I finished it."

"What did you think?"

"Remember, I told you I don't like science fiction as a rule—"

"You told me you'd never read any. That's not the same thing."

He looks down at his sandals slapping the tarmac. *"Bene disserere est finis logicis,"* he intones.

"Is that where the *Bene Gesserit* comes from?"

(John is an English writer, English teacher, twenty-five—two years my senior—with a degree from London University.)

"Eh ... what's that a quote from?" I ask.

"Your Mr. Herbert probably took it from Act I, Scene I of Marlowe's *Dr. Faustus*. It's a mistranslation of Aristotle into Latin."

"'To argue well is the end of logic' ...?" I translate off the cuff I wear to impress. "But did you like the book—"

"You must understand the Greek original has all the multiple ironies of the English. In Latin, 'end,' in this sense, can only mean 'purpose'—diametrically opposed to the ironical Greek intention. To judge the validity of the total statement *The Prophet of Dune* makes as a novel, you must decide whether you hold with the Greek or the Latin sense of this statement. If you hold with the Roman, then the book must ultimately be a failure. If you hold with the Greek, then it's a success."

"Did you *like* it, John? I want to know if you ... which sense do you hold with?"

"Greece seems to be so 'in' right now." He glances around. "Witness ourselves. Always obliged to rebel, I'll take the Roman."

"Oh," I say. "I'm afraid to ask you what you thought of the other one."

John throws back his head, laughing. "It was perfectly delightful! Now *there's* a book it's no embarrassment to commit yourself to. If you could assure me there were some dozen writers who could word as well as your Mr. Zelazny, you might make me a 'fan,' as you call them."

The first science fiction I had given John to read was my battered September 1962 edition of *F&SF*. (I had bought it the same day I received author's copies of *The Jewels of Aptor*—running along

Fourth Street, stopping outside Gerde's, Folk City panting, and flinging the six books high into December [another year, another latitude]; and a brilliant contemporary poet clapped her hands and laughed as the books flopped to the sidewalk.) I suspect John enjoyed *When You Care, When You Love* immensely. But he refused to comment because it was unfinished. On the strength of it, however, he read the other things I gave him. His comment on the Merril article included in the *F&SF* Sturgeon issue, which begins: "The man has *style*," was to narrow his eyes, smile, nod, and murmur: "*So* has the lady."

"Come on," says John. "I want to get to Petraiki's before he closes. I refuse to have a dry New Year's. Christmas was bad enough." He laughs again. "I'll never forget you and Costas running around killing turkeys Christmas Eve."

"Don't knock it," I say. "It's paying for the New Year's wine."

A number of the internationals wintering on the island had ordered turkeys for Christmas and had been quite chagrined when the birds arrived live. Costas, an auto mechanic who worked in Anó Merá, the island's other town, found out from the butcher to whom the birds had gone; we marched up the island road Christmas Eve ringing doorbells and necks. "If you'd boil up a pot of water, ma'am (monsieur, signora, Fräulein), we'll pluck it for you." My father used to raise turkeys near Poughkeepsie; Costa's father, in Sarconia. We were tipped five to ten drachmas per bird.

"How did you manage it?" John asks. "Costas speaks Arabic, German, and Greek. All you've got is French, Spanish, and English. It must have been terribly complicated to set up."

"We spent most of the time laughing at one another. That made it easier. Speak three languages and you speak 'em all." Forget cognate vocabularies. Monoglots (and even diglots) tend to get caught up in metaphorical extensions of meaning. Suspect, depend, expect: literally, look under, hang from, look out for. It's easier to communicate (by charade if necessary) the concrete meanings, letting the "foreigner" intuit the corresponding mental states implied (suspicion, dependence, expectation), than to try to indicate directly the state of mind itself. "I wrote a novel all about that sort of thing," I tell John. "It should be out by spring. Hope you get a chance to read it."

John asks, "Do you find technical-mindedness conflicts with artistic expression?" Really. We are passing the wooden gate before the art school. Behind, the mosaics of the winter gardens, the empty dorms with hot and cold running water (sigh!).

"A man once asked me," profoundly say I, "why I wanted to be a creative artist in this age of science; I told him—quoting a brilliant contemporary poet—that I saw no dichotomy between art and science, as both were based on precise observation of inner and outer worlds. And that's why I write science fiction." Then I look up. "Hey! *Ya su*, Andreas!"

Andreas the Sandy is an eighteen-year-old fisherman, with baggy pants, a basket enameled blue; his toes and the backs of his hands and his hair glitter with grains.

We go through hello, how are you, what have you been doing, fishing, writing, have you finished your book, no but come up to the house for dinner, come down to the port for ouzo, and Andreas wraps half a kilo of *maridas* from his basket in newspaper and gives them to me for a New Year's present, thank you, you know how to fry them in oil, yes? yes, thank you again, Andreas.

John waits. He can quote hunks of the Iliad in the original, but speaks no Modern Greek. The turkey venture with Costas forced me to begin learning (Costas, and the Greek for all those damn auto parts), and soon I will overhear John boasting about his clever little American who learned Greek in three weeks. Andreas waves goodbye.

We stroll down from the terraced outcropping that falls by the bloody doors of the slaughterhouse into the Aegean. This daily trip from the house to buy wine, oil, oranges, fish, and little papers of dun-colored coffee should take only twenty minutes or so. Often it becomes a full afternoon.

K. Cumbani is having a snack outside the laiki taverna on the port. Punch, beneath the chair, paws and nuzzles a shell. An old man, a big man, K. Cumbani wears a bulky, white wool jacket—looks like a pudgy Hemingway. His grandmother's bust sits on a pedestal in the town square. She was a heroine of the Greek Civil War. His family is the cultural quintessence of the island. He lets us borrow freely among his French and English books. Once a week he will contrive to say, *"C'est terrible! Vraiment je crois que je parle français mieux que grecque!*" As French is the language of the older internationals with whom he mostly associates (English is very markedly the language of the younger), this could be true.

We discuss the effect of Romantic music on post-Wagnerian opera. Tactfully politic, John and I try a few witty remarks on the Chopin-Sand affair so as to maneuver onto the correspondence between Sand and Flaubert, ultimately to change the topic to Flaubert's style (about which we *know* something). Cumbani won't bite. This sort of afternoon, vermilion on the empty winter sea, can be taxing.

"And your own book, how is that coming?" Cumbani asks.

"Slowly," I say.

"You have a very strange way of writing a novel," he muses.

Last week, on a walk at three in the morning, Cumbani saw me sitting in the moonlight on the prow of Andreas' boat, barefeet shoved beneath the sleeping pelican, singing loudly and tearing pages from my notebook, balling them up and flinging them on the water or on the concrete walk, jumping up to chase a page, retrieve a word or phrase and rescrawl it on another page. "Young man, *what* are you doing?"

"Deploying images of Orpheus by the Greek and midnight sea!"

"It's past midnight and much too cold for you to be out like this."

"Oh, look, I'm really all right—"

Cumbani made me come home with him, have some brandy and borrow a sweater, then sent me home.

Now he asks me: "Will you finish your book here?"

I shrug.

"You must send me a copy when it is published."

Cumbani's guest book, glorious upon the walnut lowboy, contains names like de Beauvoir, Menhuin, Kazantzakis, Max Ernst: His shelves are filled with their books; their paintings are on his walls.

"Yes, I will want to see this book—that you say is about mythology?"

"I'll send you a copy."

Damn Ace Books covers!

"I'm taking the boat to Delos again, I think," say I. "I want to explore the ruins some more. Out from the central excavations, there's a strange rock formation facing the necropolis on Rhenia. Do you know what it is, K. Cumbani?"

He smiles. "You are friendly with some of the fishermen. Ask them."

We return to the house early. Just before we leave the port the musicians come down, practicing for the New Year, and I am cast back to my first night on the island, when I ran up from the launch that took us in from the boat, running through the narrow streets of the white city at midnight, white, white, and white around each tiny corner; then a window: a man in a brown sweater gazed at an abstraction in orange on his easel under a brass lamp.

Artemus has already brought a rafia-covered bottle of wine and left it on the porch. I pace the garden, remembering a year and a half back when I finished *The Fall of The Towers* and saying to myself, you are twenty-one, going on twenty-two: You are too old to be a child prodigy. Your accomplishments are more important than the age at which you did them. Still, the images of youth plague me. Chatterton, suiciding on arsenic in his London garret at seventeen; Samuel Greenburg, dead of tuberculosis at twenty-four; Radiguet, hallucinating through the delirium of typhus that killed the poet/novelist/chess prodigy at twenty. By the end of this book I hope to exorcise them. Billy the Kid is the last to go. He staggers through this abstracted novel like one of the mad children in Crete's hills. Lobey will hunt you down, Billy. Tomorrow, weather permitting, I will go to Delos.

New Year's itself is a party at the house with Susan and Peter and Bill and Ron, and Costas, and John. Costas dances for us, picking the table up in his teeth, his brown hair shaking as his boot heels clatter on the floor, teeth gritting on the wood, and the wine in the glasses shaking too, but none spills. This is also sort of a birthday party for Costas, who was twenty-one last week.

Then Susan calls us to the balcony. The musicians have come up the road, with drums and clarinets, and hammers rattling on the siduri, and another playing bagpipes made from a goat's belly. And later I sit on the ladder, eating fried chicken and hush-puppies (deep-fried in pure olive oil), and talk with John till morning bleaches the air above the garden wall near the cactus by the cistern.

"Watch out with that book of yours," he tells me jokingly. "I'd like to see you finish it."

Then, a sudden depression. I am overcome with how little I have done this past year, how much there is to do.

The first days of January will be warm enough for us to wear bathing suits in the garden, read, write, swat flies against the shutters. Orion will straddle the night, and hold the flaps of darkness tight above the cold roads.

*   *   *

Some fragments of the year following?

Athens: An incredible month in the Plaka, playing guitar in the clubs at the foot of the Acropolis, watching Easter from the roofs of Anaphiotika's stone houses, at the top of the spiral stairs, while the parishioners gather with their candles at the church to march down through the city saddled between the double hills, as lines of light worm the streets toward the monastery. We made Easter eggs that night, with various leaves and flowers—poppies picked at the bottom of the Parthenon's east porch—pressed to the shells and dipped in boiling onion skins: polished floral tracery over the mahogany ovoids. *"Chrónia polá! Chrónia polá!"* and have a bright, red egg.

Istanbul: Four days' hitchhiking from Athens by the road that took me past Mt. Olympus, her twinned and hairy peaks on the left, the sea all gray to Eboiea on the right. I arrived in The City (*Eis Ton Polis—this the city*—Istanbul) with forty lepta, which is less than 1¢. A month of muddy streets and snow and gorgeous stone walls alive with carved leaves and flowers, the men stopping to wash their feet at the troughs, and mild nights on Galata bridge, the iron scrollwork, the octagonal panes of the streetlamps, and the Queen of Cities glittering under the smokey night among her domes and minarets across the water as I returned at midnight to Old City over the Golden Horn. Reconnoitering, T. described the "bay fire" to me: "A Russian tanker broke up in the harbor, sheeting the yellow water with a rainbow slick. Then, somehow, a spark! Miles of docks roared and spat at the sky. We stayed in our room, the lights out, the windows flickering. Then, *splat*, and the pane was beaded with blood—the fire-trucks were wetting down all the houses near the bay." (T. is a Swiss painter with a heavy black beard.) Rooms laced with sweet smoke, and oil reeking through the muddy streets; the Turkish bath where steam drifts through the high marble arches as you walk into the dark stalls with white stone basins and metal dipping pans; days of begging with the Danes whose hair was even longer than mine, and the strange girl dying of cancer and abandoned by her German lover in the rain, in spring, in Istanbul.

I hitched out of The City with six and a half feet of Kentuckian called Jerry, I trying to explain about love, he trying to explain about pain. He made hexes in the dirt beside the road and I fixed them on all the cars that passed and wouldn't pick us up—till a road-building machine run by Turkish soldiers stopped for us. "Get up, get up quick! We must not stop for hitchhikers, and our Commander will be up soon in his jeep! But get on quick, and crouch down—" (I had enough Turkish to figure that one out by now) at which point said jeep with said Commander arrived and he told us to get off, and the soldiers looked embarrassed, and we put the most powerful hex possible on that surplus U.S. Army jeep. Forty minutes later, when a truck hauling rock had given us a lift, we passed the jeep in flames, overturned on the road's edge. The road-building machine had pulled off beside it, and soldiers were standing around scratching their heads.

Crete: Cocooned in a sleeping bag against the cabin wall of the *Herakleon*, the wind frosting the top of my head, though it was summer, Heracleon, another dusty island city, where the "k" sounds of Northern Greek are replaced by an Italianate "ch." The two youth hostels here were op-art fantasias, one run by a madman who wouldn't let you use the toilet. I wandered down by the Venitian fountain of the lions, then past the police box to the raucous markets of the city. I made no attempt to resist the pull that forces a visitor to focus his life about the neolithic palaces. In broiling noon, I visited Knossos, descending the lustral basins, roaming through this bizarre construction, comparing the impression of ten years' reading with the reality.

Sir Arthur Evans' reconstructions are not brilliant. They are laudable for what they have preserved of the architecture. Praise him for the Great Staircase. But the Piet de Jong drawings and recreations of the frescoes (literally *everything* you have seen of Minoan graphic art is a de Jong interpretation of what *may* have been there) are a good deal more influenced by Art Nouveau, current when the reconstructions were done, than by anything Minoan. But the work of neither man is harmful, only incredibly misleading for the lay public. The single stone chair found in the palace is as likely to be a footstool for a palace guard as it is to be "Minos' Throne." The bare court that was labeled "Ariadne's Dancing Floor" is pure invention, as with the labeling of "King's room," "Queen's room," etc. The Queen's W.C. probably *is* a W.C. But to whom it belonged is total supposition. The entire wing of the palace which has been labeled the Domestic Wing, with all the charming, personalized anecdotes that have become attached to it: these are all the fantasies of a blind old English eccentric. I sat for an hour on "Minos' Throne," making notes for the book, and feeling for the labyrinth's bottom. Where would you put a computer among these stones?

Strolling with Fred near the sea by the red ruins of the palace at Malia, I asked him what he knew of the Altar Stones. (Fred is an Austrian archeologist.) "The theory seems to be they put a different plant or piece of grain in each little cup around the edge and prayed to it in some religious ceremony."

"Is this what they think, or what they know?"

He smiled. "What they think. They have to give it some explanation and it's as good as any other. Minoan archeology, even in 1966, is mostly guesswork, though they try to make it look documented."

Around the edges of the circular stones—some are thirty inches across, some several feet in diameter—there are thirty-four evenly spaced indentations, then a thirty-fifth twice as wide as the others, making thirty-six divisions in all. To me this suggests either a compass or a calendar.

Below Phaestos, the gray palace on the cliff, the shrieking children hid in the time-drunk caves of Matlá. Peacocks and monkeys played by the bay of Agia Nickoláos, and in the mountains, in the dark hut, I toasted Saint George (passing and stopping at his shrine on the tortuous cliff road, walking the edge and gazing into the foaming ravine, and further at the true Mediterranean Sea) and moved on into the central ridge of stone that bursts Crete's back. I paused, crouched beneath the curtained stones at the great cave of Dicte overlooking the mills of Lasithi in the navel of the island, after having hitched six hours into the island's high core, on the rocks, past fields so loud with bees you couldn't hear your own voice, past fields of poppies, past black orchids wild at the road's edge with purple pistils long as my forearm and blossoms big as my head: at Dicte, birth cave of Zeus, miles deep, more likely the true labyrinth than Knossos, I constructed the great rent in the source-cave for the bull-god to stalk out into my novel. The high rocks were veiled with wet moss. And later, I returned on the windy ship *Heracleon* to Piraeus, with its yacht harbors and its bawdy district and its markets where sea urchin and octopus are sold with shrimp and tomatoes and white cheese under the glass awnings.

New York? My home city, new now this trip, is the slow, blond young man who ran away from his wife in Alabama and who talked and talked and talked for nine days straight with the radio erupting pop music that became translated under the sound of his drawl. He told of his childhood suicide attempts, some dozen before he was nine, trying to drown self, drink iodine, jump out window, till he was put in a mental hospital: At five a drowning, at eight a hanging, at twelve threw himself under a car and broke his back and arm, at fifteen he drank a bottle of rubbing alcohol but had his stomach pumped in time, at eighteen he cut his wrists, at twenty-one he drank rat poison because his wife wouldn't go to bed with him, and here he was pushing twenty-four and the three years were almost up and what if he succeeded this time? and got drunk, and sick, and lay on the floor urinating all over himself, and talked about the mental hospital some more, and then about the year he spent in jail (at eighteen, where he cut his wrists) and how he tried to break open a trustee's head with a scrub brush because the man had kicked him, and the trustee had him tied to a metal bed frame and nearly cut his tongue out with a spoon; talked of how he had stood under the tree, shouting while his drunken twin brother hacked at himself with a piece of broken glass: "Cut it deeper! That's right, Alfred, cut it *deeper*! Now cut it *again*!" A northern Negro, I am as cut off from understanding the white southerner's fascination with pain as the northern white is from understanding the mental matrix in which the southern black lives.

In Cleveland: Sitting at the end of the hall of the Sheraton playing the guitar while Roger Z (at the announcement of his presence at the convention opening, the standing ovation went on, and on, and on . . .), crosslegged on the carpet, played the harmonica and the others listened. Or that same evening, gardinias floating in rums and rums, and Judith and Roger beneath plaster rocks while I tried to break the inarticulate webs, and water washed the blue lights of the stream that wound the restaurant floor. And the inarticulateness becoming, suddenly, pages and pages in an attempt to catch the forms in Roger's linguistic webbing. New and terrible, they do not answer if you call them by old names. (In this year between endings, the Judith's, Zelazny, Merril, and Blish all ceased to be names and became people.) And New York became Bob Silverberg's cats, roaming the halls and steps of Silver Mountain Castle, beneath the trees of Fieldstone.

This whole flow, fixed now by Jim Sallis's letters, contorting silences by those things unsaid, out of Iowa, out of Iowa City—RFD 3, which for me now has become part of his name. Very few things are more important than these.

The novel I was afraid might kill me is finished now, has achieved cover, print, and multiple production and distribution that creates myth. (The book, McLuhan reminds us, was the first mass-produced object. Before that, story repeated by word of mouth: creating the mass sensibility.) That which totally occupied a year is fallible and subjected to the whims of whoever will pay 40¢. How strange—did I really write it for that? But a new book has taken its place, as different from it as it was from the one before: the new one exacts responses from such dissimilar sensibilities... even the work method is totally different. Am I at all the same person?

Another New Year's staggers towards us over the temporal horizon.

*   *   *

After Christmas, I take a seventy mile drive in the back seat of an open sports car through the English December to a house of dark and solid furniture, with a stuffed giraffe in the hall, a Christmas ball hanging from its lower lip.

Every day I have risen in the dark, dressed, pulled back the blue drapes and sat down to work. Outside the window the street lamps shine up to diamond the water on the high panes. Then night drifts away from morning behind the peaked roofs across the street. The arbitrary measurements man imposes on his existence force me to consider the year, ending now. The two books I discussed in their magazine serial versions with John on the golden rocks a year ago have now been released in paperback book form. One of my dawn labors is to compare the magazine versions with the books. The first pages of *Conrad*, as far as words and word order go, are the same, without any cutting. But let me compare the editing:

Magazine:

"...you once told me that your birthday..."
"All right!"

Book:

"...you once told me that your birthday—"
"All right!"

Interruption is signified by a dash, whereas three dots signifies that the voice trails off; I approve of the book editing.

But, in the magazine:

After a time I explained:
"Back when I was a brat..."

While for some inexplicable reason in the book this has been edited to:

After a time I explained, "Back when I was a brat..."

The first is precise; the luminous generality of "explained" is focused through the colon on the statement that follows. The second is diffused, unfocused, and clumsy.

And the first line of the body of the text of the paperback edition of *Dune* explodes over a typographical blunder. (And these people are publishing the book this year has garnered?

(Damn Ace Books proofreading!

(Has anything really changed over this year?)

Later on in the day, the color of gas-fire through a glass of sherry recalls the light on late Greek afternoons.

Time magazine this week has done an article on the "generation under twenty-five" and the subject floats about London, conversations on the surface of wine glasses, over pints of bitter, and coffee cups: How is the "pop" (as opposed to the "popular") image propagated? Again Marshall McLuhan has provided the vocabulary. Trying to define the relationship of the pop image to this younger generation, I am brought up short by Jim Ballard. "You know"—he

smiles, and the fire is coke this time and the distorting lens scotch—
"you're not going to be under twenty-five forever." (Voice of draining
time.)

(Passing thought, looking at the portrait of James Pringle, red
nosed, high hatted, leering from the lobby wall: If you haven't had
opportunity to use the public health facilities of a city, you haven't
really been there. Briefly I go over the cities in which I have been...)

In Pam Zoline's apartment above the butcher's, Tom and Pam
and I drink much wine and turn the sound off on the telly while BBC-
2 presents the life story of Eleanor Roosevelt. *Revolver* is playing on
the gramophone. Her despairing and ravaged face:

"Well, well, well. He'll make you—Dr. Roberts!" the voices
warn her. The correspondences that the music and the mosaic film-
clips force from you, each image changing in time to the music, words
and music incessantly commenting on one another, is exhausting and
staggering. It becomes apparent that this will work only with shows
that are planned to utilize the incredibly high participation that TV
demands, whereas films—created for a different medium—shown on
TV fall very flat. Yet a TV newscast or a TV documentary is perfect
for this.

"Please! Please, for God's sake," Pam, her head on Tom's knee,
"it's the most exhausting thing I've ever done!" against our hysteria.

Amid the white masonite and mushroom salad, the evening
winds toward sleep. And later Pam and I discuss how Jim's letters
from over the sea have so managed to fix the rush of colored nights to
the solid structure of time. There is a soup then, sensuous, with water
chestnuts, and apricots, and grapes, and chicken, and mushrooms,
that orders the whole sensory mandala of the evening. And the
Heracleon, Life suddenly informs me as I pick up a stray copy, is sunk
with 240 people.

The next day I try to explain the soup, at least, to Mike
Moorcock. Futile.

There is a poem by the late Jack Spicer, not one of his best, but it
contains the following example:

Colorblind people can still drive because the red light is
  on the top and the green light is on the bottom.
(Or is it the other way around? I don't know because
  I'm not colorblind.)

How much more economical that would have been:

Colorblind people can still drive because the red light is
　on the top and the green light is on the bottom.
(I think.)

"Style," say I to Mike, quoting B.C.P. (brilliant contemporary poet), "is when the writer forces the reader to supply all the ugly parts of the sentence."

Mike towers over me, face framed in hair, as we move from the rugs, cushions, and clouded and flowered glass of the pub. Later, Mike ponders: "If we don't write what we seriously consider worthwhile, why bother writing?" (This is the only man I have ever met in an editorial capacity whom I can leave and not spend the next two days seriously considering giving up writing as a profession.)

These blue-draped dawns, Gloria and I battle each other as to who will get the first cup of coffee while the Brunners are still asleep. New Year's Eve morning I report at eight o'clock to Judy Merril's basement flat on Portland Street,

"I've been up since four o'clock this morning. I was just (yawn) taking a nap."

where, in a white bowl, the whisky and sugar have been soaking overnight by the stove

"And I want you to know, sir, that whisky is seven dollars a bottle over here."

and we start to play with cream

"You see, they have single and double cream here, instead of light and heavy. But the single cream is as thick as American heavy."

which is true. It still doesn't whip. It takes me twenty minutes to discover this.

"There's a little grocery around the corner. Dear me; perhaps you'd better try double..."

The proper combination (after a phone call to Hilary Moorcock) seems to be half and half.

"Mmmmm—butter, eh?"

Then we play with the eggs.

"Look, you and your old family recipes; *why* don't you separate the yolks from the whites?"

It takes much less time to whip twelve eggs

"Watch it—!"

and one egg shell than it does to whip one pint of light/single cream

"Are you sure you need six more eggs?"

—or eighteen eggs, for that matter. Alcohol (proof increased considerably by 24 hours in sugar) cooks eggs.

"Wouldn't you say this is a terribly expensive way to make an omelette?"

The rotary beater makes like an outboard through the froth of sugar and booze as drop by drop the eggs are spooned down.

"I'd like to understand a little further what you mean by the distinctions between the generation under twenty-five and—woooooops!"

It is much easier to mix two gallons of whisky & egg mixture into two quarts of English whipped cream

"It's *very* yellow, isn't it?"

than it is to mix two quarts of English whipped cream into two gallons of egg & whisky.

"Well, it *looks* like butter."

Then we lug the plastic wash tub, covered with tinfoil, into the back yard and place it under a box, in the rain.

New Year's Eve, and the party erupts in much mauve and gold corduroy mod. Tom Disch greets me at the bottom of the steps (another American science-fiction writer) in evening dress (John Sladek in military maroon, and Chris Priest, face shattered and beautiful, in jeans and blue turtleneck); Tom is handing out masks. Pam has made some umpty of them, one the size of a postage stamp, razored from a photograph and mounted on a stick to be held up in front of the eye; another three feet across, the sleeping face of the sun rayed with red, and floppy. Some of the masks are drawn, some are collage with features grafted from magazines (one gasping mouth, with crayoned lips, disgorging flowers from some *House Beautiful* advertisement) and the false faces turn, laugh, fall and rise again—

"I want you to know your eggnog is a total success! I had to save a glass behind the steps so you'd have some!"—glowing among these faces: Some have two eyeholes, some have one. There is one with three, and the sleeping sun, which eventually comes to me, as people pass them to one another, has none. The music pinions us to the instant. And later, talking to Tom (he stands by the door, his hands in the pockets of his tuxedo pants, yellow hair falling to the black silk collar of his jacket, trying to comprehend this moment past midnight), I insist: "This year, I've actually done so little, written so little, so few of the millions of impressions have been fixed by anything resembling art—I'm going to lose them,"

He laughs. "Why? Because you won't have another first night in Paris? It's not lost, Chip—"

I try to explain this way: "Some time between a year ago and now I was standing on the steps of the Blue Mosque in Istanbul, looking across the courtyard, and suddenly I realized that I could be *anywhere* within a year; there was as much chance of my being in Bombay or Tokyo, or some city or town I don't even know the name of today, as there was of my being in New York, Paris or London. There's this insane, unfixed energy—"

But it isn't explaining.

And the New Year deliquesces about our images. (How much of the noise is to convince ourselves that we can still hear? There is so much death in the "younger generation"...) Cherry colored signs with the Aldiss's on a brittle Oxford afternoon—

A few days later Tom and I go to the British Museum. It is cold, and January is still brittle on the streets.

"The gold on those gray pediment statues is really incredible," Tom says as we pass the gates and cross the sprawling pink tiles of the plaza before the steps.

The archaic statuary room is closed.

"I won't feel my trip to Greece is complete until I've seen the Elgin Marbles. Come on."

In the neoclassic hall the ruined frieze occupies and mutes us. Tom moves slowly from panel to panel, hands sunk in his overcoat.

Through reproduction, the most familiar of the panels have been erased of all freshness. Still, moments of drapery and musculature explode with the energy of a people caught in the transition from conceptual to representational art. (Passing thought: science fiction at its best takes literature back along this same route, starting at the representational as defined by Materialism, and pushes us toward the conceptual, its energy comes from the reserve latent in the gap.)

*This panel depicts the battle between the
Centaurs and the Lapiths. The head of the
Centaur is in the Louvre. An unimportant
fragment of the panel is still in Athens.*

I don't suppose assassinating Harold Wilson would get them back to Greece.

Upstairs the museum has arranged a display of fifteenth and sixteenth century Mogul prints from India.

I walk across the polished wood (ice skating through the King's Library, pulling back the purple drapes from the autographs of Keats, Byron, Shelley, Macaulay—and Tom looking at the massed volumes behind the glass doors of the two-story hall, panicing; "What are you and I making more *books* for!") toward the cases.

"Look! Look at the light!"

On their ivory mattes, sixteenth century India quivers in distorted perspective, the blacks, vermilions, chartreuses, the gold so vivid that in some prints it takes a full minute for a landscape to clear while the colors tear my eyes.

"It's as though . . ." I begin. "It's as though each object were *sunk* in light!"

No figure among the prints casts a shadow, yet each is modeled and shaded in three dimensions; each has a halo of shadow about it. Brilliant elephants cross blinding rivers. Soldiers glitter across landscapes where no discernible sun shines.

"It's incredible. The things at the horizon are painted just as clearly as . . ."

I stop.

Tom looks from me to the prints and back. "The whole scheme of color values is something that I guess we just don't understand anymore. Did they really do these? You couldn't possibly reproduce them with modern printing methods. Hey, what's the matter?"

"Nothing . . ." We spend nearly two hours in the room, wandering among the prints.

And the light . . .

MYKONOS, LONDON, NEW YORK
JANUARY 1966–JANUARY 1967